# ABOUT TANIA JOYCE

Tania Joyce is an author of rockstar, contemporary and new adult romance novels. Her stories thread romance, drama and passion into beautiful locations ranging from the dazzling lights and glitter of New York to the luscious vineyards in the Hunter Valley.

She's widely traveled, has a diverse background in the corporate world and has a love for sparkles, shoes and shiraz.

Tania draws on her real-life experiences and combines them with her very vivid imagination to form the foundation of her novels. She likes to write about strong-minded, career-oriented heroes and heroines that go through drama-filled hell, have steamy encounters and risk everything as they endeavor to find their happily-ever-after.

Tania calls Brisbane, Australia, home. She shuffles the hours in her day between family life and writing. One day she hopes to find balance!

She loves to hear from her readers.

Visit: www.taniajoyce.com

# LOST LYRICS

**The Flintlocks Rockstar Romance Series – Book 5**

**by**

**Tania Joyce**

LOST LYRICS by Tania Joyce
Published by Gatwick Enterprises 2025
Brisbane, Australia.



LOST LYRICS
The Flintlocks Rockstar Romance Series – Book 5
EPUB format: ISBN: 978-1-7635962-1-4
Paperback: ISBN: 978-1-7640950-1-3
Hardback: ISBN: 978-1-7640950-2-0
ASIN: B0DFFBJKFR

Cover Photography by: Wander Aguiar
Model: Jerrin S
Edited by: Creating Ink

For more information on the author please visit: www.taniajoyce.com

Keywords and Subjects
Rockstar romance, rock star romance, new adult romance, contemporary romance, celebrity romance, Hollywood romance, movie star romance, happily ever after, rocker, band, musician, music romance.

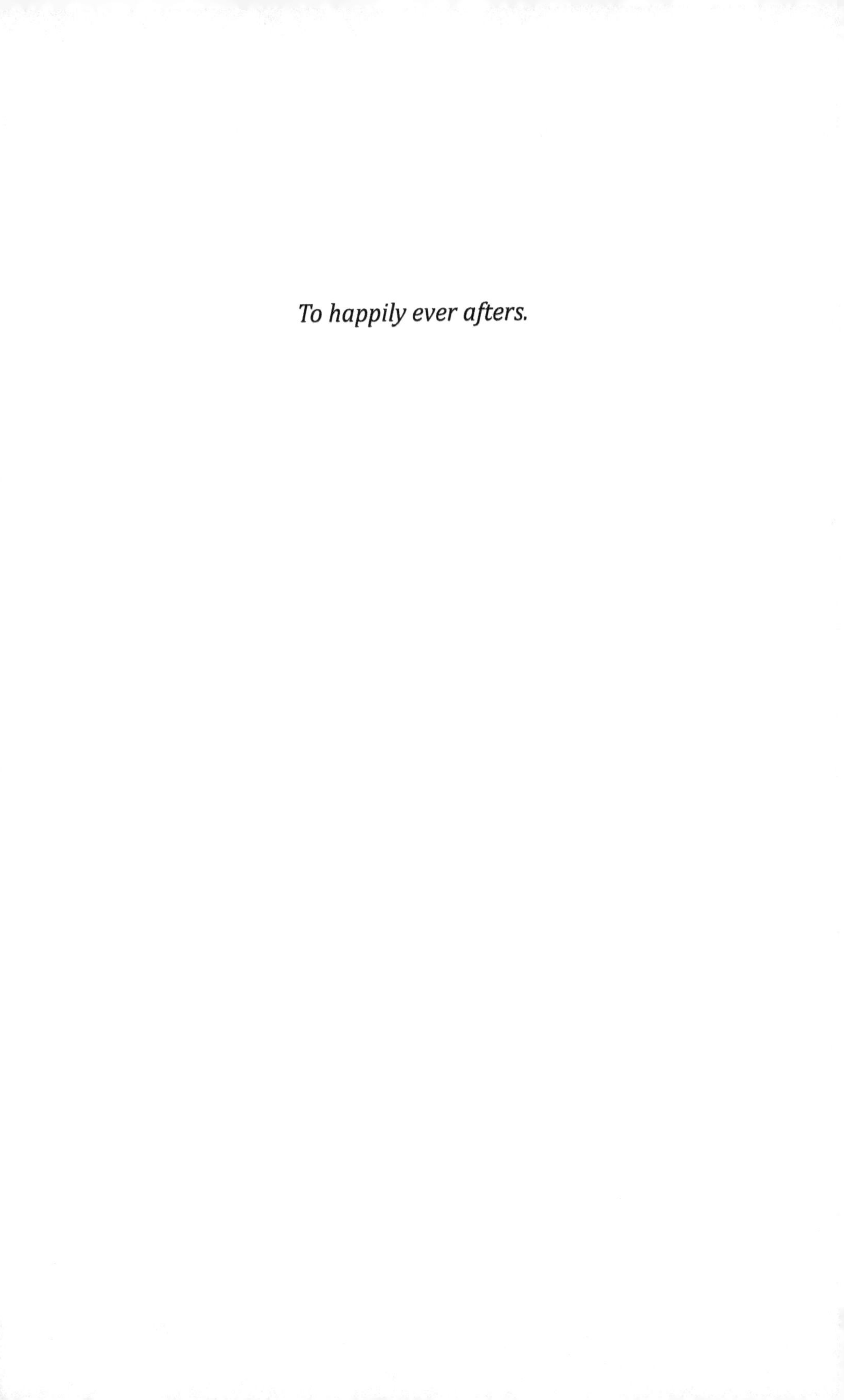

*To happily ever afters.*

# Chapter 1



It had been three years since I'd lost my brother, Phil. Thirty-six months. 1095 days. My heart and soul would be forever scarred. Not a day went by when I didn't miss Phil or see something that reminded me of him. Despite the lingering heartache, the heaviness that used to crush my chest wasn't crippling anymore. The loss and pain were easier to bear. Losing him had forced me to change, and I'd become a better man because of it.

Sitting in the passenger seat of my car, I smirked and stared at the chrome urn wedged between my legs. The good times with Phil had far outweighed the bad. *Absolutely.* I'd healed and moved on, thanks to the gorgeous woman beside me. My girlfriend, Sutton. She'd made life brighter in every way. She'd brought me out of the darkness, stood by me as my band and I had scaled to new heights, and loved me with all my flaws. I planned on never letting her go.

"Flint? Are you okay?" Heading north along the Pacific Coast Highway, she veered my Ferrari into the far lane, put her foot down, and overtook the slow dickhead in front of us. Humor caught the edge of my lip, tugging it upward. I was sure she loved driving my Portofino for the thrill and hum between her legs. But *I* did that to her whole body . . . time and time again.

In the depths of my soul, I knew I wanted to spend the rest of my life with her. I was crazy in love and had plans to propose in a few weeks. I just needed the final elements to fall into place. My idea had taken months to organize. But delay after delay had done my head in. I didn't want to throw my whole plan out the door. Sutton deserved something special. *She* was special. Every day with her was a blessing. She was the reason I was happy, thankful, and grateful to be alive.

"Yeah. I'm good." I rested my head back against the seat and swiveled to face her. Her long, golden blonde hair fell in soft waves over her shoulders. But her dark blue eyes shimmered with concern. She needn't worry. I was fine. I'd be even better once I made it through the next few hours. The reality of the drive kicked in as we headed north. "I was just remembering some of the wild parties Phil and I used to go to. He loved to cause havoc."

"Yes. So I've heard." Half-smiling, she rolled her eyes, then refocused on the road ahead. Sutton hadn't known Phil, but she'd never been impressed by the stories my bandmates—Cole and Slip—and I had often told. Fair call, he'd been a crazy motherfucker. She patted and rubbed my thigh. "But today will be hard. I'm here for you. Always."

"Thanks, Sutt. I know you are." I placed my hand over hers and gave it a gentle squeeze. Trailing my fingertips up to her wrist, I tickled her soft skin, then fidgeted with the diamond bracelet I'd given her for Christmas. It sparkled in the last rays of the day.

With a twinkle in her eye, she waggled her fingers ... specifically her ring one. "My bracelet needs another diamond to match."

A chuckle rumbled low in my throat. She was never subtle. She was itching for me to pop the question. So was I. I was running out of diversionary tactics. But today, saying goodbye to Phil again was a good deflection. "One day, Sutt. I love you and our life together. I'm not going anywhere."

"Don't stress." She jabbed her finger into my thigh, then returned her hand to the steering wheel. "There's no pressure. I'm not going anywhere either."

Oh, there was pressure. Nothing daunting, but it was there. Every fucking day. But I could hold out for a few more weeks . . . *hopefully.*

"Good." I loved Sutton was mine. She'd helped me through the worst time in my life. She'd given me something to be excited about . . . a future with her. She made facing this evening easier. "We have so much to look forward to—the rest of awards season, summer, your show's renewal. But since the tour, I haven't slowed down. I need to do that. And I will. I promise. But right now, I need to get through today."

"You'll be fine."

I flattened my palms around the urn and nodded. I hoped she was right.

This evening at sunset, my band, our partners, and I would spread Phil's ashes across the ocean, just off the rocks where he used to sit on the beach for hours and play his guitar or surf the wicked waves. We wanted to remember the fun times—not the bad. Not his addiction or substance abuse. It was time to put the past horrors behind us and be thankful for the good things that had happened since his death. Sutton had come into my life. My band and I had found Lewis, our new bassist. Tia, Cole's sister, had come home from Chicago, quit acting, and joined our sound and lighting team. The guys and I had released an album and had been on an epic world tour. We'd won some trophies during this awards season. *Freaking amazing.*

We were on a high.

We should be riding the wave of success.

But instead . . . we were on a break . . . until the end of the year.

The guys had needed it. Me, not so much.

Time off made me nervous.

Unease continually swayed through my guts like an unwavering waltz. Knots twisted tighter and tighter in the back of my neck.

Why was I so unsettled? What plagued my mind more than my pending proposal?

The answer was simple.

I missed music.

I needed it more than oxygen. More than food and water and a roof over my head. I loved to write, to create, and to play. I missed having adoring fans scream and sing along to our songs. The rush of adrenaline from performing in front of huge crowds fed my soul. I was born to entertain. But with no albums planned, and no gigs booked, the future remained uncertain.

I didn't like that. Not one little bit.

*Shit!*

This break could kill me.

Maybe I needed a new hobby. A project. But what? I had no idea.

Planning a proposal had kept me sane . . . somewhat. But it wasn't enough.

I'd lost touch with music when Phil had died, and I never wanted to lose it again. I didn't want to spiral back into the dark depths of depression or hit the bottle . . . or worse. I needed my band to reform. I needed the guys. They were my *family*. My life. A part of my soul, like music.

We'd originally planned a twelve-month hiatus, but three months had already been added, taking us to the end of the year. I prayed no more time off was required.

*Five months down. Ten to go.*

The countdown was on.

I took a deep breath to calm my thoughts and closed my eyes. Didn't help much, but it was something.

Today, my friends and I would all be together for the first time in six and a half weeks, since Christmas. But as Sutton pulled into the hilltop parking lot near El Matador Beach and stopped in the space next to Tia's Mercedes, the reason for our sunset gathering pummeled my chest. Familiar heaviness settled across my shoulders. Everyone was already here, waiting by the steps that led down to the beach.

I clutched the urn between my hands. The cold metal did nothing to chill my racing mind. *I can do this. Yes. I can.* I had to. But the backs of my eyes stung. My ribs hurt with every breath. Grief sucked. But I was okay. Sutton was there. So were my friends.

Fuck, it was good to see them.

Sutton killed the engine on my Ferrari. We opened the doors and hopped out. The ocean breeze hit my face, but for February, it wasn't unpleasant. The sun slowly sank in the west. The water glistened beneath its fading rays. Seagulls dipped and darted about. With Phil's ashes tucked under one arm, I drew my leather jacket closed across my chest. I veered around to the front of the car, joined Sutton, and stepped over to hug everyone hello.

"Good to see you, man." Slip patted my back. He sucked in a long breath and stared out across the rock formations and beach below us. "I can't believe I haven't been here in years."

"Me either." I tightened my hold on the urn, reaching, searching, feeling for Phil's presence. *Yeah, he is here.* Phil had loved surfing on every beach from Malibu to Zuma to Leo Carrillo. We all had. But none of us guys had hit the waves much . . . or at all . . . since he'd died. With time on my hands, I planned to surf with the guys once summer returned.

"Mads, how are you?" I gave her a big sideways cuddle.

"Fabulous." She hugged me back, then snaked her arm around Slip and rested her head on his shoulder. "Good to be in LA for a few days. It's so much warmer here than Vancouver."

After opting to stay in Vancouver for his birthday yesterday, Slip and Maddy had flown in this morning. Slip, the fucker, looked good. Best he had in years. Fuller face. Healthy and fit after recovering from hip surgery and overcoming his addiction to painkillers. He'd been clean and sober for five months. I was so damn proud of him, but I was still worried. He lived so far away on Bowen Island. I hated I couldn't stop by his house and make sure he wasn't drinking alcohol, swallowing oxy, or hitting the blow on repeat. None of us wanted to go through that nightmare again.

But he was here for this special day. That meant the world to me.

"Tia? Lewis? How you doing?" I stepped around the circle to give Tia a kiss hello on the cheek, then hugged Lewis.

"Same old. Same old." Lewis feigned a smile, unable to mask the fatigue in his tone. "No fresh news to report."

As I stepped back, my chest twinged. They'd been trying for a baby with no success for eight months. The strain and disappointment etched into their faces hurt my heart. They wanted a family so badly. "Hang in there, bud. I'm just glad you could make it." I gave his arm a gentle squeeze.

"Yeah. Thanks." Lewis dipped his chin.

I made my way over to Cole. "Hey, man." I slapped him on the back, then gave Ava a kiss on the cheek hello. "Ava? Always good to see you."

"You too." She smiled, but no light touched her eyes. She fell in beside Cole. But as he draped his arm across her shoulders, she tensed. A couple of inches of distance remained between them. She angled away from him and talked to Maddy about Vancouver.

*Shit. What is with that?*

Since we'd finished the tour, Cole hadn't slowed down. Instead of wild parties, boozy nights, and industry outings, he ran around, doting on Charlotte, his four-year-old daughter, Ava, and her seven-year-old son, Josh. He'd never faltered at being an awesome father. So whatever was going on in his relationship with Ava, I hoped they worked things out. They were so good for each other.

"Hey? Are your folks coming today?" Cole glanced toward the parking lot's entrance.

"No." I shook my head. "They said this would be too much for them, but they gave us their blessing." Things had gotten better with my parents. At least they talked to me now after the accident. And they adored Sutton. But the loss of Phil still plagued them. "Phil would understand."

*No, he fucking wouldn't.* He'd be pissed, wanting everyone's attention.

A pained but light giggle escaped Tia. "He'd be *really* shitty he's not here and would be missing everyone like crazy. But he'd be happy we're here celebrating him, and that we're doing okay." She sniffled and wiped her cheek. Her big, dark sunglasses didn't hide the random tear trickling down her face. Her brave smile didn't hide her heartache. She'd loved Phil as much as Slip, Cole and I had. But she, too, had moved on after losing Phil. We all had.

"Yeah. We are. Come on. Let's do this." Taking Sutton's hand, I led my friends down the long run of wooden steps onto the beach. We headed a short way south along the water's edge, over to the huge rock formation jutting out of the sand. We stopped before it and stood around a low boulder protruding out of the ground. I closed my eyes to keep a leash on my swinging emotions. The gentle rolling waves hitting the shoreline grounded me and calmed my mind.

I drew Sutton close, kissed her on the temple, then faced my friends.

Holding the urn between my hands, I ran my thumb over the engraved plaque.

*Phil Glover*
*24 May 2000—10 Feb 2022*
*Rock On Forever*

With a heavy heart, I placed the urn on top of the rock in the center of my friends. I fell back next to Sutton and entwined our fingers. She squeezed my hand and cuddled in close. *My love. My clarity.*

"Thanks everyone for coming." I smiled at the urn on the rock. "Phil, once again, you hold center stage. You are and will always be a part of our lives and hold a special place in our hearts. We often spent hours here on these beaches. The guys and I thought this was the perfect place to set you free rather than keeping you locked up in that pot. Please don't haunt us if you hate it." The muscles in my jaw ached as I struggled to keep my voice steady. I didn't want to be sad anymore. "I want you to know I will never forget you. You filled my life with laughter, crazy fun, and were the best brother a guy could've asked for. I love you and miss you every fucking day."

Sutton snaked her arm around my waist and rubbed my back. Just her touch was comforting and grounding.

Tia sobbed and sniffled as she stepped forward. She kneeled on the sand and touched the side of the urn. "Hey, Philly. It's been a while. I miss you so fucking much. Even though you broke my heart, I loved you. And I know you loved me. You always wanted to soar, live life, and never be tied down. May you ride the waves and the wind forever. Keep rocking up a storm. Love you."

Lewis took small steps toward Tia, helped her to her feet, and drew her back into the circle. He held her against his chest like she was a delicate flower. But Tia was far from it. She was one of the toughest people I'd ever known. Totally resilient.

"I got you, Tee." Lewis rubbed her arms and kissed the side of her head. "Always."

Directly across from me, Slip splayed his hand across his chest and stared at the urn. Deep grooves furrowed his brow. "Phil, I can't believe it's been three years. It's been hard. I miss that wicked laugh of yours, the partying, and the crazy shit we got up to. I miss playing beside you. You've left a huge fucking hole in my chest. Life without you got ugly before it got better. We've all fought demons and the devil to get here. If you played a part in bringing Sutton, Maddy, Ava, and Lewis to us, thank you. They saved us. Support us. Love us. You'd love them. You may be gone, but you'll never be forgotten. Love you, man. Miss you. Rest in peace."

He wiped his hand across his cheek, then his mouth, staying strong. Maddy curled her arm around his and held him close. Those two were each other's strength. I loved that. It was how I felt about Sutton.

"Phil." Lewis jutted his chin toward the rock. "I never knew you, but I know these guys and Tia loved you. I'm honored to be part of their lives and want you to know I'm taking good care of Tia. She's changed my life in so many mind-blowing ways, and we hope to have a family soon." He rubbed the back of Tia's neck. "I love her and promise to be by her side forever. Rest in peace, bro."

"Fuck." Cole eased toward the rock and squatted. "Hey, buddy. You haven't looked this good in years." Cole chuckled, but sadness punched my guts. I hated that he'd told the truth. That a shiny chrome urn on a jagged rock looked better than Phil had in the last several months of his life. "You certainly messed us up when you left. The days are getting easier, but that doesn't mean for one second we'll forget you. I'll always treasure the laughs, the music, the good times. Hope you're rocking it up there in Heaven with some sexy angels. Party on . . . Love you, man."

Cole wiped his eyes and returned to Ava's side. She touched his arm and gave it a gentle rub, but that was as far as the comforting gesture went.

*Damn. What is up with those two?*

*More drama?*

*Always.*

The girls respectfully said a few quick words, wishing Phil peace and were grateful they'd come into our lives. I couldn't argue with that.

I sniffled and drew my shoulders back. "So, bro, before we send you on your way, can I ask for one last favor? Promise me that the band will get back together before the end of the year? I miss playing with these guys so goddamn much. As much as I fucking miss you."

"Flint?" Slip grimaced as if I'd cut him a low blow to the gut. "I can't guarantee a timeframe."

"I know." I lowered my chin and stared at the urn. In the depths of my marrow, I understood why Slip had needed to get out of LA, away from the parties, the drugs, the booze. To spend time with Maddy, and work on their marriage. To focus on healing his hip and holding onto his sobriety. I supported him without question. I'd give him all the time in the world to get better if needed. But that didn't mean his absence didn't feed my anxieties. I was nervous we wouldn't reform. "I just don't want to be on a break forever."

"There are no guarantees." Slip closed his eyes and swayed on his feet. "I'll come back when I'm ready."

"I know you will. Your health comes first. I mean that." I did. But I'd be better with certainty. I wanted a concrete date for our band to reunite and hated one couldn't be set.

"I'm with Flint." Cole nodded as he tilted his head toward

Slip. "We want you to do whatever is necessary to be well. But yeah . . . I miss the band being together. We'd love you and Maddy to come home."

"Fuck, I thought Flint was the only one with issues—not you too?" Slip clutched Maddy's hand as if steadying himself. "Mads goes back to filming her show in a few months. We're not coming home permanently. You know that."

"We do. We'll work with that." Lewis splayed his hand across his chest. "But I miss you, too. I just haven't said how much."

An ache shuddered through my chest. The band meant so much to all of us. We needed Slip. We weren't complete without him.

"Don't keep shit from me." Slip shook his head like it weighed a ton. "Talk to me, all of you. About anything and everything. I don't want to go through any crap like we've done in the past three years, keeping secrets from each other ever again. Deal?"

"Okay." I bobbed my head in some way that resembled a nod, then wiped my hand down my face. "We just miss having you around. Miss playing every day. I need to work toward something, not nothing."

Music was such a big part of who I was. Without it, a huge void lingered in my chest. The unknown bred unwanted stress. I needed deadlines. Goals. Timeframes . . . to work on a new album.

"I'm not missing LA." Slip stared across the ocean. "I need this break."

"I understand that. And want the best for you. But you've gotta fucking come back." My heart hurt without having Slip only a couple miles away.

"I don't want to risk fucking up." Apprehension quaked low in Slip's tone. "My hip is good, but I don't want to re-injure it. When I'm more confident about being in control around booze and drugs, I'll let you know. Mads and I need more time together."

"That's cool." I pulled the reins back on my tone and dialed down my volume. I didn't want to upset him. "We all just love you, care about you, and miss you as much as we miss Phil."

"At least I'm still kicking." Slip threw me a lop-sided smirk.

I placed my hand across my heart and dipped my chin. "And for that, I will be forever thankful. Don't ever scare us again."

"Then don't pressure me to come back." He was serious, but so was I. Slip needed a little nudge and a ton of reassurance to let him know how much he meant to me and the guys, if nothing else.

"We're not The Flintlocks without you." I meant that with all my heart. "Our fucking lives depend on you."

He winced, stared toward the sand, then nodded. Puffing air through his nose, he smirked. "So much for no pressure."

"No. No pressure." Softening my tone, I winked at him and let the conversation rest. "Not today. It's Phil's day." I picked up the urn, hugged it tight to my chest and headed toward the low rocks that led out into the water. I stared toward the horizon, drew in a deep breath, and took off the lid.

Everything seemed to still.

No sound hit my ears. No wind touched my face. My heart dared not beat.

Images of Phil laughing, dancing, and playing his guitar flickered through my mind. As I stared at the gray ash, a calm washed over me. A lone tear slid down my face, but I smiled. *Yeah, this is right. What he wants.*

"Goodbye, bro." I whispered. "For now. Not forever. Love you."

Everyone gathered around and hugged me. They placed a hand on the urn and said their goodbyes.

After a gentle wave crashed on the shore and slowly retreated, I tipped Phil's ashes into the water. In slow, languid rolls, they drifted out, past the rocks and into the depths of the deep, blue sea.

I stood huddled next to my friends. Each one of us held a hand over our hearts and watched the serene waves take Phil toward the setting sun.

I said one silent last prayer. *Help me get the band back together. Can you do that? Please?*

If Sutton was my wife and my band was back together, life would be complete. *Perfect.*

At least I could do something about one of those things.

And I couldn't wait.

# Chapter 2



In my storage room at the back of the garage, I opened a plastic tub and took out the top notebook. Holding it to my nose, I inhaled the smell of paper, searching for a lingering scent of him . . . of *Phil*. I smiled at the faint hint of cigarette and pot teasing my nostrils. Memories flooded my mind as I smoothed my hand over the worn edges of the old spiral-bound book. Phil's messy handwriting was scribbled across the cover. Each page had turned yellow, wrinkled, and faded. But his words marked every leaf. Lyrics. Thoughts. Music.

Three more notebooks peered up at me from their resting place in the box.

I'd read every one when Phil had given them to me . . . no, thrown them at me . . . after we'd broken up. I'd tossed them, along with most of my belongings, into storage when I'd moved to Chicago. I'd forgotten I had them until I was unpacking things into my new home I'd bought with Lewis.

When I'd found them, I'd re-read them. I'd laughed. Cried. And at the beach today, I'd had an overwhelming feeling to share them. Maybe Phil was talking to me from *the other side*. Who knew? But the things Phil had written weren't just about me. There were many songs that were about the guys, too.

There were moments of happiness, darkness, and a crazy lot of fun. It was time to hand them on.

Everyone was here, at Lewis's and my place, after spreading Phil's ashes. The timing was perfect.

I gathered up the four notebooks, held them against my chest and headed into the living room where everyone lazed around on the sofas and the floor, having a drink after dinner.

I ambled over to join them and sank into the seat beside Lewis. He kissed me on the cheek and smiled. "Love you."

"And I love you." I caught his chin, touched my lips against his, then placed the notebooks on my lap. I flattened my palms against the top cover and searched my head and heart again to make sure this was right. *Yes. It is.*

"Guys?" I glanced from Flint, to Cole, to Slip. "I have something for you. For you to use, if and when, you decide to work on your next album."

Flint pinched his eyebrows together as he glanced at my lap. "What've you got there, Tee?"

I flicked through the pages of the top notebook. "These were Phil's. I've had them in storage for years."

Flint and Cole put down their beers on the coffee table. Slip shuffled forward on the sofa. Curiosity shimmered in their eyes.

I closed the book and stared at the cover. "They're full of lyrics, notes, and music. Most of them are from back in high school and when I was at college. They may be useless, but I want you to have them. You might find something you can use, or that will inspire new material."

"Tee, aren't they personal?" Cole winced and rubbed his chest as if it ached. "For your eyes only?"

*Are they? No. They were Phil's.* I traced Phil's name on the cover. "Phil was part of our lives. These belong to everyone. There are many songs about the things you guys did together. Parties. Events. *Girls.* Some of the lyrics are dark, but most were written before he got sick. When he was happy."

"Tee?" Slip leaned forward, resting his elbows on his knees. Concern edged into his tone. "Are you sure you want us to have them?"

The steady strum of my pulse didn't alter. "Yes. His lyrics shouldn't remain lost, or forgotten, or tucked away in an old box. Phil wouldn't want that. You don't have to use them. I just thought you might like to read them."

"Thank you. We will." Slip took a notebook and flicked through the pages, then chuckled. "Fuck . . . he had the worst handwriting ever."

Cole grabbed another one. "Yeah, but he had a way with words."

Flint hesitated before taking a notebook. "Thanks, Tee. The lost lyrics of Phil, huh?" He jutted the notebook toward Lewis. "Have you read these?"

"Yes." Lewis nodded as he curled his hand around my thigh. "It has given me a deeper understanding of who he was, how much he loved you, Tia, and life. Also, how messed up he was. But there's some good shit in there if we ever want to do something with them."

Trouble stitched deep lines into Slip's brow. He smoothed his hands over the cover of the book resting on his legs. "We'll see."

Like the guys, I missed Slip living nearby. He was like a brother to me. But I, out of everyone here, knew how good it was to escape the place that had caused so much pain. Sometimes you needed to run away to find yourself again. To heal the cracks in your heart. Leaving LA for three years had done wonders for me. Slip and Maddy had left town, and from where I sat, it looked like it was working for them. Both looked happy and healthy. That was worth the band having a break.

But I didn't miss the agony radiating off Flint. He'd never be the same if Slip didn't come home and the band didn't reform.

I'd learned you couldn't run away from your problems forever or stay away from those you loved and belonged with. My time acting in Chicago had been what I'd needed. It had irrefutably changed me. It had forced me to grow up. Had put much needed distance between Phil and me. I'd fallen in and out of love again, and had incurred an injury that had broken not only my ankle and half my leg but also my soul. I'd had to face the harsh fact I'd never be the same. Coming home hadn't been easy. But these people, my family, helped me navigate my way forward. I'd needed their love and support. I was beyond lucky to have found a new career working with the band and a new love. Lewis was my partner for life.

A baby would give us the family we'd always wanted.

But why the fuck wasn't I pregnant yet?

After months of trying and trying? After check-up after check-up?

Medically, there was nothing wrong. Lewis wasn't firing blanks. My hormones were on point. We were fit and healthy. I was taking pre-natal vitamins. We were doing everything right. But still . . . no baby.

*Ergh!* I flicked my doubts aside and reached for the TV remote. "I have one more thing to show you." I pointed the controller toward the flat-screen mounted on the wall and turned it on. "I made a video. If it's okay, I'd like to play it."

"Is this one of your sex tapes, Tee?" Intrigue flitted through Slip's eyes.

"Why? Do you need to learn something new?" I teased. Slip and I had always been great friends. He'd been closer to me than my actual brother. He'd helped me through my awkward teenage years and my turbulent relationship with Phil. We'd talked through every boy-girl experience and drama we'd faced. There'd never been a subject off-limits. And we'd never betrayed each other's trust.

Slip grinned a big, cheesy grin. "Tee, there is nothing on this planet you could teach me that Mads and I haven't already done."

"Okay . . . okay," Cole cut in, holding out his hand, and he paled. I loved making my brother squirm. He was protective of me and liked to think I was all sweet and innocent. "I do not want to hear about your sex lives. Tee, what's the video?"

"It's of Phil." I grabbed my phone and searched for the file to cast.

"I'd really like to see it." Cole sank back into the sofa and entwined his fingers with Ava's. The vibe coming off them had been tense all afternoon. They hadn't been as affectionate as normal. Hadn't goofed around each other like usual. Maybe Cole was emotional about today's scattering of Phil's ashes. *I get that.* Maybe they'd had a fight. *No relationship is perfect.* But there was love for each other in their eyes. There were random small smiles. Playful nudges. The gap between them was there, but not as severe as it had seemed earlier. I hoped everything was okay.

"Is everyone else alright if I play it?" I scanned my friends. No one objected.

I hit play, and the TV screen filled with the video.

I'd spent hours sifting through old footage of the guys since we were kids, from the early days playing in my parents' garage, to Phil in high school, to the two of us at prom, to the guys performing small gigs, to the last time they played together on their second tour. My edits homed in on Phil's laugh, his antics on stage, his energy, his smile. He lit up playing beside Flint, he loved outdoing Slip jumping around during a show, and he fed off Cole's electric drumming.

Something about bassists did it for me. First Phil. Now Lewis. *Maybe I should get my head checked!*

*Nah! Never.*

As the video progressed into The Flintlocks' song, *Missing You*, the frames transitioned from photographs of Phil dressed up for awards shows to stills of the four guys playing on stage. My heart hurt as my personal images of Phil and me together flickered across the screen. At the skate park. At the beach. Drunk at some party. Lying in each other's bed. His wavy, dark blond hair hung low across his hazy, I'm-stoned, hazel eyes. His cheeky grin and gorgeous lips gave off that I-know-I'm-sexy vibe.

God, I'd loved Phil.

No matter how troubled our past was, he'd always hold a special place in my heart. It had taken me a long time to get over him and move on. But I had. I'd found a new love, a deeper connection with someone who wasn't afraid to say they were mine. Someone who wanted the world to know we were together, against the odds. Lewis made me happy in every way.

He'd be an amazing father. I couldn't wait to be a mom. *Please . . . let me be pregnant.*

My video rolled into the guys on their second tour with Phil. As the degradation in Phil's health became more evident, tears stung my eyes. Dark shadows circled his now sunken eyes. His skin tone, sickly. He'd lost weight. But I ended my trip down Memory Lane with shots and footage of the band and me together, smiling. Happy. Best of friends. *Family.* That was the way I wanted to remember Phil. We were here today because of him.

At the end of the video, Flint came over, kneeled on the floor, and wrapped his arms around me. He rested his chin on my shoulder and sniffled. "Thank you. That was amazing. I miss him, Tee. Every fucking day."

"Me too. Be honest with me," I whispered in his ear. "Are you doing okay?"

"Yeah. I am." He leaned back and rubbed my arms. "Love you."

"Same."

As Flint returned to sit beside Sutton, everyone's eyes glistened with tears. The love and loss and strength we shared filled my chest with warmth. These people were my life.

Cole raised his beer. "In memory of Phil. May he live on in our hearts forever. To Phil."

Everyone lifted their drinks and chinked them together. "To Phil."

I sniffled and dabbed my fingertips beneath my wet eyelashes. "Excuse me. I need to use the restroom."

I dashed down the hallway to the bathroom and closed the door behind me. But as I sat on the toilet, my heart shattered into a zillion pieces. *Fuck. Fuck. Fuck.* I'd gotten my period. *No. No. No.* Yet another month had gone by without becoming pregnant. What was wrong with me? Disappointment hurtled through my veins and sank into the depths of my stomach. I'd failed to conceive yet again.

*Shit.*

I did my business, cleaned up, and rushed upstairs to my bedroom to change my panties. But rather than rejoining my friends when I headed downstairs, I diverted to the kitchen. I needed a moment alone. I made a cup of herbal tea and headed outside for some fresh air. Given it was the middle of February, it was chilly. I didn't care. But as I closed the door behind me, I didn't have the patio to myself. Slip sat on the outdoor sofa, staring out across the city lights.

"Hey?" I ambled over to join him. "You okay?" I curled onto the cushion beside him and cradled my cup between my hands, absorbing the warmth. Steam curled into the night air, then disappeared into nothing.

"Yeah." He patted and rubbed my knee. "I just needed a

breather. It's still hard being around alcohol. I want to get to where it doesn't bother me. Where I'm not tempted to grab a bottle. Where my throat doesn't burn for a taste. Where every cell in my body doesn't crave a hit. I'm not there yet, Tee. Just seeing bottles of beer on the table and smelling the wine on Maddy's breath before had me wanting to cave. I'm like a bloodthirsty vampire, ready to pounce and have a feeding frenzy."

"Shit. I'm so sorry. I should've been more mindful and not had alcohol tonight." I never wanted to make him feel uncomfortable. I loved him too much. "I just want everything to be right." A pathetic sob escaped me.

"Hey? I'm okay. Are you? What's up?" He hooked his arm around my shoulders and drew me against his side. "Did Phil's video get to you? It was amazing, by the way."

"Thank you. The video was fine, but I'm not okay." I rested my head against his shoulder. "I just got my period. No baby yet."

"Oh, Tee. I'm sorry." He kissed my hair. "You and Lewis haven't slowed down since the tour. You've bought a house. Moved in together. You've had a busy awards season. You need to stop. Relax. Chill. Then maybe a baby will happen."

"We've been trying for months. It shouldn't take this long."

The sliding door opened, and Lewis walked over to join us, blowing on his hands then stuffing them into his hoodie pockets.

"Tee?" Lewis sank onto the sofa beside me and draped his arm over my shoulders. I turned and curled against his side, tucking my feet up onto the cushions. I breathed his sweet, earthy scent into every cell in my body and cuddled closer to him for warmth.

He kissed my forehead. "Sweetheart? What's going on?"

"I just got my period. I'm sorry. No baby."

"Oh." The disappointment in his tone reflected my own, crushing my chest. He wanted kids as much as, if not more, than me. "Not meant to be this month. It's okay. We'll keep trying. It will happen. Trust me."

"Lew?" Slip chuckled, low and soft. "You are sticking it in the right hole, aren't you?"

"I certainly am." Lewis's soft laugh rumbled through his chest. "I was gay, not stupid. While all available options are great, I know which one to use for getting pregnant."

"Good." Slip's eyes glinted in the dim lights. "Just checking."

"Love you, asshole." Grinning, Lewis leaned behind me and play-punched Slip in the arm. "How's life in Canada?"

"Cold. Snow-ridden. But awesome." Slip rested his arm along the back of the sofa and swiveled toward us. "We've only been on the island for a month. We're still finding our way around the place and settling in."

"Can't wait to come and see it." I jabbed my foot against his leg. "Are you up for visitors yet?"

"Um . . . not yet. I need to work on this a bit more." He tapped the side of his temple. I admired his strength and resilience when it came to getting better. Rehab and recovery took time. Being here was hard on him, but today wouldn't have been the same without him.

"Slip, you do what you have to do to get better. We're not going anywhere. But we miss you like crazy. Lewis and I are busy with awards until the end of March. In April we're heading to Ibiza with Morgan, Lewis's DJ friend, for some shows, then we're going on the festival circuit with Duke in May. Maybe we could come after that?" I'd kept our calendar full to take my mind off babies. But I'd been kidding myself. Becoming pregnant was all I thought about every day.

"Maybe." Slip rubbed and patted my ankle. "I'll keep you posted."

"We'll need a vacation by then." I ran my palm over Lewis's stomach. *Hmm. Love these abs.* "Won't we, babe?"

"Sure will. But Tee?" Lewis wriggled his eyebrows, then pressed his lips to mine. "Vacation or not, there won't be any resting. There will be lots of baby-making practice. Every day if needed."

I cradled his scruffy cheek and swiped my thumb over the soft stubble. Smiling, I lowered my voice. "Good thing I'm okay with that."

"Actually . . . if I'm up for visitors by then, it would be nice if everyone came to see us around that time," Slip suggested. "We have plenty of room."

Time with our friends was always fun. Visiting Slip and Maddy's new home-away-from-home after the busy few months ahead would be perfect. I needed to unwind. De-stress. Chill out. Get fucking pregnant.

"The more the merrier." I clutched and squeezed Slip's hand. "We'll be there. With bells on."

I couldn't wait. It'd be fun.

But fuck, I hoped I was pregnant by then.

# Chapter 3



I'd been in front of some rowdy, unruly crowds in my time, but I'd never been so terrified and nervous as I was standing in front of my daughter's preschool class for meet-the-parent day. Twelve moms had turned up to voluntarily assist the teacher for the morning session. It was standing-room-only at the back of the class. I could handle the adults. I'd throw them a few flirtatious winks and smiles, and they'd be a captivated audience. But the twenty-five four-year-olds playing on the mat before me had me breaking out in a cold sweat.

I could never be a teacher . . . or a child entertainer. *No. Fucking. Way.*

The yelling and screaming, chaos and clatter filling the room was insane . . . and I played the fucking drums. The kids . . . this noise . . . created some serious decibels!

But I wanted to be there for Charlotte. My parents had never gone to any of my schooling events. They'd never attended careers days, teacher interviews, sports carnivals, or musicals. None. I was adamant I wouldn't disappoint Charlotte . . . or Josh, Ava's son, in the same way.

"I've never been in front of this many kids before." I tugged on the lapel of Ava's suit jacket to steady myself and ward off the dread loitering inside my chest. Riley, my bodyguard, stood next to her. He'd wanted to come along for a laugh. *Great.* But I prayed I didn't need him to save me from this hyperactive crowd.

"You'll be fine." Ava placed her hand over my heart and tapped it. "Just remember, they are four."

"You sure about that?" My pulse spiked as the kids jostled around on the mat, play-fighting, shrieking, and laughing. The moms stood at the back of the room whispering to each other in hushed tones, and the teacher wrote on the whiteboard.

"Yes." Ava poked the center of my chest. "You're a big kid. You'll fit right in."

"But you love me." I caught Ava's hand and winked at her. She did that sexy arch-of-one-eyebrow thing that always lured me in.

"Yes, I do." Smiling, she slipped her hand out of my hold and waggled a finger at me. *Hmmm.* I'd love to grab it, suck it, and make her quiver all over . . . but unfortunately, this wasn't the time or the place. She slapped my arm as if she'd read my dirty mind. "Now have fun. Charlotte is just happy you're here."

I was too.

I loved my daughter. And Ava. I wanted Ava in my life even more than she was at present. I'd asked her to move in with me again, for the third time, a few weeks ago, before we'd spread Phil's ashes into the ocean. It hadn't gone down well. She wasn't ready. Not after the hell her ex, Luther, had put her through. She needed more time. Didn't want to rush things.

But we'd gone slow.

We'd been together for more than a year.

How much more time did she need?

Every day, Ava and Josh melded more and more into my life and Charlotte's. We spent almost every moment together. Wasn't moving in with each other the next logical step?

Or was my FOMO playing havoc with my mind?

Flint lived with Sutton.

Tia and Lewis had shacked up together.

Slip and Maddy were married.

I was the only one who didn't live with their partner. And fuck … I wanted Ava to move in so badly.

We both hated driving through heavy traffic between my home in Laurel Canyon and her place in Los Feliz. Her house was super tiny and too noisy, and near a main road … and her dad lived there. When I stayed over, our kids had to share a room. Ava's bed squeaked … a lot. I didn't like to fuck quietly, and the walls were extremely thin.

We loved spending time together. She was the only woman I'd ever known who could keep up with me—in and out of the bedroom. She often kicked my ass, and I freaking loved it.

It wasn't a deal breaker, but hopefully by the end of summer, she'd move in with me. I'd do everything possible to make it happen. Do everything to ensure she was comfortable and confident about being together.

I could be very persuasive when my tongue was between her legs. *Hmmm. Later.*

Right then, I was in dad-mode.

Being a father was a tie with drumming as the best job in the world.

I gave Ava a quick kiss on the cheek, then jutted my chin toward Riley. "Save me if it gets too crazy in here."

"Cole, I can't wait to see how you handle a bunch of kids." Riley laughed, turned, and headed over to the side of the room with Ava.

*Shit. What am I in for?*

Charlotte jumped up off the mat from playing with the kids, ran over to me, and slammed into my legs. "You ready, Daddy?"

"Sure am." I ruffled her blonde curls.

As we took a seat beside each other on little green chairs in front of the class, a cherub smile lit her face. I was so tall my knees were bent up around my ears. Not the most comfortable position. I adjusted the drumsticks sticking out of my rear pocket and wriggled on my tiny seat. I couldn't wait to get this talk over and done with.

"Alright, class. Quiet time." Mrs. Dawn Falvey, Charlotte's teacher, stepped forward from the whiteboard and raised her hand. It took a minute for the kids to settle, sit on their asses, and face the front. Big round eyes, toothy smiles, and snotty noses loomed before me. Mrs. Falvey softened her voice and talked to the class. "Good morning, everyone."

"Good morning, Mrs. Falvey," the kids replied in unison.

"And a big hello to all the moms who've joined us." Dawn waved toward the moms, then held her hand out toward my kid sitting beside me. "Today is Charlotte's turn to bring someone in to visit. She has brought her dad in to talk to us. Charlotte, would you like to introduce him and tell us what he does?"

"Yep." Charlotte jumped to her feet. Harper, my cousin and nanny, had dressed her in black jeans, a sequin top, and boots. *Total badass vibe.* My kid had insisted on dressing like a rock star.

She lowered her red star-shaped glasses over her eyes, then jammed her hand onto her hips, struck a pose, and pointed her thumb toward me. "My daddy's name is Cole. He's a drummer." My daughter was every bit the show pony. She'd being hanging around Flint way too much. "His band is The Fhintlocks. He plays moosic really loud with Fhint, Slip and Lewis. And . . . um . . . he has a really big kit too."

I bit my lip, trying not to laugh. *Oh . . . my kit is big alright!* But I had to stay age appropriate. Ava and Riley pursed their lips, clearly trying not to laugh. Yeah, their minds were as dirty as mine.

"He's teaching me to play." Charlotte's bright green eyes glittered bright. "I'm getting good, aren't I, Daddy?"

"Yeah. You're awesome." I ruffled her hair, and she giggled.

"Thank you, Charlotte," Dawn said as Charlotte plonked down onto her chair. "Mr. Tanner, would you like to tell the children how you became a drummer and what you do on a daily basis?"

"Sure." I wriggled on my seat and wiped my clammy palms on my jeans. "I started playing the drums when I was about your age and went to lessons twice a week for years. When I was nine, I formed a band with my friends who lived on the same street as I did. We practiced just about every day, worked very hard, and started playing gigs when we were in high school. We were signed to a record label just after we graduated." Blank faces loomed before me. *Fuck, I'm boring them.* Tough crowd, and not my usual demographic.

"We've released three albums and had some hit songs. You might have heard them on TikTok or YouTube or streamed them." I got nothing other than open mouths and blank gazes, like I was speaking a foreign language. *Shit.* I scratched my cheek. What else could I say to four-year-olds? *Think. Think. Think.* "My band and I went on a huge tour last year and played lots of shows around the world. Right now we're on a break, taking a long vacation, but when I'm working, I spend every day with my band, writing and creating music. We practice and play for hours, often till very late at night. We also do a lot of promotional work which involves photoshoots, being on TV and the radio, meeting fans at events, and performing. It's great fun but a lot of hard work."

*Still nothing.*

*Fuck.*

*Great work, dick. Really connecting with these kids. Not!*

Dawn stepped forward and clasped her hands together.

"That sounds very interesting and exciting." She smiled sweetly at the kids. "Who has some questions for Mr. Tanner?"

"Me?" A boy with flaming red hair and a face of super-sized freckles shot up his hand.

Dawn pointed at him. "Yes, Floyd?"

"How many songs can you play?"

"Um . . ." *Geez.* I rubbed my forehead. *How the fuck would I know?* "Hundreds, if not thousands. I've never counted them before."

A girl with black ringlet pigtails shot up her hand. "Do you know Billie Eilish?"

"Um . . . I met her at an awards show once. She's really nice. But no."

"What about Taylor Swift?" she asked again.

"Nope. I've gone to events she's been at, but I've never met her."

The girl's shoulders deflated like I'd destroyed her dreams. I knew a lot of fucking people, but more bands than solo artists.

A boy with a big round face and glasses rose to his knees and folded his arms. He pouted and drew his brow down over his eyes. Oh, a serious question was coming. "Do you get in trouble for playing too loud?"

I chuckled and wriggled on the chair to keep the blood circulating in my ass. "When I was a kid, yes. All the time. My mom didn't like the drums, so I had to play them in the garage. But now I live in my own house, I can play as loud as I fu . . . freaking want and for as long as I want."

A girl in the front row rubbed her snotty nose, then wiped her hand on her T-shirt. Yep, I would've done that at her age too. But ew . . . *gross.* "How fast can you play?"

"Hmmm." I grabbed the drumsticks out of my back pocket. I shuffled off the chair and sat cross-legged on the floor. I tapped my sticks on the linoleum at pace. *Tap. Patter. Patter. Tap.*

*Patter. Patter,* faster and faster. My hands were nothing but a blur. "This fast."

"Wwwwow!" The kids' eyes widened. The ones at the back of the group crawled closer, peering over the heads and shoulders of the other children and getting a closer look.

I didn't stop as I asked the kids, "Do you know our song 'Fast?'"

I sang low and steady. I could picture Flint wincing and Lewis and Slip laughing at my average ability to hold a tune, but I gave it a crack.

> *How did we fall so fast?*
> *Thought this wasn't supposed to last*
> *I never thought I could feel this way,*
> *You sent my heart into disarray*

"Or what about this one?" I wound back my rhythm. "Fallen" was our biggest hit to date. I drummed my sticks on the floor and churned out the lyrics:

> *If somebody had warned me*
> *That love made you crazy*
> *I would never have fallen for you*
> *If somebody told me*
> *That love made your heart break*
> *I would never have fallen for you*

The kids giggled, laughed, and bobbed their heads. Some sang a few words, jumped to their feet, clapped, and danced. *This is cool.*

I stopped tapping and twirled my sticks around in my hands. "My band and I wrote those songs. Pretty cool, huh?"

"Whoa. That's you?" a girl in a paint-covered T-shirt asked. "So you're famous?"

I shrugged like it was no big deal. "Yeah, you could say that."

Avril, Charlotte's friend, waved at my sticks. "Do you have to be angry to play the drums?"

I chuckled at the seriousness in her tone. "No. Drumming makes me happy. It's a real rush."

"What do you do if you drop a stick?" she asked. "Do you just use your hands?"

"No." Grinning, I shook my head. "I usually have a cannister full of spares near my stool so I can grab one if needed."

Jake shot his hand up into the air. "My dad says rock stars are bad. That you party and drink too much and take drugs. Is that true?"

*What the fuck?* But I wasn't surprised a question like that had come from him. I'd met his snobby-nosed barrister dad in the parking lot a couple months ago. He'd eyed my Lamborghini SUV like it was a piece of shit compared to his Maserati. He'd invited every kid in the class to his son's birthday—everyone except Charlotte. *Asshole!* Who did that to a four-year-old?

But crap, how did I answer that question? "Not all musicians are bad. As you grow up, you'll experience many things. Some good. Some bad. You have to learn what is right and wrong. What you like and don't like. Surround yourself with good people, learn to say no, and know when to stop." I hadn't always done those things, but I'd survived. Changed. Grown up. "I gave up a lot of bad stuff to be the best dad I could be when Charlotte came into my life. Didn't I, sweetie?"

"Yeah." She gave me a high-five.

The moms let out a collective sigh, but the kids just looked at me as if I'd fried their brains. *Fuck.* This adulting and being responsible thing sucked.

Macy, another one of Charlotte's friends, tilted her head to the side and narrowed her eyes. "Do you have a girlfriend? My mom asked me if I could get your phone number. She thinks you're hot and wants to go out with you." Macy swiveled and pointed toward the back of the room. "That's my mom in the green shirt."

"Hi." I waved at Macy's mom.

Macy's mom's cheeks turned bright red as she shrank two inches and hide her face behind her hand.

But ice prickled down my spine. Ava glared at me, then spun to stare down the women. I loved how feisty and protective Ava was. Yeah, Ava was mine. "Sorry, Macy. I have a beautiful girlfriend. Her name is Ava." I pointed toward her, looking sexy as fuck in her black pantsuit. "She's over there with my bodyguard, Riley."

"Why do you need a bodyguard?" a boy with brown curly hair asked.

"Sometimes a lot of fans come to see me. So it's his job to keep everyone safe."

"Does he carry a gun?" The boy's eyes widened as he took in Riley, then turned back to me.

I nodded. "Usually yes, but not today."

"Has he ever used it?" He leaned closer, as if totally intrigued.

"No. And I hope he never has to."

"Have you ever been hurt?" His interrogation continued. This kid was on a roll.

"Yeah. I've been hit in the face with a big camera. I've been scratched, knocked over, roughed up a few times, and mushed in crowds. But I love our fans. Most are really nice."

"Okay, children." Dawn tapped her watch. "Time is running out. Let's see if there are any questions from the parents?"

Every hand shot up. *Fuck!* I flicked a finger toward Lucinda, one mom I knew. "Yep?"

"Any plans for new music?" she asked, twirling her necklace around her fingers.

"No." I shook my head. "Hopefully at the end of the year we'll start pulling something together."

She rounded her shoulders and smiled sheepishly. "Are you doing any gigs around town where we might see you play?"

"No, sorry. Like I said, we're on a break."

A short, curvy lady in a red dress raised her hand. "Is it true Slip quit?"

"What?" I grimaced and shook my head. "No. He's just spending time with Maddy, his wife. That rumor is bullshit." But nausea pummeled my gut. Like Flint, I wasn't convinced he'd come back, and it fucking killed me.

"Mrs. Falvey?" a kid hollered from the floor and pointed at me. "Charlotte's dad said a naughty word."

"Yes." Dawn threw me a stern glare. "Mr. Tanner, please watch your language."

"Crap. Sorry. I mean . . . shit . . ."

The kids broke into fits of laughter, rolling around on the floor.

"Daddy." Charlotte laughed and slapped me on the leg. "Don't be naughty."

"Charlotte?" Jake, the little shit, spoke again. "Why didn't you bring your mom today?"

"I don't have a mom." Charlotte leaped from her chair, whimpered, and curled into my shoulder. She buried her face into my neck and strangled me with her tight little arms.

Struggling to breathe, I peeled Charlotte off me. I drew her into my lap and cuddled her against my chest. I kissed the side of her head and stroked her hair. "Hey. It's alright." I turned to the kids. "Charlotte lost her mom last year. But she is very lucky to have me, Ava, and other family and friends who love and take care of her."

"I don't have a mom either," another boy said. "But I've got two daddies. They're awesome."

"I don't have a mom either." The snotty-nose kid wiped and rubbed her nose again. "I live with my grandma."

"See?" I nodded and kissed Charlotte again. "Everyone is different. And special."

The lunchtime bell buzzed. *Thank fuck!*

"It's time for morning break." Dawn stepped forward. "Thank you for coming in today, Mr. Tanner. It's been very interesting to hear about being in a band." She smiled at the kids. "What do you say, children?"

"Thank you, Mr. Tanner," the class hollered, then they jumped to their feet and rushed into the adjacent room to have their snacks. It took me a couple of minutes to ease Charlotte off me. I hated that she still missed Shelby, her mom, and Keith, Shelby's partner. But I understood. I still missed Phil after three years.

After chatting with the inquisitive, overzealous moms and escaping the classroom, Riley drove Ava and me back to my house. Harper would pick up Charlotte later in the day.

Ava and I headed into my living room and sank onto the sofa. Damn, I'd never savored the peace and quiet so much. Preschool was a whole new level of chaos and noise I could barely comprehend. *Fuck!* Was I getting old? *No. No fucking way.* I was twenty-seven next month. I was still in my prime.

Ava curled toward me and kissed me on the cheek. "You were amazing with the kids. They loved you."

"I think I bored them with the real-life shit, but they loved the drumming." I hooked my arm around Ava's shoulders and drew her against my side. "I hated seeing Charlotte get upset about her mom. It kills me. She still misses Shelby."

"Yeah. Let her feel that. Let her talk about her mother."

"Yeah, I do." I kissed the side of Ava's head and breathed her in. Her hair smelled so good, of something sweet and rosy. "Just seeing Charlotte crumble in front of the class hurt my chest. I wish I could take that pain away. You're awesome with her, too. I hope I'm the same with Josh. I love that little guy."

Ava ran her hand across my stomach in soft, slow strokes. I loved her touching me, anywhere and everywhere. She smiled at me. "Do you think being a dad is your calling?"

"God no. But I love it and I'm doing my best." I rolled toward Ava and kissed the small of her neck. "Would you like to give this daddy some loving?"

Giggling, she pushed me away. "Later. I have to get back to the office. You guys may be on a break, but the workload hasn't stopped. There's the tour documentary to finalize, events to get you to, socials to maintain, fans to keep happy, and your everyday lives to run. Travel bookings and emails are never ending." She sighed, sinking deeper into the sofa. She bit her lip and wrinkled her nose. *Too sexy.* "And I'm helping Flint pull together a certain you-know-what for you-know-who."

I jabbed my finger against her arm. "I can't believe you won't tell me what he's got planned. Is it gonna happen soon? Sutton is dying for that ring on her finger."

"Trust me. I know." Ava rolled her eyes and laughed. "She keeps asking me if I know something she doesn't. It's so hard not to say anything. It's stressful."

"I have a solution." I swiped my fingertips down her cheek, then brushed the tip of her nose. "Move in with me. It would ease the stress. You'd be closer to work. With Charlotte and me. Closer to the band. Closer to Josh's new school." I leaned forward, eased her jacket aside, and kissed the top edge of her shoulder. "And I could do many things to ease the tension in these sexy shoulders of yours."

She clutched my hair and drew me back. She caught my chin and softened her tone. "Cole . . . we've talked about this. I like the way things are for now. I don't want to burst our bubble."

"It won't burst." I took her hand and entwined our fingers. "We'd make it better."

"I love you. I really do. You're the best thing that has

happened to me in years." She swept her fingers through my short hair. "But we're still new. I'm finding my feet. After the hell Luther dragged me through, I need to take this slow. I want to be more confident in my job. In us. In this new life. Ensure Josh is okay."

"I understand that. I'm the same about Charlotte. I don't want to pressure you, but at the same time, I do. I'd love for you and Josh to move in here. We can be a family." That scared her. I understood that. Trusting someone again was hard, but I would do anything and everything for Ava. Being patient wasn't easy, but a must.

"I want that too. But I don't want to mess this up."

"You won't." I was more worried about me fucking up things rather than her. "But if you do, or I do, we'll deal with it. Together. I want a life with you."

She pressed her lips to mine, lingered there for a few seconds. *Hmmm.* I loved the taste of her mouth on mine. She broke our kiss and licked her lips. "I'm yours. We're good. I promise. But can we just enjoy dating for now?"

"Yes. But why delay the inevitable? Is there anything I can do to change your mind? Speed up the process? Or am I missing something?" That wouldn't be a first.

"No." She swept her fingers through my short hair. "You're amazing. It's been so long since I've had a boyfriend. We have fun together. I like having you woo me."

I slid my hand up her thigh and gave her a sexy smile. "If I have to court you, may I take you out tonight? Dinner. Drinks. Dancing. Harper can mind the kids."

"I'd like that."

"Hmmm. Good. But you know I like a challenge. If I have to make love to you every day to prove that we belong together, I will gladly do so."

"Better start convincing me."

I popped open the button on her dress pants and slid my hand into her panties. "Gladly."

# Chapter 4

---



*What the hell?* Someone had parked in my spot. Couldn't they read? What the fuck did the sign "RESERVED FOR SUTTON SUMMERS" mean? *Damn it.* It was April Fool's Day, but this wasn't funny. I was already late, thanks to Flint. He'd had a restless night, couldn't find his favorite Green Day T-shirt to wear this morning, and had needed my help to find it. He'd then left in a hurry with Cole and Lewis to go to a meeting. I'd never seen Flint care so much about a T-shirt. Weird . . . but whatever.

I pulled into a spare parking spot, four rows away from the front of the studio. Flustered, I rushed through the rear entrance and headed for my dressing room. I swung the door open to find my fellow *Angels in LA* castmates, Mia and Peyton, dressed and ready for the day. Farrah, our hair and makeup artist, stood resting her butt against the counter, pulling the hair out of a brush, laughing with them. Mia sat in her chair with Peyton standing, wedged between her legs. They kissed, giggled, touched each other, and canoodled like love-struck teenagers. Clearly, they'd made up after their huge fight yesterday. Their third one this week. *Ergh.* I loved them, but they continually did my head in. I'd spent more than an hour yesterday after work consoling Mia. She'd sworn they were over. Today, it was as if nothing had happened.

I'd never survive in a turbulent relationship like that.

Mia and Peyton had been dating on and off since our show started two years ago. It was *on* at present, but who knew for how long? I was so glad Flint and I weren't like that. We'd had our moments, but damn, we'd never had a walk-out-on-each-other, I-need-some-space fight like those two often did.

"Hi." I dumped my purse on the counter. "Sorry I'm late. Someone parked in my spot. I had to walk a mile to get here." *Well . . . half a mile.* I dashed behind the privacy screen and stripped down to my underwear. As I slipped into my fluffy robe and put on my soft slippers, I eyed the gorgeous red evening gown I'd wear for today's shoot. *Holy shit!* Was that Valentino? It hung like liquid silk on the front of the clothes rack, loaded with outfits for this week's shoot. Alice in wardrobe had excelled. Our budget for clothing was getting better and better with each season. Designers wanted us to wear their outfits, carry their bags, be adorned with their jewelry, and be seen in their shoes. I loved that. With a huge smile on my face, I sank into the swivel chair, ready for Farrah to perform her magic. I was having a bad hair day, so she'd have her work cut out for her.

I turned toward Mia and Peyton and circled my finger at them. "This is good to see. You girls make up?"

"Yeah." Mia rested her head against Peyton's belly. "Sorry for causing a commotion yesterday. I didn't like her flirting with Austin Williams after she'd made out with him on set."

*I would've gladly taken her place, but no such luck.* "I think everyone was envious."

Peyton's scene with Austin had been steamy and a load of laughs. With our show focusing on the disastrous, often funny, dating and working lives of our three career-oriented characters, we always had fun when popular actors made cameos.

Peyton swept her hand over Mia's hair and tugged on a long strand. "Babe, I like it when you get crazy jealous. I can't help it if the studio casts hot guests to play my next dating nightmare. He was funny and nice . . . and an awesome kisser."

Mia rocked back in her chair and shot a fiery look at Peyton. "Okay. Don't push it."

"I won't." Peyton winked and blew Mia a kiss. "Love you."

Farrah grabbed a makeup cape, draped it over the front of me, and fastened it behind my neck. "I could give you a recap of their make-up sex if you wish."

"Ah, no thanks." I slumped in my seat and swung to face the mirror. "I don't need details."

"Hey?" Mia reached over and rubbed my arm. "Are you okay?"

"Um . . . yeah. I'm fine." I wriggled in my chair, struggling to get comfortable. I tugged and pulled at the neckline of my cape. It didn't loosen. *Okay, just strangle me.* "I just hate being late. Flint was off this morning. He has been for a few days. Something is bothering him, and he hasn't told me what it is yet." The tension in my brow hadn't eased all morning.

"Trouble in paradise?" Peyton raised a concerned eyebrow.

"No. God no. We're good." *But are we?*

The past few months, awards season had kept us busy, attending events for my show and for his band. Now it was over, he moped around the house. He cleaned. Gardened. Cooked. Watched endless hours of TV. He missed hanging out with the guys, playing music, and not having Slip nearby. He hated the uncertainty of The Flintlocks' future. I didn't want him to fall back into the depths of depression, hit the bottle, and laze around our home all day. He needed a new interest. A project to work on. Something to look forward to.

And I had a plan to give him that.

There was only one thing that would make our life

better . . . marriage. We'd talked about it. He'd reassured me it was in our future. When the timing was right, he'd ask. For now, he just wanted to enjoy being together. But I had a deadline. I wanted a ring. To be his wife. If he hadn't asked me by our third anniversary in June, I'd pop the question. Our wedding would give him something to focus on.

But the niggle in the back of my mind raised its ugly head.

What if he said no?

What would I do?

What if he still wanted to be with me and just wasn't ready to tie the knot? Would I be okay with that? If he said '*No, I don't see my forever with you anymore,*' I'd be crushed. Inconsolable. Totally devastated. I was so in love with him, I didn't want to . . . no, couldn't . . . think about a life without him.

*Crap.* I couldn't worry about proposing. I had a busy day filming ahead.

"Men are so much moodier than women." Mia threw me a you-can-have-them smirk. "I don't know how you put up with them. But I'm sure Flint is fine."

"I'm sure he is," I said, to reassure myself more than anyone else. But Mia shouldn't talk. She had more mood swings than Dr. Jekyll and Mr. Hyde. I loved her and Peyton. We'd become great friends. But damn, I missed Maddy. She'd been away, working in Vancouver, for years. Now she was on a break, spending time with Slip. I missed her coming home on weekends and catching up. That gave me more time with Flint, though. And I'd never complain about that. "I'll take Flint out to dinner this weekend and get to the bottom of it."

"You always do." Peyton clutched and rubbed my shoulder. "But it's time for you to get ready. Are you looking forward to your scenes with Ethan today? Roll out more of that sexy tension, you two do so well."

"Absolutely." My head bobbed as Farrah ripped her brush

through the long strands. My character, Sienna, had a crush on her boss, Braxton. Ethan fit the role well. He played clueless perfectly. Fans adored him. He was handsome, tall, and had a Ryan Reynolds vibe about him. But . . . he was no Flint. "We're filming the scene where I rush back to the office to work with him on an urgent client presentation first, then we're doing the dinner function I bail on, right?" Many scenes weren't filmed in order. Today was no different.

"Yep." Mia grabbed her script off the counter and flicked through the pages. "We couldn't make it through the table read on Monday without falling into fits of laughter."

"I know." Giggling, I glanced sideways at the girls. "Ethan makes it impossible to keep a straight face when he's trying to be serious. He does this little lip twitch and eyebrow-archy thing." I did my best to impersonate his look, and the ladies burst out laughing. "See? It's so hard to stay in character."

"Nah. You nail every scene." Peyton giggled. "We need you two to keep that boss crush going on forever if it keeps our ratings skyrocketing."

"I'll do my best." God, I loved my job. After nearly being destroyed financially by my father three years ago, and after struggling to find a new role when my previous show ended, I was back on top. I was in my element, being on a popular TV show about empowered, professional women. It continually challenged me and taught me new things, in front of and behind the camera. I was no longer stuck in a dead series or typecast as a high school sweetheart. Dating Flint had renewed and revamped my career, and I had revitalized his. Damn, we were good for each other.

"Sutt, we'll go grab a coffee. You want one?" Mia eased herself from Peyton's clutches, stood, and straightened her suit jacket.

"No, thanks. I had three at home." Was that why I was on

edge? Too much caffeine? *Maybe I haven't had enough? Three cups isn't overdoing it. Is it?*

"Okay. We'll see you soon." Mia took Peyton by the hand, led her out the door, and closed it behind them.

"Let's get to work." Farrah tied my hair into a high ponytail, then grabbed her set of hot rollers. "Ready for an updo?"

"Sure am." I sank lower into my chair and closed my eyes. As Farrah set my hair, I ran through lines in my head. But my mind kept drifting to Flint. Something had distracted him for days. He'd left the room to take calls. He'd paced the garden. Kept emailing and texting madly. But last night, he'd been okay, like whatever had been bothering him had been resolved. A small smile curled across my lips. He'd cooked dinner. We'd made love on the sofa while watching TV. We'd cuddled in bed before falling asleep in each other's arms . . . but around two, he'd tossed and turned until my alarm went off at seven.

I hated he was worried about something. We talked about everything. So this weekend we'd sort things out for sure.

An hour later, Peyton and Mia hadn't returned. Where the hell were they? Maybe I didn't want to know since they were still in making-up mode. Farrah had miraculously transformed my mass of long golden hair into a stylish bun on top of my head and had plastered it into place with a ton of hairspray. She'd done my makeup, giving me perfect smoky eyes and a smear of bright red lipstick across my lips. *Very glam.*

There was a loud knock on the door.

"Can I come in?" our production assistant, Jerome, hollered from the other side.

"Sure," I called back as I admired Farrah's work in the mirror. I pouted and pressed my lips together, smoothing out my lipstick. *Damn. She is good.*

The door swung open. Jerome's large frame filled the doorway. His headphones hung around his neck like a foam medical brace as he greeted us with his big, warm smile. "Morning, ladies. Sutton, Frank wants you on set. He's good to go. Are you ready?"

"I sure am." I twinkled my fingers at him. "Give me five minutes to get dressed."

"Great. Can you please come via the back? There are some boxes blocking the path to the main floor."

"Sure." There was always crap lying around the place—everything from tables and chairs to props to stage lights. That was nothing new.

"Alright. Let's get you frocked up." Farrah recapped the lipstick and put it on the counter. "I have no idea where Alice is. She must be still dressing the guys."

"It's okay. I can put on a dress and pair of shoes." I eased out of the chair, shrugged off my robe, and draped it over the privacy screen. I ran my fingertips over the gorgeous, silky red gown. My skin tingled as I slipped on the strapless dress and buckled on the towering matching stilettos. *Wow.* This dress was more magnificent than anything I'd worn during awards season. How was I supposed to film a scene where I had to be annoyed at my boss in this spectacular gown? I felt amazing, beautiful, ready to bedazzle the night . . . at ten in the morning.

*Shit.*

I had to clear my mind. Focus. Get into character.

*Easy, right?*

I grabbed my script out of my purse and headed for the set, stepping over cables and meandering down the narrow corridor. The silky skirt swirled around my legs with each step, brushing my skin with the softest of touches. *Note . . . go to Valentino for my next few gowns.*

But as I passed the break room, my skin prickled. Half a dozen crew with coffees in hand stopped their chatter, filling the air with a disturbing quiet. Their eyes set on me, giving nothing away. What was that about? That had never happened before. I glided on by, ignoring the unease in my gut.

I rounded the corner of the set, and my breath shot out of my lungs.

I stopped dead in my tracks.

My mouth hit the floor.

Frank, our director, stood by a camera and monitors, chatting with the camera crew. *That wasn't unusual.* Other technicians, assistants and operators hovered about, preparing for the day. *As they should be.* Mia and Peyton were perched on their chairs, flicking through their scripts. I was filming first, so that was fine too. But the set totally frazzled my mind. Braxton's office was adorned with candles and bunches of huge roses. Ethan, dressed in a sleek black suit, leaned against the desk, reading through his pages, cool, calm, and collected.

I charged over to Frank and waved toward the set. "What the hell is this?"

"Sutton, get into position." Frank put one hand on his hip and flicked the other at Ethan. "We don't have all day."

"Uh . . . no." I stood my ground. Our scene was supposed to be full of flustered, stressful tension, not a candle-lit romance. "Can someone tell me what is going on? Has the script changed?" I glanced over at Shona, our producer, and Rhonda, one of the show's writers, sitting at a desk, typing away on their laptops. "I didn't get any update."

"There was no need for an update. There is only one small change." The constant presence of irritation in Frank's voice didn't alter. Deep down, he was a sweetheart. Most of the time. He stepped closer to me and folded his arms. "Rhonda and Shona want to see if a small shift in the dynamic between Sienna and Braxton works. If it does, great. If not, we'll kill the idea. Ethan has a few new lines. Yours haven't changed. If you feel the need . . . ad-lib. You're good at that."

"Yes, but Braxton doesn't know Sienna likes him. Romance isn't their thing."

Frank shrugged half-heartedly. "Time for him to not be so clueless."

"But . . . that doesn't fit the storyline." Frustration coiled beneath my skin. "Doesn't any change like this need to be approved by the entire team of writers? The studio?" I pleaded with Shona for an explanation but got nothing from her other than a blank poker face.

"Sutton?" Frank rubbed his brow. "It's one test scene. Work with me. I have to make this happen. It is what the writers want to see for future planning. Are you able to do this or not?"

"Yes. Yes, of course. But . . ." *Shit.* "Are you sure my script hasn't changed?" It would've been nice to have had some forewarning. But I could do this. I just had to focus. Get in the zone.

I tossed my script onto my chair, walked over to my entry spot stage-left behind the closed office door, and closed my eyes. As I smoothed my hands over my dress, I took a deep breath. I was Sienna. Marketing executive. Ready to be flustered . . . *that is easy* . . . and have an evening full of slow burn tension in the office with my clueless boss. *Yep. Here we go.*

After lighting was adjusted, hair and makeup were checked, and boom mics were in position, the crew gave the thumbs up to Frank.

"Awesome. Alright, let's go." Frank took a seat behind his monitor, then called out, "Quiet on set. Action."

I knocked on the door to Braxton's office and rushed inside. "I'm here. I came as fast as I could." I panted like I'd run a mile, then swallowed hard, halting in my tracks, and took in the office overflowing with beautiful candles and gorgeous pink roses. *Crap. I have to ad-lib. It is called for.* "Um . . . Braxton? I'm sorry. Am I interrupting something? Didn't you call me back to work on tomorrow's Hamptons presentation?"

"You're not interrupting anything. I called you in." Ethan, in his suave suit, slowly came around to the front of his office desk. Okay, I could see why the fans of the show raved about his good looks. He had sexy, short salt-and-pepper hair and a charming smile, but no one was hotter than Flint. Ethan took my hands in his and softened his voice. "There is something I wanted to talk to you about first."

In character, I swallowed hard, delivered my line. "Is it about the promotion?"

"No." Ethan shook his head, slowly.

*What?* He should've said yes. *Damn it! Think.* What would Sienna say? She didn't take shit from anyone. "Well, this is a bit of an overkill to show me how much you appreciate my work in the office and the amount of overtime I do. Nice touch, but I would've been happy with takeout Chinese."

"This is more than a show of appreciation, Sienna." He took a tiny step closer. "Please tell me if I am crossing the line here. But you're impossible not to notice. I've seen the way you look at me. I'm not blind. Tell me I'm not imagining things."

"Braxton." *Shit, this is so off the script.* "I don't know what you mean."

"Yes, you do. Every time I'm in the same room as you, I feel a connection. Tell me you feel the same way. That *this* is something."

"Yes. But . . . fuck." My blood pressure spiked. "Cut." I stepped three feet away from Ethan and spun to Frank. I waved my palms in the air. "What the hell is this? None of this dialogue is what Braxton would say."

"Sutton, that was fantastic." Rhonda stepped in beside Frank. But was that a twisted, evil, yet humorous glint in her eye? She was having way too much fun with this. "Keep going. I wanna see if this works."

"What am I working with, Rhonda?" I jammed my hands on my hips. "We're supposed to be working on a client's presentation, not wining and dining. Braxton is supposed to be oblivious to Sianna's crush on him. This is changing everything. Why wasn't I told?"

"I'm telling you now." Rhonda shrugged, grinning with too much satisfaction. "Let's have some fun with this scene, please?"

*Fun? This isn't fun. This is just ridiculous.* "Fine," I groaned. Did we have the budget to waste studio time? I didn't think so. I turned on my heels and got back in to position. I wriggled my knees, my toes, then stretched my neck from side to side. "Sorry, Ethan. This is just weird."

"Nah, we can do this." Grinning, he wrinkled his nose. "You're great at ad-libbing. I'll give you all the cues you need. I got you."

"Thanks." I took a deep breath and smoothed my hands over my dress. That helped clear my head. "So, where are we picking up from?"

Ethan straightened his tie. "Tell me you feel the same way. That *this* is something."

"Okay." *Crap.* How could I make this scene work? I was supposed to be annoyed with Braxton. My lines hadn't changed. I had to stay true to my character. Stick with the storyline. Sienna liked Braxton, but she wouldn't fall into his arms even if things changed. There'd be no fucking on the desk. If Braxton was suddenly interested in her, she'd be flattered and remain professional. She'd play it cool, not willing to risk her chance at promotion or jeopardize her reputation in the office. That would be believable.

"Action," Frank called out.

Ethan repeated his line. "Tell me you feel the same way. That this is something?"

A dull throb pummeled the back of my brain. But I ignored

it and played along. "Braxton, you're a great boss. Fun to work with. There might be something, but whatever it is, it can't evolve into anything."

"Why not?"

*Because clearly Rhonda was on some weird, potentially drug-induced trip and is messing with the fucking storyline.* I summoned a sweet smile, turning on the innocent charm. "I'm next in line for a promotion. I don't want to be the talk of the office or for you to treat me differently."

Ethan took my hands in his. Was that a tremble? Yeah, he didn't like this change either. But he never broke character. "I can't hide the way I feel about you anymore. I can't wait to see you each morning. Your laugh and smile brighten my day. Your voice intoxicates me." He swept a loose strand of my hair behind my ear and softened his voice. "Sienna, regardless of what people within these gossip-filled walls will say, I'd love to go out with you. Take you on a date. I see my future with you."

*What the fuck?*

"Sienna, please. Be my girlfriend."

"No." I yanked my hand free and took a step toward Frank, but Ethan caught my arm. I yelled from the center of the set, "Frank, why are you going along with this crap? This is utter bullshit. Am I been pranked? It's April Fool's Day. Please tell me this is a joke." There had to be some explanation for all this craziness.

"Sutton, it's not a joke. You're doing a great job." Frank patted the air. "Your reactions are on point. Roll with it. Keep ad-libbing. Please?"

"Shit." I shook my head to erase the frazzle. "No."

"Yes." Frank pointed at me. "Keep going. Action."

Ethan stepped in behind me and placed his hands on my arms. "Sie, I like you." His tone was serious. How could he stay so calm when this was so off the mark? I preferred things when he was clueless. "Sit down with me. Help me change this presentation while we have a drink or two. Then, let me take you out to dinner. Please?"

I dug deep. This was so freaking ludicrous. My blood had overheated. Frank had done nothing like this on set before. Why now? I spun to Ethan and glanced up at him. There was no lip twitch or sexy eye. Fuck, he was deep in character. Okay. I was a damn good actress; I could do this. I took a steady, lung-filling breath, let it out slowly, and found my inner calm. "We'll see. Let's get this presentation done first, okay?"

"Yes, we will. But Sienna, you're all I've thought about for months." Ethan never faltered in his delivery. "I want to be with you, grow old together."

I jerked my chin back a fraction. "That's being a little hasty, isn't it?"

"No. I've heard the office gossip. You're into me. I'm into you. So why not manifest the future I want? You're ambitious. Beautiful. Run some of our biggest accounts. You're funny. And sexy. And in line to become the next senior executive. I like strong women. I can definitely see us getting married."

"Married?" I swayed on my feet and winced. "Brax, the problem is, I don't believe in marriage." My character was hellbent against settling down thanks to her parents' ugly divorce.

He cupped the side of my face. "I'll make it my mission in life to change your mind."

This definitely wasn't in the storyline. But fuck, this day was so weird. I didn't know where to go with the dialogue.

There was a knock on the door. I spun around, but no one entered. I turned back to Ethan. "Braxton? . . . Are you expecting someone else?"

A sly glint flared in his eyes, but he ignored the knock. "Sie, everyone wants to get married. Everyone wants to spend their life with someone they're in love with. I honestly believe that might be you."

I shook my head and took a step back. "You don't know me well enough to make that call."

"Fuck, Sienna." Ethan stormed past me and stopped by the door. "I'm trying here. I've told you how I feel." The low, angry fire in his tone prickled my skin. *Holy shit.* He was on a roll. "But if you don't want to be with me and don't want to marry me . . . then what about this guy?" Ethan yanked open the door.

*Oh. My. God.*

My heart faltered. My knees buckled. Tears sprang into my eyes.

Flint stood there, dressed to the nines in a tuxedo, holding a huge bunch of pale pink roses.

I crushed my hands against my chest to hold my thundering heart in place and laugh-cried.

Flint, my handsome, tall, sexy man, stepped toward me. "I'm glad you didn't say yes to Braxton. Because there is only one person you belong with, and I hope that is me."

"She's all yours." Ethan slapped Flint on the shoulder, slipped to the side and left me alone on the set with Flint. I couldn't see the cameras, the booms, the production crew . . . just the love of my life.

He handed me the flowers. "You look so beautiful."

"Oh my God." I took the bouquet, inhaled the sweet scent, then cradled the flowers in my arm. I trembled from head to toe. "You . . . you organized all this?"

"Yeah, I did." He dipped his chin. "I've been planning this for months. Everyone was in on it. Especially Frank. Rhonda. Shona. The girls and Ethan.

"I knew this scene was bullshit." My heart raced at a million miles an hour. Flint had gotten me good. We always stirred each other, but this was a winner, hands down.

"But this next bit isn't." A sexy glint flashed across his eyes. "Are you gonna give me a chance to say my lines?"

I hugged the roses against my somersaulting stomach and nodded.

His cheeks were flushed. He fidgeted with his bow tie.

I could hardly breathe.

It was happening. I'd been waiting for this moment for more than a year. It was finally here. And it was perfect.

He took my trembling hand and got down on one knee.

A blissed-out sob escaped me.

"Sutton." He grinned, then cleared his throat. "The moment Blake and the guys suggested we date to save our careers, I thought it was a ludicrous joke. When I met you, I swore you were too innocent to be with someone like me. But you annihilated my preconceptions. I never expected you to be so strong. Determined. And desperate as I was in need of change. You broke down my walls. You opened my heart. You brought me out of my darkness into the light. You have calmed the chaos in my mind and grounded me. Somehow, you put up with my band and all of my shit and theirs too. I love your smile, your laugh, the home we're making, and the life we have together. I love you with every ounce of my soul, with all of my being, every cell in my body. I want to spend the rest of my days making you happy, giving you everything you have ever dreamed of." He dug into his jacket pocket and pulled out a black velvet box. He opened it. The most gorgeous emerald-cut diamond sparkled in the light. "So, Sutton Summers, down on one knee, will you do me the biggest honor and marry me?"

"Yes. Oh my God, yes."

He slid the rock set on a white-gold band onto my finger. It fitted perfectly. It glittered. It was the most beautiful ring I'd ever seen.

Flint rose to his feet and kissed me. He dipped me backward, and I squealed. He smiled against my lips. "I fucking love you, Sutt."

I cupped his cheek; warmth filled my chest and soared through my heart. Dizziness spun through my head, and tingles skipped across my skin. I was so happy I couldn't stop crying. "I love you. So much."

The cast and crew erupted with cheers, whistles, and woohoos. From the back of the crowd, our friends rushed forward with champagne and balloons and glasses.

"Oh, wow. Everyone is here." Tears blurred my vision as I hugged Tia and Ava.

"We didn't want to miss it." Cole handed me a flute of champagne. "Congratulations."

"I wanted the people who are a huge part of our lives to be here." Flint snaked his arm around my waist. He drew me close and kissed my cheek.

Maddy weaved her way through the crowd, and I shrieked. I slipped out of Flint's hold and flung my arms around her. "You're here. I miss you so much."

"Me too." She held onto me like she didn't want to let go. "Congratulations. Quick. Show me the ring."

I held out my shaking hand. I couldn't take my eyes off my diamond. It had to be at least eight carats. *Wow!*

"It's stunning." Maddy eyed my bling, then threw Flint a playful wink. "About time, hey?"

"Yes. It was time." Flint grinned, a big, beautiful, relieved, thank-God-that's-over-with grin.

"Where's Slip?" I whispered to Maddy.

"He's at home." Concern flashed through her eyes before she gave me a warm smile. "He's okay. You'll see him tonight before we head back to the island tomorrow."

"I can't wait." There were so many people hovering around us, cheering, drinking, and congratulating us. I was drawn into the celebrations. I'd love to catch up with Maddy, but now clearly wasn't the time.

The past few minutes slammed into me.

Overwhelmed, I swayed on my feet. My heartbeat thundered against my ribs.

*Oh. My. God . . . I'm engaged.*

Flint edged in beside me, cradled the back of my neck, and gave it a gentle rub. "Sutt, I've stressed for months on how to blow your mind. You're all Hollywood. I like the simple things in life, so I combined the two." He patted Frank on the back. "Frank was in on the plan the moment I came up with the idea. We had to find a spot in the storyline where we could twist things around. Ethan was a true champ." He raised his glass to my co-star, then turned to the gathered crowd. "A huge thank you to everyone who kept this a secret and played their part in organizing today."

"It was fun." Peyton stepped from the group and hugged Flint, then me. "Congratulations, Sutt."

"I can't believe it!" I shrieked, jumping up and down on the spot. "I'm engaged." *Holy shit.* "I'm so freaking happy!" I wiped tears from my eyes, then curled my arm around Flint's, steadying myself. "I think I'm still in shock."

"I'm glad I surprised you." He touched his lips to mine, then wriggled his sexy eyebrows. "But this day isn't over yet. You're wearing that gorgeous dress for a reason. It's for the next part of the surprise. There is a helicopter waiting outside in the lot to take us to lunch. We'll be home to have dinner and drinks with these guys." He waved his hand at our friends. "So, if you are ready, I'm going to steal you away for the afternoon."

He'd blown my mind. Stolen my heart. Owned my very soul. I'd follow him anywhere, to the ends of the universe, if needed.

I glanced at Frank for his okay. He chuckled and nodded. "Go. Get the hell out of here so Flint can stop fucking with my filming schedule and messing with my writers. We will re-shoot the original scripted scene with no weird-ass changes tomorrow."

"Oh, thank God." I tilted my head back and laughed, then pointed at Ethan. "I knew that scene was messed up."

"No shit." Ethan sashayed over and hugged me. "But it was fun. Congratulations."

"Ditto." Rhonda stepped forward to give us her well wishes and waved her champagne toward me. "I was stressing Ethan wouldn't pull it off. But he did. The look on your face was worth it."

"It was priceless." Shona veered around her and embraced me. "I knew I loved working with you for a reason. You stay true to yourself and your character. Somehow Ethan pulled it off and Flint . . . well . . . anyone who goes to such extremes to propose, gets down on one knee, and confesses his love like that is definitely a keeper. Congratulations."

"Thank you." I gave her a warm hug, then slid back into Flint's arms.

Grinning, he kissed me on the temple and murmured softly, "I love you."

I couldn't stop smiling. My love for him filled the whole sound stage. I leaned into him, never wanting to let him go. "I love you, forever. But first, where are we going for lunch?"

Sexiness blazed in his gorgeous eyes. "You'll have to wait and see."

I didn't think this day could get any better, and as long as I was with Flint, I didn't care where we went. "I'm all yours. Lead the way."

He took hold of my hand and drew me down the corridor. After ducking into my dressing room to grab my purse, we dashed out the door.

I couldn't wait for my next surprise.

# Chapter 5



After flying in the helicopter for forty-five minutes, we landed on the lush green lawn outside a small vineyard just north of Santa Barbara. The host, Barkley, greeted us and we followed him through a gorgeous garden to a private dining area underneath a beautiful wooden pergola. Hundreds of pale pink roses—my favorite flower—and twinkle lights adorned the exposed beams. In the center of the covered area stood a table set in fine white linen and crystal glassware.

*Oh my.*

"Congratulations." Barkley grabbed a bottle of champagne out of the ice bucket and popped the cork. He poured two flutes and handed them to us. "We're honored to host you for lunch today. Please, enjoy your drinks. I will return in fifteen minutes with your first course."

"Thank you, Barkley." Flint nodded.

After Barkley disappeared through the garden, Flint took my hand and drew me close. My heart still soared through the clouds. He swept loose strands of my hair behind my ear, then placed a soft kiss against my mouth. As he eased back, sunlight glistened in his ice-blue eyes, and he stole my heart all over again. "I'm glad I surprised you. I thought of every possible way to propose, from taking you to some romantic place overlooking the city lights, to flying you to somewhere exotic in the world and having a candlelit dinner, to just asking you one night at home, but I wanted something unique. Something a little crazy. Something different. Something all about you. You are so beautiful, Sutt. I can't imagine life without you. Don't want to."

I took a small sip of my champagne and stared at my diamond as it sparkled in the sunlight. I put our glasses on the table, closed the gap between us, and linked my fingers behind his neck. His gorgeous gaze melted my insides. "This has truly blown me away. I'm beyond impressed. You have given me so much I will always be grateful for. A found family. Your unwavering support. Unconditional love. Together, we found our strength, rebuilt our confidence, and breathed new life into our dreams. From our very first date, we set out on a path I'd never expected. Now, I can't imagine being anywhere else but with you. I can't wait for the next chapter of our lives. Together. Forever."

He brushed his thumb down my cheek in featherlight strokes. "Sutt, there are days I still struggle with losing Phil. But I promise I will do everything and anything to keep the darkness at bay. I know I can do that because I have you. Tell me off if I'm ever an asshole, get too depressed, put a foot out of line, or do something stupid. Life isn't perfect—we both know that. But with you, it's pretty damn close. I love you. So fucking much. I can't wait to make you my wife."

Fresh tears prickled my eyes. My heart swelled to the size of the moon. I was so happy. So lucky. So blessed. "Today was amazing. It was weird and crazy and confusing, but now . . . it's perfect."

"Thank you for saying yes."

Giggling, I wrinkled my nose. "As if I wouldn't."

"True . . . so, I have another big question for you."

I held my breath. What could he need to ask?

"Do you have any ideas about when and where you'd like to get married?"

"Oh my God," I threw my head back and laughed. My heart beat so fast, I felt like I was going to explode. *I'll be a bride!* "I'd marry you tomorrow if I could."

"We *could.*" He tugged me closer and wrapped his arms around my waist. "At City Hall. But I know that's not what you want, Sutt. I want to give you the wedding of your dreams. Anywhere. Anything. At any time."

"Really?" I arched one eyebrow at him. Devious mischief took hold. "Okay then. I've always wanted the fairy tale." I laid on a dreamy tone. "I'd love to get married at Disneyland. Arrive in a horse-drawn carriage. Have a wedding party of twenty people. Invite hundreds of guests. I want to fill the night sky with fireworks. I want every inch of the venue to be covered in flowers and twinkle lights, and to have big chandeliers sparkling overhead. We'll hire the best photographers and designers and have an exclusive magazine deal. I'd love a cake so big it touches the ceiling and an ensemble of ten violinists and cellists playing. We're going to outdo any celebrity wedding that has come before us. I want our day to be the talk of the town for years to come."

With each item I listed, blood drained from Flint's face. "Really. Wow. Um . . ." He swayed on his feet and swallowed hard. "Okay. If that's what you want."

"Yes." I jumped on the spot, ramping up my excitement. "I can picture you and the guys in pale pink top hats and tails. And me in a huge wedding dress fit for a princess with a tiara and a train that is a mile long."

"Hmmm. Okay." He closed his eyes and rubbed his furrowed brow. "Anything else?"

"Flint?" I stilled and caught his hands, holding them

between us.

"Yeah?" He winced.

"I'm fucking with you." I burst out laughing and shook my head. "That's not me. Or you."

"Oh, thank God." He let out a relieved breath.

"I like the finer things in life, but I'm no princess. Not anymore." I cupped his cheek, brushing my thumb against his smooth, freshly shaven skin. "Our wedding day will be for both of us. It is our day. A nice venue with family and friends is all I need."

His shoulders relaxed and light returned to his eyes. "Now that, I can do."

"I'd love our wedding day to be elegant but chill. On the news, but private. Big, but reasonable. But most of all, a fun celebration with those closest and dearest to us."

"That sounds perfect. We'd better get Ava onto it, then?"

"Yes." I ran my hands around his shoulders. Damn, he rocked a tuxedo. "But I want to enjoy being your fiancé, too. I know how hard it is to find venues in this town, so how does in twelve months sound?"

He jerked his chin back. Surprise widened his eyes. "You sure you want to wait that long? We could go anywhere in the world to get married."

"I know, but this is our home." I slid my hands down his chest, then placed them on his waist. "I love Cali. We'll find somewhere amazing and have a spectacular wedding."

"We will. I can't wait." He kissed me, stealing my breath. His hand roamed down my arms, around my waist, and across my back. With every touch, my knees weakened, and heat rushed to my core. Just as I tugged him closer, deepening our kiss by flicking and tasting his tongue with mine, footsteps clicked on the pathway. *Crap.* Flint groaned, pulling me against his hardness. Then he cursed and took a step back. "Sutt, I want to do many sinful, dirty things to you, get you out of that gorgeous dress, taste every inch of your skin, but . . . later. I'll make the wait worth it, I promise."

"You sure?" I panted as the ache between my legs begged for relief. "We could get Barkley to come back in half an hour."

"Trust me, I'm going to need more than half an hour." A devilish smile curled across his lips as he eyed me up and down. He moaned as if in agony, sighed, then tilted his head toward the table. "But right now, I'd love to discuss more ideas for the wedding over food. I haven't eaten all morning, and I'm starving."

"Food works." We made our way over to the table and took our seats just as Barkley walked around the corner with our first course.

He placed steaming plates of spinach and ricotta ravioli on the table. "Enjoy." He bowed and left.

Flint took hold of my hand across the table, drew it up to his mouth, and kissed my ring. "I love you, my fiancé."

"I love you, my future husband." Heat blazed in my cheeks, and I couldn't stop smiling. I took a sip of my cold champagne and savored the sweet taste on my lips. "Was proposing the reason you've been off for the past few days?"

"Yes. I kept checking and rechecking in with everyone. I went over and over the script with Ethan and Rhonda. So many elements had to fall into place. I had no plan B."

*Damn . . .* "Were you nervous? About proposing?"

"Shit yes." His eyes widened as he nodded. He picked up his flute, chinked it against mine, then took a long sip. "I was sweating and shaking the whole time. My gut was in knots. I was so tempted to fly through the door, tell you to stop calling cut, and just pop the question."

"Any option would have worked."

"It fell into place. I'm stoked you said yes."

"Yes. I can't wait to be your wife." *Arrrrgh!* I wanted to shout from the mountaintop. Holler across the ocean. Scream at the top of my lungs. *I'm getting married. I'll be Mrs. Flint Glover. Yay!*

As we ate the melt-in-your-mouth, buttery ravioli, Flint and I threw around ideas for our wedding, venues, dates, and wish list items. Every time he smiled, or the breeze teased his hair, my heart beat just for him.

Our wedding would be perfect. It could rain, hail, or be blistering with heat. I wouldn't care. All that mattered was that by the end of the day, I would be his wife. He, my husband.

I couldn't wait to get a gorgeous dress, a cake, pick a theme, select decorations, and make sure we had every trim and treat for our nuptials.

I stared at the enormous rectangle diamond sparkling on my finger. My heart filled my chest.

I was engaged. To my love.

*Oh yeah!*

Bring on the wedding plans.

Nothing was going to stop me from marrying the man of my dreams.

*Absolutely nothing.*

# Chapter 6

SLIP

As the elevator headed up to the rooftop bar at the Waldorf Astoria Beverly Hills Hotel, I wiped my clammy palm on my suit pants. Beneath my long hair, sweat broke out on my brow and trickled down the back of my neck like I had a rampant fever. It had been four weeks since Flint had proposed to Sutton. Tonight, at their engagement party, it would be my first time around a lot of alcohol and possibly drugs since I'd been out of rehab. Nothing I'd said to myself had settled the unease swirling through my gut or stopped the fear lurking in the depths of my mind. I didn't want to give in to temptation, be lured back to the bottle, cave to cocaine, or taste one pill on my tongue.

*Fuck!*

*I'm okay. I can do this. I can.*

*Maddy's here.*

The more time I spent with Maddy, away from LA, the more I liked it. The move to Bowen Island had been what we needed to get healthy, to strengthen our relationship, and lay a foundation for our marriage. I'd promised Flint, Lewis and Cole the band would get back together, but I had no timeframe in sight. I wasn't ready. They'd been so supportive of my need for a break, even if they gave me a nudge to come home now and then. I loved them for it. It meant they cared. But I refused to give them any false hope. I'd missed hanging out with the guys, but not enough to return to Cali permanently. Not yet . . . maybe never. I didn't want to return to LA without being certain I could handle the shit the music industry and life in the public eye threw our way. Therapy had done wonders. My sponsor was great. I didn't want to damage the good work and progress I'd made toward getting better.

Maddy had been the main key.

It had been months since we'd gotten dressed up to go to an event of any kind. Tonight had called for us to venture out of our jeans, sweatpants, and hoodies and put on something more suited to the occasion. Maddy had outdone herself. Glamorous, as always. Just one look at her in her yellow party dress stole my breath. She radiated pure warmth and sunshine through her big, bright smile. Her long, dark hair shimmered as it caught the light.

We stepped out of the elevator. With a bounce in her step and a hurry-up tug on my hand, Maddy dragged me across the rooftop promenade toward the bar. Her excitement at seeing Sutton bubbled in the air as we approached the mass gathering of guests. There must have been about one hundred people there.

Maddy drew me to a halt beside the oversized array of pink flowers.

"Are you sure about this?"

I didn't miss the anxious edge in her voice. "Yeah, Mads." I set reassurance into my smile and drew in a deep breath to clear my head. *Shit. That's beer. And champagne.* The sweet scent drifted in the air, burning my throat like wild fire. I swayed on my feet but fought the urge to drink taunting my insides. "I wouldn't be here if I wasn't." But how long I could stay was questionable.

She rubbed my arm. "If at any time you need to leave, just say so."

"Will do." I gave her a sly smirk, then kissed her on the lips. "Does that include the need to take off so I can do wicked things to your gorgeous body?"

She caught my chin and arched one sexy eyebrow. "Yes, but later."

"Deal." I kissed her again, just because I could. "I love you, Mads."

"Always." She slid her hands down my black button-up, toyed with a button, then took me by the hand. Just as our fingers entwined, a loud, excited shriek pierced the air.

"MADDY!" Sutton charged forward, flung her arms around Maddy's shoulders, and hugged her tight. "You made it." With tears glistening in her eyes, Sutton laughed. Her infectious energy zapped the center of my chest. *Yeah.* It was good to see her.

"Ohhhhh." Maddy reciprocated Sutton's overzealous embrace, and they rocked from side to side. "It's so good to see you. I miss you soooo much." She shuffled back a step and flapped her hands at Sutton. "Show me the ring again."

Sutton beamed as she held out her hand. The huge diamond glittered in the golden lights.

I hadn't had the chance to see it close up before. *Fuck. It is a huge rock.*

Maddy and I hadn't spent much time catching up with everyone during our last visit. When Sutton and Flint returned from lunch after he'd proposed, they'd been tipsy, wanting to drink more champagne and down some vodka shots. I'd had to leave. Maddy didn't have to, but she'd gone home with me. The craving for a drink had hit hard. It'd burned too much. I'd been sober for eight months. I didn't want to blow it. But I had to take small steps toward returning to a normal life without succumbing to drinking. Tonight would be a good test.

I had my therapist on speed dial. And my sponsor.

But Maddy was all I needed.

Flint swaggered over from the bar to join us. I flicked a finger at Sutton's ring and jutted my chin toward him. "You've done good."

"Thank fuck, right?" An I'm-cool smile inched across Flint's face as he drew me in for a hug and slapped my back. "It's good to see you, man. Real good."

"Same." I patted his shoulder and fell back a step. "Congratulations again. Shall we grab a drink to celebrate?"

Flint stilled. Concern rippled across his eyes. "Are you drinking alcohol again?"

"Nah, man. I'm still sober and loving it." I did. But nothing stopped my taste buds from begging me for just one shot as I glanced toward the bar and the mass of people with champagne, wine, and beer in hand. *No . . . I can do this. I'm in control.* "Tonight I'll find out if those thousands of dollars I've spent on therapy have been worth it."

"We'll make sure of it," Flint said, reassuring me.

"Slip, we love that you and Maddy are here." Sutton rested her head against Maddy's as they embraced. "But if being here gets too much, if you have to leave, or take a break, we'll understand. We don't want you to be uncomfortable."

"Sutt, thanks. I'm okay." I threw her a wink. I loved how my friends cared, but I wished they'd stop worrying. I'd be better off if no one asked if I was drinking again. And even better if there weren't ten types of vodka on the shelf behind the bar. Tito's. Grey Goose. Absolut. Yeah, I'd counted them. Yeah, I wanted a shot. But would I have one? . . *no.* I was good. "Don't worry about me. You just have a fabulous night. Enjoy your engagement. Let's celebrate."

"I'm down for that." Flint thumbed toward the partygoers.

"Let's go mingle."

"After you." I waved him forward. He took Sutton's hand and drew her into the crowd. Maddy and I followed.

After hugging our friends hello, we grabbed drinks from a waiter. I opted for soda and lime. As long as I had something in my hand to keep me occupied, I'd be fine.

Sobriety was a daily battle, but it was one I'd keep fighting. I'd survived eight months; I planned on many more.

Maddy only indulged in a drink or two when we ventured out to dinner or caught up with these guys. She never drank at home. We had no alcohol in the house. But tonight she'd no doubt have a few drinks. Thank fuck kissing her didn't break my sobriety. If it did, I'd be fucked.

She grabbed two flutes of champagne from a waiter passing by and handed one to Sutton. "So, have you set a date? Found a venue?"

"No. Not yet." Sutton's shoulders sank two inches as disappointment swayed in her voice. "Since we announced our engagement, we've had hundreds of messages from companies offering help, suggesting venues, and offering honeymoon packages. It's so exciting. But then . . . everything we've looked at is booked out for at least two years. It's crazy. I need to find a wedding planner *like* yesterday. Ava's too busy with stuff for the band. I don't want to add to her workload."

"I'm happy to help." Ava tilted her head toward Cole, Lewis, and Flint. "These guys are busy, but don't have too much travel over the summer. I'm still run off my feet, but I'll do what I can."

Good thing she hadn't included me in that gesture. I wasn't rushing back to be involved in appearances and publicity events for our band just yet. I needed this break, and if I wanted more time off, the guys wouldn't hesitate to give it to me. Even though it'd kill Flint.

Maddy sipped her champagne, then licked her lips. "Sutt,

if you want a small wedding like Slip and I did at our house, you could use Raya. She was an amazing coordinator. But if you want big and flashy, have you contacted Quill? He's the guy who organized my first wedding and only does high-end events. I'm sure if you drop your name, he'd take you onboard in less than a heartbeat."

It still did my head in that Maddy had come close to marrying someone before me.

Sutton's smile couldn't get any bigger. "Oh . . . I loved Quill. He'd be perfect."

Maddy crooked her head to one side and injected sarcasm into her tone. "Just as long as *your* wedding day doesn't end up like *my* first one did."

"Mads." I threaded my fingers underneath her long hair and massaged her neck. "Noah was an asshole for leaving you at the altar. But I, for one, am glad he did. Now you're mine, and I'm never letting you go." I turned to Flint and jabbed my finger at him. "You and Sutt belong together. Don't you ever hurt her. Don't fuck this up."

"I won't." Flint slid his arm around Sutton's waist. Warmth flooded his eyes as he gazed at her. I loved seeing him happy. "Sutt is my forever. I can't wait to get married. But it's her day. I've just got to wear the suit she wants me in and turn up on time. Isn't that all I have to do?"

"Uh . . . no." Sutton counted on her fingers. "We need to find a venue, pick a theme, decide on decorations, colors, and flowers, select a cake, sort out food, transport, accommodation, and guest lists, plan our bachelor and bachelorette parties, organize the rehearsal and reception dinners, work out who's going to play for us, register for gifts, and book the honeymoon. And I'm sure there are a million other things we'll need to add to that list."

*Fuck.* I was so glad Maddy and I hadn't taken the traditional route. Gotta love a spontaneous Vegas wedding for some things. No stress was at the top of the list. The party we'd had when we renewed our vows was small and intimate . . . and hassle-free.

Flint scratched and rubbed his chest like he was about to have a heart attack. "There is a lot to organize, but you love that stuff. We'll hire a wedding planner to help you. Call this Quill guy."

"I will." Smiling, Sutton jabbed her finger against his arm. "But you're not getting out of anything. This is your day, too."

"Yes, but I've already told you what I'd like. No church. On or near the beach. A big party to celebrate. As soon as possible."

"I want those things too." Sutton's electric excitement was contagious. "After we've enjoyed being engaged for a while."

*Hmph.* I hadn't expected that. I'd thought she'd want to walk . . . no, run . . . down the aisle and marry Flint as quickly as she could. But she'd changed since we'd first met. Flint had been good for her. Sutton had a new confidence and strength that couldn't be reckoned with. She didn't take shit from anyone. Her wicked sense of humor rivaled Flint's. They kept each other's feet on the ground . . . well . . . except for tonight. They were both on a high, celebrating.

"Being engaged is overrated." Maddy giggled and bumped her hip against mine. "Less than an hour was good for us."

*So true.* "Perfect amount of time." I kissed the sensitive skin on Maddy's neck, just behind her ear, inhaling the sweet cocoa-butter scent of her shampoo. *Mmmm. Mio bel girasole.* My beautiful sunflower, who kept *me* grounded.

She flinched beneath my touch. Goose bumps shot over her skin, and she blushed. I loved that.

"I'm liking that notion more by the second," Flint groaned, then grinned.

"Hey!" Sutton flicked Flint on the chest with the back of her hand. "We're going to enjoy being engaged, and we're going to have a fabulous wedding."

"Yes. We will." Flint caught her hand, kissed it, and drew her close. "I just can't wait to marry you."

"Me either." Sutton smiled, melted into his side, and kissed him on the cheek.

"Well, then." I raised my glass toward the center of my gathered friends. "To Sutton and Flint. Congratulations on your engagement. We look forward to being part of your celebrations and your future together. Cheers."

"Thank you." Sutton dipped her chin, then took a sip of her champagne. She turned to Maddy and caught her by the hand. "We will have to line up some weekends to go dress shopping. I can't do that with anyone but you. Will you please be my maid of honor?"

"Really?" Maddy stood two inches taller, towering half a head over Sutton. "I'd love to."

"There's no one else I'd rather have by my side. I wish you lived closer. I want you to be part of everything. I'm so freaking excited."

"I'll be here as often as I can." Maddy hugged Sutton, but I didn't miss the falter in my wife's tone. "I promise."

An ache stabbed the center of my chest. Maddy always missed Sutton, but was she missing LA? That was new. We'd kept in touch with everyone, but other than two quick trips home for the spreading of Phil's ashes and Flint's proposal, we hadn't been here for months.

Maddy didn't miss rushing home every two weeks to care for her mom like she used to do before we'd moved to Bowen Island. Valerie had been away when we'd been here visiting. Valerie's lupus still wasn't under control, but during her brief phone calls, she'd insisted she was stable and doing okay. Bridget, her former home nurse and now live-in companion, had kept her in line. Bridget had been a godsend, giving Maddy a much-needed break from looking after her mom. Maddy's mental health, eating disorder, and worries seemed to have disappeared since we'd been living on the island. Like me, she'd needed to escape.

I hadn't missed parties or going out. It was strange how content I was just hanging out with my wife. Walking. Talking. Reading. Kayaking around the island. I'd gotten back into repairing old guitars after finding some for sale at the local markets. Maddy had taken up landscape painting. She was so fucking good. Our new interests were part of our therapy and recovery, and we loved the creative outlet. But maybe Maddy was ready for things to change. Our travels would amp up once she returned to filming her show in Vancouver at the end of next month. I wasn't looking forward to our getaway coming to an end.

But we were here in LA for two days.

I planned to enjoy every moment of the weekend, catching up with friends.

After our drink, the guys grabbed fresh vodkas and the girls, champagne.

As food came around, we fell into telling old stories, cracking jokes, and throwing digs at each other. I missed this element of our friendship.

But as the alcohol flowed and people got drunk, just looking at the bar became hot torture. The smell tantalized my nostrils and spun through my head. The recollection of the taste on my tongue made my mouth water. My veins hummed as I recalled the buzz. The high. The fun. The kick. The rush.

*No. Stop. Don't go there.*

I grabbed another soda and lime from the bar, excused myself, and made my way to the far end of the rooftop. Taking a seat at one of the small tables, I took a slow, deep breath to clear my head. *That's better.* I stared out across the endless blanket of LA lights, the traffic meandering along the boulevards, and the black silhouette of the mountains in the distance.

Pity LA wasn't always this quiet, scenic, and calm.

"Hey?" *Cole.*

I jumped as he slapped me on the shoulder and took the chair beside me. Lewis and Flint fell onto the seats opposite us. All had bottles of water, no booze. *Thank fuck.*

Cole nudged his elbow against my arm. "Everything okay?"

"Yep." I fidgeted with my glass on the table, twisting it from side to side and picking at the etched logo. "Just needed a moment."

"Take all the time you need. I'm just glad you're here." Cole ruffled the top of my head, flicking my long hair over my face. I didn't miss that.

"Yeah. Me too." Chuckling, I swept my hair back into place and pushed his hand away.

"You're looking better every time I see you." Lewis waved his water bottle at me before taking a sip.

"Thanks, man. Feeling it too."

"I'm really happy for you." Flint reached across the table, slapped my arm, and laid it on. "So, does being here ignite the fire under your ass and the need to get the band back together?"

Never subtle. Not his style. "The fire hasn't gone out. It never did. Unlike you." I smirked, giving him a dig in return.

I understood the desperation and need for music. Our friendship and our band were life. Cole and I had been gutted when Flint lost his connection with music after Phil died. Sutton had been the key to getting it back. But I'd never lost touch with music. I just needed time out. The alcohol and drugs and pain had broken me. I'd pushed myself too hard. I didn't want to find myself in the gutter again. "I play nearly every day. But Bowen Island is where I need to be for now."

"I know you do. I want nothing more than for you to be well.

But just so you know, I've been writing songs." A spark stirred low in Flint's tone. "I'm creating tunes. Coming up with new riffs. Recording progressions. I can't wait to get back together so we can turn them into something amazing."

Cole slumped in his chair. Anguish drifted across his eyes. "Flint, why haven't you asked Lewis and me over?"

Flint jiggled his leg, fidgeted with a coaster, and furrowed his brow. His voice fell to a pained murmur. "It wouldn't be the same without Slip."

The weight in his tone pressed against my chest.

Me being away was hard on everyone, especially Flint. I understood that. But they had my back.

"Thanks, man." I stared at my drink to avoid Flint's heavy gaze. "That means a lot to me." But *shit* . . . a wild notion popped into my head. How did I feel about it? I had no clue. I had to put it out there . . . for Flint. I cared about him too much to not say anything. My stomach cinched and swayed like a sail in the breeze. "If you're that hungry to create new music, why don't you do something that isn't related to the four of us? Work on a new project. Maybe . . . *shit* . . . have you considered doing a solo album?" I held my breath as I glanced from Cole, to Flint, to Lewis and back again, gauging their reactions. All three jerked backward like I'd stabbed them in the fucking hearts . . . and their backs. *Fuck.* I backpedaled a fraction. "Or what about writing songs for other artists? Do a collaboration. Work with Kyle, Gem, Hayden, and Hunter. Everhide would love you to work with their signed artists. You need to keep busy. Keep writing."

"Are you fucking with me?" Blue fire shot through Flint's eyes. "No. Other musicians do that when they want to explore alternate music styles and sounds that differ from their band's vibe. That's not me. I'm not me without the three of you. I don't ever want to go down that road."

It'd kill me too, but I never wanted to hold my friends back while I focused on fixing myself. "Flint, none of us want you to lose your gift again. It's just a side project. Just . . . think about it."

"No." His jaw tensed and ticked. If looks could kill, I'd be dead.

"Whoa. Breathe, dude." Lewis nudged Flint on the arm. "It was just a suggestion. But . . . it's an interesting one." He shrugged and bobbed his head. Then, clicking his fingers, he straightened. "What about that chick you told me about? The one you introduced me to at the LA Music Awards after-party? What's her name? . . . Reba? She was looking for a songwriter, wasn't she?"

*Reba?* She'd lost on the Discovered-On-YouTube contest that had shot Everhide to fame several years ago. She'd had a great solo career since then but hadn't had any big chart-topping hits for a couple of years. We often caught up at events. She was quirky and wild and would be fun to work with.

"Whoa." Cole eased forward, rested his arms on the table, and clasped his hands together. He took a moment to breathe as he studied Flint. "It's not a horrid idea. We'd support you if you wanted to do it. Although it would be like you're cheating on us."

"See?" Flint thrust his palm at Cole and glared at me. "I couldn't do it."

"Fine. Don't." I leaned back in my chair, stretched out my legs, and crossed my ankles. There was no skin off my back. I just didn't want him to resent my time off. I couldn't handle that. Not ever. "It was just an idea. But regarding us, as a band, please bear with me. I'll come back when I'm ready. I promise." I just wasn't there yet, and I was scared I never would be. My love for these guys and music were the only things that kept me optimistic.

"Slip? Ignore Flint. He's got other things to worry about." Cole snickered and jutted his chin at Flint. "You're gonna be inundated with wedding plans. You won't have time to contemplate doing anything else."

"Yes, I will. Sutton will have everything under control. She's incredible and knows what she wants and loves organizing parties. If I help, I'll just get in her way and stress her out. I don't want to do that." He swiveled his water bottle around on top of the table, staring at it. Trouble etched deep into his brow. "It's just weird not having music to work on. After our second tour, we had a contract to deliver another album. Now, after our third, we have nothing. No goal. No deadlines. And I don't like that. I need music and to play in front of crowds and to be with you guys."

My chest ached, low and deep. I'd crave those things too . . . when I was better.

Flint knew that. Respected that. But that never stopped him from having a crack at testing me. *Asshole, but I love him.*

"Flint, come hang out with Tia and me." Lewis changed the direction of the conversation. "We're off to Ibiza next week, then traveling with Duke and his band up the West Coast doing the festival circuit. It will be fun."

*Oh yeah.* Festivals were wild . . . often full of drugs, booze, and raging parties. When Flint struggled after Phil's death, Cole and I had played with friends at some festivals to help them out as needed. It had been a gig here and there—nothing serious. Nothing long term. Not our music. We were The Flintlocks. No other band or venture could replace that. We were tied to each other for life.

But until my soul healed, and my mental strength returned, I couldn't mend the hole I'd caused in our band. I wouldn't let Flint, or anyone else, sway my decision.

"Damn. I love a good festival." Flint slowly broke out into

a smile. He glanced over my shoulder at the partygoers and chuckled. "But I'll pass. I was away from Sutt too much during the tour. She'd kill me if I took off again."

"Who's under the thumb?" Cole kicked Flint's ankle underneath the table.

"I'm not afraid to admit I am." Flint grinned with no shame. "But you can't talk. How many times have you asked Ava to move in with you now?"

"I've lost count." Cole slouched back in his chair and gulped down his water. He placed the empty bottle on the table and crushed it. "I've given up asking. I don't like not getting my way. Why the fuck did I fall for a woman who doesn't kiss my feet?"

"Because there's no fun in that." I shrugged. "Ava's good for you."

A cool smile inched across his mouth. "She drives me fucking crazy, but in a good way. I'd do anything for her and our kids."

"Then the best thing you can do is to be patient." I spoke to Cole but directed my comment at Flint. He just grinned and nodded. He knew that was meant for him. I flicked my gaze back to Cole. "Give Ava the time she needs. Shock fucking horror, but sometimes people need that to figure things out. They need to make sure any big life changes are right and to be confident in those choices. Not everyone processes things at the same pace. Give her some space or you'll drive her away."

"When did you become such a wise old fuck?" Grinning, Lewis waved and pointed his water bottle at me. "Don't go off at me for being the oldest one in the group."

"Rehab did me wonders." I couldn't deny the fact. The journey back from hell had changed me. I honestly didn't think I'd be here if I hadn't. What kept me going every day was Maddy.

But I'd sensed a shift in her. Her mom's deteriorating health and her own return to work no doubt played on her mind. Our escape was coming to an end.

*Shit.*

I wanted to hold on to our life away for as long as possible. But I knew if . . . no, when I came back—I had to be more optimistic—these guys would be there for me. *Always.*

I took in each of my friends. "Guys, stop worrying. Things are good. I'm doing everything I can to get better. I mean that." I pinned Flint with my gaze. "But you need to take care of yourself and each other, too. Flint, think about writing for Reba. Talk to Everhide. You're getting married. Be involved. Enjoy every moment. Don't fuck this up."

He stared at me. He took a big breath, and a warm smile inched across his face. "I won't. And . . . maybe you're right. I'll consider contacting Reba and Everhide. No promises, but it might give me something interesting to work on."

"Good." I was right. He knew it. I jerked my head toward the partygoers. "Sutton is amazing. You deserve to be happy."

"I am. But I'd be even better if the band was together."

A low laugh rumbled through my chest. Fuck, I loved him. "Patience, my padawan."

"Yes, Master. But you know I have none. Fuck . . ." Flint groaned as he rubbed the back of his neck and stared up at the sky. "I've turned into Sutton, haven't I?"

"Somewhat." I bobbed my head slowly. "But you're good. We're good. And that's what matters. We're The Flintlocks. Together for life."

But more change was coming.

I felt it in my bones . . . and my soul.

I prayed I was ready and strong enough for whatever lay ahead.

# Chapter 7



The electric festival energy hummed through my veins. Flashing lights flooded the concertgoers in a kaleidoscope of colors. The sweet aroma of weed drifted on the gentle breeze. Booze flowed. Thousands of people were in party mode. DJ music thrummed through the speakers as stagehands made equipment changes for the next band to play . . . for Duke and his boys. In twenty minutes, they'd close out the last night of the festival circuit.

I sat on an old equipment trunk behind the control panel, sucking on a cold beer, absorbing the festival vibe, and ogling Tia's sexy ass. She stood beside Chloe, Duke's wife, performing final light and sound checks. With her headset on, Tia rocked a pair of leather shorts and a vest that tied at the center of her chest. Her mid-calf biker boots, long legs, black makeup, and dark brown hair in a messy ponytail gave me a solid boner.

Tia never ceased to amaze me. The change in me since meeting her was beyond astounding. After struggling with my initial attraction since I'd only ever been with men, I now only had eyes for her. She had changed the course of my future. I was still attracted to men, but I didn't want to be with anyone else but her.

She was my soulmate. My life partner.

We wanted a family.

It drilled a hole in my chest she hadn't become pregnant yet. We'd had a ton of sex. But none of my squiggly fuckers had gotten through. They were probably fighting with each other for front-row position. *That's my boys . . . and girls.* But none of them had made it to the finish line. *Damn it . . . stupid fuckers.* I couldn't wait to be a dad. But with each month that failed, a dark sadness ate away at the light in Tia's gorgeous green eyes.

I didn't want her to worry . . . but we both did.

We'd agreed once we got back to LA tomorrow, we'd start monitoring her ovulation cycle and bang it out wherever and whenever we needed to, so we upped our chances of conceiving. But for now, I wanted us to both chill and enjoy the last night of the festival.

Just have fun.

The past four weeks, we'd sweltered in the sunshine, laid low, and avoided too much public attention which we often encountered in LA. Tia loved working alongside Chloe. I'd spent half my time flirting with Tia during Duke's shows, the other half stepping in as an instrument tech and stagehand for the band.

It had been a welcomed change of pace after touring the world, attending award season functions, and showing up to meetings with my band's management team to plan for the future. But if Slip didn't come home by the end of the year, The Flintlocks schedule was thin. I wanted to spend the rest of my days playing with those guys. For that not to continue scared me. It had played havoc on my mind. Money was no longer an issue, which was one less thing to worry about, but not playing together again wasn't an option. I wanted The Flintlocks to be my forever band and to have a baby with Tia. But both were in limbo . . . for now.

I had faith things would work out. I held onto hope. And

prayed like a goddamn motherfucker.

Slip's absence had put a pause . . . and a big question mark . . . over *when* we'd reform. He'd said he'd come back, and I believed him. I just missed him like crazy. He'd become my best friend on the West Coast. I couldn't lie. I wanted him to come home.

The Flintlocks and Tia were all I needed.

At nine o'clock, Duke and his boys were minutes away from hitting the festival stage. I threw a sexy smile at Tia. She usually flirted profusely before a show, throwing me winks and kisses, and making dirty, suggestive gestures with her mouth and sways of her hips. But not today. She just turned back to the soundboard and played with some switches. *What the . . .?* She'd been quiet. Off.

The last day of being on the road was always a mix of emotions. There was the high of performing the last show, the excitement of the after-party, and the thrill of heading home— then there was the sadness that it was ending, that you'd be saying goodbye to newfound friends and would miss playing in front of fans. Guessed tonight had gotten her down. I'd make damn sure I'd put a smile on her face by the end of the night.

Five minutes from showtime, the crowd chanted, '*Crimson Dukes. Crimson Dukes. Crimson Dukes*.'

But a commotion at the security barrier caught my eye. Joi, Duke's stagehand, rushed up to the control panel, spoke to Tia, saw me, then dashed over.

"Lewis," he panted, his face contorting as he raked in jagged breaths. *Fuck! How fast did he run?* "Evan is puking his guts up. He reckons the fish tacos he had for lunch were off. It's going both ends. Are you able to fill in?"

"Shit. Are you serious?" My heartbeat tripled and skipped. *Fuck yes, but oh shit!* I'd only played with Duke and the boys a couple of times when Tia and I had gone to his and Chloe's place for dinner. I knew a few of their songs, but not their entire set list. Jumping on stage in front of several thousand people without ever having played their tracks was ludicrous, right?

"We've got no backup bassist." Joi keeled over, clutching his knees. Dude was unfit as fuck. We weren't that far from the stage. "Mila, our usual guy, can't get here in time. Please? Duke is begging."

I rubbed the back of my neck. I was a damn good bassist, but could I do this?

Tia tossed her headset on the panel, ambled over, and slid in beside me. "What's up?"

"Evan is sick and can't play." I tugged on the bottom of her vest, just so I could brush my fingers against her bare stomach. "They want me to fill in."

"You can do that." She patted and rubbed my thigh. "You'll be great."

After playing with The Flintlocks and touring the world, I no longer suffered from stage fright, but churning out songs I didn't know injected nausea into my gut.

But I could do this. Hold the rhythm. Easy.

"I can. But Tee, are you okay?" I caught her hand, pleading for her to tell me what was wrong. I wished she'd smile. Stop stressing about babies, and the gig, and running the lights. She'd worked on enough shows to do this with her eyes closed.

"Yeah." She swiped her troubled brow. "I'm just not feeling the best. I'll be fine after the show."

"Did you eat the fish tacos at lunch?" Concern swung in my voice. "That's what's hit Evan."

"No." She shook her head.

I drew her closer to my side. "You want me to stay with you?"

"No." She swept her hand down my cheek, then gave it a gentle pat. "Go. Have fun."

*Fun? Hell yeah.* "Alright. I'm happy to help." I slid off the trunk and dusted my hands on my jeans. "But Tee, please don't flash any lights in my eyes." Humor rippled through my tone. She often did when I played. It was our thing—for her to let me know she was watching. I secretly fucking loved it.

"No guarantees." A playful glint flickered through her gaze as she pressed her lips against mine. "You love it when I do."

I caught her around the middle and drew her close. "I love you watching me."

"Always do. Love you." She kissed me again, smacked my ass, and shooed me away. "Go. I'll make you shine, babe."

"Okay. But be backstage when we finish."

"I'll see what I can do."

After one more kiss, I followed Joi around the outer rim of the crowd into the backstage area. I flashed my VIP access pass and headed up the metal steps and joined the band waiting on the side of the stage behind the gigantic screens. Duke was running through warmup drills. Wolf, their drummer, and Ezra, their lead guitarist, stood at a table, putting on their transmitters and ear monitors.

"Lew. So sorry, man." Duke dashed over and slapped me on the shoulder. "Are you able to help us?"

"Sure." I wasn't usually cocky, but smugness slipped into my tone. "Not sure if you've heard, but I'm okay on the bass. I can hold a rhythm and keep up with the beat."

"Smartass." Grinning, he shoved me on the shoulder. "But that's what we need. Attitude. Fire. Let's rock this joint."

"Fuck yeah." I clapped. Joi handed me Evan's bass and ear-monitors. I put them on, adjusted the neck strap, and strummed the strings, getting a feel for his guitar. It wasn't as heavy as mine, but it would do.

We hit the stage. The crowd roared, cheered, and danced. I played in time with Wolf's heavy drumbeat, concentrating on each change in the song, adding in depth, rhythm, and melody on the bass. But my thoughts drifted to Tia. The whole baby thing had stressed us out. Conceiving hadn't happened. We needed a vacation. We'd had no downtime since the tour had finished. I needed to take her somewhere nice—Hawaii or Cabo or the Caribbean—and visit Slip and Maddy, so we could relax and do nothing but try for a baby.

Done.

That would be good.

As I glanced across the mass of people toward the control panel, a light flashed in my eyes. A huge grin inched across my face. *Tia.* It was awesome to be on stage, performing in front of a huge audience. I'd never miss this side of being a musician. But I was a Flintlock. My life, heart, and soul belonged to Cole, Flint, Slip . . . and Tia.

They were my family. My future.

At the end of the show, I raced off the stage in a pool of sweat. Tia rushed to meet with her arms open wide. I drew her into my embrace and hugged her tight. Her beautiful smile snagged my breath. So did her glassy eyes, full of tears.

"Hey?" I cupped her face between my hands and pressed my forehead against hers. "Tee? What's going on?"

"I'm okay." Her voice was barely audible over all the cheering and hollering from the band and crew celebrating the end of the festival. "I'm just glad the last show is over."

"Me too." I smoothed my hand over the back of her hair. "That was awesome. But different. It's not the same high as playing with my guys, but still . . ." I wriggled my eyebrows. "It's made me horny as fuck."

Tia closed her eyes, then swayed on her feet. She sobbed and shook her head.

"Tee?" My gut hit the floor. "Shit. I'm sorry." *Me? Thinking with my dick. Idiot.*

"No. Don't be." She placed her hand on my chest and met my gaze. "I love you. I'm just happy."

"Well . . . that's good." Worry still spiked through my veins. "So why the tears?"

"I can't hide it anymore." Her chin trembled. Her face paled. She clutched onto my arms as if steading herself. "All day, it's been killing me. I found out this morning. I wanted to wait until after the show to tell you. To surprise you . . . Lewis . . . I'm pregnant."

"What?" My heart leaped toward the stage lights, boomed in my chest, and spun through my head. Warmth flooded my soul. "You are? You mean it? We're gonna have a baby?"

Tears glistened and shimmered on her cheeks as she nodded.

"Arrrrgh!" I picked her up and spun her around. "Oh my God. This is brilliant." I put her on her feet and kissed her, kissed her with everything I had, every ounce of love I held for her. *Best. News. Ever!*

But we were interrupted.

"Hey, Lewis?" Duke slapped me on the back. "Thanks for tonight. You were awesome."

"Dude, you can play with us anytime." Wolf fist-pumped me. "Totally nailed it, man."

"Incredible." Ezra half-hugged me. "I don't know how the fuck you pulled that off, but you did. It was great to share the stage with you."

"Well, put your party shoes on, boys. We have reason to celebrate." I clapped and rubbed my hands together.

"Last night of the festival. Woohoo!" Duke pumped his fists into the air.

I raised my brows at Tia and whispered, "Can we tell them? Is it too soon?"

She'd just found out she was pregnant. Was it too early to

share the news?

"It is. But I don't care." Tia turned to the guys. "We have another reason to pop the champagne. I'm pregnant. We're going to have a baby."

"Argh!" they all screamed, jumped around, and hugged us.

"That is fucking awesome." Duke laughed but shook his head. "Oh, man, I can't wait to see you two slow down and become parents. It will be a shock to the system."

"Nah." I hooked my arm around Tia's waist and kissed the side of her head. "This is what we've wanted for months. We can't wait."

"Congratulations." Duke bowed, then pointed toward the after-party tent. "Let's go fucking party."

"You up for it, Tee?" Concern crept through my tone. Tia's face hadn't regained any color.

"For a while." She rubbed my stomach. "But this is why I haven't been well for the past two days. I've had morning sickness. I peed on a stick after breakfast. I didn't believe the result, so I did two more tests to make sure. It's killed me not telling you."

"Tee? Don't apologize." I drew her against my chest and wrapped my arms around her. The scent of her jasmine perfume swam through my head. "You've made all my dreams come true. Any happier, I'll burst."

"Don't do that." She rested her cheek against my shoulder. "I kinda want you to stick around."

A big grin pinned onto my face. "Good, because I'm not going anywhere . . . unless it involves taking you somewhere private so we can celebrate, somewhere here or back to our hotel. My balls are aching to do so." That was no lie.

"Can we do both?"

"I like your thinking." After a quick drink with Duke, Chloe, and the guys, I took Tia's hand and led her out of the tent, past the portable toilets, and down the row of dressing room trailers set up for each band. The last one was Duke's he'd barely used.

I drew Tia inside. We had each other's clothes off within seconds and veered into the shower. After a quick freshen up, we made our way into the bedroom with a freshly made bed and shut the door.

As I kissed Tia, I laid her on the mattress, then hovered over her.

"My God, you are beautiful." I kissed her lips, her neck, her boobs, then made my way down to her belly. I trailed a line of soft kisses across her abdomen. "We did it, Tee. You take good care of our little one."

"I will." She combed her fingernails through my bobbed hair and swept it back off my face. "No booze or party drugs from now on."

"That sucks, but I'll stop too. I'm in this with you, Tee." I kissed her tummy again. "Every step of the way. I want this just as much as you do."

Fresh tears welled in her eyes as she nodded. "Then you'd better show that baby some loving."

"Oh, I plan to." I dipped my tongue into her belly button, then swirled around it in a slow circle. "Forever, Tee."

She cupped my cheek. "Lew . . . we're gonna have a baby."

The crack in her voice snared my heart. *A baby.* After so many months of trying.

I made my way back to her lips. With a stroke of my thumb, I wiped away the tears dampening her temple. "You don't know how happy that makes me."

"I do. Because I feel the same way. I love you, Lew. So much."

"I love you, Tee."

I covered her body in licks, nips, and tiny soft kisses. I dragged and swept my fingertips across her smooth skin. As I delved between her legs, a soft moan tumbled from her lips.

She writhed beneath my touch. Her warm arousal on my fingers made me salivate. I wanted her. All of her. To taste her. Fuck her. Make her come.

"Fuck, Tee. I love that you're always wet. It makes me so fucking hard."

"That's great. But . . ." She let out a soft belch. "I need to move." She wriggled underneath me, pushed against my shoulders, and sat upright. "Lying flat isn't good. It's making me more nauseous and spins my head."

"You want to stop? . . . Or be on top?"

"No." She blinked slowly, then threw me a devilish smile. "Maybe from behind?"

"Mmmm." I leaned forward and kissed her sweet lips. "You know I love that."

"And touch me." Her hot breath teased my mouth. "I love it when you touch me."

"Always willing to do that."

As Tia rolled over and positioned herself on all fours, I moved in behind her. I licked my lips, hungry to taste her juices, play with her ass, and fuck her hot, wet pussy. My dick twitched in agony, wanting to be inside her.

I slid my hand down her back and over her round ass as she widened her knees. I edged closer and slid my hard cock between her legs, teasing her folds, her opening, her clit.

She pushed back against me. "Lewis? Don't play. Just fuck me."

*Shit. She'll be the death of me.* "Tee, I'm so hard. I don't want to hurt you, or our baby, or upset its little home inside you."

"I'll hurt you if you don't fuck me now." She growled through clenched teeth.

I gave her a spank on her cheek, then smoothed my hand over the mark. "Are you going to be this bossy for the next nine months?"

"Yes, if you don't give me your cock when I need it."

I gave her another tap—a touch harder this time. "What was that?"

"Argh. Yes," she moaned, laughed, and wriggled against me. "I will always boss you around. But spank me later. You can tie me up. Cuff me. Plug me. Do anything you want. But please, just fuck me now."

"Tee?" Hissing through my teeth, I rubbed the head of my dick against her hot opening. My God, she felt like heaven. We loved to play. Loved our toys and tricks. We drove each other wild. But my balls cinched and screamed in anticipation. I needed to be inside her. With a gentle thrust, I entered her—all the way in. "You can have this anytime you want."

"Oh . . . fuck yes." Her head fell forward, her long hair curtaining her face. "Finally."

"This what you need, Tee?" I pulled back a fraction, then drove into her again. Harder.

"*Ohhhh.* Yes." Her pleasured moan jolted through my cock as I thrust into her deeper . . . *oh yeah.* "More. Like that."

I slapped her butt cheek again. "Did you forget something?"

"Please. More like that. Please." She clawed at the bedding and rocked back against me, taking all of my hardness inside her.

I loved making love to her. Loved it when she wanted . . . *me.*

I drove into her again. Hard. Slow. Steady. In and out. Waves of heat coiled through my veins, spread across my chest, and spiraled up my spine. Fucking Tia altered my heart every damn time.

With each drive, she embedded herself deeper into my soul.

With each plunge, I belonged to her more and more.

With each beat of my heart, I lived for her . . . and our new growing baby.

I kissed my way up her back, jumping from freckle to

freckle. "Tee?" I grabbed onto her hips. "Is faster okay?"

She nodded. "Please. Don't hold back."

I splayed my fingers over her hips and tightened my hold on her hips. I eased back a fraction, then slammed into her sleek hotness. Shit, I wasn't going to last long.

"Argh" Tia cried out, flicking her hair back. *God*! What a gorgeous sight! "Yes. That. Don't stop."

*Shit . . .* I set the movement on repeat. Eased out. Slammed in. Eased out. Slammed in.

But I needed more. Faster. Harder. Faster. Harder.

The trailer rocked and squeaked. The bed hit the wall. *Fuck.* Anyone passing by would know what was going on. I didn't care. This woman was my everything.

My breath quickened, rasping through my teeth. My heart thundered against my ribs. I pounded into Tia time and time again. My groin slapped against her butt.

"Lew, touch me," she panted. Glancing over her shoulder, she reached for my hand.

She guided my fingertips across her fiery flesh and around between her legs. I slid my fingers into her wet slit and rubbed her swollen clit. That only made me fucking harder.

She rolled her hips. My balls ached for release.

"Lew. There." She clenched around me.

*Fuck yeah.* "I'm with you, baby." I'd held on for as long as I could. "I'm gonna come."

I drove into her, hard and deep. Every muscle in my body burned. With a quick jerk, I came as her body convulsed.

Pulsing and throbbing and shuddering, I spilled into her. My body quaked and quivered in sync with hers. Riding out the wave of bliss, I savored being inside her, feeling her warmth around me, imprinting this moment, this day she'd given me the best news ever into my memory bank.

I withdrew and crawled across the bed to lie beside her.

I pulled her into my arms and swept her hair back over her shoulders.

"I needed that." She nuzzled against my neck and kissed beneath my ear.

"So did I." Grinning, I cupped her face, lifted her chin, and kissed her. "I love you, Tee. I can't believe it's finally happening. We're gonna have a baby."

"Nine months will fly by." She swept my hair back off my forehead. "Are you ready for our life to change?"

"The moment I auditioned for The Flintlocks, and they picked me, my life changed. The moment I met you, my life changed. The moment I kissed you and fell in love with you, my life changed. Now, having a baby with you is a change I can't wait for. I want to be a dad. I want a family. I want to spend my life with you. That okay?"

"Yeah. I love you." Tears loomed in her eyes as she smiled. "I can't wait to get back to LA tomorrow and tell everyone."

"Me either. They'll be stoked." I brushed my thumb across her cheek. Charlotte was going to have a cousin. Our Flintlocks family was growing. And I was a part of it. I'd never felt so loved before. I'd found where I was meant to be. For the first time in my life, I truly felt like I had a home, and it was in LA, with Tia.

There was a loud slap on the side of the trailer. "You guys finished fucking?" Duke's voice hollered from outside.

"Yeah," I called back. "Give us five minutes to get dressed."

Duke laughed. "I'll give you two."

Unable to stop smiling, I smoothed my hand over Tia's hair. "Do you want to stay here at the party or go back to the hotel?" I was down for either option.

"I'm feeling better, so we can stay awhile. Let's party like rock stars, only with no drugs and booze or groupies."

I chuckled and kissed her again. "Yeah. Like fucking rock stars."

# Chapter 8



"I didn't sign up for this shit." I sat across from Beckett at the café next to my old office in Melrose, having lunch. I'd just spent five minutes laughing, with tears in my eyes, giving him an update on some errands I'd done for the band over the past few days. I'd sourced Haigh's Chocolates from Australia for Flint's dad's birthday present. They were decadent and worth it. I'd called a plumber for Lewis to fix a blocked drain. The foul stench had been rank. I'd made a reservation for Cole at an impossible-to-get-into restaurant . . . Okay, that was for our date night, and he'd wanted to take me out. I was okay with that. I'd had the guys' dry-cleaning picked up and returned. Scheduled three photoshoots and fittings with designers. I'd booked flights and hotels, organized cars, drivers, and security for an awards show they'd attend in Las Vegas. The list went on and on.

"Yes, you did." Chuckling, Beckett stuffed a fry into his mouth and chewed. "You could've turned down the job and not worked for the band."

Faking a grimace, I jerked my chin back. "Yeah, I'm not crazy." Or maybe I was. Some days, I missed being a bodyguard . . . others not at all. Taking on the executive personal assistant role for The Flintlocks had its pros and cons. "This job offers better pay. Has more benefits. I have a nanny, and Josh can travel with me. It's full of interesting tasks . . . most of the time. There is rarely a dull moment. However . . ." I sighed, smoothing my napkin across my lap. "It can be stressful. No day is the same. It's not just the four guys I have to look after—it's their partners too. That includes me . . . which is weird."

But being Cole's girlfriend had a lot of perks. I tried not to smile as I wriggled in my chair, pressing my thighs together. My pussy still throbbed after he'd fucked me senseless this morning. My legs still struggled to function. I wasn't complaining about that. Or the job. No, talking about my work kept my mind off Cole . . . somewhat.

He'd asked me to move in for about the tenth time this morning, after he'd made me come so hard I'd seen stars. But I had a theory. If I kept avoiding the topic, I wouldn't have to make a decision. I liked the way things were between us. After the hell I'd been through with my ex, Luther, and a bitter divorce and custody battle, I needed to make sure moving in was the right decision for my son and me. I didn't want my heart, or Josh's, destroyed again. There was nothing wrong with taking my time. I needed to be more confident and secure in my relationship before I took that next step. Catching up with my best friend was the perfect distraction.

I scanned the busy café again, out of habit. Tables, full of people eating lunch. Waiters, busy taking orders. The coffee machine, brewing. But no one was loitering outside. No paparazzi either. I got the odd glance, no doubt being recognized as Cole's partner, but nothing that was cause for concern. Once a bodyguard, always a bodyguard.

My cell phone pinged again for the fifth time since Beckett and I had ordered coffees and burgers. I peered at the screen. Another meeting request from Blake, the band's manager. Just because the guys weren't working on a new album, life hadn't slowed down. Cole, Flint, and Lewis had a bunch of events coming up over the summer. The tour documentary was nearing the final cut. April, the band's publicist and my coworker in crime, was preparing the media kit and promotional campaign for the release on Netflix. The entire Flintlocks team had held several meetings over the past several months to discuss new projects, sponsorship deals, brand ambassador opportunities, and marketing promotions. But Flint had shut down many conversations, refusing to agree to anything without Slip's involvement.

I hit *accept* on the notification, picked up my chicken burger, and took a mouthful. My phone pinged again. This time it was an email from Quill. Yeah, he could wait. Some days, I didn't have time for lunch, but I hadn't seen Beckett in two weeks. We needed a good catchup.

"Does that thing ever stop buzzing?" Beckett pointed to my cell phone.

"No." I covered my mouth with my fingertips and finished chewing. "Not for very long, anyway. I spend half the day on administrative tasks, like paying the guys' bills, helping April with content for social media, booking travel, and running personal errands. The other half is spent helping with wedding plans. I'm a highly overpaid travel agent and event coordinator."

Tiny crinkles formed at the edge of Beckett's eyes, and he bobbed his head. "So not much different from before other than a huge pay rise?"

"Yeah, I guess." I missed field training, specialized security operations, and going on assignments with my team, but I didn't miss the long days and being on constant alert. I still got plenty of exercise. Cole was a fitness freak like I was. He tried to outdo me on our morning runs, racing ahead and sprinting home before me. I let him beat me occasionally. I didn't want to damage his ego too often.

"Do you like organizing the wedding stuff?" Beckett took a sip of his hot coffee.

"Yes and no." I licked some burger grease off my fingertips. "It brings back nightmares of being married to Luther."

"Understandable. That guy was a psychotic, narcissistic prick."

"So . . . you really liked him?"

"Uh, no."

"Good." God, I loved Beckett and his wife, Opal. They'd helped me through some difficult times. "But Sutton and Flint are like two loved-up squirrels. They're excited and know what they want, which makes life easier. Although Sutton gets pissed and frustrated with Flint. He wants nothing to do with the finer details. He wants to leave everything up to her and Quill." I took another small bite of my burger and talked with my mouth half-full. "Their wedding planner knows his shit. He knows everyone in town and where to get the best deals on anything you need. He has dozens of venues, function centers, fashion designers, stylists, top-end suppliers, and hotel managers on speed dial. This guy is the bomb. The wedding is going to be huge."

"So, why are you involved?" Beckett quizzed as he picked a piece of lettuce out of his teeth.

"Sutton is so busy with work, filming late most days. Quill CC's me in on everything so I can discuss things with her when she's home. He's often running other weddings or events in the evening, so it's easier for me to relay any updates."

"You're the middleman?"

A little giggle escaped me. "That . . . and so much more." But what I did really dawned on me. I drew in a deep breath and my chest swelled. These people had entrusted me and placed their lives, personal details, and everyday existence into my hands. I didn't take the responsibility, their privacy, or the honor lightly. I was in my element. "Nothing happens with any of The Flintlocks without me knowing about it."

He let out a low laugh and waved a fry at me. "You always liked to be in control."

I couldn't argue. He was right.

He popped his fry into his mouth and chewed. "Have Flint and Sutton found a venue?"

"Yes. Thank God." I put down my burger, grabbed the ketchup bottle, and squished sauce over my fries. "It's going to be at Romans, that wedding venue on the beach at Santa Monica."

Beckett pinched his eyebrows together. "Isn't that place old, decrepit, and rundown?"

"Yeah, it is . . . *was.*" The old art deco place had been built in the fifties and hadn't been maintained. "It was recently sold to Eriksons, a high-end restaurant group. They've closed it and are doing a full renovation." Sutton wouldn't even consider the place at first. It wasn't modern and stylish or to her liking. But once Quill had shown her the designs and concept artwork for the restoration and rebuild, she'd fallen in love with it. Romans was on the beach, which was what Flint had wanted. And since they'd had so much trouble finding a venue with availability within their desired twelve-month timeframe, they'd jumped at the chance to have the wedding there. "It reopens in April next year. Sutton and Flint have secured a date in May."

"Wow. In eleven months?" Beckett's eyebrows shot skyward. "I didn't think they wanted to wait that long to tie the knot."

"Neither did I. But they've been realistic about setting a date. They want to enjoy being engaged. So unless something more amazing comes up beforehand, that's it." One item off the long to-do list.

Beckett tilted his head to the side and smirked, puffing air through his nose. "So there's no chance of you quitting and returning to security anytime soon? Sam and Wells would take you back in a heartbeat."

"Nice try. But no. I love my job. However, so many of the things the band is planning are subject to Slip coming home."

"Do you think he will?" Beckett licked the salt off his fingertips.

"I hope so. But life changes. We all know that." I was no different. I had changed careers. Was dating Cole. Had full custody of Josh. I never had to deal with my ex ever again. Some changes were for the better. "You know Slip as well as I do. You've covered him more than I ever did. He's no doubt scared of succumbing to booze and drugs again. He wouldn't want to go back to rehab. Or re-injure his hip. He adores Maddy and doesn't want to jeopardize his relationship. He seems happy and content with where he is. If that's what he needs to live a good, clean, healthy life, I'm all for it."

"Me too." Beckett nodded, then lowered his chin. "But I miss covering him. The random people and events we're working on during the band's downtime aren't as entertaining or exciting as The Flintlocks were. I miss traveling, and the fun the guys had, and the commotion we ran into everywhere we went. I look forward to every outing they have to attend. Those guys take the fans, the fame, and madness in their stride."

"Well . . ." I threw him a sly smile. "Maybe everyone but Slip."

"True. He got a bit messed up. But I'm glad he's doing okay."

"Yeah, he is." I picked up my burger and took a huge bite.

"And you?"

Oh, there it was. My diversionary tactics had come to an end. And Beckett knew it.

A big grin inched across his face. "How's Cole?"

The topic I'd wanted to avoid. *Damn it.* "How's Opal?" Could I deflect the subject? Talk about his wife instead?

"She's fine. But you know that. You saw her last week and told her nothing about Cole. So spill. I won't let you get away with it."

My phone pinged with yet another message, this time from Cole.

My heart fluttered against my ribs, but the knot in the base of my gut yanked tight. I wished the latter would stop. God, I wished it would.

I swiped open my phone and checked the image he'd sent. A selfie of him in a park, sitting between Charlotte and Josh, lit the screen. The kids hugged his neck. Big chocolate-ice-cream-covered smiles covered their faces. Cole's goofy grin struck something deep inside me. Warmth spread through my entire body and pooled between my legs. I loved him. And the kids.

But a dull ache throbbed in my head.

*Shit.*

"Ava?" Concern drifted through Beckett's voice.

I couldn't take my eyes off the photo, unable to comprehend the mix of emotions swirling through me.

"Ava?" Beckett kicked my foot. "What's up?"

"This?" I spun my phone around to show him. "See what I have to put up with?"

"Um . . . messy kids on a sugar high . . . or Cole?"

"The kids are great . . ." My shoulders sagged. "So is Cole."

"So, what's the problem?" Confusion rippled his brow. "Is there one?"

"Yeah. Me." I pushed my half-eaten burger away and slumped back in my chair. "He keeps asking me to move in."

"Why don't you?" Beckett finished his burger, picked up the remains of mine, and demolished it.

I closed my eyes and took a breath. "Becks? I'm so fucking afraid." I placed my hand on my stomach to ease the nausea. "Scared it will all turn to shit, like my first marriage."

"Ava." He wiped his fingers clean on a napkin. He reached across the table and clutched my hand. "Sweetheart, Cole's not

Luther. But don't be pressured into doing something you're not ready for. You take all the time you need. You'll know when you're ready. When it feels right. If he loves you, he'll wait."

"He is. We love each other. That's not the problem." I clung onto Beckett's hand, trying to make sense of the doubts spinning around in my head. "I wake up next to him most days and feel like I'm in a dream. I'm afraid one morning, I'll open my eyes, and it will all be over. That he'll turn into an asshole like Luther." I'd never forgive Luther for treating me like I was worthless, for taking custody of my son when I struggled after losing my mom, for being cruel and vindictive. I'd fought Luther for so long, I'd forgotten what it was like to be loved, respected and treated well. Then I'd met Cole. He was nothing like Luther. I had Josh back, thanks to him. After years of court battles and time apart, I'd wanted to spend every moment with my son. Cole had interrupted that plan . . . No . . . he'd changed it. He stole more and more of my time. More and more of my heart. He'd embedded himself deeper and deeper into my life.

I hadn't felt like this about anyone for so long, if ever. It was hard to comprehend. Somehow, I had to kill the lingering doubts and fears from my mind. But how?

"Oh, Cole's an asshole." Beckett ate another fry. "He's talented. Funny. Underneath all those good looks, and fancy clothes, and laid-back charm, he's a great guy. He adores you and loves his daughter and Josh. He owns a huge house, has awesome friends, and isn't short of a few dollars. He's a total fucking asshole, right?"

Giggling, I pegged a fry at Beckett, hitting him on the chest. "Don't you be sarcastic with me."

"Ava?" He picked up his coffee and glared at me over the rim of the cup. "What have you fought so fucking hard for every day since we met? Even before that . . . since your divorce?"

"To have full custody of my son. To be a family."

"Bingo." Beckett flicked an eyebrow upward, took a sip of coffee, then placed his cup on the saucer. "Thanks to Cole, you've got that. Cole and those friends of his are the tightest fucking family I've ever known. That is what you've always wanted. You deserve that. Don't be afraid to take a chance on something amazing when it's right in front of you."

"Becks, I just can't seem to take that step to move in together. Something is holding me back. Maybe Luther is still messing with my head. He knocked me up, and we got married, thinking it was the right thing to do. He promised to love me forever, and sold me a dream, and look how that turned out?"

"Yeah. Luther was a fuck fest. But Cole isn't."

"I don't want to screw this up with Cole."

Beckett's eyes darkened with understanding. He nodded and rubbed my hand again. "You won't. Trust me. You'll know when the time is right. One day you'll wake up and go, 'Fuck, I can't live another day without this person. I can't breathe or stop thinking about them.' You'll want to spend every second with them and want to build a life together. You'd sooner risk being hurt again rather than lose them. You'd take a fucking bullet for them." He softened his tone. "It's okay to be cautious. Careful. But don't be afraid to live or love someone with everything you have to give." He stabbed a finger at me. "You need to own this, bitch. Cole fucking Tanner loves you."

The back of my eyes stung as I nodded. "I know. It's crazy. And good. But this isn't just about me. It's about Josh too. I need to be one thousand percent sure that this is right for him. He's been through enough heartache with Luther. Josh needs someone to love him, give him a safe home, and be a person who he can look up to."

"Isn't that what Cole does?"

"Yes. You're not helping."

"Yes, I am. I'm eliminating your doubts."

"You wish."

"Stop overthinking this. I've never seen you this happy. That has to mean something."

"It does." I nodded, then pinched my eyebrows together. "I don't want to be stuck in limbo. So . . . I've given myself until the end of summer to sort my shit out." I didn't want to think about the consequences if I didn't.

"You okay with that?"

*Am I? Yes.* "Yeah. I like deadlines." I loved Cole. No question. I just needed to make sure my heart was strong enough for whatever the future held. "He's a good man, isn't he?"

"Total asshole, remember?" Beckett chuckled and wiped his fingertips over the sides of his mouth.

"No . . . he's not." I stared at the photo still displayed on my cell phone. My heart wanted to wrap around him and our kids. Love them forever.

Was that on our cards?

I loved dating Cole, being his girlfriend, and hanging out with the band. I hadn't laughed or traveled the world or made new friends in years. Cole had given me a new lease on life. Sex with him was fucking phenomenal. My pussy quivered just thinking about it.

Was it wrong to want it all? Him. A family. Our kids to be together. *Shit no.*

So when would the calm come?

I closed my eyes and took a deep breath to clear my head.

Visions of Cole flickered through my mind. His infectious smile. His will to never give up. His confidence, thinking he could take me down in a fight. *No chance.* His love and passion for his music, family, and friends. His devotion to our kids . . . and me.

Yeah . . . we were good. I loved him.

Could I take that leap and move in with him?

*Hmmm.* Guessed I'd know by the end of summer.

# Chapter 9

MADDY

"No! It's too early," I moaned, ignoring my cell phone vibrating on the nightstand.

Slip curled his body in behind me, his chest to my back, and nuzzled into my neck. "Don't people know not to call before midday?" His sleepy voice whispered into my ear.

We rarely got up before noon. I loved sleeping in. Relaxing. Being with him. We'd been in our new house on Bowen Island for six months. Neither of us had tired of the views, the walks through the forest, hiking around the island, or kayaking along the coastline.

But Slip had been playing more often. He was jotting down lyrics. Recording melodies and progressions. I had this niggling feeling that the pull to be with his band had grown stronger. I loved that. It also twanged my heartstrings. I didn't want our time here to end. Having to return to reality, work, music, travel, and life in the public eye daunted me. But one thing didn't. I no longer doubted being with Slip. Time together had given me the confidence in our relationship I'd needed. We had each other and would survive anything.

Just as I drew Slip's arm across my chest and cuddled it against my breasts, my cell phone buzzed again. It was 7:08

a.m. It really was too early for calls. I picked up my cell, blinking to focus on the screen. Bridget's name blazed across it. It wasn't like her to call unless it was urgent.

*Oh, shit . . . Mom!*

I shot upright, knocking Slip's arm off me, and answered the call. "Hey, Bridget. What's up?" I tried to keep the worry out of my voice, but it had taken hold of every cell in my body. Mom wasn't well the last time we'd spoken. Her lupus had flared severely, giving her a terrible fever and wheeze.

"Maddy?" Bridget sniffled. "It's your mom. She's in hospital again and not good. I mean, really not good. The doctor wants to talk to you."

"Okay." My hand shook as I flicked the cell phone onto speaker so Slip could listen in.

"Hi, Maddy. This is Dr. Raithna. How are you?"

"I'm fine. What's going on?" Rubbing my chest, my fingers trembled. "You're making me nervous. Is Mom okay?"

"I'm sorry. It's not good news. It's time."

"Time?" Haze muddled with my brain. "Time for what?"

"Maddy?" Confusion edged into the doctor's empathetic tone. "The infection your mom got in her lungs after surgery is back. It has worsened and isn't responding to treatment. We've tried for weeks to get it under control, but her lupus has won. Adding in the years of Valerie's excessive intake of strong prescription medication and alcohol abuse, her body can't take anymore. It's shutting down."

"What? Shutting down? What infection?" My voice quaked. "What are you talking about? She had a bad flare-up last week, but that's not anything unusual. She's okay, isn't she?"

"Maddy, no." Dr. Raithna's tone softened. "She's been on a rapid downhill path for months."

*Months? No. No. No.* The doctor didn't know what she was talking about. "But we talk all the time. Take out last week, she's been well."

"You must have caught her on a rare, good day." Dr. Raithna's voice remained level but compassionate. "Bridget has done an amazing job taking care of her, but I'm sorry. There is nothing else we can do."

*What?* Tears rolled down my cheeks. Mom had told me she was getting better. That she was living a healthier lifestyle, thanks to Bridget. No drinking. Fewer pills. Better meds. She'd said it was fine for me to go away with Slip. To work on our marriage. I'd always wanted to spend time with her because she'd been so sick, and I hadn't wanted to miss a moment with her. Now this?

My whole body shook. My head throbbed, unable to fathom the news.

Slip wrapped his arms around me and let me sob against his chest.

"Maddy?" Dr. Raithna dialed down her tone. "We're administering morphine to make Valerie as comfortable as possible. She's slipping in and out of consciousness. In my honest opinion, she only has a few days left. A week, tops. If you want to see her, I suggest you come as soon as possible."

"Oh my God." My chin trembled. "Yes. I'll be there as soon as I can. By early afternoon at the latest."

"Okay. I'll be at my practice for the rest of the day. I'll catch up with you tomorrow morning here at the hospital around eight."

"Yes. Yes, I'll be there."

I ended the call and dropped my cell phone onto the bed. "Mom lied to me. Bridget too. She's dying . . . like, really dying." The day I'd dreaded had come. I'd known it would, but not like this. Anger, fire, heartache, and hurt burned through my veins and singed every cell. This was so my mother. She'd kept the truth from me. That *was* nothing new. Why this time? I didn't need protecting. *Fuck!*

"I'm sorry, Mads." Slip pressed his lips against the tip of my shoulder and rubbed my back.

"Slip . . ." Unable to move, I stared at nothing, my eyes too full of tears to see.

"Sweets, I've got you." He slid off the bed and drew me to my feet. He wrapped his arms around me and held me close. Just the woody cedar scent of his bare skin cleared my head. His warmth soothed my heartache. "Everything will be okay. Why don't you have a shower, and I'll get everything organized?"

"Thank you." I sniffled and nodded.

Somehow, I dragged my feet into the bathroom, bathed, dressed, and packed. We were on a plane by nine-thirty, in LA at one, and walked into the hospital by two.

I rushed down the corridor, gripping Slip's hand so tight I was sure I'd cut off his blood circulation. He never complained. I burst into the private room and my heart faltered at the sight before me. Mom lay stretched out on the bed, hooked up to oxygen. An IV drip hung beside her, the tube leading to a bandage on her wrist. She struggled for every breath, wheezing and coughing with each rise and fall of her chest. Her eyes were closed. Her cheekbones protruded. Her skin, pale. Her arms, limp by her side.

Bridget shot up from the chair beside the bed and rushed over to hug me. "Maddy." Then she gave Slip a hug too. "Hey."

"You okay?" he asked.

"Yes and no." Bridget wrapped her arms around herself and glanced at Mom. Dark shadows circled Bridget's puffy eyes. It looked like she hadn't had a decent sleep in weeks. "It's been a long couple days."

I slid over to Mom's side. I sat on the edge of the bed and took her cold, frail hand in mine. She'd lost more weight than I'd noticed during our video calls. "Mom? I'm here."

Mom blinked her eyes open. A pained smile quivered across her lips. Tears welled in her eyes. She wheezed through her oxygen mask. "Oh, Madison. You came."

"Of course I did." I stroked her hair. With no makeup on, Mom's cheeks were covered in red blemishes, but the rest of her face and bone-thin arms held a mix of yellow and gray hues. Her eyes that used to shimmer were now dull and sunken. The nasal gastric tube hanging from her nose ran behind her ears and was full of some creamy-colored fluid. "Why didn't you tell me?"

She clutched my hand against the mattress. "I didn't want you to worry."

I'd worried about her for fucking years; a bit more wouldn't change anything. "If I'd known your health was this bad, and you only had several months left, I would've stayed in LA."

"I know you would've. But I didn't want you to. You needed to start your life with Slip. You needed each other. You've taken care of me for so long, I didn't want to be a burden anymore. I knew I didn't have much time left, and I wanted to spend it with Bridget. You didn't need to see me go downhill anymore."

Was that selfish or selfless? I couldn't think straight. "But you were fine on our calls. You looked well." I hated I hadn't seen her in person for months. She'd always been away whenever I'd been in town. Had that been a lie, too? Knowing my mother . . . *yes*.

"I only called you when I felt strong enough to do so." She sucked in a wheezy breath. "I put on makeup to cover my blemishes." *Raspy cough.* "Took meds or oxygen beforehand to disguise my failing health." *Hard swallow.* "We never chatted for long. I was just too weak and in pain." She winced and wriggled on the bed, gasped for air, then coughed, phlegmy and loud.

My chest ached just watching her.

"Hi, Valerie." Slip came to stand beside me. "How you

feeling?"

"Like shit." She smirked.

Ever since Slip and I had gotten back together after his stint in rehab, renewed our vows, and decided to spend time in Canada, she'd been nice to him again. She'd made him promise to take care of me. That would've had a whole new level of weight to it if she'd known she didn't have long. *Fuck!*

"Are you in pain?" Slip eyed all the equipment on the other side of the bed. The IV, heart-rate monitor, and other machines I'd never seen before, all with screens displaying numbers and flashing with lights. None of it made any sense to me, but none of it looked good.

Mom squeezed my hand tight. Her chest heaved, but panic flashed in her eyes like inhaling air was impossible. She gasped and wheezed and coughed. I rubbed her hand as tears tumbled from the rims of my eyes.

After a few weak breaths, Mom sank against the pillow as if exhausted. "The pain is tolerable thanks to the morphine and whatever else they are pumping into me. But everything hurts when I cough."

"Mom?" I struggled to form words. "The doctor said days. Is that right?"

She closed her eyes. A lone tear escaped and slid down her temple. She nodded. "All my organs are failing. Too far gone for treatment or surgery."

I clenched my jaw until my teeth hurt. Anger spiked through my veins. Mom had refused so many treatments over the years. Refused to change her lifestyle. It was like she'd wanted to die. And I hated that. Hated that she could've had such a happy, healthy long life, but chose to destroy her body instead. "You could've avoided this. You could be enjoying life. Not lying here, dying."

"Madison. Baby girl." She touched my hand with the weakest

of soft taps. "Don't cry. It's okay."

"It's not okay."

"It is." She slumped deeper into the pillows. "I didn't realize how much my depression affected you, or how much I'd burdened you with my illness and hurt you with my inability to get better until you met Slip." The faintest of twinkles glittered in her eyes as she glanced at him, then turned back to me. "You changed the moment you met him. I saw how happy he made you. I was jealous at first, but then, I didn't want to stop you from living your life anymore. I knew before my lung operation my liver was failing, my kidneys were weak, and my lungs were too damaged. The surgery was only a temporary fix. The doctor gave me twelve months. I've gotten ten."

*Oh no.* My heart shuddered. I sobbed, wiped my tears away on the back of my hand, and turned to Bridget. My shoulders slumped. "Why didn't you say anything?"

She stepped in beside Mom on the other side of the bed. "Because I love her and respected her dying wishes. What I did was part of her palliative care agreement. What she requested."

Mom's eyes closed, and she seemed to drift off into sleep. I shuddered and turned into Slip's embrace.

Bridget leaned over and kissed Mom's forehead. Then she wiped her own cheeks, straightened, and put on a brave face. "She comes in and out of awareness. But over the next few days, those moments of being awake will become less frequent as her body shuts down. She can't eat. Her body can't absorb any nutrition. Her lungs are beyond damaged." Bridget's voice never faltered. Never broke. I didn't know how anyone, medical professional or not, could remain calm when someone they'd loved and cared for was so ill.

I collapsed against Slip's chest. He just held me, rubbed my back, and let me cry.

"Maddy?" Bridget sniffled but remained strong. Love and

care for my mom welled in her eyes. "The next time she comes 'round, I'd say your goodbyes. She was good just now. I think she's been holding on to see you. She'd only let me call you home when the doctor said it was time." How Bridget remained so stoic, I'd never know. I was a complete mess.

How could I say goodbye to my mom? Someone who had frustrated me, angered me, used me, and lied to me all my life. She'd abused strong pills to control her depression. She'd popped addictive meds to manage her deteriorating lupus condition and pain. She'd become a functioning alcoholic and never listened to me or any doctor. But I loved her. I'd loved taking her shopping, out to lunch, to dinner, and to events for work . . . before I'd met Slip. She'd been my excuse to come home to LA.

What was I going to do without her?

I closed my eyes and curled deeper into Slip's chest.

Slip's touch, his hands circling my back, and his steady heartbeat calmed me. I had to be grateful for the good times I'd had with Mom. I was blessed she'd helped me pursue my acting career and taught me to be independent. I had to be at peace with the fact that soon she'd no longer be suffering. After twelve years of taking care of her, I'd be finally free of those responsibilities. But that hurt my ribs. Crushed my heart. I'd do anything to have her stay, be healthy, be here. Be my mom.

"Are you okay?" Slip asked Bridget.

She nodded. "It's hard. I really love her, so it hurts to watch her suffer and fade away."

"How long has she been really bad?" he asked.

"Since Christmas. The couple times you came to LA, she insisted we go away somewhere so you couldn't see her." Tears pooled again in Bridget's eyes, but none fell. "Maddy, Val loves you, and she wanted to make sure you had someone in your life who'd love you just as much as she did."

So many mixed emotions hurtled through me. I was upset I hadn't been here. Shocked my mother had thought of someone other than herself. Blown away that she loved me so much she'd let me go.

*Fuck!*

"Yeah. I know she did." I sniffled. "It's just hard to comprehend. She seemed so good two weeks ago."

"It was her decision to hide her deterioration." Bridget clutched Mom's hand against the bed. "You know your mother. She was stubborn and set in her ways."

"Oh, that's for sure." I couldn't argue with that.

"Why don't I grab you ladies some coffee?" Slip smoothed his hand over my hair. "Sound good?"

"Actually," Bridget sighed, "I'd love to go home and get a few hours' sleep, then come back tonight. Maybe we can take it in shifts, just so someone is here when she wakes . . . or doesn't." Her chin trembled, but her voice never faltered. "We can call each other if things get . . . to that point . . . when they'll up the morphine."

Nausea flooded my stomach. The end was too close. Too real. *Shit.* "Okay." I nodded. "I'll keep you posted."

After Bridget left, Slip and I had an early dinner at the hospital café, then returned to Mom's room. We sat beside her bed, sipping coffee. But Mom never roused.

Bridget returned at ten in the evening and we swapped shifts.

Nothing changed with mom's condition overnight.

But I'd barely slept. After crying in Slip's arms, I'd finally found my peace. This wasn't a sudden illness. It was just sad the end was finally here.

We returned to the hospital the next day at eight to see the doctor.

After Dr. Raithna checked Mom's vitals, machines, and

reports, she shook her head. "She doesn't have long. Her blood is poisoned with toxins. Her lungs are barely functioning. Her heart is struggling. If she doesn't come 'round today, we will up the morphine administration tonight."

Bridget and I nodded. I wouldn't be so calm and understanding if it wasn't for Slip holding me upright.

During visiting hours, Sutton, Flint, and our friends came by and said a quick hello but didn't stay long to give us time with Mom. She'd drifted in and out of consciousness once late in the morning but had been barely comprehensible. At four o'clock, she had a huge coughing fit that seemed to wake her up.

But there was no light in her eyes. It was as if she were almost gone.

"Mom?" I clutched her hand and held it against my cheek.

"Oh, Madison. I love you. So much."

"I love you. I don't want to tire you or talk long. Just know I hope you find peace." She had so many demons and had never fought them off. "Thank you for being a great mom." *Most of the time.* "We had a few hiccups, but that's okay. Life isn't perfect or easy. But we always had each other. And now Slip is part of our family too. My life. We're in a good place. He takes care of me and vice versa. He makes me so happy, Mom."

"Just know that's all I've wanted . . . You to be happy . . . and loved." She wheezed and winced. Her raspy, rattly breath seemed to slice her chest. "I love you. And Slip. Always be there for each other. But promise me one thing? Live life. Cherish every moment. Love your family and friends. Don't go down the path I did."

"I promise."

"I'm so tired."

"It's okay, Mom. You don't have to fight anymore."

"Is Bridget here?"

"No. But she can be within thirty minutes."

"Please. Call her."

Twenty-three minutes later, Bridget shot through the door. Slip and I headed out into the corridor to give them a moment alone.

By five-thirty, Mom had slipped into unconsciousness. Her monitors beeped and flashed red.

We called the nurse. She called the doctor.

At ten o'clock that night, Dr. Raithna dialed up the dosage of morphine.

My gut cinched. My heart cried. I kissed Mom on the forehead . . . *goodbye*.

Within an hour, her breathing slowed.

Her rasping eased.

Peace washed over her face.

We stayed with her all night.

Surrounded by the people who loved her, Mom passed away at 7:02a.m.

*** 

Five days later, after Mom's memorial service, family and friends came back to my house in Sherman Oaks, where Mom and Bridget had lived. Mom had pre-planned everything—the service, the wake, the catering. It was hard to comprehend that something involving my mother had been stress-free.

As I cleared some empty glasses off a table and headed into the kitchen, Sutton drifted over to me. "Hey, Maddy? You don't need to do that." She took the glasses from me and handed them to one caterer, and mouthed '*thank you*' to them. The lady smiled and left us, picking up more used dishes and glassware on her way back to the kitchen.

Sutton hooked her arm around mine and drew me across the room. "Let's go outside and get some fresh air."

*Is that possible in LA? Doubtful.* But outdoors was what I needed.

I swiped a bottle of water off the table, and we headed outside. We joined Tia, Ava, and the guys on the lawn.

"How are you holding up, Maddy?" Sadness hooded Ava's eyes as a small, concerned pout touched her lips.

"I'm okay." Numbness had set in. I wasn't sure whether that was a good thing or not. "It's still sinking in. It's hard to believe she's gone."

"Do you need our help with anything?" Tia asked as she nibbled on a mini cupcake. Mom had loved her sweets.

"No. Thank you. Timothy's here for a couple days. We only have a few things to finalize." My brother didn't care about Mom's affairs. They hadn't been close for years. Mom had gotten rid of so many of her belongings and had her will, finances, and insurance in order. Bridget had made plans to live with friends. They'd known the end was coming. All I had to do was move the last of my things to Slip's place before I sold the house. I didn't need it anymore. Although I owned it, it had been Mom's home more than mine. I hadn't lived there full-time for years.

I stared at Mom's favorite potted azaleas, sitting in a row at the end of the patio. They were blooming with tiny pink flowers. She'd spent hours fussing over those stupid plants, trimming them, talking to them, watering them. "I already miss her."

No more shopping outings and long lunches. No more wildlife shows on TV. But it was weird. I wasn't miserable. Mom had been sick for so long that her passing hadn't come as a total shock. I'd been angry she'd lied again, hurt she'd kept information from me, but in the end, I was glad she could rest in peace. "Today isn't a sad day. Mom's no longer suffering or in pain. I can't be upset about those things." I glanced at each of my friends, grateful for how lucky I was. "And I can't thank you all enough for being here."

"We'd do anything for you, Mads." Ava snaked her hand around Cole's waist and rested her head against his shoulder. "We're here for you and Slip. Always. But we miss you. After things settle down, we'd love to come and see you if you're finally up for it. The kids are on summer vacation. We've wanted to visit you guys for ages."

I glanced at Slip. We hadn't had any visitors yet. We'd delayed having any guests to make sure we took the necessary time to get better. We were still a work in progress but doing well. If Slip needed more of a break before we faced reality again, I would support him one thousand percent. But he smiled and gave me a subtle nod. I turned back to Ava.

"We'd love that." I slid my hand into Slip's and gave it a gentle tug. My handsome husband hadn't left my side. "We're ready. Aren't we?"

Slip's eyes glinted as he drew me against his side. "We sure are. But why don't we make it a big event?" He skipped his gaze across our friends. "We'd love everyone to visit. Would you all like to come for July Fourth?"

"Only if you stay away from the grill." Flint chuckled, but was dead serious. "I don't want burned sausages and steak again."

"Hey?" Slip drew his chin back and laughed. "I've learned to cook . . . kind of."

That element of our time away had been fun. We were much better in the kitchen now thanks to YouTube videos. We'd mastered some amazing dishes. Thai chicken was our go-to favorite. Making cookies often ended up in a sticky, sexy mess. *Hmmm.* Especially ones that involved chocolate. He didn't call me *sweets* for nothing.

"But are you okay if we drink? Not a lot. Just something." Caution veered through Cole's tone. "I can't do July Fourth without beer. It would be criminal."

"Yeah, it should be fine." Slip nodded. There was no quake or hesitation in his voice. "It'll be another good test. I don't want to drink anymore, but you're more than welcome to."

"Count us in." Lewis rubbed Tia's lower back. "We've wanted to visit for months, too."

"We certainly have." Tia stuffed the last bite of cupcake into her mouth, then patted her lower belly. "The three of us will be there."

"It's a date." I giggled and flicked my finger towards Tia's abdomen. "So, how is the baby coming along?"

"So far, so good." She stuck out her tummy and smoothed her hand over her barely there bump. "I'm ten weeks. Am I showing?" Tia turned sideways, one way, then the other.

"Ah . . . a little." Not really, but, hey. I was so happy for Tia and Lewis. Smiling, I swiveled my head to Sutton and Flint. "And what about you two? Can you come?"

"Abso-freaking-lutely." Sutton wrapped her arm around mine and hugged it tight. "We'll be there. I've been itching to see your new house. I can't wait."

"Me either." I rested my head against her shoulder. But something hard yanked low in the depths of my stomach. Something I hadn't felt in a long time. I missed this—hanging out with our friends. I had to go back to the studio in two weeks. Then life would be different yet again. I wouldn't have to come to LA to see Mom anymore. I wouldn't have to run her around to appointments. I didn't need to plan secret rendezvouses with Slip anymore. So would I make the trip home as often as I used to?

*No? Maybe not?* I didn't *need* to . . . and I didn't like that.

My best friend was getting married.

Tia and Lewis were having a baby.

Cole's and Ava's kids had grown so much in the past few months.

I loved Slip. I loved our life on Bowen Island, but . . . for the first time in years, I missed LA and being close to our friends.

What was with that?

Was Sutton's wedding and not being a part of every step the root of the problem? Or was it not seeing Tia's belly grow each week? Or was it missing out on playing with Cole's and Ava's children? I didn't have baby fever in any way, but I loved Charlotte and Josh.

For the past few years, I'd been so consumed with working in Vancouver and flying home to LA to take care of Mom, I hadn't had much time to myself or to think. Slip had been my element of fun; Sutton, my grounding. But now, after having time away, I'd reevaluated what was important to me. Losing Mom had hit home hard. These people were my world—my life. Sutton was my closest friend. She couldn't wait to marry Flint. We'd seen each other through more relationship ups and downs than I cared to remember. Now . . . we were both happy. In love. Facing new chapters with the men who'd changed our lives. Flint was perfect for Sutton. I wanted to be part of her celebrations. I wouldn't let her down. I'd be there as much as I could.

"Sutt." I swept her hair back over her shoulder and smoothed it down her back. "I'm here for three more days. Once today is over and Mom's affairs are finalized, I'll have some spare time. Would you like to do some wedding stuff? Dress shopping? Lingerie hunting? Cake tasting or anything else you'd like?"

"I'd love that." Excitement flashed in her eyes, but then she softened her tone. "But it's okay. There is no rush. You just lost your mom. When you're ready, we'll sort out some dates to catch up."

I appreciated her thoughtfulness, but I didn't miss the longing in her voice. Time was ticking. Her wedding was in eleven months. She'd want to get as much done as soon as she could. And I wanted to be there for her. "I'm okay. I'd actually like something else other than losing Mom to focus on. I'd love a day out. Do you know how long's it's been since I've been shopping?" I hadn't been to a mall since Slip and I'd set up house in January, six months ago. No clothes stores, day spas, or specialty retailers. My God . . . my hairdresser was going to have a fit when I saw her next week. I had to get my hair cut and colored before returning to work. I couldn't wait. I looked forward to being pampered again. Bring on the manis, pedis, facials, and salon treatments. They were the perks of my job I loved.

"Too long, right?" A playful but cautious smile lit her face as she nudged her hip against mine. "I'm always up for some retail therapy. But only if you're sure."

She didn't have to tiptoe around me. I needed this.

"Yes, I'm sure. It's a date."

"Perfect. I really need to get things moving for my wedding. Time is ticking, and Flint has been less than useful." She slumped her shoulders and shook her head. "He thinks everything will just happen like magic."

*Well* . . . he had people waiting on his every whim, so I understood that.

"Sutt?" Flint slipped his hand underneath Sutton's hair and rubbed her neck. "I know you're behind it all. I don't want to get in the way. I'm happy with anything you want."

"See?" She rolled her eyes and sighed. "Useless."

The wedding meant so much to Sutton. She was hurting. I didn't want that. I'd do everything I could to help.

As the afternoon lingered on, guests began to leave. By five o'clock, everyone had gone. I shut the front door behind my neighbor, the last person to head off, and ambled down the hallway into the living room. Bridget headed upstairs to rest.

Slip drew me to a halt by the sofa. "Mads, are you okay?"

"Yes." I lowered my chin and nodded. But then I met his

gaze. I couldn't lie. "Actually . . . no. I miss everyone."

He drew me into a hug and kissed the side of my head. "Yeah. Me too. Why don't we stay in LA for a bit longer? We don't have to go back to Bowen Island straight away. Not until you start work in two weeks."

"Really?" Light filled my chest. My pulse did a quick skip. "You want to do that?"

"Yeah. We can take more time going through and packing up your mom's stuff. You can spend time with Timothy before he heads back overseas. We can catch up with our friends. And most of all, enjoy some fucking sunshine and heat."

That would be good. We'd had nothing but rain and gray skies for weeks on the island. Summer heat hadn't hit. We needed some Cali sun.

I snaked my arms around Slip's waist and rested my head against his shoulder. "I miss your . . . *our* house here."

He combed his fingers through my long hair. "Then let's stay."

"Are you sure you're ready to do that?" I pressed my lips together and met his gaze, searching for signs of doubt, worry, and concern, but found none. He'd been sober for ten months. There had been a change in him recently. When we'd gone to the local restaurant for dinner or headed to the mainland for a night out, he hadn't had to have a timeout away from people who were drinking. He hadn't constantly fidgeted with his wedding ring or stress-bead bracelet to keep his mind off the alcohol. I wasn't naïve—maintaining sobriety was a constant battle—but now it didn't seem to be as hard as it used to be for him. Damn, I loved my man.

"Yes." His confidence never cracked. "It's just an extended visit."

"I'd love that." I gave him a quick kiss, then tugged on his shirt. "And I love you."

Slip always seemed to know what I needed, when I needed it. I'd lost my mom. She'd left a huge gap in my life, and I wanted to fill it with spending more time with friends. Mom may have been very ill for a long time, but she'd lived life to the fullest and had a great group of friends. I had that too. They were my family, and I wanted to be around them more often.

When I returned to work, Slip and I would have to find a balance between my job in Vancouver and our life in LA with our friends and Slip's music. I was confident we would because we had each other.

Today I may have laid my mom to rest, but she'd given me the greatest gift. I'd been given a new lease on life. A life that was my own. One I could devote to my husband, my friends, and my career. One that I would not waste.

# Chapter 10



"Flint, are you hanging with us just to avoid more wedding talk?" Cole sat before me in the tiny patch of gritty sand on the stony beach, attempting to make something that resembled a sandcastle for Charlotte. She was farther down the shoreline in front of Slip and Maddy's house with a bucket in hand, exploring the rocks with Ava, Tia, and Josh.

Lewis, on his hands and knees, patted and smoothed the pebbly mounds Cole had made, trying to make them look like towers. Slip lay beside me, sun baking on the stones. *Yeah, this is no Californian Beach.* But being here on Bowen Island was nice for a change. The private stretch of the shoreline may have been small, but the water was crystal clear. I could handle mountains and trees and being on an island for a few days. Over the past seven months of our hiatus, the four of us hadn't had many opportunities to hang out together and just do nothing. We hadn't sat in the same room and played music as a band.

That sucked.

But chilling was good. This was what I needed.

Bowen Island had turned on the sunshine and warmth for the Fourth of July weekend. We may not have been in the States, but we were here to celebrate.

I leaned back on my beach towel, closed my eyes behind my sunglasses, and turned my face toward the sun. The bright rays warmed my cheeks and heated my skin. The gentle ocean waves teasing the shoreline soothed my racing mind.

"I'm not avoiding wedding talk . . . I just needed to get out of the house." Who was I kidding? Yes, I needed a break. Since I'd proposed three months ago, Sutton had gone wedding mad. Tying the knot was exciting, and I looked forward to our big day, but now every conversation focused on the occasion. It was doing my head in. We'd hired Quill to take care of the details. It should have been stress free. But it wasn't. So while Sutton and Maddy were at the market, I'd jumped at the chance to spend time with the guys. "And yes. I needed a breather. Our wedding isn't until May, but Sutton wants everything done now."

Slip play-punched me in the arm. "Makes getting married in Vegas on the spur-of-the-moment sound better by the day, doesn't it?"

"Fuck yeah." I couldn't argue. He and Maddy may have had the right idea. "You should see my house. Half the living room has turned into a shrine to all things wedding." Fabric swatches, piles of magazines, and pictures had taken over every surface. Sutton had even bought a carry-on bag full of magazines and folders on this trip to show Maddy.

"What did you expect?" Slip ripped off his shirt, then shaded his sunglass-covered eyes with his arm. I smirked and shook my head. His physique certainly hadn't suffered during his time off. He was more buff than ever. He could give Cole a run for his money in the abs department. But then . . . so could I. Slip peered at me from underneath his arm. "Sutton's been itching to marry you since you moved in together. She's just excited."

"I am too." I drove my hands into the gritty sand and let the tiny stones fall through my fingers. Sutton used to calm the chaos in my mind—now she was causing it. "But I don't care about picking colors, decorations, and flower arrangements. It's more her day than mine. I'm happy to wear what I'm told to, rock up at the set time, and be done with it."

"You can't do that." Lewis cut out windows in the stony towers with a stick. "It's your fucking wedding, man. You're only planning on doing this once, so suck it up. Be involved. It'll make her happy."

My head wobbled into some form of a nod. "Yeah, I know. It may kill me, but she's worth it."

Just thinking about Sutton brought a smile to my face. I'd promised her the wedding of her dreams, so I had to ensure she got that. Rather than dwelling on tasks that didn't interest me, I'd suck it up, make the process fun, and be infected by her contagious excitement. I'd do whatever she needed me to do. Easy, right?

*Fuck! I hope so.*

"Sutton is more than worth it." Cole slammed another bucket of gravelly sand next to his ever-growing castle. It was now two-foot square and getting bigger. "I don't think we'd be sitting here if it wasn't for her."

"She's helped us through a lot. She's stuck around, and I don't plan on letting her go." A small grin tugged at the corner of my mouth. Sutton had gotten under my skin since the day I'd met her. Now she was tattooed on my soul. I was hers. And I wasn't afraid to admit that. "Anyone who puts up with my shit is a keeper."

"We all put up with your shit." Chuckling, Slip rolled onto his side and propped his head on his hand. "That's what we do and will always do. But enough about weddings. What else have you been up to?"

I was more than happy to change the subject. I scooped up another handful of gravelly sand and squashed it into a ball. "I've been gardening. Cleaning. Cooking. Going to occasional work meetings and events with these two idiots." I jutted my chin toward Lewis and Cole. ". . . And I've been writing." I carefully placed my ball of sand on top of Charlotte's castle, but it collapsed. *Yep, not sand.* "I took your advice, Slip, and considered other projects. When Sutt and I were in New York a couple weeks ago, I met with Everhide. They've signed two new artists and asked me to write some songs. I've been in my studio, working on new material, but nothing has clicked. It doesn't feel right. Music isn't the same without you guys."

I'd lost touch with my creative spark when Phil died, and I was terrified of that happening again. I respected everybody's need for a rest after touring. I wasn't an asshole. But this break was killing me. I craved to be back working on music with these three guys, my band. Patience wasn't my forte. I'd give them time off until the end of the year as planned, but not a moment fucking longer. Otherwise, I'd be giving them an ultimatum, like they'd given me.

"I wish I had time for music." Cole stuck a stick into the top of one of his sand mounds like a flagpole. "With Harper away on vacation with Sloane, I spend most of my days with the kids. By the time Ava and I get up and she goes to work, I feed the kids, dress them, play with them for a bit, then it's time to repeat everything for lunch and dinner. It's a full-time fucking job. I can't wait for Harper to come home at the end of the summer. I need to get back behind my drums. It's killing me. An hour playing here and there isn't enough."

"Maybe not, but you love playing dad. Don't deny it." Lewis patted and smoothed sand over another section of Cole's castle.

"I won't. But you, my friend . . ." Cole pointed a pebble-covered finger at Lewis. "Enjoy your freedom while you can. Parenting is exhausting. In eight months when your baby comes, you'll know what I mean." The biggest smile spread across Cole's face as he glanced towards the kids, exploring some rocks. "But it's the best job ever . . . next to drumming and playing with you guys." An even bigger smile spread across his face when Ava waved at him and blew him a kiss. I chuckled, stoked their relationship had settled over the past couple of months.

Cole turned to me. "I'm glad you're getting in the studio, though. If you write any good songs, let us know. We get first dibs, okay?"

"Always." Our dibs rule used to be over girls—now it applied to songs. Music was much easier to deal with than women. "But you've nothing to worry about. You guys are the only option. So anytime you want to jam, let me know. I'm always down for that." I yanked the rim of Slip's baseball cap lower over his eyes. "That includes you."

"Thanks." He tapped my hand away. "But fuck off."

I just laughed. So did he. "Never."

"I'm glad you're not moping around." Slip sat upright and realigned his cap and sunglasses.

"God, no. I'm busy." I'd made sure of it. I didn't want to slip into bouts of depression again, or hit the bottle hard, or lose my connection with music. There was too much to live for. Thanks to these guys . . . and Sutton. "Since I can't even seem to stop talking the wedding for very long, there is one important detail we need to discuss. We need to plan my bachelor party."

"Leave that up to us." Cole dusted the gravelly sand off his hands. "There is only one option, and that is Vegas. It will involve strip clubs, lots of tits, booze, and partying until dawn."

Slip nodded as he threw us a sly grin. "I'm all for scantily clad women dancing on stage, but let me tell you, the shows Mads does for me are so much better. They're freaking hot. I swear, I'm going to install a pole in every home we own. Last week, when Maddy put on music and gave me a lap dance . . . *fuck!* At strip joints, you have to behave. At home, you don't. She was naked. And horny. And she went to town on my dick." Grinning and wincing, he adjusted his crotch. "I swear I got friction burns from her tongue ring."

"Ouch!" My dick flinched as the thought of pain erupted inside my head. "Is that worse than chafing?"

"Both suck." He shrugged and winked at us. "But I'll suffer for the pleasure."

Lewis arched an eyebrow and hummed low and deep. "*Hmmm.* I'm all for a bit of pleasure and pain."

Cole picked up a handful of gritty sand and threw it at Lewis's chest. "I do not need to hear about you and my sister's kink fetish."

"You sure?" Chuckling, Lewis swept off the dirt and shrugged, unashamed of his bedroom escapades. "Tia's taught me a lot of shit."

"La. La. La." Cole covered his ears with his hands. "Nope. Don't want to know."

Lewis leaned back on his hands and stretched out his legs. "Never took you to be so vanilla, Cole."

"Fuck, I'm no missionary-all-the-time guy. But Ava and I don't need toys, or ties, or tricky shit. My dick, hands, and tongue are more than satisfying. I can get Ava off in a hot minute, but I'm more into endurance and love fucking her for hours."

"Gotta agree. Long sessions are the best." Thinking about Sutton naked brought a dirty smile to my face. "Those nights, or days, when you just fuck each other senseless, are the best. You think you're done, lying in bed, spent, exhausted, and you think your dick will never work again, but your girl gives you a sexy how-about-doing-it-again look, touches your balls or her tits, or flashes you her pussy, and you're back in action."

The guys sighed in unison and bobbed their heads. "Yep."

I straightened my sunglasses and injected a touch of smugness into my tone. "Face it, we're all pussy whipped, and we fucking love it."

"I can't believe I'd ever be saying that." Lewis puffed air through his nose and grinned. He tilted his head to the side and glanced toward Tia playing with Ava and Josh on the water's edge. "But yep . . . I do."

A loud shriek cut through the air.

Laughing and giggling, Josh and Charlotte ran towards us, holding hands. With one big leap, they landed on top of the castle mounds, stomping and destroying them into ruins.

Cole slumped back on his haunches and mouthed, '*Fuck*'. All his hard work, gone in a couple of seconds. He pointed at the pile of sand. "Char, that was for you to play with."

"I am playing. Josh and I are dinosaurs." She stomped on another tower, giggling and roaring with each step. "Can you build another one?"

"Please, Cole?" Josh fell to his knees and demolished the last remains of the castle, pushing it flat with his forearms. "Can you make the next one bigger?"

"Nope." Cole's second of being pissed disappeared as he grabbed Josh around the waist, tackled him onto the ground, and tickled him. Over their laughter and wrestling, I couldn't tell who was having more fun, Cole or Josh. Cole reached for Charlotte and dragged her into their play flight. "You're both monsters. No more castles." Cole leaped to his feet, brushed the pebbly sand off his arms, chest, and shorts, then held out his hands. "I'm going for a swim. Who's coming?"

"Me." Charlotte bounded off the castle remains and clutched Cole's hand.

Josh scrambled to his feet and took hold of Cole's other hand. "Yeah."

It still did my head in how much Cole loved being a father. I loved he was happy. That Charlotte, Ava, and Josh gave him purpose and the love he deserved.

I'd leave them to enjoy their swim.

"On that note, I'd better go up to the house." I eased to my feet. "Sutt will be back from shopping soon, and we're cooking dinner."

"You got it bad." Lewis shook his head, grabbed the bucket, and filled it with pebbly sand, no doubt to rebuild the castle.

"No, man . . . I've got it good." I picked up my towel and shook off the tiny stones. I slapped Slip on the shoulder. "It's good to be here. This place is awesome."

"Yeah." Slip nodded. "It certainly is."

I waved farewell to the girls still ambling along the beach. I looked forward to a quiet night, hanging out with everyone, and hopefully playing a few tunes. But as I walked inside the ground floor of the house and strolled along the hallway to my bedroom, noises made me falter. *Sobs? Cries?* I opened the door to my room and found Sutton curled into a ball on the bed. Tears streamed down her face. Her bundle of wedding magazines and folders were scattered across the navy quilt.

*Change of plan.*

My stomach flooded with nausea and hit the floor. I hated seeing her upset.

"Sutt?" I tossed my towel onto the chair, rushed to her side, and squatted. "Babe? What's wrong? What's happened?" I smoothed my hand over her soft hair, wiped her tears away with my thumb.

"There's been a fire. Romans. It . . . it burned down. There's nothing left. Not a thing. No one was hurt. But . . . we've lost our wedding venue."

*Shit.* That wasn't a part of our plans.

*Fuck.*

Now what the hell were we going to do?

# Chapter 11



*Romans has burned down? Fuck!* I'd really liked that place. "Will it be rebuilt in time?"

"No." A fresh waterfall of tears cascaded down Sutton's face. Blotches of red covered her cheeks and shone on the end of her nose. She tossed her used tissue next to the other ones scrunched in a pile on the nightstand. "Quill called twenty minutes ago. Supposedly faulty wiring sparked during the renovations. The whole venue is destroyed. There's nothing to rebuild. We had so much trouble securing a place a couple months ago. What are we going to do now?"

"Hey. It's okay." I leaned forward and kissed her forehead. *Shit. We need a miracle.* "We'll find somewhere. At the end of the day, it doesn't matter where we get married as long as we get married."

"Yes . . . but no," she sobbed. "That was the perfect place. In the perfect location. With the perfect view over the beach."

*Yeah. It was.* "Hey?" I rubbed the back of her head. "Let me grab us a wine, and we'll come up with another plan. You want red or white?" *Stay calm. We'll find somewhere. Fuck! But where?*

"White." She sniffed and sat upright. "How come you always know what I need?"

"Because I love you." I pulled a fresh tissue out of the box on the nightstand and handed it to her. "So dry those tears. I'll get us a drink."

"Thank you." She dabbed her eyes and wiped her cheeks.

I dashed upstairs, grabbed a bottle of Sauvignon Blanc from the wine fridge, and poured two big glasses. My head throbbed. *Wedding venue? Think.* I'd held enough big parties in my time. Surely, I could come up with ideas for our wedding.

*So much for having a break from nuptial discussions.*

But I'd promised the guys I'd suck it up and be involved. Time to grow a set and help.

I returned to our bedroom, closed the door behind me, I took a seat next to her, and handed her a wine. "Okay, so Romans is out. Did Quill offer any new alternatives?"

She curled her legs underneath her, rubbed her brow, and shook her head. "No. He says if we want to stick with our date in May, and don't want to get married in the city, the only option is to do a private ceremony on the beach. I don't want to get married on the sand. I want to see the ocean but not be on it. I don't want to get dirty feet or get wet or ruin my dress."

I pressed my lips together to contain my smile. She really wasn't a beach person. Why she used to live in an oceanfront condo in Santa Monica still amused me. She couldn't swim and loathed sand, dirt, and holiday crowds. But like me, she loved the view of the water.

I took a sip of my drink and licked my lips. The dry white wine was cool and refreshing after a hot day. "Has Quill tried every hotel, country club, ranch, and function center between San Diego and Santa Barbara?"

Sutton bobbed her head, smoothed her short sundress over her legs, then rested her glass on top of it. I'd preferred her skirt where it had been, resting higher up her thighs. "Within our specifications, yes."

*Damn!* "And you don't want to get married in Downtown, Hollywood, or Beverly?"

"No." She flicked a lone tear off her cheek with the tissue.

"Sutt?" I placed my hand on her knee, just so I could touch her . . . and tease her skin just beneath the edge of her dress. "Is there anywhere else in the world you'd like to get married? London? Italy? Paris? New York? If you're set on a beach view, we can look at Hawaii, the Bahamas, Tahiti, or a gazillion other locations."

As she closed her eyes, a troubled groove formed between her eyebrows. She took a few deep breaths, her shoulders rising and falling with each one. But then she stared into her wine and shook her head. "I love those places, but no. I want to get married in LA. It's where we met. Fell in love. It's home. And most of our friends and family live there."

*True.* I raked my brain for a solution. "What about Cole's house? There's no beach view, but he has a huge garden. It's high in The Hills, overlooks the city lights, and has room for a couple hundred people." Our yard barely had room for a cat. We had a decent-sized outdoor entertainment area and a big pool, but otherwise, the house took up the entire block. The few square feet of grass and hedged fence line could hardly be called a garden. And it definitely wasn't large enough to hold a wedding. Cole's place, on the other hand, was an over-the-top extravagance.

She shook her head. "He has a beautiful home, but that's like us getting married in our own house. I don't want that."

"Okay . . . what about Kyle and Gem's joint in Pacific Palisades?"

She squeezed my hand, and her lips drew into a strained smile. "It's gorgeous, too, but not big enough for a large number of guests."

I wouldn't object to scaling down her first draft of the

guest list to less than one hundred, but Sutton wanted to invite everyone—friends, family, and important people in our lives. So be it. "Alright, so if there are no venues or hotels available, we'll have to find a house we can take over for a few days."

She took a big gulp of wine and swallowed it down. Her whole body slumped as if exhausted. "Yes. At this point, I'll consider anything. But who do we know who owns a home with a massive garden that overlooks the beach, that will accommodate a wedding for over two hundred people?"

The cogs in my brain kicked into top gear. The wheels turned and whizzed, but then they clicked into place. *Shit.* "I . . . might." But I didn't want to get her hopes up. "It's a really, *really* long and *very* thin shot, but Andy, the owner of our old label WestTyme Records, owns a place on the hills in Malibu. It overlooks the beach. I could see if we could have it there. He's rarely in LA these days. His latest dick-warmer is some eighteen-year-old British pop star, so he spends most of his time in London."

Hope flickered in her dark blue eyes, but it was quick to fade. She wrinkled her cute, reddened nose. "But you didn't end things well with WestTyme. Do you think he'd let us use his house?"

I swayed my wine through the air, tilting it this way, then that. "Andy's okay . . . *just.* He's ruthless and will do anything for publicity. He'll no doubt take this as an opportunity to beg, grovel, and promise the guys and I the world to re-sign with them. But there is no way we'd ever do that." I was positive WestTyme regretted dropping us after seeing the hits we'd had under Everhide's label, and the tremendous success we'd had selling out our global tour thanks to the Ashlem Entertainment Group. But tough shit. They were the consequences of not giving me more time to process losing Phil. Severing ties with WestTyme had been the best thing that had ever happened to my band. We'd grown, had gotten bigger, and would never look back. "If Andy agrees, we'll have to drop his name during some PR, but I'm okay with that. Are you?"

A meek smile played across her lips as she shoved my thigh. "I am all for publicity. You should know that."

*Yes, I do.*

Light returned to her beautiful eyes. She straightened and swiped her damp cheeks with her fingertips. "Do you know the address of the house? Can we Google it so I can check it out?"

"Sure." I grabbed my cell phone out of my shorts pocket, typed in the address and clicked on the image tab. "This is it." I turned the screen toward her. "As far as I know, no one else has ever gotten married there. We'd be the first."

A huge grin lit her face. "I'd love that." She scrolled through the pictures of the exterior. "Wow. This place is gorgeous."

The huge, two-story Spanish-style mansion, with its manicured lawn and immaculate gardens, stood high on the cliff overlooking the Pacific Ocean. It was elegant, like Sutton. Built to entertain, like me. It would be perfect . . . if we could get it.

"I've been there a couple times." A dull thud drilled low and deep into the depths of my mind. Memories of the cocaine-high, pill-popping, alcohol-overloaded, groupie-filled parties Andy used to hold bombarded me. They'd been fucking wild events. But I didn't want that kind of gig for our wedding. *No. Definitely not.*

"It's really nice inside." I scanned the image results, but there weren't any recent photos online of the interior. "He totally gutted and rebuilt the place when he bought it. It's modern. Has big, black fancy lights. It's decked out with beige furniture and dark floors and has a huge arched staircase inside the entrance. We could get married at sunset on the lawn, then have the reception in an event tent."

"I'd love that." Sutton stopped scrolling through the photos and lifted her chin. Desperation welled in her eyes. "Can you call Andy?"

"Yep." I glanced at my watch and did a quick calculation. "Tomorrow. It's close to one a.m. in London. If Andy says yes, we'll go check out the house and see if you like it."

"Flint?" She slapped my thigh. "We both have to like it. It's our day—not just mine."

I caught her hand and entwined our fingers. "I'd marry you out our front door on the curbside, but that's not your style." I kissed her fingertips. "Is it?"

"No. I want our day to be perfect. Something everyone will remember and talk about for years to come."

I wouldn't be marrying her if I had expected anything less.

I leaned in and gave her a soft kiss. "I'll certainly remember it. Forever. Guaranteed."

*Too smooth?*

*Never!*

I was just stoked that I, some kid from Pasadena, who liked singing and playing the guitar, could now afford to give my fiancée the wedding of her dreams.

Silver flecks sparkled in Sutton's eyes. She grazed her teeth across her lower lip. Yeah, I'd made her day. She curled her hand around my leg and gave it a small nudge. "Since we're discussing the wedding, and I know it's not your favorite topic, but would you mind doing one or two other things with me . . . maybe three?"

I took a quick sip of wine, then threw her a saucy grin. "Is that the number of orgasms you want me to give you? I'm down for that."

"No." She blushed. I loved it when she did. "I meant discuss a few wedding details."

"Sure." Anything for her. "But remember, we've got to cook dinner soon."

"I know. We have plenty of time." She grabbed her folder and took out a bunch of printouts. "So, first, what kind of suit do you want to wear? That will influence the overall theme, colors, the style of decorations, the flowers, and the girls' bridesmaid dresses. Since we aim to get married near the beach, do you want to go casual in linen?" She shuffled and moved the photos, laying them out on the bed. "Or wear semi-formal dinner suits, or go all out in black-tie tuxedos? And what colors do you like?" She pointed at a pile of floral arrangements printouts. "Bright reds, pinks or yellows, soft pinks and creams, or white?"

*Wow.* This was a lot to take on board. I really didn't care about this shit. But Sutton did. And when I looked at the photos, I winced. Maybe I did care. I put my wine on the nightstand and sifted through the images spread out across the bed. Some suits in the pictures weren't me. A few of the flower bouquets were ugly. So . . . yeah, I had to have a say . . . and a bit of fun.

"Sutt, none of this works. I want the guys and I to wear bright blue dinner suits and have the place decked out with big pink flowers, silver balloons, and huge ice sculptures. I want real flamingos walking around the garden and have a classical pianist playing. Oh, and doves. We've gotta have a fucking shitload of doves."

Sutton choked on a mouthful of wine and giggled. "Ice sculptures? Flamingos? Doves? What the hell? Since when have you liked them?"

I swooped in and kissed her lips. Hovering an inch away from her mouth, I lowered my tone and chuckled. "Never. I'm fucking with you."

She caught my chin between her thumb and index finger, shook my head, then tapped my cheek. "I know." She touched her lips to mine and smiled. She combed her fingers through my hair, swiping the long strands off my face. "I know you, Flint Glover. But I can get you flamingos if your heart is set on them."

"No." I grimaced. "Please don't. I definitely don't want flamingos."

"I was kinda liking the idea." Her playful tone threaded through my heart. *Damn, she's beautiful.*

"No, you weren't. They'd shit all over the lawn, and you wouldn't want that."

Her eyes glinted as she pressed her forehead against mine. "I hate that you know me so well."

"Likewise." I kissed her again, then scanned the pile of pictures once more. "Okay. So let's do this wedding thing."

"Please." She shuffled in close, her arm and leg brushing against mine. *Yeah . . . perfect.*

I sifted through the printouts. "How's this? I like black. So no linen. I'd prefer a dinner suit and tie over a tux." I grabbed the picture of the Hugo Boss design that had caught my eye and placed it in front of Sutton, then shifted through more of her photos. "Roses are your favorite flower, so ignore all these peonies, tulips, orchids, and whatever these spikey looking things are." I tossed those pages aside. "And you like light pink more than any other color." I picked up a couple of pictures containing pink decorations and flowers and put them beside the suit photo. "So my suggestion would be black dinner suits, light pink roses, and decorations similar to this." I pointed to an image of a table decked out with a black tablecloth, white plates, candles, crystal glassware, and a low centerpiece of pink and white flowers.

"Oh my God." Sutton splayed her hand across her chest and rested her head against my shoulder. "Black and pale pink are perfect. You're so good at this. I've been stressing about themes and colors for weeks. You really need to be more involved."

"I will. I promise." I kissed the tip of her shoulder. "I'm sorry I haven't been. I just want you to have the most amazing day and have everything you want. I don't want to get in the way.

But from now on, if you need my help, just ask. Although . . . I don't think I'll be very useful when it comes to your dress." The excitement of our pending day simmered through my veins. "I'm actually looking forward to that surprise. To see you dressed up as a beautiful bride. *My* bride. But I'd also be very happy if you wore nothing." I twisted toward her and ran my hand over her bare thigh. "Or if you chose something short and sexy. Nothing skanky, but something that shows off these gorgeous legs."

She raised a saucy eyebrow. "I won't be in nothing. I already know what I want for my dress." All traces of her tears disappeared as glitter shimmered through her eyes.

"You'll look amazing in anything, but I have one simple request." I dipped my head and kissed the small of her neck. "Make sure it doesn't have a million buttons or lacing. I'll want to get you out of whatever you're wearing as quickly as possible. Deal?" I slid my palm higher up her thigh, dragging the hemline of her dress with it. She giggled as my hand disappeared underneath her skirt and my fingertips brushed across the front of her panties. "Make sure it's . . . this easy."

She turned to face me and smiled against my lips. "What happened to discussing the wedding?"

"Oh . . . we are." I took her wine and placed it next to mine on the nightstand. "This is part of the wedding is non-negotiable. Practice is essential before our wedding night."

"*Mmmm*. I won't argue with that." She ran her hands over my shoulders, down my sides, and took hold of my T-shirt. She eased it upwards, yanked it over my head, and dropped it on the floor. Hunger flared in her eyes as she raked her gaze over my chest. *Total boner material.* She leaned forward and kissed along the length of my collarbone, up my throat, and met my lips. "I love you."

"Will you love me when I'm an old, fat, and frumpy musician?"

"I will never stop loving you. Not ever."

"Sutt." I cradled the back of her head and buried my fingers into her hair. "We are going to have a spectacular wedding. With our friends and family. And music. And laughter. I want to give you everything you've ever wanted. All I ask is for you to be mine."

"I already am." She untied the cord at the top of my beach shorts and ripped the Velcro open. She eased them off my legs along with my briefs. One eyebrow curved upward as she scanned my straining cock. "And this is mine." She wrapped her hand around my hard dick, stroked it up and down, then dragged her thumb over the tip.

"*Hmmm.*" I hummed, pulsing into her touch. I pulled her dress over her head and tossed it aside, then ripped off her panties and bra. Snaking my hand around her hip, I guided her back onto the bed. As I hovered over her, kissed her, and licked the tips of her gorgeous tits, I took in every inch of her gorgeous body. There was nothing more beautiful than this woman before me. Her smile lit my world. Her touch grounded me. She owned me, heart and soul.

I'd been in love twice before, but neither of those times came close to how deep, satisfied, and complete Sutton made me feel. She was the calm to my storm. The light to my darkness. The fire to my ice. She'd brought me back to life and made my heart beat again. For her.

There were days when my grief overwhelmed me. Days I didn't know how I would face the hours ahead. But every time I heard her voice, saw her smile, touched her hand, and kissed her lips, every wrong in my world righted.

She'd seen me at rock bottom. Helped me find music. Loved me and my friends with all our faults and flaws. I'd fallen in love with her time and time again. I couldn't wait to marry her.

As I nestled between her legs and braced my forearms

beside her head, my heart pounded in time with hers. Life had tested us, dragged us through hell, and we'd survived. We were troubled souls who'd healed each other. She'd saved my life. I was indebted to her for this lifetime and every one after that.

She wrapped her long legs around me and drew my hips against hers. She brushed her fingertips down my cheek and whispered, "Together forever, okay?"

"Yeah, Sutt. Forever."

My lips found hers. With a flick of my tongue, I tasted and teased and explored her sweet mouth. She was the only drug I'd ever need. Burying myself inside her, I thrusted, rocked, and plunged slowly into her hot depths. Each drive made me harder. Hotter. Hungrier for her. She clenched around me and rocked her hips in time with mine. My breath snagged, hissing through my teeth. As I drove my hard cock into her pussy, a low groan rumbled deep inside my throat. "Fuck , I love you. I can't wait to marry you. I can't wait to call you my wife."

Tears welled in her eyes as the biggest smile curled across her lips. "Then we better find somewhere to say *I do*."

"On it. In the morning. But right now, it's time to practice making you come . . . at least twice."

"Then what are you waiting for?"

"Nothing . . . absolutely nothing."

Grinning, I withdrew, kissed my way down her body and headed between her legs.

*First one, coming up.*

***

In the morning, I made a call to Andy. After his initial shock that I'd contacted him—and he'd thrown a few rude comments and dirty jokes my way—I'd gotten down to business. His house was available. He'd love us to have our wedding at his place in return for some publicity. *Done.* We could check out his home at any time. One of his new artists, Cheri Rose, was staying there until mid-April while she recorded an album and performed some gigs on the West Coast. The place was ours after that. *Yes!* Sutton and I could keep our early May wedding date. *Perfect!*

We had a deal.

One task ticked off the wedding plan list.

One happy fiancée.

One less stress.

I prayed that was the last drama for us before the wedding . . . but somehow, I doubted it.

# Chapter 12

COLE

I clutched onto a handful of the bedding, placed my other hand on Ava's head . . . and slowly pulsed my hips in time with her divine, delectable rhythm. Waking up with Ava's lips wrapped around my cock was the way I wanted to see every Sunday morning in.

No . . . make that every day.

I'd wanted Ava to move in with me for months. I hadn't looked at another woman since I'd met her. She was it. How could she not want this? To be together every day. We were good. This was good.

*Fuuuuck!*

She licked and slayed my dick with her hot, wet tongue. My whole body tensed. Ached. Pulsed. *So fucking good.*

I thrusted into her mouth, pushing deeper. Her head bobbed in a slow, lazy rhythm.

I hissed through my teeth. "Yeah, baby. Like that. That's it. I'm gonna . . ."

My balls cinched, begging for release.

But just as I was about to come, Ava stopped.

*Fuck! NO!*

With a dirty grin smeared across her lips, she crawled over

me and plunged my dick into her hot pussy.

*Hell yeah. Just as good!*

"You shouldn't have stopped what you were doing," I pathetically complained as I spread my hands around her slender hips and tugged her forward just so I could bury myself deeper inside her.

"I'm not." She flicked her tongue into my mouth and rode me, slow and steady.

*Nope. Fuck that.* I wasn't in the mood for snail-pace anymore.

I grabbed her, flipped her down on the bed, and hooked one of her legs underneath my arm, pinning it between my shoulder and hers. I plunged back into her. I loved this angle, so I could penetrate her hard and deep, just the way she liked it.

"You like being in control? Don't you?" Her eyes fluttered closed as I drove into her.

*Yeah, I do.* She knew that. But she was just as bad. Our games of outdoing each other often ended in fits of laughter. "Yes, because I like fucking you."

Warmth glinted in her dark brown eyes. "I like loving you."

I threw her a devilish grin and pinned her against the mattress.

"Oh, geez." Her hot breath teased my face. "That's good."

*Yep. It is.* My cock was rock hard from her mouth working me into a frenzy. Her pussy clenching around me drove me to the point of no return.

The heat from being inside her took over.

"Ava . . . No control this morning. I gotta go."

"Just stay there, Tanner." She gripped my hips, digging her fingernails into my flesh. "Don't move. Let me rub . . ." Concentration etched her brow as she rocked her pussy upward, pulsing, claiming, fucking my dick with each move.

*Yep. I'm gone.*

"Fuuuck." I came, hard and fast. Spilling into her had never felt so good. *Damn, I needed that.* This woman had a power over me like no other before. Jolts of electricity coursed through my body, zapping every muscle. I sank into her, giving her everything she needed. Contact. Pressure. Friction. I fucking loved her body giving in to mine. Giving her pleasure. I loved making Ava come.

She laughed and quaked, panting and smiling and shuddering beneath me. She wound her fingers through my hair and tugged on it. Tingles shot over my skin. My heart filled my chest. This . . . being here with Ava . . . was bliss.

"Good morning." Grinning, I released her leg and hovered over her, brushing the tip of my nose against hers. "Love you, Aves." She was the only woman who bossed me around. Who had control of my heart. And I loved it. Loved her.

I kissed her sweet mouth, then lowered onto the bed and curled in beside her. She rolled to face me and swept her fingertips down my stubble. "Morning, handsome. I didn't mean to wake you."

"You can fucking wake me like that any time. I will never complain."

"Me either." She drew the black sheet over us and sank deeper into the pillow. "Can we stay in bed all day?"

"Okay." I swept her blonde hair off her face and tucked the loose strands behind her ear. "We don't have any plans." Harper was due back from San Diego tomorrow. The kids started school next week. I wanted to savor every second I had with Ava, Josh, and Charlotte before the summer vacation ended.

We'd fallen into a routine. Charlotte and I often spent one night a week at Ava's place. They stayed at least four nights a week at my joint. I missed Ava like crazy when she wasn't by my side. My house wasn't complete when she and Josh weren't within its walls.

But she was here right now.

I ran my hand over her hip, tugged her forward, and edged my cock against her crotch. "You want another round?"

"Hmmm." A playful glint shimmered across her eyes. "Can I please be on top this time?"

"If you insist."

As I leaned in to kiss her, thundering steps and giggling shrieks came charging down the hallway toward my bedroom.

The double doors flung open and banged against the wall. In rushed Josh and Charlotte. They jumped onto the bed and crawled up to give us morning kisses and cuddles.

"Daddy. Wake up." Charlotte straddled and jumped on my stomach.

"Hi, sweetie. I'm awake."

She slapped my bare chest. Luckily, the sheet was between us. "Why aren't you wearing your pajamas?"

"I was hot cuddling Ava." I tickled Charlotte's tummy. "But I'd better put my boxer shorts back on, hey?"

"Okay." She leaped off the bed and grabbed them from the floor and handed them to me. "Here you go."

"Thanks." I pulled them on underneath the sheets. *So much for another round with Ava.*

"Mommy?" Josh kneeled beside her, folded his arms, and gave her an inquisitive glare. "Were you having Mommy-Cole time?"

"Yes." She patted his legs, then pointed to the floor on her side of the bed. "Grab me my jammies and I'll get dressed, too."

The kids understood Ava and I had time-out, not-to-be-disturbed moments. They were too young to understand what that fully entailed. But they rolled with it. Normally Harper would be here to keep them entertained, or they'd be at school, or asleep. Luckily, I hadn't been in the middle of rocking Ava's world when they'd barged in. I'd pick up where we'd left off later.

Josh swiped Ava's silky pajamas off the floor and handed them to her. She slipped her camisole over her head. Then wriggled on her shorts.

Charlotte clambered to the end of the super-king bed, stood, and jumped up and down. "Daddy, can we go to the beach today? I want to build a sandcastle."

After my efforts on Bowen Island, I'd resorted to tipping out a long line of sand mounds for the kids to stomp on during our beach visits. Anything fancier was a waste of effort.

"No. Not the beach" Josh joined Charlotte, springing up and down. Thank God for the high ceilings. "Let's go for a bike ride."

"No." Charlotte leaped higher, waving her arms in the air. "To a park to play on the swings."

"Yeah." Josh plonked on the bed beside Ava's feet. "Can we, Mom?"

"Please, Daddy?" Charlotte ran up to me and flopped across my chest.

I cuddled her tight and roared softly, nuzzling into her neck. "A park?"

Charlotte shrieked, giggling and flinching within my hold. I wasn't letting her go anywhere.

Waking up to these two kids filled my whole soul with warmth. The light and love in my chest I had for them and Ava was like nothing I'd ever experienced before. *Fuck* . . . I was honestly fucking happy.

Ava laughed and tickled Josh with her toes. "Which park?"

"One with water." He giggled as she continued her onslaught.

"But Cole has a pool." Ava stopped tickling Josh and waved toward the full-length window that overlooked the garden. "We can swim here."

"And bounce on the trampoline." With a bright smile, Charlotte crawled off my chest and jumped on the bed beside me. I grabbed her around the waist, lifted her above me, and blew a big raspberry against her belly.

"Daddy. Stop. Put me down." She squealed and wriggled and laughed. Best sound ever.

"Do that to me." Josh bounced up the bed and wedged himself between Ava and me. "I want airplanes."

"Alright." I placed Charlotte down. With a pounce, she made her way over to Ava and cuddled against her chest. *Wow! That . . .* stole my heart.

I raised Josh into the air. He stretched his arms wide, and I swayed him from side to side. He flew like a plane, complete with roaring effects. *But damn*! He was twice the size and weight of Charlotte.

"You're getting too big." I lowered him down.

He flung his arms around me and gave me a kiss on the cheek. Then he rolled toward Ava. "Mommy?" he whispered at a close-to-normal volume. "Can I ask you something?"

"Sure." She nodded as she swept her hand over Charlotte's long blonde curls.

He leaned over to Ava and spoke into her ear.

Tears welled in Ava's eyes. She smiled a beautiful smile, then nodded. "Well, maybe we should ask Cole first."

"What's that?" I shuffled onto my side.

Josh sat back on his haunches beside our legs. Charlotte slid off Ava's chest and stretched out between us, hogging half my pillow. Having moments like this, with family, was something I'd never thought I wanted. Now I couldn't imagine life without these three people. I didn't want to contemplate existing anywhere without them.

Josh swiveled to face me. He pouted. Deep furrows etched his brow, and seriousness washed over his face. "Cole, can Mommy and I stay here? Like . . . every night?"

My breath hitched. My heart hit the roof. Every cell in my body hollered, *'Yes!'* . . . but I played it cool. "As in, you'd like this to be your home? Every day?"

"Yes." He nodded once. So sure of himself.

Was it wrong I wanted to leap to my feet and jump on the bed with the kids? *Fuck no.* "I would like that very much if your mom is okay with it." Hope filled my chest. "Ava?"

Tears shimmered in Ava's eyes, but the biggest smile covered her face.

My heartbeat skipped around the room. "Is that a yes? Will you finally move in with me?"

She reached for my hand and entwined our fingers. "Yes, Cole. We'd love to move in with you."

"Yeah!" I leaned over Charlotte, clutched the back of Ava's head, and drew her lips to mine. As I breathed her in, kissed her, and drew her sweet scent into every cell in my body, I couldn't help but grin. "About fucking time."

She cupped my cheek and nodded. "This . . . our kids. You. Us. It's what I want. Everything's aligned. The time is right. I love you, Cole."

Josh and Charlotte scooted to the end of the bed and bounced around on their hands and knees.

*Fuck it.*

I rose to my feet on the mattress and drew Ava to stand. As we held hands with the kids, we jumped up and down and around in a circle. Ava's smile stole my heart all over again. "Woohoo!" I cheered. "We're going to live together."

"Yay. I have a sister." Josh clapped.

"And I have a brother," Charlotte cheered.

A tear slid down Ava's cheek. I kissed it away. "I love you. So freaking much."

"I know. This is so surreal. I'm so happy."

"We've got it good." I sank onto the bed with Ava and took her hands in mine. The kids continued to run around us. "We're a family. I've always had Tia and the guys. But this . . . here with you . . . and the kids . . . is the best feeling ever."

"I didn't know love like this existed until you came along."

"Neither did I."

"Daddy?" Charlotte flung her arms around my neck, cuddling me from behind. I loosened her hold. I didn't need to be strangled. "When can we get a baby sister?"

*What?* I thumped my chest. I'd just lost ten years of my life.

"No, a baby brother." Josh laughed, jumping on the spot.

A burning fever washed over me. My head spun. *Whoa! More kids?* I'd never contemplated any to begin with, but now I had Charlotte, life had changed.

Ava's eyes bulged white. Her mouth fell open. She stared at the kids, then swallowed hard. Her voice came out in a tiny, quivering whisper. "You . . . you want another brother or sister?"

"Yeah." They jumped in unison.

*Wow!* I loved Charlotte and Josh, but this was a whole new level of holy-fucked-ness. Did I actually want more kids? *Do I?*

Ava pursed her lips. Her gaze softened, and the sun shone behind her glassy tears.

"Ava?" My pulse strummed, fast and erratic. With a dry gulp, I dislodged the lump in my throat. "Do . . . do you want to have more kids? One day?"

She fidgeted with my fingers and my signet ring. "Um . . . maybe . . . one day. *Shit* . . . yes."

I couldn't breathe. Blink. Budge. "With me?"

She scrunched her nose and smiled. "Kinda love you, so that might be a plan."

My heart pounded at a gazillion miles an hour. Giddiness swam through my head. Excitement skipped through my veins. My future with Ava was clear. "I think I'd like that too. So does that mean one day you'd like to get married? Is that an option?"

"First time was shit." She smirked, lowered her chin, and stared at our entwined hands. I didn't need the reminder that

Luther was an asshole.

I turned toward our kids, tackling each other on the pillows. My chest expanded so much, I felt like it would burst. "But look at our kids. Ava? This is our family. One I will always love, protect, and cherish. I want this forever."

She tilted her head to one side and studied my face. She wouldn't find doubt there. Not any. "You're serious, aren't you?"

"Yes." Losing Phil had been the wake-up call I'd needed to clean up my act. I still loved partying and going out, but I didn't drink as much, never touched drugs anymore, and didn't miss hooking up with girls, the regulars, or the randoms. "Charlotte changed me. So did you and Josh. You're all that matters now."

Another lone tear caught on Ava's cheek. She smiled and swiped it away. "Trusting you with my heart and, more importantly, my son, has been life-changing in more ways than one. I love you, Cole. Love this life with you. I'm terrified, but excited and happy." She swiped her thumb across my lips. I kissed them and took her hand in mine again. She held it tight. "I would love to have another baby . . . one day. When the time is right, when it feels right, we can talk about marriage. But for now, let's just enjoy being together. Living together. We'll take the next step, and navigate every new path, together."

I leaned forward and kissed her. Smiling against her lips, I eased her back onto the bed. I hovered over her. I drew in a deep breath and took every inch of her beautiful face in. Ava was mine. Fuck, I loved her. "Everything about you is right, Ava. I will follow you down any path you want to venture. I will kick your ass during every run. I've known since our tour, when you turned the world upside down to find my daughter, I wanted to spend the rest of my life with you. So you'd better get used to the idea. You're stuck with me."

She combed her fingers through my hair and shook my head. "You're crazy, but I love you."

"I love you."

"Um . . . Ava?" Charlotte plonked down on her bottom and fidgeted with the bottom of her T-shirt. Concern and love swam in her big green eyes. She gnawed on her bottom lip, then lowered her chin. "Does . . . does this mean, if you live with Daddy, you will be my mommy?"

"Oh baby, come here." Ava pushed me off her and sat upright. She drew Charlotte onto her lap and held her close. "Your mom will always be your mom. She's in Heaven watching over you and sending you love from the stars above. Me moving in means I will love you just as much as your mom did. I will give you just as many cuddles and kisses as she gave you, if not more. You can call me Ava or Mommy, or whatever you're comfortable with."

Charlotte played with her shirt. Her little brow strained as if her mind struggled to comprehend what Ava had said. My chest hurt. No child should lose their mother. But I would've never known Charlotte existed if Shelby hadn't been killed in an accident. I'd promised to be the father she deserved.

Charlotte sucked in a big breath. She turned to Ava, smiled, and nodded. "How about Avy? Like Ava and Mommy together."

Fresh tears welled in Ava's eyes . . . and in mine. *Fuck!* My kid was fucking amazing. Ava hugged and kissed Charlotte on the cheek. "I'd like that very much."

"Cole?" Josh ran over to me and plonked down on his knees. "Will you be my dad? My real dad is a jerk."

"Hey!" I ruffled his hair. "Luther is still your father, even though you're right. He isn't very nice. So always remember how he made you feel and never treat people in the same way." I looked square into his big brown eyes, and my heart flooded with warmth. "But Josh? I love you. And your mom. And Charlotte. If it's okay with your mom, I'd be honored to be your dad."

"Yes." Ava sniffled and nodded. "I'm okay with that."

I drew Ava, Charlotte, and Josh into a group hug and cuddled them close. "We're gonna be a family. Awesome."

Two kids . . . and Ava.

*My family.*

This was living. This was love. This was my future.

# Chapter 13

SLIP

In Maddy's condo in Vancouver, I tinkered on my guitar, waiting for her to get home from work. There was nothing unusual about late September rain falling constantly, the ocean forming a dark blanket across to the islands, or the busy road noise drifting up from the street below. But the twang tightening in my chest was new. So was the pull in the pit of my gut.

I stared at the pile of notebooks scattered across the chaise. One of Phil's peeked out from underneath my pads full of lyrics and music. I hadn't been able to open it. I was too afraid of what it might contain. Phil's private thoughts. His lyrical prowess. Or just too many heartbreaking memories. But now the faded book called me. Called me in a way I hadn't anticipated or expected.

It had been a year since my band and I had finished touring. I'd been sober every day since. The craving for a drink or a hit of drugs no longer ruled me. Going out with friends and being around others indulging in booze had gotten easier. I didn't want to get wasted or wake up hungover. I was good. I had more energy, slept well, and lived healthily. But now my notebooks and Phil's had sparked a new addiction inside of me . . . something that burned hotter and brighter every day. Something I had no power over, no control over, no way of stopping ever . . . The need to work on new music had ignited, and I couldn't switch it off.

Since moving to Bowen Island, I'd played nearly every day, but I hadn't written many songs, composed any great tunes, or created anything serious. I'd jotted down random lyrics and notes here and there just to capture what was in my head. But since Maddy had gone back to work in early July, and we'd spent time here in the city, new melodies and words kept me awake at night.

So did Maddy's unrest.

She hadn't told me what was bothering her. We talked about anything and everything. There was no problem with our communication. I guessed she needed time to process whatever was troubling her before she could discuss it with me.

I put down my guitar, hauled myself off the sofa, and ambled into the kitchen. I grabbed an alcohol-free beer from the fridge and resumed my position in the living room. As I cracked off the lid, Phil's notebook caught my attention again.

*Shit!*

What was with that?

Maybe it was time.

Was I ready to read his words?

I took a sip of my drink, closed my eyes, and inhaled a deep breath. Memories of Phil's smile and laughter, and us playing music together, danced through my mind. *Fuck.* I missed him. But grief no longer crippled me. I had a lot to live for. Be grateful for. I'd beaten my addiction. I had a beautiful wife. I had fantastic friends.

The break after the tour and rehab had healed me physically, emotionally, and mentally. I was in a good place.

But . . . could I do this? Open his notebook?

*Yeah . . . I can.*

With a shaky hand, I reached for Phil's lost lyrics. Sinking back into the sofa, I rested the pad on my legs and ran my hand over the cover. I smirked at Phil's scraggly, messy handwriting scribbled across the front:

*Property of Phil Glover*
*PRIVATE*
*FUCK OFF!*

I turned to the first page full of inked words, with random lines crossed out and new ones written above them. The page was dated six years ago.

*I promised you the world, but somehow that came undone*
*I promised to love you, but somewhere it all went wrong*
*I promised to be yours, but something else had a hold on my heart*
*I promised to stand by you, but every day I fell apart*

*You deserved to be loved by someone better than me*
*You deserved to shine, not be held back by the likes of me*
*You deserved to be happy, something I couldn't give you*
*You deserved honesty, and that is why I'm telling you . . .*

*I loved you*
*But I was nothing but a fool*
*I loved you*
*But I wasn't strong enough to fight*
*I loved you*
*But I let you go to follow your dreams*
*I loved you*
*But every day without you kills me inside*
*Kills me inside*

*Knowing you could've been mine*
*But the darkness in my mind*
*Overruled every time*
*The drink keeps it down deep*

*But it has a hold on me*
*I'm losing my mind as it consumes and binds*
*Into my soul and takes me into the unknown*
*I miss the fun that we had*
*And making love to you in bed*
*The pills stop the pain*
*Other girls aren't the same*
*There is only one you*
*But there is nothing I can do*
*You deserve to be free*
*Not stuck with someone like me*
*Every day without you hurts me like hell*
*Hurts me like hell*

*I said I'd never leave you, but here I am, all alone*
*I said I'd be yours forever, but you broke my heart*
*I said I wanted you to be happy; please pick up the phone*
*I said I was sorry, but we were doomed all along*

*I loved you*
*But I was nothing but a fool*
*I loved you*
*But I wasn't strong enough to fight*
*I loved you*
*But I let you go to follow your dream*
*I loved you*
*But every day without you kills me inside*
*Kills me inside*

I wiped my hand across my mouth and rubbed the tip of my chin. The backs of my eyes stung.

*Shit!* Were these lyrics about Tia? Their breakup? *Fuck!*

We'd all had some tumultuous relationships in the past. We'd all gone through too much heartache and pain. I hoped that was behind us. We'd found incredible partners. We'd settled down. Every time I talked to my friends, everyone seemed happy.

I was.

But as the days passed, it was impossible to ignore the draw I had toward the guys. When we were in the same city, the same venue, the same room, we gravitated toward each other. Our unwavering friendship and music had united us in irrevocable ways. *Fuck!* For the first time in months, my very bones craved playing with them. My body ached to feel the music reverberating through my veins. My soul hungered for fans to scream our names.

*Shit!*

I wasn't ready to go back.

*Am I?*

I continued through the book, reading song after song. Each one stabbed my heart but filled it with warmth. Phil had been my best friend for fifteen years. I'd always love and remember him, the good times more than the bad.

Then, one page with lyrics and guitar chords written above them caught my eye. I grabbed my guitar and plucked out the tune. I read the words over and over again. What I strummed was Phil through and through. This song could have been about anyone, but deep down, I sensed it was about us guys.

*If you're feeling down, you know you just gotta holler*
*If you're happy, I'll be the first to cheer ya*
*If you're sad, I'll be the shoulder for you to cry on*
*If you're in the mood to party, I'll bring over the liquor*

*So we can laugh, dance, and drink until your worries disappear*
*Or we can sing, scream, and shout until the neighbors call the cops in*
*I'll stand by you for every up and down we face*
*We'll take on the world together, every challenge we'll embrace*
*We'll soar through the stars, never let our feet touch the*

*ground*
*Let's rock this life together. You're the best thing I've ever*
*found*

I closed the book, rested my head back against the sofa, and hugged my guitar across my chest. Phil had been right. The guys and I had faced every up and down together, we'd taken on the world, and we rocked this life together. We'd all grown, changed, and survived because we had each other.

*Fuck* . . . I missed them.

I texted them in our group chat.

> Me: You read your notebook of lyrics from Phil? Just started mine.
> So many memories. Good and bad.

No one replied. *What?* It was still weird not knowing where each of them was and what they were doing every day. Everyone was busy doing their own thing. We no longer lived in each other's pockets. But the growing pull toward them had me on a new edge. One I had to be certain I was ready to face.

The elevator bell dinged. There was a rattle of keys. The front door opened. In walked Maddy. My chest swelled, and my heartbeat did a quick step and a skip just like it did every time she walked into the room. Her smile, full of sunshine, made my day. But today, it wasn't as bright as normal. Tiredness clouded her eyes.

"Hey, hon." She dumped her purse on the console table. Ambling toward me, she dragged her feet like they weighed a ton, then sank onto the sofa beside me.

I put my guitar down, hooked my arm around her shoulders, and drew her against my side. I kissed her troubled brow. "Rough day?"

"Long one." She sighed and snuggled into me. Yep, I knew what twelve-hour-plus days felt like. "Hilary is still in a bad mood. She has been for weeks. She's ordering retake after retake when we've executed scenes perfectly. The writers argue constantly over dialogue cuts, changes, and storyline directions. The girls are distant and seem extra bitchy. I am constantly frustrated. And Mills, who I used to get on so well with, has turned into an asshole. He's always making rude jokes and smartass comments at me for taking time off, for not handling the gossip that surrounded us when we first got married, and for being Hilary's pet. He's trying to be funny, but he's not."

"Well, fuck him." Six months off work had done wonders for our marriage and Maddy's health. She was no longer bone thin. She ate well. We were solid. But clearly not everyone felt the same way. "Is that what's been bothering you? I'd love you to break up with your on-screen boyfriend." I threw her a lopsided, hopeful smirk. "Mills can fuck off the show. I'd be very happy with that."

I'd have a word with him the next time we saw each other. No one messed with Maddy. What had happened to him being Maddy's friend outside the show? Maddy loved her castmates and crew, but yeah . . . something had been off since she'd returned to the studio.

Maddy rested her cheek against my shoulder. "Mills has become arrogant. But it's not just him. I've tried to ignore the show's changes, and the different vibe on set, and not let anything get to me. But it has. It's not the same anymore. The dynamic has shifted . . . died. The fun we used to have as a group has disappeared. Is it me? Or them? Or was I blindsided about how good it was?"

"Mads . . . you've been through a lot." I rubbed her arm, still overwhelmed sometimes by what we'd endured. "The rough start to our marriage, your health concerns, my stint in rehab, and losing your mom have been a lot to handle. Don't be so hard on yourself. Maybe you need more time off."

"No. I was ready to go back. It's just hard when it's not the same."

"Been there. Done that." I'd had similar concerns with my band during our last tour. Being on the road wasn't the same without Phil, but Lewis had fit in perfectly. He'd become one of us. And now . . . after time apart, new anxiety had crept into my mind. I was scared the guys and I wouldn't reconnect in the same way when we got back together. Maddy was clearly going through those motions at work. "Mads, if everything has changed on the show, if people aren't respecting you, or they're causing havoc, you don't have to put up with that."

"I know. I won't." She curled toward me and draped her arm across my waist. I buried my nose into her hair and breathed her in. *Mmmm. Mio bel girasole.* "This show has been a part of me for so long. I love living here. I love my castmates and crew . . . well, I did. But it's like a different world now."

I played with her long hair and rested my cheek against the top of her head. "Maybe it's not just the world. Maybe it's us. We've both changed. The best part is we now have each other."

"Yeah. We do. I love you." She kissed the small of my neck, then pointed to Phil's notebook lying open on the chaise. "You writing again?"

"No. That's Phil's. It's the first time I've opened it since Tia gave it to me." I took a deep breath as his words filtered through my head. "It's been hard to read some of the lyrics. He loved Tia so much, but he was too much of a mess to be serious. Too wild and out for fun. Maybe being too young played its part as well. The drugs, booze, and women certainly did." I waved a finger toward the book. "But some songs have chords penned in them. I was tinkering with a couple tunes."

"Can you play something for me?" She eased forward out of my hold. "I'll grab a drink. You want another one?"

"Sure."

As Maddy glided over to the kitchen, I picked up my guitar and strummed the strings. The sad, soulful tune I'd been playing filled my head. The notes tweaked and shuffled through my mind. I altered several chords. Reworked the bridge. Yeah . . . the melody flowed so much better this way.

"Wow." Maddy returned and slid onto the sofa beside me. "I love that."

"It's good, isn't it? Sad but good." I plucked at the strings, worked my fingers over the frets. "I've tweaked Phil's chords here and there."

"You're so talented."

"Me? Nah." I churned out a wicked lick. "I just pick up a guitar and fuck around."

"Don't do that." Maddy slapped my thigh. "You're gifted. Own it."

"You're right." I nudged my knee against hers. "I'm the fucking shit."

She smiled over the rim of her drink. "Yes. You are."

I kept playing, swept up in the reverberations coursing through my fingers. Maddy sat there sipping on her lime-infused mineral water. Her gaze locked onto mine and calmness rained over me. I had music, my beautiful wife . . . but then my chest twanged again. The need to play with the guys burned hotter.

*Fuck!*

Maddy smoothed her hand over my leg. Concern hovered low in her tone. "You miss them, don't you?"

"Who?" *Can I play naïve? Nope.*

"The guys. Playing. Hanging out." Maddy got me.

"Yeah . . . it's been brewing stronger over the past couple weeks."

Her brow furrowed. She pursed her lips, then nodded. "It's been a year. Do you think it's time?"

"For what?" I didn't want to hear it. Admit it. Say it out loud. *Do I?*

"To get back together. Start writing new material. Record."

Nausea pooled in my guts. My leg jiggled. "Just thinking about that makes me nervous."

"Why?" she whispered.

"Like you, what if it's not the same?" What if we've grown apart? What if we didn't get along anymore? What if we'd changed too much? . . . What if I can't make music without getting fucked up?

"It won't be the same. It will be better." Reassurance set in her tone. "You guys are inseparable. You need them like they need you. You need music."

I closed my eyes, pursed my lips, and nodded. But I had to be honest. "Yes, but it's not just the guys I'm worried about, or the writing and recording—it's the life that comes with it. It's the time and commitment. The energy needed. The promo, touring, being on the road. Performing. The parties. The press. I don't want to fall off the bandwagon. I don't want to lose you again."

Sadness swallowed the light in her eyes. "We didn't handle being apart, did we?"

"No."

"But we're in a much better place." She drew her shoulders back. Love and certainty returned to her gaze. "You're stronger than you think. You have me, your sponsor, a great therapist, and people around you who love and care about you. I know you can do this. I trust you won't falter . . . but I'm here if you do. The difference now is we're solid. Have faith in us, in yourself, and focus on what is truly important to you."

I placed my guitar down on the chaise and took Maddy's hand in mine. "Mads, that's easy. I live for you, the guys, and music." I scrunched my eyes shut and tapped the side of my temple. "But I can't switch this off. Tunes are burning inside my brain. I don't want to leave you or be apart again. It's too soon to go back."

"No, it's not. I think the fact that you can't switch it off is a sign you're ready." She lowered her chin and fidgeted with my fingers. "We said we'd always be honest with each other, right?"

"Yes." *Shit. Be honest.*

*With Maddy and myself.*

*Am I ready to go back?*

*Fuck!*

"So, I'm going to throw something on the table." She entwined our fingers and rested our hands against her thigh. "It's been niggling inside my head for a couple weeks, and it won't go away."

My stomach twisted into twine. "What?"

"I love living on Bowen Island but not here in the city. I love acting, but my show has changed. My castmates, people who I thought were friends, have shown their shallow, true colors. I don't want to hang out with them anymore. I love being with you no matter where we are." She lowered her chin and fidgeted with my beaded bracelet. "I miss Sutton and our friends like crazy. She's getting married and I'm not there for her. So . . . next time we're in LA, I'm going to meet with my agent. It's time I sniff around for a new role."

My heart jolted against my ribs. *Holy shit!* "You want to leave *Vancouver Heights*?" I hadn't seen that coming.

"Yes. I haven't been happy since day one back on set. This condo doesn't feel like a home-away-from-home anymore. My priorities have changed. I've changed. My life is with you. You need your band. I need something fresh. So . . . what do you say? Are you ready? Are you ready to go back to LA?"

*Whoa! Wait!* "Just LA? You don't want to look at roles that may be filmed in a different state or country?"

She shook her head slowly. "No . . . just LA."

The back of my eyes stung. "You want to go home?"

"Yeah . . . it's time."

I swept my hand underneath her hair and cradled her neck, and drew her mouth to mine. I kissed her soft lips and breathed her in. With Maddy by my side, I could do anything. This was what we both needed.

"Yes." I was strong. I was ready. I had Maddy. "It's time. Let's go home."

# Chapter 14



Being pregnant was nothing like I'd expected. My ankles were swollen after the flight home from New York. I was horny all the time. That wasn't new . . . and Lewis *never* complained. I couldn't stop eating. My clothes were tight. My five-month baby bump seemed excessively huge, bulging like I was near due. At this rate, by the time I reached full-term, I'd be as big as a humpback whale. My newfound craving for salty Australian Vegemite spread and grilled cheese sandwiches didn't help my waistline. The toasted treat had become my weakness. I should've never tried Vegemite when we were Down Under during the tour. Now, I couldn't live without the stuff.

Nor Tim Tams.

*Oh. My. God.*

Those chocolate biscuits were pure evil.

I could never just have one.

Last week, Lewis had driven to three different grocery stores across LA to track down the Aussie items for me. I would've screamed bloody murder if he'd come home without them. He hadn't let me down.

He was a keeper.

*My baby daddy!*

Tonight, we'd rocked up to Flint and Sutton's for dinner and a catchup. Sutton had let us in, and we followed her to the music room, where soft music was playing.

Since July, Cole, Lewis, and Flint had gotten together once a month to jam. The only thing missing was Slip. It had been just over a year since the tour had ended, but there had been no talk of getting back together. I was certain it burned on everyone's brain, like mine. I missed working with the guys. I couldn't wait to be back on the road, even when I had a baby.

Sutton opened the heavy door to the music studio and the three of us strolled inside. Ava lazed on one of the black sofas at the far end of the room, drinking a glass of wine. Cole sat behind the drum kit, hammering out a wild rock beat. Flint stood before him, slaying his electric guitar.

Lewis's fingers twitched in mine.

Giggling, I drew him close and smacked his hot ass. *Love him in Levis . . . in leather is even better.* "Go. Play. You know you want to."

"Thanks." He gave me a quick kiss. "We won't be long. Promise."

I patted the center of his chest and shook my head. "Don't make promises you can't keep."

His eyes glinted, and he wriggled his brows. "I always keep my promises. I promise to give you a foot massage and fuck you any way you want when we get home."

"I'll hold you to that."

"I'm counting on it." He kissed my tummy, then walked backward toward the guys. "Just a few songs. Half an hour. Tops."

That meant at least an hour. "It's okay. Go." I had the girls for company. We wouldn't be with these guys if we couldn't tolerate them playing for hours on end. They hadn't had a good jam session in weeks, so we'd better let them have their fun.

"Hey, you." Ava waved me over to join her, then patted the sofa beside her. "How was New York?"

I placed my tote down on the floor and lowered onto the seat beside her, tugging my T-shirt that was now too short over my baby bump. "Fabulous, as always. It's so beautiful there in the fall." Spending a week catching up with Lewis's old friends, Hayden, and the rest of the Everhide crew, had been full of laughs. "Crashing at Hayden and Lexi's place was an eye-opener. Having a toddler in the house was a whole new level of crazy. Charlotte and Josh are tame compared to Declan. I was exhausted watching him run around. Lewis loved every second."

Lewis had so much love in his heart for everyone. After growing up with parents who didn't support his homosexuality-cum-bisexuality, he'd run away from home as a teen and had always stayed true to himself. He'd followed his heart. He was one of the strongest people I knew. He'd found a new band. A new home. A new family. *Me.* Was there something more to life than being blissfully happy and excited about our future together?

We'd bought a house. We were about to have a baby. We loved each other.

We were soulmates for life.

*Oh, whoa.* A wave of heat washed over me. I let out a slow breath and pursed my lips to contain my smile.

Was there something I could do to make our life even better?

*Maybe.*

"How's Kara? How's my dress coming along?" Sutton interrupted my train of thought as she topped up her wine.

"She's good, and she's on track with your wedding dress." I tucked a cushion behind my back. It already ached. Not sure I wanted to be pregnant anymore. "I saw some of the flowers she was making for your skirt. They're beautiful."

The biggest smile lit Sutton's face. "I know. Kara keeps snapping me photos and sending updates. I can't wait for my first fitting after Christmas."

"I won't fit into anything by then other than stretchy leggings and hoodies." Luckily, it was coming into winter. I could at least be comfortable in what I wore.

"You look gorgeous no matter what you wear." Sutton handed me another cushion for my feet. "Tell us more about your trip. Are Gem and the other guys good?"

"Yes. They're back in the studio recording again." I put my aching feet up on the old coffee table, propped the cushion under my heels, and stretched out my legs. *Oh . . . that's better.* "Lewis and I spent a day in the studio with the four of them. They're working on a new album. It was so freaking amazing to see them lay down tracks. They're magic to watch. Lewis jumped at the chance to work with them to refine some riffs and progressions for one of their songs. Reynold, their producer, showed me around the studio's new channel mixer and recording equipment. That was incredible." I was certain I'd never return to acting. I loved light and sound engineering and working for the band too much. I couldn't wait to tour again. "But a week away was long enough. Like always, it's good to be home."

"Hmmm. Not for long." Ava raised her glass and took a big gulp. "We're about to hit awards season again. The next few months are flat out with invites and functions. I've got everyone scheduled for fittings at Gabrielle's boutique in two weeks."

"You're an angel. Thank you." I'd go with Lewis to his events as long as pending motherhood didn't cause me grief. But lately, every position I sat, stood, or lay in had gotten more and more uncomfortable. Where had *that* information been in the baby books I'd read? Where did it say you'd be tortured from the moment you became pregnant—morning sickness, having to pee all the time, and having sore tits? Those things weren't fun, but I still couldn't wait to have a baby.

"Have you had an update from Slip and Maddy? Are they coming home for any of the functions?" I asked. Last time I'd talked to Slip two weeks ago, he'd said he had no plans to attend anything. That plan had better change soon. Wasn't the end of the break approaching?

"April's talking to Maddy's publicist." Ava sighed and relaxed back onto the sofa. "We haven't had a final confirmation on anything yet."

"Mads has said nothing to me either." Sutton swept her long hair back over her shoulder. "She hasn't been happy at work. I worry about her."

"*I* worry about these guys. Look at them." I jutted my chin toward the three of them playing. Heads bobbing. Bodies swaying. Totally in sync with each other. "They need to get back together."

Christmas was only two months away. I prayed Slip was ready to make the move in the new year.

There was a loud knock on the door.

*Wait. What?* I knew that knock. *Didn't I? Holy shit!*

Everyone froze.

I looked at the girls, then the guys. They knew that rap as well as I did.

Or did I have baby brain?

*Ergh!* Highly possible.

The door flung open and in rushed Slip and Maddy.

"Argh! Surprise," Slip hollered and jumped through the doorway. He charged over to the guys and hugged them.

I was right! Only one person banged on the door like Slip.

"Oh my God." Sutton leaped from the sofa and charged toward Maddy. She flung her arms around Maddy's neck and hugged her tight, rocking from side to side. "I didn't know you were coming to LA this weekend."

"So good to see you." Maddy clutched onto Sutton for dear life.

With a skip in her step, Maddy dashed over to Ava and me and gave us a huge hug. Maddy hovered her hands toward my tummy. "Oh. You're getting so big. May I?"

"Sure." I didn't mind when people asked to touch my tummy, but I hated it when they just dived on in and rubbed it without permission.

She flattened her palms over my bump and her eyes widened. "It's so hard. I thought your belly would be mushy. Sorry. You're the first person I've known to have a baby."

"You want one?" I pointed to my stomach.

"Hell no." Maddy grimaced and shook her head. "But I'm happy for you. You look amazing. Definitely have that glow about you."

"Thank you. And how are you?" I clutched her hand.

"I'm..." Smiling, she swiveled her head toward Slip, catching up with the guys. "We're really good."

Within seconds, Slip had a guitar in his hands and had joined the jam session. *Ooooh!* My eyes watered. My chest quivered. *Holy shit.* I placed my hand over my heart. The guys were playing. Just like old times. But why the fuck was I so emotional?

"How are you, Ava?" Maddy sank onto the sofa opposite Ava. Sutton returned to sit beside Maddy. "How's living with Cole?"

"It's loud. Crazy. Non-stop." Ava's gaze drifted to Cole and a warm smile curled across her lips. "Waking up every day next to someone that good-looking is tough, but someone has to do it. I'm okay to take one for the team." She shrugged one shoulder and giggled. "But it wasn't much of a change. We basically lived together anyway. Dad loves having my house all to himself. He's actually started dating. I'm happy he's finally moving on after losing Mom."

"That's awesome." Maddy shuffled around on the sofa and turned to face the guys.

As they played, hope filled my chest. *Please get back together.*

The boys churned out another three songs before they joined us on the sofas, squishing in beside us.

"That was incredible. Damn, it's been too long since the four of us have played together." Lewis leaned forward and rested his elbows on his knees. He jutted his chin toward Slip, sitting opposite us. "It's fucking great to see you, man. Why are you in LA without letting us know?"

"We had some shit to take care of." Slip twisted and fidgeted with the lid on his water bottle. "Mads had to meet with her agent and has put her house on the market . . . and I wanted to talk to you guys about something."

"As long as it's good news." Cole wiped his sweaty face on a towel he'd grabbed from the basket beside the drums, then hooked it behind his neck.

Slip winced, grimaced, and rubbed the tip of his chin. Then a big cheesy grin inched across his face. "I was wondering if anyone is fucking ready to get back together?"

"Holy shit! You mean that?" Flint yanked his arm from around Sutton's shoulders, knocked her in the head, and shot forward like a bullet. "Sorry, babe." He patted her knee, then refocused on Slip. "Are you serious?"

Slip splayed his hands wide. "I'm here, aren't I?"

"Fuck yes!" Flint hollered. My pulse skipped in time with his energy. This was what we'd been waiting for.

"We're in." I waggled my finger between Lewis and me. I couldn't wait to get back behind the soundboards and control panels, working with these guys.

"Me too. One thousand percent." Cole pumped his fist. "Fuck yeah." But then he drew his shoulders back, cracked his neck, and patted the air with his hand. "Can we think this through for a sec though? We've got events coming up before Christmas. Lewis and Tia will have a baby in mid-February. My kids are in Kindy and school. Flint and Sutt, you're getting married in May. Slip and Maddy, you're still in Canada. Before we jump into this, we need to put a solid plan together. If Blake gets a whiff of this, he'll have our next tour planned before we've written our first song."

"Then let's talk." Lewis rubbed his hands together. The vibe radiating off him and the guys filled the room with a contagious buzz—totally addictive and adrenaline-pumping. "How are we going to do it? When? Where?"

"I don't want to rush this album," Slip said calmly. "Like Cole said, we've got a lot on in the coming months."

"True, but first . . ." Flint caught his breath and scanned the guys, as if readying himself to gauge their reactions. "We all need to be on the same page. Have the same mindset. I can't wait to record again. I've got lyrics coming out of my ass. But we have to think about where we're going to take this. How big do you want to go?" Fire blazed in Flint's ice-blue eyes. "Everhide and Ashlem will need to know for scheduling ahead. So for me? Singles and promo are a given. Tour? *Fuck yeah.* But do you want indoor venues like last time or push for larger arenas and stadiums? I'm all for bigger shows. I want to sell out the likes of Wembley and MetLife, and perform in front of enormous crowds. So if you want something different to that, say so now. We all need to agree and commit to this. There'll be no turning back. So if you need a few days to think about it, do so. But I'm all in for fucking big." Flint slapped his thighs, stomped his feet, and yelled, "I can't freaking wait."

"I don't need to think about it." A buzz hummed through

Lewis's voice as he edged forward in his seat. Any farther and his ass would be on the ground. "I'm with you. Count me in. Stadiums would be wicked."

"The bigger, the better." Cole clapped, then nudged his elbow against Ava's arm. "Are you ready?"

"Yes, absolutely." She kissed him on the cheek.

"I wouldn't have bought it up if I wasn't ready." Seriousness hovered in Slip's tone. "Ashlem promised us to make us as big as Coldplay, so they'd better fucking deliver. But when we tour, our breaks need to be longer. I don't want to burn out again. We need to accommodate Sutton's and Maddy's schedules. Lewis will need time with Tia and their baby. Cole and Ava with their kids. So if you're okay with that, I'm in. My hip is better. My head is straight. I want this. Let's go as big as fucking possible."

"Whoa! Yes!" the guys hollered in unison, jumped to their feet, and hugged each other across the coffee table. After some back-slaps and fist-pumps, they flopped back onto the sofas.

Flint couldn't wipe the smile off his face.

Neither could I.

Sutton curled her hand around Flint's leg and kissed him on the lips. "I told you to be patient. And I'm with Slip. Longer breaks would be nice."

"We'll do that. I promise." He sat three inches taller, unable to contain his electric energy, and took everyone in. "So, when can we start? Planning. Brainstorming. Writing. Playing. Slip, are you going to join us via Zoom or be here? We could come to Bowen Island for some sessions. What do you think about that?"

"Whoa!" Cole butted in. "Slip, your house is really nice, but at this time of year, it's fucking cold. If I can't snowboard, I don't want to be near the snow. I need sunshine, man."

"It's coming out of your ass." Chuckling, Lewis flicked his finger toward Cole's backside. "I can see it from here."

"You want a closer look?" Cole went to stand, but Ava caught his hand and pulled him back onto the sofa. Cole just grinned and kissed Ava on the cheek. "Spoilsport."

"No one wants to see your lily-white ass." Ava covered Cole's face with her hand and pushed him away.

Maddy cleared her throat loudly, capturing everyone's attention. "Um . . . actually . . . as of Christmas . . . Slip and I will be in LA. We're moving back home."

"ARGH! What?" Sutton shrieked, turned to Maddy beside her and clasped Maddy's hands. Tears welled in her eyes. And mine too. *Damn hormones.* "You are? Oh my God. That is amazing . . . but why? What's happened?"

"My show's changed too much." Maddy's lower lip sank, but she kept her tone light. "I don't like the new direction. So, I quit. I finish this season in mid-December. I've talked to my agent, and he'll hunt down a new role for me. I'm in no rush. I'm going to enjoy more time off. Be with Slip. Fall back into LA life."

Sutton wiped tears from her eyes. "This is the best news ever. I've missed you so much."

"Same." Maddy entwined her fingers with Slip's and held their hands against her thigh. "Since Mom died, I've realized how important family is, and time together is precious. You guys are my family. I've been away for far too long."

"It will be so good having you home." I splayed my hands across my chest. I loved that everyone would be together again. I loved Maddy and Slip. This was where they belonged. "We are family. Always will be."

Tears glistened in Maddy's eyes. "It's time to come home."

I understood that more than anyone. After being away filming in Chicago for years, the pull to be with Cole and the guys had become overpowering. I'd come back to LA to be with them.

"So, guys?" Flint rubbed his thighs. "Can we start now?"

He'd start right that minute if the band wanted to.

"Honestly and realistically, after the new year would be best." Slip didn't hesitate. "That's only two months away. We can have some initial discussions over the coming weeks and make plans, but I don't see us hitting the studio before then. Maddy has to finish her show. We need to sort out what to do with her condo in Vancouver and move back to LA. Does that sound okay?"

"It sure does. It absolutely does." Flint rubbed his hands together, then slapped them against his thighs. "I can't fucking wait."

Lewis hooked his arm around my shoulders and cheered with the guys. The tension that had been present in his brow for months had disappeared. Deep down, he'd been concerned the band wouldn't reform. That he'd have to find a new venture to work on or a new group to play with. But he'd always been optimistic. And he had every reason to be. These guys were solid. They weren't going anywhere. Lewis belonged with them. He was a Flintlock.

So was I.

And so was our growing little one.

After dinner, drinks, and too many laughs, Lewis and I headed home.

We ambled into the kitchen, and I eased onto a stool to get off my swollen feet. Lewis switched on some soft music, then made me a cup of peppermint tea. He hadn't stopped smiling since Slip and Maddy had given everyone the good news.

Neither had I.

My boys were ready to rock up a storm, write, record, and tour. *Yeah!*

Every step would take months to deliver, but I couldn't wait to see what direction their new music took and hear the songs they created. The material Lewis had written was incredible.

But I was even more excited to be with them every step of the way, working in the studio, running their front-of-house, and traveling with them when they performed live.

*Damn* . . . I'd have a baby when we hit the road.

That would be life-changing.

As Lewis placed my cup of hot tea in front of me, my belly twitched. I shot my hand over the weird sensation. My breath hitched. What was that? It was like butterflies, coming in soft waves of little pops and flutters.

"Tee, you okay?" Concern swayed in Lewis's voice.

My eyes widened as I slid my hand across my abdomen.

The tiny, barely there flutters happened again. I'd felt something similar before, but I'd thought I'd had gas. But this movement felt much different, lighter, not uncomfortable.

"Lewis." Tears welled in my eyes as I waved at him to come around the kitchen counter. "Come. Quick."

"What's wrong?" Panic flashed in his silver eyes, and he dashed to my side. I'd never seen him move so quickly.

I took his hand and held it beneath mine against my belly. "It's the baby. I can feel it. He's kicking."

"*He?* He is?" Lewis ran his hand from side to side, staring at my belly.

Then the little pops jumped to life again.

"Holy shit." The biggest grin slid across his lips. "That . . . is so weird, but freaking awesome." He bent forward and kissed my tummy. "You be nice to your mommy."

I combed my fingers through Lewis's hair, drawing the long strands off his face. "You're going to be an amazing dad."

He straightened and drew another stool closer. He rested his butt against it and cupped my face. "All thanks to you. You've given me more than I could've ever imagined. Being here with you, watching our baby grow, blows my mind every day. There is no place in the world I'd rather be. I love you, Tee."

"Love works in mysterious ways."

"It certainly does."

I stood, drew him to his feet, and took a couple of steps clear from the stools. I wrapped my arms around him and rested my cheek against his shoulder, and we danced, swaying slowly to the music.

"This is perfect." I shuffled from side to side, our bellies pressed together. Love already surrounded our baby. I eased back to meet Lewis's gaze. My heart thudded with happiness. The band was back together. The year ahead would be exciting. I was with the man I wanted to spend the rest of my life with. Lewis and I had always wanted the same things.

There was only one piece we'd missed.

We hadn't been ready before.

But now we were.

I felt it in my soul.

I took Lewis's hands in mine. "I love you." My voice came out soft and held a tiny tremor. "With every part of me and all my heart. We have music, a family of incredible friends, a baby on the way, and each other."

He rested his forehead against mine. "Life couldn't get any better."

My pulse quickened, tapping faster and faster throughout my entire body. "What if it could?"

He leaned back. Intrigue flitted across his eyes. "How so?"

I took a deep breath, filling my lungs to capacity, then squeezed his hands. "Marry me?"

"What?"

"I'd get down on one knee if I could, but my tummy's too big. Remember, I said I'd ask you when the timing was right? Now . . . is right."

After Emilio had dumped him when Lewis had proposed, Lewis had sworn he'd never ask someone to marry him again.

I'd said I would if and when the time came about.

I held his hands against my chest. "Lewis King, I love you. You're the father of our child. We have this incredible life together . . . and it's only going to get better. So please, will you do me the honor and marry me?"

He caught me around the back of my neck and drew my lips to his. His tongue flicked into my mouth. He breathed me in and moaned. It was like every kiss he claimed from me was the best fucking thing he'd ever had, tasted, and craved. He drew back. His heart pounded beneath my touch. His eyes glinted with warmth, love, and tenderness. "Yes. Yes, I'll fucking marry you."

I kissed him again, unable to stop smiling.

His love bound my heart to his. He was my soulmate. My life.

He was mine. I was his.

From then until the end of time.

# Chapter 15

MADDY

"And that's a wrap." Hilary, my producer, stepped out from behind the camera.

Instead of cheering, or clapping, or that-was-a-great-day-everyone praises from the crew, solemnness hung in the air.

Tears prickled my eyes. My chest pressed tight around my heart. But as I drew in a fresh breath, the weight on my shoulders disappeared. Light filled my steps as I headed off the studio set. After five and a half years of dedicating my life to *Vancouver Heights,* I'd filmed my last scene. Stepped off set for the last time. Delivered my last lines.

Hilary ambled toward me with her arms held wide. Sadness clouded her eyes. Her bottom lip jutted forward. "Maddy, amazing take."

I gave her a warm, tight hug. *Of course it was. But oh my God! I'm done.*

I'd loved my show until I'd needed six months off to save my marriage and get better. My work was no longer the reason I got out of bed in the morning. Slip was. *I* was. My found family was. What was important to me had changed.

I held nothing but respect for Hilary. She'd always been kind, supportive, and an incredible producer, even if she'd been difficult to work with since I'd returned for this season.

"Thank you." I stepped back and placed my hand on her forearm. "For everything. For believing in me and helping me when needed."

She bowed her head. "It has been a pleasure working with you. I'm sorry to see you go."

"Me too. But it's time. New opportunities are waiting to be discovered." My agent hadn't found me another role yet, but I had a meeting with him in LA in four days. Hopefully, he'd have some updates by then.

"You'll shine no matter what you do or where you go." Hilary's words were always encouraging. "I'm already envious of whoever casts you."

"Thank you." I gave her one last hug.

My castmates and the crew gathered around me. The tears, hugs, and wishes overwhelmed me. These people had been great friends and fun to work with, but they weren't family. Not like Slip, Sutton, and the band. I'd denied it for so long, but LA was home. I no longer had to distance myself from the heartache and humiliation I'd experienced several years ago when Noah had left me at the altar. I didn't have to worry about Mom. She was no longer sick and suffering. I didn't have to stress about gossip surrounding Slip and me. It had died down. We were blissfully, happily married. We'd given each other time and had put effort into our relationship and were excited about the next chapter in our lives.

I had no job and no solid plans, but I was confident I'd pick up a new role. I was fortunate to be an A-lister and ambitious, and I'd been in demand by casting agents. I'd wait for the right role, though. Slip had come to Canada to support me. Now it was time to return the favor while he and the guys wrote their new album.

Slip, carrying a huge bunch of red roses, meandered

around cameras and booms, and made his way through the crew to me. He slid his arm around my waist and kissed me on the lips. "Congratulations. To the end of an era and on to new beginnings. Love you."

"You'd better take care of Maddy." Geraldine, my fellow castmate, flicked Slip's shoulder with the back of her hand. "Or I'll come to LA and kick your ass."

"I promise I will." Slip chuckled as he stood beside me.

"Gonna miss you like crazy, Maddy." Mills, my on-screen boyfriend, hugged me. "You take care."

"You, too." *Asshole.* But we were cool. I wouldn't miss his shitty jokes. Or his cherry cola breath. *Nope. Not one bit.*

Slip sneered at him. "I'm not gonna miss you making out with my wife on the show anymore."

I loved that Slip was a touch jealous and protective of me. *Possessive.* It was hot.

"I won't miss you visiting the set and glaring at me. You intimidate the fuck out of me, bro." Mills's voice pitched high. Had my badass rock star with long hair, tattoos, and a ripped body made Mills nervous? *Good.* "Thought you'd storm onto the set and deck me every time I had to get close to Maddy."

Some days, I'd wished Slip had.

"Believe me," Slip jested with a twitch of his lip, "I've thought about it."

Mills let out a nervous laugh, then cleared his throat and straightened his stance. "But Maddy was the best on-screen girlfriend a guy could ask for. Always professional. Always fun. Always amazing."

*Aw!* Mills could be nice. Pity it was too late.

The group shuffled around and formed a wide circle in front of me.

"Maddy?" Lotti, one of the other girls from the show, stepped forward and held up a Cartier gift bag. "We all chipped in and got you a little something to remember us by." She handed me the bag. I pulled out the red leather box and opened it, revealing a gold watch encrusted with diamonds.

"Wow! This is way more than I'd expected. Thank you. It's beautiful." So much better than the pen Kwan had gotten when he'd left. *Yay!*

"Now." Lotti clutched my hand and swayed my arm gently from side to side. Her big, beautiful Julia Roberts-smile took over her face. "Go take on LA. We'll no doubt see you at events." Then she pouted and waggled her finger toward my face. "But don't go stealing any awards from us."

Giggling, I shook my head. "Sorry, babe. I can't make that promise." That was true. I had no idea where or what show or movie I'd work on next. That was scary and daunting but exhilarating.

After more speeches and stories from the cast and crew about my time on the show, everyone headed out to dinner. We laughed over good wine and great food. It was a fun yet emotional night. I wasn't just saying goodbye to everyone I'd worked with; it was farewell to Vancouver too. This place had been my home-away-from-home for more than five years. I loved this city so much. But we'd be back. Slip and I would stow away to Bowen Island on a regular basis. That was our place to escape.

After way too much champagne and wine, we headed home just after midnight to my condo that overlooked the harbor.

I woke, naked, wrapped in Slip's arms, and to the view of the gorgeous glistening expanse of water and rare sun-filled skies outside my window. Vancouver had turned on the perfect send-off. But I wouldn't be fooled. It'd be freezing outside. December always was.

I rolled out of bed, showered, and dressed in comfy leggings and a sweatshirt. Sitting on the floor in my room, I packed the last few items into my suitcase. Shoes. The clothes I'd worn last night. A couple of books. *Done.* As I unplugged my alarm clock, wound the cord around it, and stuffed it in between some clothes, a mix of sadness and excitement pummeled my chest. The door to my life here was closing, but a fresh one awaited me in LA.

I was ready for the change.

I closed and zipped up my bag. As I rolled my suitcase toward the door, Slip came out of the bathroom to help me with my luggage, freshly showered and dressed in jeans and a T-shirt.

"Is that everything?" He put the case next to the rest of our belongings lined up for the movers. The small travel bags for our four-day road trip to drive our McLaren Spider home sat separately by the dining table.

I drew in a long, deep breath. Calmness washed over me. "Yes." I snaked my hands around his waist and stuffed them into his back pockets. As I rested my cheek against his shoulder, I looked around my bare apartment. No pictures. No trinkets. No traces of us. Just the basic furniture remained, ready so we could rent the place out.

I wasn't sad about leaving.

My heart had left this place the moment I'd quit my show. Now, I just wanted to get to LA and live life with Slip.

"You okay?" He kissed my head and circled his hands over my back.

"Yes." I swiveled my head and kissed the small of his neck, then brushed my nose toward his ear. He smelled delicious, all citrusy after his shower. "I'm excited to be going home."

"Me too." He rested his head against mine. "Time I got my ass back to work."

"I do like your ass." I gave his butt cheeks a firm squeeze, then slipped my hands out of his pockets, up underneath his

T-shirt, and across his lower back. His skin was cool against my touch. I dipped my fingers into the waistband of his jeans and ran them around to the front, tickling his flesh in their wake. I popped open the button of his fly. "I like what's down here, too."

Slip caught my hand and held it against his stomach. Heat simmered low in his eyes. "Mads, the movers will be here in ten minutes."

"So?" I arched an eyebrow. Mischief coiled through my veins.

"Maddy?" Slip grinned. His voice and smile betrayed his attempt to be serious.

"Slip?" I caught the bottom of his T-shirt and lifted it a couple of inches. Lowering my head, I kissed the bottom of his stomach. I licked along the line of his happy trail, dipped my tongue into his belly button, then headed higher toward one nipple. Glancing up at him, I threw him a saucy smile. "We need to say goodbye to my condo. One last time."

He laughed; his belly quaked beneath my touch. "Didn't we do that last night when we got home?"

"Yeah, we did." I bit my lip and scrunched my nose. Sex on the table had been hot. "But I was tipsy. Now, I'm not." I yanked his T-shirt over his head and dropped it on the floor. He didn't put up a fight.

Fire simmered in his eyes as he glided his warm hands over my arms and shoulders. "You, my beautiful wife, are trouble."

"No, I'm just happy." I reached for the button on his jeans again. I lowered his zipper and slid my hand over his hot, bulging erection. "And . . . I love you."

"Hmmm." Smiling, he cupped the side of my neck and brushed his lips against mine. "*Ti amo. Mio bel girasole.*" He skimmed his thumb along the line of my jaw and teased it down my throat. "And I love this bit." He shifted his head to one side and kissed the soft skin beneath my ear. His wandering hands skimmed over my sweatshirt and cupped my boobs, tweaked my nipples. "And these."

"I love all of you." I dipped my hands into his boxer briefs and took hold of him. After circling my thumb over his hot head, I smeared his pre-cum up and down his groove. "But right now, I want this bit inside me."

A soft moan rolled through his throat. He caught my hands, withdrew the one from inside his pants, and wound my arms around his neck. He took hold of my waist and guided me backward until my butt connected with the wall by the fireplace. His lips touched mine, soft yet needy. "Stay."

He ducked and yanked down my leggings, taking my panties with them, and pulled them over my socked feet. As he straightened, he ran his hands up my bare legs. I'd love to wrap them around his head, but we didn't have time. This was just a quickie.

I wriggled his jeans and boxer briefs lower, freeing his thick, hard cock. With a sexy smirk curling across his lips, he closed the gap between us. I hooked my leg around him and pinned him against my body. Curling his palm around my thigh, he gripped it tight and bent his knees. He took hold of his cock in his other hand and nudged it against me, stroking my opening up and down, teasing and taunting me.

Giggling, I swept his hair off his face and tucked it behind his ear. "This is familiar." *Half-naked. Pinned against the wall.*

"How so?" He pressed his lips together to contain his smile.

"This is where you fucked me after you convinced me to stay married." Running away from him after we'd wed in Las Vegas had been a mistake. I knew that now. Him coming after me and pleading with me to give us a chance had been crazy . . . but agreeing to do so had been the best decision I'd ever made. I couldn't imagine life without Slip.

He pushed inside of me, stealing my breath. Warmth coiled

up my spine, around my heart, and through every vein as he touched his lips to mine. "I knew we belonged together. It just took you a while to believe that. I would've kept fighting for us, Maddy. I always will."

"Same." I ran my hands around his shoulders and linked my fingers behind his neck. "This is where we started our marriage. Now, we're saying goodbye to this place to move onto new adventures. I can't wait. Just you and me. Together."

"I like the sound of that." He pulled back a fraction, then drove into me slowly and set the motion on repeat. Again. And again. *Oh yeah.* "Fuck, you feel good."

I sank down the wall an inch or two and tilted my hips so he could penetrate me deeper. "So do you."

My head drifted to one side, giving him access to my neck. He nipped, licked, and sucked my flesh. His hot breath sent goose bumps shooting across my skin.

I needed more. More of him.

I buried my fingers into his long hair, drew his lips back to mine, and kissed him hard. Hungry to taste him, I flicked my tongue into his mouth. Each touch flooded my system with fire. Each tease quickened my pulse. Each taste was a pure high. Kissing him was addictive. *My fix.* Slip and I had become dependent on each other. But that was a good thing. That was what marriage was about. We could lean on each other. Trust each other. Would always be there for each other. We'd learned from our painful pasts and wouldn't make those mistakes again.

I breathed Slip into my soul. I rocked my hips and fucked his cock, driving him toward the edge. He hammered into me, thrusting harder and faster.

*God. This is good.*

*We* were good.

He eased one hand between us and taunted my clit. His body tensed tighter and tighter. "You with me?"

I moved in time with him. His drive to my tilt. His rubs to my pulses. "Yeah."

Lost in our kisses, touches, thrusts, and rocks, I came at the same time as Slip. Shuddering. Quaking. Jolting. My pussy throbbed around his thudding cock. My heartbeat thundered against his. Panting, we smiled over our kisses, perfectly in sync.

*Gotta love a hot quickie!*

He pressed his forehead against mine. "Are you ready, Mads? For LA and everything that city and our life will throw at us?"

"Yes." I ran my hands over his broad shoulders. "We have a beautiful home. We have incredible friends and family. We're ready for the next stage in our lives. I love you. Nothing will ever tear us apart."

"*Ti amo.* Let's go home."

Just after we cleaned up and redressed, the intercom buzzed.

The movers loaded our belongings into the truck and drove off. I took one last slow stroll around the living room. I took one last glance across the gorgeous harbor. I took one last deep breath within these walls.

Yes, it was time to move on.

I entwined my fingers with Slip's and led him out the front door. I locked it for the last time.

We jumped into our Spider and headed south.

Life was about to change yet again . . . but I had a good feeling about it.

Whatever it was, I was ready.

*Look out LA. We're coming.*

# Chapter 16



There was only one thing I enjoyed as much as planning my wedding . . . and that was Christmas. The magic in the air, the streets, and shops full of decorations and twinkling lights, and carols playing in every store gave me a high. It was impossible not to be caught up in the cheer. I loved shopping, giving gifts, and spending time with friends.

This would be my last Christmas as Sutton Summers. Next year, I'd be Mrs. Glover.

The big day was getting closer and so much had to be done. Flowers, table settings, and decorations had to be finalized. Cake had to be ordered. Dresses were being made. The guest list kept growing longer and longer.

But today wasn't about our wedding. It was Christmas. At Cole's.

Loaded with gift bags and presents galore, Flint and I entered Cole's house. My mouth fell to the floor as we entered the foyer. Cole's entire entrance and living room and been transformed into a winter wonderland, covered in green garlands, twinkle lights, baubles, fake snow, and gold wreaths. The most stunning Christmas tree covered in lights and decorations stood by the gas fireplace and nearly reached the top of the atrium. There were Santa Clauses and elves, reindeer, angels, and nutcracker statuettes dotted around the room.

"Cole?" I crossed the room, fell to my knees, and placed our presents under the tree. "This looks amazing. Is all this for you or the kids?"

"Me, of course." He grinned goofily as he helped me with my gifts.

Flint placed his load of boxes wrapped in bright, festive paper next to mine. "Dude?" He stood and slapped Cole on the back. "Christmas will always be at your place from now on. You don't do things half-assed, do you?"

"Nope." He straightened his Santa hat and flicked the pompom over his shoulder. "Plus, I have a girlfriend who likes to organize everything." He waved to Ava, who was cooking up a storm for lunch in the kitchen.

I should help her, but I'd probably burn something. Like I'd done to the pumpkin pies on Thanksgiving. I didn't want to ruin any of her delicious dishes again. It was best if I stayed clear of the kitchen.

"Are the others here yet?" Flint scanned the games room and the yard.

"Not yet. They'll arrive soon." Cole jutted his chin toward the garden. "The kids are outside playing with their new swing set from Santa. I do not rate putting that up in the dark and fucking cold on Christmas Eve. I followed the instructions, but somehow I have six spare bolts, three washers, plus the packet of spares. It hasn't fallen yet. So win, right?"

"Totally." Flint chuckled. "Why didn't you pay someone to put it together?"

"I'd thought it would be easy, but I had to get Sloane out of bed to help me. I'll blame him if it breaks." Cole yawned, no doubt tired from his late-night construction efforts and early start to the day with the excited kids. "How are your folks?"

"Good." Flint flopped onto the sofa and stretched out his legs. "Sutton and I managed not to kill anyone with our cooking."

I eased in beside him and patted his stomach. "Babe, you cooked. I watched. That's why everyone is still alive."

Steven, my brother, his girlfriend, Kate, and Flint's parents had come to our place for Christmas Eve. We'd all drunk way too much wine over dinner and presents, but it had been an awesome catch-up.

The door swung open, and Lewis and Tia charged toward us. I burst out laughing.

"Ho. Ho. Ho," Lewis hollered, dressed up as Santa, carrying a sack full of presents. Tia wore an elf outfit that stretched tightly over her baby belly.

Tia deposited more gifts by the tree and Lewis put down his bag. A loud shriek pierced the air outside. Charlotte and Josh rushed inside, ran over to Lewis, and collided into his legs.

"Uncle Lewis, did you bring us presents?" Charlotte looked up at Lewis with big, bright green eyes.

No fooling them. He wasn't Santa.

"I did." He tickled Charlotte's tummy, then drew both kids into a hug. "But you have to wait until after lunch for your gifts."

"Okay." Josh pushed out of Lewis's hold and grabbed Charlotte's hand. They ran into the games room on the other side of the kitchen, where toys and books lay spread across the floor—no doubt their haul from Santa this morning. With more gifts waiting for them, those two kids would be spoiled even more.

Flint and I jumped off the sofa to say hi.

Lewis stepped over to me, lowered his beard, and kissed me on the cheek. "Happy holidays."

"Merry Christmas." I straightened his Santa hat. "I love the outfit, Santa."

He grinned but scratched his cheek and chin. "It's itchy and hot. But it's all for the kids." He was as bad as Cole—a big kid at heart who'd do anything for them.

"Tia, happy Christmas." I hugged her hello. Her huge baby bump was the size of a watermelon, and she still had two months to go. "Are you sure you're not having twins?"

"Nope." She swayed from side to side, rubbing her lower back. "Just one. Feels like twenty."

Flint's cell buzzed. He grabbed his phone out of his jeans pocket, glanced at the screen, then stuffed it away again. "Um. Cole? We need the kids."

"Shit. Yep. On it." Cole strode over to the games room, clicked his fingers at Ava as he passed, fetched the kids, then returned to the living room. As the kids took a seat by the tree, Ava joined us.

*What is going on?*

The doorbell rang.

The huge glass door swung open and in stepped Maddy and Slip, wearing ugly reindeer Christmas sweaters and carrying a big box each. Slip's present was twice the size of Maddy's.

"Merry Christmas, everyone." Maddy made her way over to us. Flint lightened her load, taking the box from her.

"Who's ready for more Christmas presents?" Slip hollered and handed Cole the enormous gift.

"Me!" Charlotte and Josh pounced on all fours.

The box tilted in Cole's hands.

Was that a rustle? A whimper?

*Oh, my.* My heart skipped a beat. Cole hadn't, had he?

"Okay." Cole held the box in the air above the kids. "This one is for the two of you. It's actually from Ava and me."

"And this one is for you?" Flint held his present out for me to take.

*Me?* I'd already gotten a diamond necklace and Prada purse from him. I didn't need anything else. The box moved, tipping to one side. *Oh crap!*

Cole placed his box on the ground. The kids yanked the lid off and out leaped a tiny ball of black and white chaos . . . a Dalmatian. The puppy whimpered and whined as it licked and sniffed Josh's and Charlotte's faces. Its tail wagged at one hundred miles an hour, thumping against the box.

"A PUPPY! We got AHH A PUPPY!" Charlotte grabbed the dog around its neck and crushed it against her chest. It scrambled from her hold and dashed over to Josh.

*Oh gosh . . . what do I have?*

I put my box down and eased off the lid. A beautiful, yet frightened, black kitten shivered in the bottom corner. "Oh. She's beautiful." I picked up the tiny cat, stood, and cradled it against my chest. I patted her back and kissed her head.

"It's actually a him." Flint edged closer and scratched its ears.

"And it pissed and shat all over our bathroom last night." Slip grunted as he gave the kitten the evil eye and then did the same toward the puppy. "The dog was just as bad, peeing everywhere in the laundry. They both cried all night. Maddy and I have had no sleep. You can thank us at any time."

"They weren't that bad." Maddy curled her arm around Slip's and rested her head against his shoulder. But judging by the dark circles under her eyes? Yeah, she hadn't had a decent sleep.

"You're champions. Thank you." Cole squatted and patted the puppy. "So, kids, you now have to take care of this little guy. But first, you have to give him a name."

"Spot!" Charlotte giggled as the puppy licked her face.

I winced and shook my head. Too obvious, right? But whatever.

"No. Rex. Like a T-Rex. Roooar!" Josh clawed his hands and hollered at the dog. The puppy just licked his nose.

"Yeah. Rexy." Charlotte wrapped her arms around the puppy's tummy and kissed his head. "I love you, Rexy."

Ava bobbed down next to the kids and smoothed her hand along the puppy's back. "Sounds like his name is Rex."

"Very cool name, kids. I love it." Cole ruffled the puppy's head, then stood. "Do you want to take him outside for a play before lunch?"

"Yeah." The kids stood. Josh picked up Rex around his middle and carried him outside at somewhat of an awkward angle, but the puppy didn't seem to mind.

*Too cute.*

"What are you going to call this little ball of fluff?" Flint asked, rubbing one of the kitten's tiny paws.

"Why did you get me a cat?" I kissed its face and brushed its soft fur against my cheek. I was already in love with the thing, but I'd never wanted a pet. I lowered my voice so only Flint could hear. "I thought I was the only *pussy* you wanted?"

Flint stroked the kitten's back. It purred and curled against my chest. He leaned in and whispered in my ear, "You definitely are, *Kitten*." Too much heat flared in my cheeks and between my legs. *Damn.* He eased back and a sexy smile played across his lips. "This little guy is just a pet. I've always liked cats, but my parents would never let me have one. When Phil nearly hit a cat on the night he died, I've always wondered what happened to it since it was never found. In a warped and weird way, I've always wanted to know whether it was okay or not. That cat played a part in bringing you to me."

I arched an eyebrow. "So we need to call him PTSD?"

"What? No?" Flint grimaced and chuckled. "But you knew I was fucked up before we started dating."

"We both were."

"Yeah." He softened his tone. "But we're good now." He rubbed the kitten's ears again. "This little guy is from the rescue shelter. He'll keep you company when I'm traveling or working, and vice versa. He's perfect, just like you."

"I'm not perfect, but thank you." I guessed now I was a cat lady. That was a change I hadn't seen coming.

I held the kitten against my breast and stroked my fingers along his back. I scratched the top of its head. "So, what should we call you? You're a Flintlock. A little rock star. Relish attention. You're handsome. Clearly like black. And you would look great in a leather collar. *Hmmm*. Sounds like someone else I know." I winked at Flint, then held the kitten in front of my face and stared into his yellow eyes. "You're just like a Danny Zuko, aren't you?" I met Flint's gaze again. "Like you on the night I got you to sing at Hayley's. When we sang 'Summer Nights.' So it's Zuko."

Flint closed the gap between us and threaded his hand around my waist. A playful smile curled across his lips. "Not Greasy? Lightning? Putzie?"

"No." I giggled. "Zuko."

"I love it. Zuko it is." He kissed me on the lips, lingering there for a few seconds. *Hmmm*. "Love you. Merry Christmas."

"Love you. And thank you."

*Wow*. Our family was expanding . . . and changing. Two new members had joined us today—Rex and Zuko. They'd no doubt be a handful. But life was good. Maddy and Slip had moved home two weeks ago. The guys had discussed their writing schedule. My show was a hit. We'd all jetted around the country to awards shows and events and still had more in the coming weeks. In a few months, I'd be married. I honestly don't think I could get any happier.

After lunch, we sat around in front of Cole's huge gas fireplace, laughed, and told stories. We opened presents. Torn paper, gift bags, ribbons, and boxes covered every inch of the floor.

As the kids played with new toys on the rug, Maddy tapped

me on the arm. "Hey, can I steal you for a moment? I need to discuss something with you. Can we go outside for a sec?"

"Sure." I handed Zuko to Flint. His eyes lit up—clearly happy I'd finally handed Zuko over. He laid the sleepy kitten against his chest and scratched its ears. Zuko purred away. I rose to my feet and followed Maddy outside. She ambled across the lawn and stopped by the hedge.

"Mads? Is everything okay?"

"I hope so." Excitement and worry skipped in her voice. In the cool air, she tugged the sleeves of her sweater over her hands and fidgeted with her wedding rings. "So . . . I had a meeting with my agent yesterday. Carlos has come across a role that I'm interested in . . . but it's subject to you."

"Me?" I buttoned my glittery Christmas cardigan. For LA, it was freezing today. "Why me?" Her agent was a powerhouse in this town. Maddy was an A-list star. If he'd found her a role, it'd have to be for a fabulous hit show. Money and fame had never come between Maddy and me, and it never would. Our friendship meant the world to me. I wished her every success and would support her no matter what.

Maddy closed her eyes. She sucked in a deep breath, then blurted. "Because it's for *Angels in LA*. To start the next season in March."

"ARGGGGH!" I jumped up and down, then flung my arms around her neck. My heart skipped and danced through the clouds. "Yes. Oh my God. Yes! I'd love to work with you again." When Tia had left the show at the end of our first season, they hadn't replaced her. We'd had guest stars come and go, but no one had stayed long-term. There'd always been talk about adding a new main character, someone who'd blend in perfectly with our cast. Maddy would be perfect. "That would be brilliant."

Here I was thinking life couldn't get any better. But this was definitely another leap forward.

"It's not guaranteed." Maddy stepped back and wiped her happy, teary eyes. "The studio wants me to audition. So before I even contemplate doing that, I needed to make sure you'd be okay if I did."

She met my gaze, no doubt looking for any concerns or fears, but she wouldn't find any. I'd loved Maddy since we'd met on a show when we were twelve. Our friendship had stood the test of time. We'd survived drama, love, and heartache, ups and downs and more. We were unbreakable.

Maddy clutched my hands. "I'd love to be on screen with you again, but I won't go where I'm not wanted. I don't want to rain on your parade, step on your gown, steal any of your light. Your show is your baby."

"It's not just *my* show." I shook my head as happiness exploded in my chest. "You will add to it—not take anything away. Peyton and Mia and I are on an even playing field. No one outshines the other. You already know the girls, so if you join us, we'll have so much fun. Just like old times."

"Yeah." A hopeful smile inched across her lips. "I'd like that."

Happy tears burst from my eyes. I hugged Maddy tight. "I love you, Mads. Please do the audition. You shouldn't even have to do one. I'll put in a good word for you. You'd be the perfect fit for *Angels*."

"Thank you." She stepped back and rubbed my arm. "You don't need to say anything, but yeah, that would be nice."

"Done." I jumped and clapped my hands. "I'm so excited. This is the best Christmas ever."

Warmth shimmered in Maddy's eyes. "And the new year is going to be even better."

"It certainly is. You're home. The guys will be together, working on new music. Tia and Lewis are having a baby. I'm getting married. There are so many amazing things happening, my head keeps spinning."

"We've got it pretty fucking good, don't we?"

"We do. We absolutely do."

Maddy's stunning smile was contagious, but then reality slammed into my chest. There was still so much to organize, plan, and book for the wedding. My to-do list was a mile long. "If I could stop stressing about the wedding, everything would be fine."

"Why are you stressing?" Maddy winced, as if she didn't believe me. "You have everything under control and a team of people to help. There is no need to worry." She gave my hand a gentle shake. "Your wedding will be a beautiful day where we celebrate you and Flint. Have fun planning it. Be excited. You don't need the best of everything or need to outdo every other big, fancy wedding ever held in Hollywood. Be prepared for things to go wrong, because they will. But it's Quill's job to have backup plans. I'm sure he'll have several in place." Reassurance set into her every word. "We know you love Flint and are committed to each other. At the end of the day, it's just a big party."

*True.*

"Everyone who loves you will be there. We'd come if you served sausages on paper plates, and soda in Solo cups, and you wanted to get married in T-shirts, surf shorts, and flip-flops."

I sucked in a sharp breath and gaped, laying on the shock. "There will be no flip-flops at my wedding. Not ever."

Maddy laughed. "I know. But Sutt, I'm here for you. We have five months to meticulously plan everything and make sure the day goes off without a hitch."

"Thank you. I'm so glad you're here. And I am excited. Our next task is to decide on flower arrangements for the ceremony. And we need to brainstorm ideas for our grand entrance. I want to make it fun and dance and wow the guests."

"Sutt, of course I will help you. But most people won't remember what decorations were on the table, or the flowers you had, or the food they ate—only how much booze you put on at the reception, and if you're lucky, maybe the dress you wore."

*Really?* I sifted through my memories. I'd been to a couple of weddings, but yeah, the only ones I remembered were a cousin's reception where everyone had gotten rotten drunk, and Maddy's special days—her heartbreak and tears at her first wedding. And how big her smile had been and how happy she'd seemed with Slip at her second.

But I wanted my wedding to be burned into people's brains. "I want it to be beyond fabulous."

"It will be. For you . . . and Flint . . . That's all that matters. But I assure you, I'll remember it, too, because I'm your best friend, and I can't wait."

She was right. I didn't need it to be over the top. Just special. The day was taking shape. I was counting down the days until I married the love of my life.

But before then, we had more awards ceremonies to attend, birthdays to celebrate, Valentine's Day to enjoy, and a baby was due. I had a show to film. The guys had an album to write. Oh, and now, there was another wedding to look forward to. Lewis and Tia aimed to wed in September, a few months after their baby was due.

I had to stop stressing. Enjoy the ride. Be thankful I was there, surrounded by my friends I called family.

The year ahead would be exciting.

I couldn't wait.

*Bring it on.*

*Bring it on, now!*

# Chapter 17



The day I'd been dreaming about for more than a year had arrived. I'd looked forward to this moment more than my pending wedding. I was back in my home studio with the guys, ready to write a new album. It had been just over fourteen months since we'd agreed to take a break. Now, we were here, together again. I couldn't wait to get started. Music was a huge part of who I was. I wasn't complete without my band.

We were set. Ready to work.

At the far end of my studio that overlooked the garden, we took seats on the two large sofas that faced each other. Lewis, beside me, Slip and Cole, opposite. I'd stowed my acoustic guitar next to me, leaning it against the edge of the armrest. Everyone pulled out their notebooks and laptops from backpacks or satchels and dumped them onto the coffee table in disarrayed piles. Lewis grabbed his electric bass. Cole drew out a set of drumsticks from his backpack. Slip sank onto his knees beside the coffee table and opened the guitar case he'd brought with him . . . one I'd never seen before.

"Holy shit." I didn't need to see the logo on the head to know what brand it was. The classic vintage sunburst acoustic body and long, dark neck with signature mother-of-pearl fretboard inlays screamed *Gibson.* But that was no ordinary guitar. "Is that a Lab '57?"

"Yep." Slip spun the guitar around in his hands. "Found it online near our place on Bowen Island. This old guy had it sitting in his garage, collecting dust, for years. He'd never used it and had no idea what it was worth. It had a broken tuning key and bridge and some bad scratches. He had it listed for five hundred dollars. I offered him five grand and he wouldn't take it. I showed him online what she was worth, and he didn't believe me. After much negotiation, we settled on three. I still feel bad I got such a bargain."

"Shit. You got a seven-thousand-dollar guitar for three grand?"

"Actually, this one is probably worth closer to eight-and-a-half. It didn't take much to restore it. She's a beauty, isn't she?"

Slip handed me the guitar. I placed it across my lap, struck the strings, and admired his incredible restorative handiwork. "Dude, it looks brand fucking new. And sounds . . . amazing. Is this my late Christmas present?"

"No fucking way." He puffed air through his nose and shook his head. "She's mine."

"You sure?" In my collection of more than twenty guitars, I had a few Gibsons, electric and acoustic, but I could always add more. I didn't have a Murphy Lab '57.

"Yes." He held out his hand and flapped his fingers. "Give her back."

I tinkered away on the steel strings, loving the sound and feel. But before I got too attached, I handed her over. "She's awesome. Can't wait to see what you create on her."

"Me too."

"Alright then." Cole shuffled forward in his seat and rolled his sticks between his palms. "Let's write an album. Where do you want to start? Look? Feel? Sound? Anyone got anything they want to lay on the table?"

"I do." I wrung my hands together, cracked my knuckles. The first two albums I'd penned with Phil, then Cole and Slip had joined us to flesh out and compose the music. I'd written our third album with Cole and Slip after Sutton and I had broken up . . . and then, when Sutton and I had gotten back together. There had been way too much alcohol involved. But I'd loved the process and their input every step of the way. "I want this album to be written like our last one. We're all together, for every word, every line, every note. Is everyone cool with that?"

Fire ignited in all the guys' eyes as they nodded.

"I have a million ideas zooming around inside my head." I leaned forward and rested my elbows on my knees. "I've written a bucket-load of new songs and composed some cool music, but I'd also like to do something with Phil's lyrics. Have you read your notebooks?"

"Sure have." Cole grabbed the one Tia had given him and flicked through the pages.

"Yep." Slip tapped his hand on top of his pile of pages and pads.

"I've read all of them." Lewis dipped his chin. "The guy had a way with words."

"He certainly did." I remembered how we fed off each other, coming up with lines, stories, and rhymes, trying to outdo each other, creating song after song. Phil was truly talented. His lyrics were incredible. I didn't want them to go to waste. "I'd love to swap each notebook around and we can read each one, tagging the songs we like . . . like this." I pulled mine off the coffee table and showed them the colored Post-it notes sticking out the top. "Green is awesome." *There were three.* "Blue is 'I can work with it.'" *Four of them.* "We see which ones we agree on and turn those into something."

"So you want this album to be Phil's work?" Concern drilled

into Slip's brow. "I'm not sure about that. I want to write new music. This is a fresh start for all of us. I don't want to look back."

Cole closed his book and placed it on the table. "I don't think the album should consist entirely of his stuff. But there are some really good lyrics in my notebook. Raw shit that hits hard, that I know we'll turn into phenomenal songs. A mix of old and new would be good. Does that work for everyone?"

"I'm not making any promises about using Phil's songs." Slip ruffled his hands through the back of his hair. I understood his hesitation about not wanting to write an album of depressing songs or using all of Phil's words. He shrugged, not totally killing the idea. "Like always, we'll see how things unfold as we write."

"I'm cool with that." Cole nodded and scratched his scruffy cheek. "I'll mark up my book tonight and have it ready to swap tomorrow."

"Awesome, and yes, I'd like a mix, too." I skimmed through a few of the pages in Phil's notebook. There was some great stuff in there. I couldn't wait to work on the music for several of these songs. "We've come so far, but I don't ever want to lose sight of where we came from. I don't want to dwell on losing Phil anymore. The aim is to honor and remember him in a positive way. To not let these lyrics go to waste. I'm so grateful for where we are, what we have, and what we've achieved. I'm excited about the years ahead." I closed the book and held it against my chest. "Our last album was about breakups and falling in and out of love. This album is about us . . . what we've lost, what we've found, and our friendship that has stood the test of time. I want it to be full of good vibes. We're gonna write some incredible rock songs and legendary music."

"Ooh." Lewis clicked his fingers. "We could give the album a working title of *Lost and Found*? I kinda like that."

"Yeah. Me too." I bobbed my head.

"That works." Cole picked up a drumstick and twirled it around his fingers. He was super chilled most of the time, but always fidgeted with something.

Slip rubbed his forehead. Too much worry had embedded there. I didn't want to see any. "Fine. But if we go down the path of using some of Phil's material, I don't want to focus on losing him or the darkness. Most of the lyrics in my notebook are depressing and painful. Most of them were written just before he died. I'm happy to honor Phil—you know that. He was my best friend. But anything we use has to be fun and positive. A song or two is fine. If we find more, we can always record them and keep them in mind for future albums. We've turned our lives around in the past couple years. All for the better. I want to look forward, not backward. I have a new fire burning inside me. Fresh rhythms and tunes are hammering my head. The break has given me a new lease on life. Let's make this a fun album."

"Absolutely." I clapped my hands together, then held up one finger. "But . . . with a couple love ballads and heart-breaking tracks thrown in."

"If they weren't our bestselling songs, I'd beat that crap out of you." Cole shook his head, but his eyes glinted. "I'd prefer upbeat party tracks. Much better for drumming."

"That is true . . . but our bestselling hits have been the emotional ones." I counted on my fingers. "Angst-filled love, being hot for a girl, sexy innuendo, and crushing heartbreak sells."

"I know. But write the soppy ones from memory, not reality this time." Cole jabbed a finger at me. "Just promise me you won't fuck things up with Sutton. We don't want to see either of you hurt, or for you to fall into the depths of depression and hit the bottle again. Or have to write another album totally about her."

Grinning, I bobbed my head. The guys and I had been through so much shit together, but we'd survived. We were stronger. I was better. "We won't . . . not the whole album anyway. I'm in a good place. Sutt is my one. I'm ready to take on the world again. Are you?"

"Fuck yeah." Cole twirled his sticks around his fingers, then tapped them against his books. His energy filled the room, a clear sign he was itching to write and play.

Shards of silver light shimmered across Lewis's eyes. His electric vibe was as contagious as Cole's. "The album has to tell a story. The story of us. That after hard times, there is good. After heartache, there's love. Hope. A bright future. Our friendship has been key." He straightened and slapped his thighs. "So let's do this. Let's write an album."

"Yes, please." Slip strummed the strings on his guitar and jutted his chin toward me. "We always come up with the best songs when we just jam and follow a beat, or you get all fucking emotional. Have you worked on anything good recently? We gotta start somewhere, so what have you got for us?"

"I have so many bits and pieces to show you." I shuffled through some books. "I don't know where to start."

"Same." Lewis scrolled and clicked on his laptop. "I've got some great ideas. Let me see if I can find one."

"Actually . . ." I drew my shoulders back and rubbed my hands up and down my thighs. "I know where to start." This day was what I'd been living for. I wanted to capture it. Capture our feelings, our thoughts, our goals. I grabbed my laptop, opened it, and turned it on. Damn thing took forever to load. "Gemma told me to do this years ago, and I never have. So you're gonna suck this up and go with the flow. It's a quick activity for us to understand each other. I want everyone to say why you're here. Why do you want this? Or why the fuck you can't breathe without music? Or what's driving you to make this album, get back on stage, and follow this dream?"

"That's a no-brainer." Cole leaned back on the sofa and stretched out his legs.

"Good." I opened Google Docs and a new file, ready to type. "I'm gonna wing this and write shit that comes into my head. You first, Cole."

"Fine." He rolled his sticks against his leg. "I'm here because my life is better with the three of you. Drumming and you guys are my world. . . Ava and the kids are my everything. Taking care of my family is my priority. I want to give them the best life possible, travel with them, and be the best father and partner I can be."

I rolled my hand through the air, coaxing him to give me more. "Can you give me a moment, or a time when something happened when you knew you couldn't live without Ava and the kids?"

His gaze softened. "Yeah. It's been right since our last tour. But a couple months ago, we were in bed. It was early. We'd just finished fucking when the kids came charging into our room and jumped all over us. We had to quickly get dressed, but then the four of us just lay on the bed and talked, hugged, and goofed around. It was the day Ava agreed to move in. Every day since then just keeps getting better and better. That's the day we truly became a family."

I closed my eyes. I didn't want to picture him fucking Ava, but I'd sensed they'd been truly happy the past few months since they'd lived together. I'd felt that way when Sutton had moved in with me. Words and feelings tumbled around in my head. My fingers glided across the keyboard as I typed. Tunes and words formed in my head, then the lines rolled off my tongue:

> *The sun . . . woke us*
> *Sweet kisses . . . Hot love*

*Knotted sheets . . . Soft touches*
*Your smile . . . perfect*
*My heart . . . surrendered*
*This life . . . with you*
*Is all . . . so new*
*Our family . . . has grown*
*Let's see . . . where this goes*
*Bold steps . . . A home*
*Our love's . . . so strong*
*We can't . . . be wrong*
*This is . . . so right*
*I'm yours . . . You're mine*
*Every day . . . and night*
*I'm yours . . . You're mine*
*Together . . . for all time*

"Fuck." Cole smirked. "You just came up with that? This is why you write most of the lyrics."

"I can just spin more shit than you." I chuckled, fixing my typos, and saved what I'd written.

"That's true." Slip laughed and placed his guitar over his legs. He tinkered at the strings, mimicking the way I'd read the lines. "You are full of shit."

My laugh rumbled low through my chest. Fuck, I loved these guys. "Don't make jokes. You're next."

Slip thumbed a string and stared at his fingers. "Me? Okay. I'm honestly happy to be alive. Clean. Sober. With Maddy." He rested his arm on top of his guitar and spoke from the heart. "I was so fucked up at the end of our last tour. It took a long time to get better. But I did. I'm confident I won't relapse. I'm here for me, to prove that I can do this sober. I'm here because I love you guys and music. I need you to survive. And Maddy. She inspires me to be the best person I can be every day. I've known she's the one for years, since the first time we slept together. But that feeling grew stronger when we went public with our relationship, and she said yes to marrying me . . . both times . . . in Vegas and after rehab. She is it. Forever."

"You two are meant to be." I tinkered on the laptop keys, the words flowing.

"We are." Smiling, he strummed his strings. "She's the best."

"How's this?" I read my words with more of a storytelling beat:

> *Sunset . . . Vegas*
> *The lights . . . endless*
> *A slow dance . . . Champagne*
> *Diamonds . . . A veil*
> *Morning . . . Goodbyes*
> *Your tears . . . Heart break*
> *Cameras . . . Cruel words*
> *Rumors . . . that hurt*
> *But you . . . and I*
> *Are ride . . . or die*
> *Our love's . . . so strong*
> *We can't . . . be wrong*
> *This is . . . so right*
> *I'm yours . . . You're mine*
> *Every day . . . and night*
> *I'm yours . . . You're mine*
> *Together . . . for all time*

Slip played a few chords, then shot forward and jotted down some notes on his new notebook. "I like the beat. The lyrics, not so much, but it's a start."

Slip didn't totally shoot me down, so that was good.

"Lewis?" I swiveled my laptop toward him. "You?"

"Me?" He scratched the tip of his chin. "Fuck, guys . . . I'm here because finding you was my destiny. I've had so many amazing experiences since moving to LA. It's been mind-blowing, life altering, incredibly good, and totally crazy. From auditioning for you, to now being a Flintlock, to meeting Tia, to having a baby soon. I've found the family I've always wanted. I have a home. I was born to play with you. Nothing beats doing what I love with my best friends. I'm here for you. For Tia. To make music, perform on stage, entertain the fans, and tour. Fuck, you could write a novel about those things, not just a verse."

He wasn't wrong there.

"Let me give this a crack." I tapped my finger against the side of the laptop, pinched my brows together, and mulled over what Lewis had said. "How's this?"

> *The stars . . . night sky*
> *New city . . . New life*
> *I was . . . so scared*
> *But then . . . you appeared*
> *Your touch . . . so new*
> *One smile . . . and I knew*
> *Your kisses . . . profound*
> *Heartbeats . . . so loud*
> *Music . . . our souls*
> *I've found . . . my home*
> *Our love's . . . so strong*
> *We can't . . . be wrong*
> *This is . . . so right*
> *I'm yours . . . You're mine*
> *Every day . . . and night*
> *I'm yours . . . You're mine*
> *Together . . . for all time*

"Wow." Lewis splayed his hand against his chest. "Flint, that's amazing."

"Thanks." I loved writing lyrics. I loved letting my mind search for a feeling, home in on it, and write whatever words jumped into my head. Some songs came easily. Others took days to nut out or were never finished.

Slip added more chords. Lewis strummed his bass and joined in, feeling and finding a rhythm to match. Cole tapped away on the table, drumming in time with their tune. I felt the vibe; it was my turn. I pounded on the laptop keys. Mine was easy. There was nowhere else I wanted to be. I was here for Sutton, music, and these guys. I wanted to write and perform for the rest of my life and spend every day with Sutton. Having the band reform after our break had saved my soul and sanity. Finding Sutton, living with her, proposing to her, and having her say yes had healed my scarred heart.

I finished typing and read my lines to the guys:

> *Moonlight . . . Our fate*
> *From our . . . first date*
> *We were good . . . then lost*
> *Drowned sorrows . . . the cost*
> *But we found . . . our way*
> *Grow stronger . . . each day*
> *Each song . . . I write*
> *Is for you . . . my love*
> *My soul's . . . on fire*
> *You take . . . me higher*
> *One door . . . I opened*
> *My heart . . . exploded*
> *Got down . . . on one knee*
> *You are . . . my everything*
> *One ring . . . for you*
> *Can't wait . . . to say I do*
> *Our love's . . . so strong*
> *We can't . . . be wrong*
> *This is . . . so right*
> *I'm yours . . . You're mine*
> *Every day . . . and night*
> *I'm yours . . . You're mine*
> *Together . . . for all time*

"Damn." Lewis play-punched me in the arm. I just grinned as I stared at the words pasted across my screen. He then shoved my thigh. "Not bad for our first effort."

"Thanks." I hit save. Those moments had brought us here. They were why we were here. It was what we lived for. I loved that.

But what impressed me more than the lyrics I'd written was the fact the guys had come up with a sick beat. My words would probably never see the light of day, but I liked the music. I picked up my guitar from its rest spot against the side of the sofa and positioned it on my lap. I zoned in on Lewis's and Slip's fingers and listened to the beat. The rhythm. The chords they were playing.

I joined in. Cole tweaked his tempo, drumming his sticks faster and faster against the coffee table. Lewis hit record on his laptop to capture the tune.

"Fuck this. I need to play on the kit." Cole leaped to his feet, raced over to his drums, and took to his stool. His pedals captured the beat. His sticks snared the drums.

How could we not join in?

I put down my acoustic, dashed over to my rack of guitars, and grabbed my electric Fender. I plugged it in and stood in front of Cole. Lewis glided over with his bass. Slip picked up his electric guitar off the stand beside his mic and jumped in.

But after a few minutes of us playing, finding the chords and rhythm and beat, Cole caught his cymbals, silencing them. "That's awesome. It's something we can work with. But . . ." Fire blazed in his eyes. "Can we just jam?"

"Fuck yeah." I stuck the strings on my guitar. The need burning in the guys' eyes matched the fire skipping through my veins. Slip and Lewis nodded. My fingers quivered against the fretboard, ready to glide across the steel stings. "Let's go for thirty minutes, then it's back to work."

"Yes, boss." Slip slayed a wicked riff on his guitar. *Show-off.*

Laughing, I stepped over and clipped him over the head. I

hated it when he called me *boss*. I was the lead singer, but we were an equal team. *Always.* "Are you able to keep up for that long? If you don't, you're buying lunch."

"Oh, I'll keep up." He adjusted a tuning key. "Let's play."

"Lewis? Cole?" I jutted my chin at them. "You in on this?"

"What? Play for thirty minutes without stopping? That's not even a challenge." Cockiness swaggered through Cole's tone. "I'm in."

"I'm always down for playing before work." Lewis strummed out a rapid beat on his bass. "I'm good to go."

"Alright then." My fingers hovered over my strings. This, playing with the guys, our friendship and having fun, were more reasons for living. "Let's play 'Motion,' 'Love Makes You Crazy,' 'Follow You,' the medley from tour, and the songs we played for our encore. That should be about half an hour."

"Yes, boss." Slip saluted me.

*Asshole, but I love him.* "Fuck you."

"Love you. Now let's play." He positioned his fingers over his strings.

Cole tapped his sticks together, beat his bass drum four times, then hammered out the intro, leading us into our set. Lewis, Slip, and I struck our electric guitars. The music reverberated through our amps, my feet, and my soul. Cole's cymbals shattered the air. The booming beat struck the center of my chest. I sang, but not in front of the mic.

We stood in a circle, feeding off each other's energy. Slip and Lewis banged their heads in time with the music, flicking their long hair over their faces. I laughed out loud, rocking from side to side on my feet. Cole's hands were a blur as he struck his drums. It was wicked to be back together again. Playing. Joking around. Living and breathing music.

For thirty minutes, we rocked out our songs. We sweated. We panted. But no one called timeout. Cole struck the last note, threw his sticks in the air, and caught them. "Hell yeah. That's what it's about. Us playing. The music. That rush."

He raced around from the back of his kit to join us.

We huddled in a circle, draping our arms around each other's shoulders.

"Cole's right." Fire burned hot inside my chest. "Music is who we are. We're going to write an incredible album. Tour. And keep doing this for the rest of our days."

"Absolutely." Lewis wiped his sweaty face on the shoulder of his T-shirt. "But I'm starving. I'll buy lunch. Then let's get to work. I've got a bunch of songs I've been working on and want you to hear."

"Me too." I tilted my head toward the door. "Food, then work."

"Deal." Slip took off his guitar and placed it on the stand. "I've got lots of verses and ideas to throw at you guys. I've written some cool riffs, and other bits and pieces. They just need to be paired with some awesome lyrics."

Cole grabbed a towel from the basket next to his drums and wiped his face. "I've worked on some new cool beats. I can't wait for you to hear them. But once we sit down, fuck around, play with some lyrics, and I get a feel for the song, that's when I fire. That's when the drumming comes to me. You know that."

"We do. I want to hear everything, but let's eat first." I set down my guitar and led everyone out of the room.

We headed out to the kitchen and living area. I grabbed icy-cold beers for Cole, Lewis, and me, and a lime and soda, now a permanent item in my fridge, for Slip.

We sat around my dining table and told stories and rude jokes while we waited for the pizzas Lewis had ordered to arrive.

I loved these moments—hanging out with the guys, talking shit, and laughing—just as much as playing music.

We had the best job in the world.

We had an album to write.

We would. I had no doubt.

*Lost and Found* would be another epic chart-topper.

I felt it in my bones.

I pictured us performing in front of thousands of people at Wembley, MetLife, and even the MCG in Melbourne. Yeah, that would be epic.

We'd work toward making that dream a reality . . . after lunch . . . and another beer or two.

This time together, enjoying each other's company and having fun, was just as important as our job.

I was a fucking good boss, wasn't I?

*Hell fucking yeah!*

# Chapter 18



I used to dread attending film industry functions when I was married to Luther. The stuffy, snobby, shallow chitchat with executives, investors, producers, directors, and celebrities had often done my head in. The snooty glares and upturned noses from people when they'd found out I was a cop had been draining. I'd avoided cameras and the spotlight. But going to events with Cole and the band had completely changed my opinion. Now, I liked to be seen . . . with Cole. I couldn't wait to be styled and dressed, pampered, and glammed up for an evening of fun. At every lunch or dinner, Cole was always determined to transform the occasion into a sexy, flirty, and often steamy affair, full of laughs.

He talked dirty, fucked dirty, and liked to *get* dirty when we went for a run through the hills or worked out in the home gym, or after he'd had a session on the drums. There was something about his sexy smile, his hot body covered in sweat, and his laid-back swagger that drove me crazy. Every day we grew closer, fell more in love, and made our life together better.

I'd grown comfortable and confident in our relationship. I never wanted to lose what we had.

After spending most of the day with Tia, Maddy, and

Sutton in our hotel suite, getting our hair and makeup done for tonight's Grammy Awards, I slipped into my long, maroon beaded gown. The plunging neckline was daring and bold but elegant and sexy. Some days I missed my simple security uniform and heavy flat boots, and carrying a concealed weapon or two, but today was not one of those days.

As Maddy and I sat on the sofa, sipping on champagne, Liliana, our new personal makeup artist and hair stylist, touched up Sutton's gorgeous smoky eyeshadow and lipstick at the table. Tia stood beside us, swaying from side to side on her feet and rubbing her lower back. She was due to pop in two weeks, but had insisted on coming tonight. FOMO ran in the family.

There was a knock on the door.

"That's the guys." April rose to her feet from the desk and made her way over to the door. She opened it, and in strolled the guys in their suave designer dinner suits.

As Cole came toward me, my breath skipped through my lungs and my heartbeat doubled in speed. *Every damn time I lay eyes on him.* He wore formal attire like it was a second skin. He radiated pure perfection in Armani, Valentino, or Versace. But tonight, he was sex on legs in Dolce and Gabbana, with a black glittery shirt, tie, and pocket square.

*Super sexy. Damn hot!* I'd be the one instigating the dirty talk tonight.

Cole halted in front of me and held out his hand. I slid my palm into his, and he drew me to my feet.

"Ava?" His green eyes darkened as his gaze raked over the arch of my breasts. He slid his hands around my waist and kissed my lips. "You look beautiful."

"Thank you. You're very handsome too." I leaned forward and whispered in his ear, "Are you going to keep your hands where I can see them tonight? And your eyes off my boobs?"

He shook his head. "No fucking way."

"Good." I placed my hands on his hips and pulled him forward so our bodies were flush, and my groin pressed against his cock. "I'm gonna need that before the night is out."

"Hmmm," he moaned, low and soft. "How about now?"

"Can't." I straightened his pocket square, then gave his chest a tap. "We have to go."

Flint, Lewis, and Slip greeted their ladies with a quick kiss. Whatever Flint whispered in Sutton's ear made her blush . . . which she did often.

Slip's soft murmurs to Maddy left a sexy smile stitched onto her lips.

Lewis sank onto the cushion beside Tia, bent down, and kissed her baby belly, then her cheek. "Hey, Tee. You good? No weird aches or pains? Don't really want you to go into labor on the red carpet."

"I'm in constant pain and uncomfortable, but I'm fine." She ran her hands over her belly. "I'll let you know if anything changes."

I loved how close I'd grown to the girls, especially Tia over her pending motherhood and our constant talk about children. It was hard not to love her. Her dirty mouth, quick wit, and sexy banter had her outdoing the guys on many occasions. She was a female version of Cole . . . *God help us*. But the four of us had become inseparable. I spent more time with them than my sister, who was more of a workaholic than me.

Cole played with one of my Cartier dangling earrings he'd given me for Christmas and softened his voice. "Have you called the kids?"

"Yeah. They're good." I struggled to contain my smile as images of mayhem at the kitchen table flitted through my mind. "Rex ate Charlotte's dinner. Josh had a sore stomach after eating twelve chicken nuggets and two slices of pizza. Harper dropped a full bottle of ketchup on the floor, but otherwise, had everything under control. She was about to put the *Super Mario* movie on for the hundredth time."

"Sounds like a typical evening." Chuckling, he leaned in and pressed his lips against my temple.

"Yeah." I slipped my hands inside his jacket, placed them on his waist, then rubbed them up and down. His silky shirt, cool beneath my touch. "Wish we were there."

"No. It's a work and date night." Fire simmered low in his eyes as he arched one eyebrow. "You're mine. Harper will be fine."

"I know. She's amazing." Harper was the best nanny I'd ever come across. After a rough start with Maddy over her past relationship with Slip, they too now got along . . . well, they tolerated each other and were civil. Harper's involvement with Sloane had eased the friction. They basically lived together in Cole's guesthouse. I never had to worry about the kids, knowing they were in the best of care. So tonight, I could enjoy the evening with Cole, the band, and the girls.

Working for The Flintlocks had changed my life. It had tested my skills, my patience, and my time-management capabilities, and I'd added new areas of expertise to my resumé. I'd met some incredible people and couldn't have gotten to this point without April's and Blake's help. I was now on a first-name basis with stylists, makeup artists, designers, flight and accommodation specialists, private jet operators, and car service providers across the globe. I'd never envisioned that happening within my lifetime. *Yet, here I am.*

My old security team was always on-hand when needed. I worked alongside event managers, production crews, and function organizers, executives at the Ashlem Entertainment Group who managed The Flintlocks tour and promotion and marketing campaigns, and the crew at Everhide's record label.

My cell phone had so many contacts in it to cater to the guys' needs, I was sure it would melt down if I added one more number.

I could give Quill, Sutton and Flint's wedding planner, a run for his money.

But I was in my element. I loved helping the guys, getting them to places, and ensuring their safety and that everything went off without a hitch. I was ready to step in and deal with any mishap or drama when it arose. But best of all, when it was time to enjoy an outing, I often joined my friends. I worked beside them, not from the sidelines.

I had the best of both worlds—work and play. Business and . . . *oh, my . . . pleasure!*

How had I gotten so lucky? How fortunate was I to find someone as kind, caring, and loving as Cole?

Now I'd found him, I never wanted to let him go.

"Are you ready to walk another red carpet with me, Aves?" Cole's soft voice hummed in my ear.

"Always." I entwined my fingers with his and drew him toward the door. "But before April cracks her whip, we'd better get out of here."

The eight of us headed out of the hotel suite, with April and our security close behind. We slipped into a limousine and were chauffeured to the Dolby Theatre. The short drive was slow. The car queue, long. The waiting crowd of fans and photographers, huge.

After we stepped out of the limousine, Cole took my hand. Our group shuffled along the carpet, smiling and posing for the photographers. The guys weren't up for any awards tonight, so they could just relax and enjoy themselves. But Flint's energy skyrocketed when reporters asked him about plans for the next album, and he could finally say new material was in the works.

Oh, it was. *Big time.*

Over the past few weeks and after several meetings with their executive team, the band, Everhide, and Ashlem had locked in dates. The guys would record after Flint and Sutton's May wedding and release their first single in November. Promo would roll out across the following months and into the new year, with their next global tour kicking off in September. Their schedule wasn't rushed, crammed, or pushed to the limit. We'd get to spend a lot of time . . . together.

Cole kept his cool charm in place as we cruised down the carpet. Lewis and Tia gloated to anyone who asked about the approaching due date of their baby. Slip and Maddy glided along beside us, cracking jokes and posing when needed. There was never a dull moment.

As we reached the main media area, the camera flashes continued to blind me. The hollering reporters and photographers deafened my ears. Production crew and publicists hovered around us like shepherds herding sheep toward the entrance. But every time we had to wait in line to progress along the carpet, one devilish glance from Cole sent a fiery heat through my veins.

He drew flush against my side and smiled against my ear. "Every time you lean forward, I can see your nipples. That's such a fucking turn-on."

*Shit!* I lowered my voice so only he could hear. "The Hollywood tape isn't sticking to the fabric." I pressed my breast into his arm, trying to get the stupid tape to re-stick, but it didn't work. I had some spare stripes in my clutch, but I couldn't change them in the middle of the red carpet. "As long as it's only you that sees my tits, I'm okay with that."

"I want to do more than just see them." His voice dropped to a dangerous, sexy low. "I want to lick them. Suck them. Fuck them."

"*Shhhh.*" My nipples hardened, itching against my beaded

dress. Heat pooled between my thighs and crept into my cheeks. My body had a mind of its own around him. "Later. Behave." I forced a smile onto my face and turned Cole toward the cameras. We waved, posed, and moved on.

Throughout the ceremony, Cole slid his hand up and down my thigh, inching dangerously close toward my panties. *Tease.* But each time he gave me a suggestive look, our arms brushed together, he ate something off my plate, or he kissed me, a wave of pure happiness washed over me.

I honestly couldn't remember a time I'd felt like this before.

By the time we got to the after-party, champagne skipped through my veins and hummed through my soul. As a DJ pumped out the tunes, my friends and I hit the dance floor. Under a sea of disco lights, we laughed and swayed. Cole twirled and spun me 'round. Our bodies drew close, and we dirty-danced up a storm.

"When I get you to our room, I'm going to fuck you on every surface." Cole growled low in my ear. "Is that okay?"

I ran my fingers up his suit-clad thigh, digging my nails into the fabric. "Will you be slow and gentle? Or rough and dirty?" Okay, maybe I'd had too much to drink . . . or not.

"Ava?" He tightened his hold around my waist. "Don't tease."

I grabbed his ass. "Will there ever be a time when I don't make you ravenous?"

"I hope not. You fucking do it for me." He pressed his hardened dick against my crotch. Only the thin layers of fabric stood between us. "You want me to make you come? Here, on the dancefloor?"

My body temperature dialed up ten notches, but I kept my voice calm and collected. "I'm sure you could, but the other guests might get jealous." *Or upset.* I didn't want the security team to haul us out of the room for indecent behavior.

"I don't want that." His hands circled my back, my shoulders, my arms. "So, how about the second we leave?"

My breath entwined with his. "We're staying here in the hotel, so I'm sure we can make it to our room."

His eyes narrowed into sexy slits. "Or the elevator. Whichever comes first."

"I know the security team, so turning off the cameras can be arranged."

"Hmmm." He rocked his hips against mine again. My core clenched, craving to have more of him. *Damn . . .* "I knew I loved you for a reason. But I don't care who sees us."

"Me either, but without video evidence would be nice."

"True. Although . . ." Sexiness embedded in his grin. "I'd keep a copy if we were filmed."

"That doesn't surprise me."

I wrapped my hand around his tie and drew him closer. Our lips met. Our tongues teased and touched. Tasting the vodka on his mouth intoxicated me even more. His spicy cologne filled my head with a dizzy high. The music slowed. In the middle of the crowd, our dancing turned from provocative sexiness into a gentle sway. Our friends shuffled nearby. I slid my hands beneath Cole's jacket, ran them around his waist, and pressed them against his back. My heart beat in time with his.

This was nice. No . . . this was *perfect.*

Cole cupped my neck. Kissed me. Held me close.

Every touch was soft. Sexy. Seductive.

"I love you," he whispered against my mouth.

Could the night get any more superb? We'd laughed. We'd had fun. When I was with him, there was no one else in the room. He only had eyes for me.

I was his. He was mine.

Butterflies fluttered low in my belly. Warmth spread across my chest. There was only one thing that could make our relationship better. I'd never thought this day would come, yet . . . here it was.

Everything felt right. Aligned. Clear.

I touched my lips to his, then smiled from the bottom of my heart. "Ask me."

"Ask you? What?" Confusion flitted across his eyes. "Would you like to sit down?"

"No."

"Would you like another drink?"

"No."

"You want to get out of here?" Hope shimmered in his eyes.

"No. Not yet." My tone softened with seriousness. "Cole? . . . Ask me."

His mouth quirked at one corner. "You want something to eat?"

"No . . . wait . . . yes, but later."

"Then I'm not sure what you want me to say?" But then . . . he paused. His lips parted a fraction, and his eyes widened. He sucked in a slow breath that shuddered through his chest. His heartbeat quickened beneath my touch. He knew what I meant, but he shook his head like he had no clue. His gaze softened. A small smile touched his lips. "We have two amazing kids. You love your job. The guys and I are working on the next album . . . We live together. What more could you possibly want?"

"Cole . . . don't be an asshole." I yanked on his tie—a gentle but decent jerk.

He caught my hand and held it against his heart, drew me close, but a pinch formed between his brows. "A guy can only take so much rejection. You've said no to me many times."

*Shit . . . really? Crap . . . I had.* "Are you serious?"

"No." He grinned, running his thumb across the back of my hand in soft, swirling strokes. My past refusals hadn't put him off. *Thank goodness.* "But are you sure?"

"Yes. I am."

"So am I. I have been since the first time I asked you to move in." He drew my hand to his mouth and kissed my fingers. Fire, love, and warmth flared in his eyes. "Ava, I have no ring. Have nothing prepared. It's too crowded to get down on one knee. I wish our kids were here to be part of this, because fuck . . . I love you and them so much. So . . . in the middle of this room full of friends, colleagues, and people I have never met in my life, I would like to ask you *one* question. With my hand on my heart and giving you all that I am . . . Ava Matthews, will you please . . . marry me?"

Tears prickled my eyes. My heart swelled, filling my chest so much my boobs nearly popped out of my dress. My cheeks hurt from breaking out into the biggest of smiles. "Yes, Cole Tanner. I would love to marry you."

He raised his arms into the air, pumped his fists, and hollered, "Fuck yes!"

Grabbing me around the waist, he lifted me, spun around on the spot twice, then lowered me back onto my feet.

Laughing, I brushed my fingertips down his cheek. "I love you."

"Love you too, Aves. Woohoo!" he cheered, then kissed me.

Flint stopped dancing with Sutton and slapped Cole on the shoulder. "What's up?"

"I proposed, and she said yes." Cole hugged him sideways. "We're going to get married."

"Argh! Congratulations." Sutton flung her arms around my shoulders, and we jumped up and down. Our other friends joined our celebrations.

The news spread like wildfire around the room. A few minutes later, the DJ bellowed into his mic, "Well, folks, it all happens at the after-party. The word is out, so let's be the first to wish the very best to Cole Tanner and Ava Matthews. They just got engaged. Whoa! Alright! Yeah! Someone grab those two some champagne, and let's celebrate."

As music blared, people hugged and congratulated us. By the time we made it to our table, a waiter had brought us a bottle of champagne and had filled several glasses.

My heartbeat and head hadn't come down from cloud nine.

I'd found the man I wanted to spend the rest of my life with.

My friends and I took a flute each—Slip grabbed a water—and we chinked our glasses together.

"To Ava." Cole raised his glass to me. "Life works in mysterious ways. It brought me Charlotte, Josh, and you. We've become a family, one that I will love and cherish forever. You're a Flintlock, and I can't wait to spend the rest of our lives together. Cheers."

"I look forward to kicking your ass forever more." I nudged my elbow against his ribs. "But most of all, I want to love you every day. Love our children. Follow our dreams and be happy."

"Cheers to that." Maddy tapped her glass against mine, then downed a sip of her drink. "Congratulations."

"Thank you." I took a decent mouthful of my champagne, savoring the sweet, cold bubbles as they tingled on my tongue.

I would always be grateful these people had come into my life . . . and for Cole.

For him, being a decent, kind, and loving man.

I cuddled into his side. He draped his arm around my back, held me close, and kissed me on the cheek. My heart doubled in size.

I'd found love. Happiness. A home.

This was true love. *Family.*

After the hell I'd been through, I deserved to be happy.

*This* was my happily ever after.

# Chapter 19



"Lewis? Wake up. Oh shit. Shit. SHIT. *Arrrrgh*!"

Tia's slap on my head, cursing, and shaking of my shoulder had jolted me from my sleep. "Tee? What's up?"

"It's time. We have to go. Now!"

"Now?" My pulse spiked, hitting my skull with a thud. "You sure?"

"Arrrrgh!" Tia rolled onto her side, drew her knees up, and clutched her belly. Her breath hissed through her teeth. "Fuck yes. It's coming. I haven't slept. My lower back is killing me."

"Has your water broken?"

"No." She winced and keeled forward. "Lew, our baby is coming. My contractions are five minutes apart."

"Fuck. Okay." I blinked and wiped the sleep from my face. *Yep, I'm awake.* The bright LED light from the clock on the nightstand burned my retinas. 2:23 a.m. *I got this.*

I swung my legs off the bed, but paused. I turned back to Tia, leaned over, and kissed her. Excitement and fear skipped through her gorgeous green eyes. It did the same in the base of my gut. "Are you okay?" I asked.

"I'm fucking terrified. Somehow, this thing has to come out of me."

*Yeah.* I wasn't looking forward to that part either.

She flicked her finger toward the walk-in closet. "Just help me get changed, grab our bags, and let's go."

"On it." I dashed across the room, changed, and grabbed Tia her favorite stretchy comfy sweatpants and hoodie. Tia had packed and prepared her hospital bag. I hadn't. I zoomed around the room and stuffed a few things into an overnight bag. In less than five minutes, we were dressed and out the door.

As I drove out of the Hills toward the Cedars-Sinai Medical Center, my pulse hadn't returned to normal. Not sure it would. This was it. Today, we'd meet our baby. I reached over and rubbed Tia's thigh. "Are you ready for our lives to change?"

"Too late if I'm not. *Arrrrgh!*" she cried as her hands circled her belly. "Fuck! It hurts."

"Hold on, Tee. We're nearly there."

With my foot to the floor, I broke every speed limit on the way to the hospital.

We'd called ahead and were met at the front door by a nurse waiting with a wheelchair. While Tia was taken to the delivery ward, I sped our Mercedes to the parking garage, pulled into an empty space, and sprinted back to the reception area with our bags in hand. Tia had just finished checking in when another contraction hit.

She glanced at her watch. "They're three minutes apart."

"Okay." Nurse Loretta patted and rubbed Tia on the shoulder. "Let's get you onto a bed and see where you're at."

I followed the nurse wheeling Tia through a set of secure double doors and into a monitoring room. I dropped our bags just inside the door, then helped Tia to stand. After she changed into a hospital gown, she clambered onto the bed. As the nurse attached a heart-rate monitor to Tia's finger, Tia clenched her teeth, grabbed her belly, and cried. It was so loud, I was sure she woke the rest of the band miles away. "*Arrrrgh!* Get this thing out of me."

I wished I could. My ribs ached with every breath. I'd been to all of Tia's obstetrician appointments. Watched our baby grow day by day. I had the 3D image from one of our baby's scans saved as the background image on my phone, but we didn't know whether we were having a boy or a girl.

I'd read every baby book Tia had bought. I knew what was supposed to happen at every stage. We'd visited the hospital, so we knew where to come on the day. But nothing had prepared me for the pain spearing Tia's cries when her contractions hit. It jolted my stomach, flooded me with nausea, stabbed my chest, and filled me with total hopelessness.

"Tee?" I kissed her forehead. "Can I get you anything? Water? A cold cloth? Want me to rub your back?"

"No." Tia grimaced, grabbed my hand, and gripped it tight. "Just don't leave me for a second."

*Fuck!* Did she have to crush my fingers? Clearly . . . yes. "I'm not going anywhere."

After attaching more monitors and cables to Tia, the nurse turned to me. "I need to check how far along Tia is. Would you mind stepping outside for a second?"

Tia shook her head. "No. He stays. He's seen everything down there."

"True." A sly smile slid across my lips. "I'm here for all of it." Except the smell of hospital disinfectant and the sight of medical equipment. Wooziness ran through my head in a feverish wave. If I kept my focus on Tia, I'd be fine. *Hopefully.*

"As you wish." Loretta slipped on a pair of disposable gloves and draped a sheet over Tia's waist. "Tia? I need you to pull up your knees, then widen them."

I happily stayed beside Tia's head. Right then, I didn't need to see everything.

Loretta's hand disappeared beneath the sheet. Tia winced

and wriggled on the bed.

"Tia, you're about eight centimeters dilated." Loretta ripped off her plastic gloves, tossed them into the trash can, and then washed her hands at the sink. "This baby wants out. We need to get you into a delivery room."

*Holy shit!* How long had Tia been in labor? She'd been fine when we went to bed at ten. She'd said her lower back was aching, but that wasn't anything unusual. But clearly, it had been.

Tia lowered her legs and straightened her hospital gown over her tummy. "Don't we have to call my doctor?"

"Yes." Loretta nodded as she typed notes into the laptop beneath one monitor. "We'll call Dr. Mila, but I'm not sure she'll get here in time. She lives about an hour away."

"No. No. No." Tia shook her head in short, sharp jerks. "I'll wait. She has to deliver our baby."

Loretta placed a hand on Tia's shoulder and gave it a gentle rub. "Remember, you have to be prepared for anything and do what is best for your child. You may want to wait, but I don't think your baby does." A comforting smile flitted across Loretta's face. "We have other doctors here if needed. You're in good, safe hands."

"I know." Tia winced. "But I want Dr. Mila."

It wasn't like Tia to be anxious. But having a baby warranted anything. The panic in Tia's voice seared my brain. Somehow, I found a thread of inner calm. "Loretta, I can call our doctor if it helps."

The nurse glanced at the monitors blipping away. Flashing lines and numbers blazed across the screens. There were no alarms going off, so that was a good thing, right?

Loretta nodded at me. "Thank you, but I will. Everything is fine, but the baby is close."

"Wow." I drew my shoulders back. "I thought the first baby

was supposed to take a long time."

"So did I." Furrows grooved Tia's brow as she pressed and rubbed her tummy. *Our little munchkin wants out.* "But I won't complain if this is over with quickly." She glanced at the nurse. "What about pain relief? An epidural?"

*Shit!* Tia had wanted to go drug-free. But yeah, I would've taken anything that was on offer. I hated that this hurt her.

"You're too close for an epidural, but you can have gas." Loretta pointed toward the levers and gas lines at the back of the bed.

"Yep." Tia flapped her fingers at Loretta. "Give it to me. Now!"

Loretta smiled and nodded as if understanding and hooked up a tube for Tia. She handed Tia the plastic device. "Okay. Gently inhale through this mouthpiece at the beginning of a contraction. Not too much, or you'll get head spins."

Tia snatched the tube from the nurse and sucked on the gas. Bliss hit Tia's face.

Loretta's eyes glinted, and she patted Tia's shoulder. "You're doing fine. When I get back in a couple minutes, we'll transfer you to a delivery suite. I'll be quick." Loretta pushed the laptop trolley clear of the bedside and dashed out the door.

Just as it clicked closed, Tia curled onto her side and wailed. "Ow!" She held her belly.

I dashed around to the other side of the bed and massaged her lower back. "Does this help?"

"Yeah. But I think I've changed my mind. I don't want a baby anymore."

I chuckled. "Bit late for that. But you got this."

"Ooooh." Concentration etched her brow, and she breathed in and out. In and out. In and out. "You reckon? I'll gladly trade places."

"I'm no good with pain." I wasn't. I was a total wuss. I hated paper cuts. There was no way I'd handle labor. Just seeing Tia in pain twisted my insides into knots. "You're the strong one—not me."

Five minutes later, Loretta returned and transferred us to a delivery suite.

Withing thirty minutes, Tia's contractions were down to two minutes apart. Her sweaty hair clung to her face. She puffed through her breathing exercises. Rolled from side to side. Cursed and cried, groaned, and screamed . . . a lot.

I never left her side, totally blown away by what was happening and the miracle of life. Our baby would come into a loving home, be cared for, adored, and supported, no matter who they grew up to be. They'd never be abused, rejected, or disowned like my parents had done to me.

I wiped Tia's forehead with an icy-cold cloth. Rubbed and massaged her back. I held her hand. Breathed through the contractions with her. Gave her encouraging words and kisses. But with every minute that passed, I felt more and more useless.

Tia was just fucking amazing. She kept going. Kept finding new grit, strength, and determination.

Thirty minutes later, Loretta examined Tia again. She was fully dilated.

Loretta was about to buzz for a doctor, but the door to our suite swung open and in swept Dr. Mila and another nurse, Pamela. For someone who'd been woken at three o'clock in the morning and made it to the hospital in just under an hour, Dr. Mila looked incredible, as if she were prepared for a normal workday. Neat hair in a bun. Neat scrubs. Neat touch of makeup. *Wow! She's superwoman!*

"Well, this is an exciting reason to be woken up for in the wee hours of the morning." Dr. Mila came over to the bedside. "Hi, Tia. Lewis? You hanging in there?"

"Just." Smirking, I puffed air through my nose. Tia's

gorgeous green eyes shimmered, and she found a smile for me. As I kissed her clammy hand, a new wave of anxious excitement quivered through my veins, but so did fresh concern for Tia. With the doctor here, the hardest stage for Tia was yet to come . . . delivering our baby.

Dr. Mila grabbed a set of disposable gloves out of the box on the wall, snapped them on, and stepped in beside Tia. Loretta gave the doctor a quick update.

After Dr. Mila did a quick examination of Tia, she nodded. "Tia? Are you ready to meet your baby?"

"Please? Get this thing out of me."

"You have to do that part, but I'll be with you every step of the way. Are you ready to push?"

Loretta stayed monitoring the machines. Pamela wheeled a trolley of implements toward the far end of the bed. The blood drained from my face. I hoped the doctor didn't have to use any of them. *Ergh!* I wasn't looking forward to this.

I squeezed Tia's hands. "Tee, I'm sorry for knocking you up."

Her grip tightened around my fingers. "I'm not. We want this. Just don't let go of my hand."

"Never."

"Arrrrgh! Fuck!" Her pain-filled cry punched my gut. "We're only having one kid this way. This sucks."

"One is more than I could've ever dreamed of, so I'm okay with that."

"I know. But if we have a second, it will be via C-section. That has to be easier and less painful than this."

*Another child? Wow!* We hadn't talked about more than one. But I was down for whatever she wanted. I kissed her sweaty forehead. "Let's start with this baby first."

"Okay," she said through clenched teeth and dipped her chin. Exhaustion had already drained the light in her eyes. "One baby, coming up."

Dr. Mila moved into position, seated between Tia's raised legs, and wriggled her facemask into place. She patted Tia's knee. "On the next contraction, I want you to push."

Tears sprang from Tia's eyes as she nodded. She monkey-gripped my hand super tight, cutting off my circulation. I didn't care.

"You got this, babe. I love you." I swiped the damp strands of hair off her face.

"I'm scared." She squeezed her eyes shut.

"Don't be. I'm here. You can do this."

The lines on the monitor waved. The contraction hit and Tia pushed, screaming as she curled forward. My stomach cinched as if I felt every contraction, but I knew mine didn't come close to what she was going through.

"That's it, Tia," Dr. Mila bobbed her head. "You're doing great. Let's do the same again."

"ARRRRGH!" Tia screamed and pushed. "Lewis, why the fuck do you have to have such a big head? This baby has taken after you."

"I don't have a big head." *Do I?* But yeah, the baby was above average in our previous scans.

"Wanna bet?" Tia hissed.

She strained and pushed. Her cries reverberated off the walls. Tia collapsed, exhausted, against the pillow. The same motions went on and on. Push after push. Contraction after contraction.

Tia was spent. I was drained, but didn't falter in giving her words of encouragement, holding her hand, soothing her brow with a cloth, or loving her with all my heart.

Somehow she kept going, digging deep to find new strength, and tapped into her energy reserves. She was my pillar of strength more than I was hers.

An hour later, Dr. Mila gave Tia the thumbs-up as she

nodded. "That's it. I can see the head. We're almost there." Fiery encouragement charged through the doctor's tone. "You can do this. Give me a big push."

"I can't," Tia sobbed. "I'm tired. Just cut it out of me. Fuck this shit."

"Tee?" I kissed her hand. "I want to meet our baby. Don't you?"

"Yeah." Her chin trembled. "I do."

The contraction hit, and she cried. Cried and pushed. "ARRRRGH. YOU MOTHERFUCKER."

"That's it, Tia." Dr. Mila added grit into her tone. "Use that energy and push. Push hard."

"FUUUUCK!" Straining and groaning, Tia clenched her teeth and curled forward over her chest.

Tears welled in my eyes. The agony on her face and her pained howl speared my soul, but her unwavering determination ignited it. God, I loved her. "Come on, baby. You can do this."

"Yes, you can, Tia." Dr. Mila's eyes widened. "Here it comes. Keep going. Keep going. Yes. That's it."

Tia pushed and pushed.

"Yes!" Dr. Mila hollered. "You did it."

Exhausted, panting for air, Tia collapsed against the pillow and cried. Sweat trickled down her blazing-hot face, but she'd never looked so beautiful. I kissed her forehead, and she threw me a tired smile.

"And it's a beautiful baby girl." The doctor's eyes shone over her mask. She lifted a bloody, gooey baby into the air. The slimy umbilical cord hung from her middle.

Sweat broke out on my brow. My queasy stomach rocked. Dizziness swam through my head. But my heart soared to the stars. *Holy shit. We have a daughter. But oh crap . . . am I going to faint? Throw up?*

Then the sweetest sound I'd ever heard filled the room.

Our daughter cried.

My nausea disappeared. Fresh tears welled in my eyes. One escaped as I leaned over and kissed Tia. "You did it. We have a baby girl."

"Oh my God," Tia sobbed as the doctor placed the baby on Tia's chest. "Hi, little one." She cradled our child, and the most gorgeous smile lit her face.

My heart exploded.

Nurse Loretta quickly placed a blanket over our baby for warmth and cleaned her face, since she was covered in a lot of goo.

As the doctor performed checks on our child, and the nurse tended to Tia, I somehow buried my nausea and scurried around to cut the cord. I was glad Dr. Mila had already done the bulk of it. Mine was just a token gesture. And nope, I didn't need to do that again.

Tia kissed our daughter on the forehead and brushed her fingertip down our baby's cheek. "Lewis, she's beautiful."

"She is." I leaned over Tia, taking both my girls in. "So does the name we chose still fit?"

A fresh, glistening tear slid down Tia's cheek as she nodded. "Yeah. She's Winter. Winter Mavis King."

We'd talked about and tossed around so many ideas, but the first one we'd come up with had stuck and grown on us more and more each day. Tia and I had met three years ago in December at a club after I'd just joined The Flintlocks. We'd connected during my first few days with the band in the snow at Big Bear and then in New York in January when we'd recorded. Tia had twisted my queer life upside-down. She'd changed me forever. That year I'd found a new home, a new band, and had fallen in love with her. We'd had many magical nights during the nine months of tour, but some of the most memorable were in winter when we'd performed in the US and Canada. Winter had brought us together. Had changed our lives. And now, our love had brought us our own precious little girl . . . *Winter.*

Cuddled against Tia's chest, Winter yawned, blinked her tiny lashes, but then squeezed her eyes shut, not ready to face the light.

I draped my arm over the pillow behind Tia and rested my head against hers. I placed my trembling hand on Winter's back and gave her the softest of pats. She was so tiny. So fragile. So perfect. My heart couldn't be any fuller. This was living. "Tee, she's gorgeous."

"We did it," Tia sniffled. "We made a baby."

"Yeah. We did."

We certainly had. *Wow!*

After all the heartache and pain I'd endured growing up, the many career highs and lows I'd weathered, and the struggles that had tormented me when I'd fallen for Tia, I'd survived . . . I'd truly found my soulmate. I was so fucking happy. I'd found where I belonged. I had everything I'd ever wanted. A band. A home. A family.

"I love you, Tee." I kissed her soft lips. "You've made all my dreams come true. We have a beautiful daughter. I have you. I promise to love both of you forever. Okay?"

"I love you. And Winter is perfect."

"She is. Just like you."

Moving across the country was the best decision I'd ever made.

I'd found my future. Nothing was ever going to change that.

Life in LA fucking rocked!

# Chapter 20



The day I'd been counting down to had arrived. Today, I'd marry Flint. But instead of glorious sunshine and endless blue skies, LA had delivered wild wind and raging rain. It had begun last night during our rehearsal dinner. I'd checked the weather app every hour and there'd been no sign of it easing.

Of all the days to rain!

I'd gone through every emotion . . . from being distraught, devastated, and frustrated, to elated, ecstatic, and carefree. *I am getting married! Who cares about the weather?* But it was torrential. There was too much time to kill until I walked down the aisle. My nerves played Tetris in my stomach. I fidgeted with the tie on my slinky white dressing robe with the word *'Bride'* embroidered across the back and paced the length of the living room. The girls and I had slept at Kyle and Gemma's house in Pacific Palisades last night. We'd get dressed here for my big day since it was only a short drive to Malibu. The guys had stayed at Andy's mansion—our wedding venue.

"Sutt, will you stop worrying? There is nothing you can do about the rain." Maddy threw me a reassuring smile as she sat at the dining table, getting her hair styled into a high bun of barrel curls. Her stunning makeup of glittery eyes and soft pink lips highlighted her beautiful face. *Totally gorgeous.*

I loved I got to spend almost every day with Maddy now she worked on *Angels in LA.* She'd been on the show for two months and had fitted in from day one. Having her by my side meant the world to me.

"I'm not worried, Mads." A little, but not a lot. Nothing would stop me from marrying Flint. Not even this insane downpour.

Liliana, our hair and makeup goddess, and her assistant, Prue, had already worked their magic on Tia and me, and had nearly finished Maddy and Ava.

Ava closed her eyes for Liliana to dust glitter on them. "Isn't it supposed to be good luck if it rains?"

"It's not just raining, though." I thrust my hand toward the window. Gutters overflowed. Rain hammered the panes. The wind whipped through the trees. "It's a one-in-one-hundred-year event." I honestly didn't know whether to laugh or cry.

"It'll make the day memorable, won't it, Winter?" Tia cooed as she sat her daughter on her lap, rubbing and patting her back after feeding. Winter yawned wide. Her little eyes fluttered, as if she was totally milk-drunk and ready for another nap. *Lucky her.* I'd barely slept last night. Too excited. Too anxious. Too concerned about the weather.

So much for a sunset wedding!

But everything would be fine. *Yes . . . No . . . Maybe.*

I'd been out of bed since seven o'clock that morning. The girls and I had been pampered all day . . . manicures. Pedicures. Massages. We'd had a fabulous champagne-and-chicken-salad lunch. It was now three. Three hours until the big event. I'd been on my cell phone throughout the day, talking to Quill about plans A, B, C, and D. His meticulous planning, calm manner and being prepared for every scenario kept my anxiety on a leash . . . *just.* He took rearranging the day to accommodate the weather in his stride. Not sure he'd even broken a sweat. He'd texted three times before lunch with progress reports, reassuring me his crew were working overtime to set up more tents, and getting more space undercover for our guests.

Total miracle worker.

I'd called Flint several times, but he hadn't answered. He hadn't replied to my messages. Had he lost his phone? Forgotten to take it with him? Was he hungover? Passed out somewhere? Stuck out-of-town thanks to the weather? Visions of *The Hangover* movie flashed through my mind. What had the guys done last night when we'd left them? Flint had promised me they were going straight to bed. So where the hell was he?

My blood pressure inched higher as the weather worsened. I'd put on a brave front, laughed, and tried not to let the rain get to me. But with each passing minute, it did. As my bridesmaids were being attended to, and Kara, Gemma, and Lexi floated around getting ready, I needed a moment to pull myself together.

*I'm okay. Yep. Absolutely . . . maybe . . . not!*

"You girls look amazing. I'll be back in a few minutes. Just ducking to the bathroom . . . upstairs." I didn't need the toilet—I just needed somewhere quiet to clear my head. Walk. Pace. Refocus. The weather was out of my control. There was nothing I could do about it. Flint would be okay. His cell phone location said he was—well, his phone was—at Andy's house. I just needed to breathe.

But the second I walked into my room upstairs and closed the door, torrential rain bucketed down in thick curtains, slamming onto the roof with deafening pelts and overflowing the downpipes. I stepped over to the window. Waves of water flooded the pavements. Rivers ran down the driveway and along the curbsides. Puddles the size of reservoirs formed on the lawn. *Shit.* As I turned away from the deluge, I caught sight of my beautiful wedding dress hanging on the front of the closet door. My chin trembled, and I burst into tears. It would be ruined in the wet. *Shit.*

I sank onto the window seat, covered my face with my hands, and sobbed. I was allowed to be a little emotional, wasn't I? It was my fucking wedding day.

I just needed to have a cry, release my frustrations over Flint not calling, and erase my disappointment in the weather. Then I'd be okay.

*Yep. I'm good.*

*Absolutely.*

*I was strong. I got this.*

I sniffled, sucked in a deep breath, and dabbed my eyes with my fingertips. *Yep. Better.* I didn't want red eyes on my wedding day. I didn't want to ruin my makeup.

Car tires splashed through the water and pulled into the driveway. I knew that engine. *Flint's Ferrari.* What was he doing here? *Shit! What has happened?*

The car door slammed. The doorbell rang. Before I had time to rush out and meet him, Flint charged through my bedroom door. He stopped six feet from me. Water dripped from the long ends of his black hair. His ice-blue eyes rippled with concern. "Sutt?"

"Flint?" I closed the gap between us, flung my arms around him, and held him tight. I didn't care that he was wet. "What are you doing here?"

"I had to see you." He rubbed my arms up and down, then massaged my shoulders. "I knew you'd be stressing and upset about the weather."

I placed my hand on his chest. His heartbeat raced beneath my touch. "It's shit, isn't it?" A laugh-cry escaped me. "It's so bad. Maybe we should call it off? Get married another day." *Yeah, there is no chance in hell I'll be doing that.*

"What? No." He drew me into another hug. *God*, he smelled so good, all citrusy. He kissed the side of my head. "It's under control. Everything is ready."

"Why didn't you call?" I rested my cheek against his shoulder. "I've been going out of my mind."

"I'm sorry." He rubbed my back. "I've been busy helping Quill's team. I left my cell phone upstairs in my room. When the extra flooring and tent arrived, the guys and I rushed around, helping them set up and change things around." He tightened his embrace. "Sutt, I'm so sorry. When I saw all your missed calls and texts, I thought it would be best to come see you in person. To let you know everything is okay."

Shaking my head, I eased out of his hold. "We have to face reality. It's crap outside. We can't get married in this." *Oh, yes, we will.*

"Yes, we can." Certainty set in his voice. "We won't be in the rain. We set up a new tent and flooring between the house and the main tent so no one will get wet. Our guests will have drinks in there and along the patio we enclosed with clear blinds, not down on the beach. The tents are so tied down they won't blow away, even in this wind. Quill's got everything under control."

Before he took another breath and rattled on any further, I placed my finger over his lips. Smiling, I softened my gaze. "Flint? . . . I'm fucking with you. We always said we'd get married in the rain, hail, or sunshine. We got rain. It's not ideal, but it's okay."

The weather was far from perfect, but it was no deal-breaker. I'd gotten overwhelmed, but nothing, not even a Category Five hurricane, could stop me from marrying Flint. I would traipse through knee-high mud, get soaked through to my skin, and say '*I do*' in the downpour if I had to. But wow . . . he'd been so concerned he'd driven over here to make sure I was okay. To reassure me that everything was fine. God, I loved him.

"Why, you . . . ?" Chuckling, he gave me the sauciest evil-eye, then hugged me. "I was so worried. You wanted this perfect day, and it's insane out there."

"It is." I leaned back, still locked in his arms. "But I've learned from you to chill and take things in my stride. We were prepared for the unexpected and had backup plans in place. You and Quill have helped to keep my stress levels under control during all the preparations for today. They're up there but not bubbling over and turning me into a wreck." *Not completely anyway.*

"Sutt, you amaze me." Light sparkled in his eyes, making my heart flutter. "We're going to have a fabulous evening. The flowers arrived, and looked incredible. There are twinkle lights everywhere. Catering was setting up in the kitchen when I left. The only thing we have to change is where we have photos taken after the ceremony." He toyed with a bouncy curl brushing the side of my cheek. His eyebrows did a cute flick upward. I loved the way he looked at me, when heat simmered in the depths of his gaze, like he couldn't wait to have his way with me. It wouldn't be long before we could have each other . . . forever. "We can have pictures taken upstairs in the house in that really nice living area, or in the main tent with all the decorations around us, or we say, '*Fuck it,*' and have them done in the garden as planned. I don't care about getting wet."

"I do. I'm not getting rained on in my dress." *Shit. My dress.* He hadn't obviously seen it hanging on the closet door behind him.

The sexiest, most suggestive smile I'd ever seen slid across his lips. His mischievous gaze ran down the front of my robe. "Is this what you're wearing?" He caught hold of my sash and tugged on the ties. "I do like it. I wanted you to wear something I could get you out of quickly."

I slapped his hands away and tightened the knot. I didn't want him to see my wedding lingerie before tonight. "You shouldn't be here. Isn't it bad luck to see the bride before the ceremony?"

"Never." He slid his hands around my waist, clutched my ass, and rested his forehead against mine. "Sutt, tonight will be amazing. I will be there at the front of that tent waiting for you. I can't wait to get married." He swiped his thumb down the length of my cheek, then kissed my lips. "Regardless of the shitty weather, let's have fun this evening."

"We will. I don't care if no one comes other than you, me, the officiant, and Maddy and Slip to be our witnesses. I mean that. I just want to marry you." But shit . . . we'd invited one hundred and seventy guests; they'd better turn up.

"I love you." He touched his lips to mine, then eased back and whispered, "My very, *very* soon-to-be wife."

"I can't wait." I tapped him on the chest. "But you'd better go. It's nearly three-thirty. I have to get dressed, have photos with the girls, and then get my ass to Malibu."

"You do that. I'll be there, ready and waiting."

"I'll see you soon, husband-to-be." I kissed him, smiled against his lips, then covered his eyes with my hands. "I'm gonna guide you out of the room. I don't want you to see my dress. Okay?"

"Shit. Yeah. Okay."

I walked him out the door, gave him one last deep, long kiss, just to give him something to look forward to, then waved him off. "Love you. Drive safe. See you at six. Don't be late." I was a stickler for being on time. I'd be there. Guaranteed.

"I won't be late, I promise." Flint slipped out of my hold, skipped down the stairs, and rushed out the door, back into the rain.

I drew in a deep breath and placed my hand over my stomach to settle the butterflies. *Damn.* I was so lucky to have found someone so amazing.

Maddy ambled into the foyer, then leaned over the glass panel at the bottom of the staircase. Her hair and makeup were complete. "Was that Flint? Is everything okay?"

"Yeah, it is." I nodded. "He came to make sure I wasn't having a meltdown over the weather."

"Oh . . . that's so sweet." She pouted and splayed her hand across her chest. But then worry furrowed her brow. "Are you?"

"No."

"Good. You don't need to worry about anything. That's Quill's job." She smiled her sweet smile and pointed at me. "You just have to enjoy yourself."

"That's what Flint said. I am and I will." I filled my lungs with air, feeling lighter every second. If this evening went off without a hitch, Quill would be worth every excessive dime.

I leaned against the top glass panel and rounded my shoulders. "I had my little cry, but I'm okay now." I really was. "We're going to make the most of it and have a fabulous time."

"We certainly are. Would you like a quick snack?" She waved toward the kitchen. "Diego and the kids have made protein balls and a fruit platter."

*Good. Nothing to make me bloat.* I didn't need a bulging tummy in my wedding photos. Everhide's nanny had his hands full looking after the band's five children. He'd been amazing, entertaining them, keeping them busy while the girls and I had gotten our hair and makeup done. But now . . . my bladder called to me. I *needed* the bathroom. "Sure. I'll be down in a sec. I still need to pee."

Over a quick snack, the girls and I had another champagne. It helped to calm my jittery nerves and bubbling excitement.

I finished my drink and glanced at the clock. Four o'clock. It was time. Time to be a bride.

The girls and I headed upstairs to get dressed. Kara and Gemma helped us while Lexi flitted around, taking photos. Our main photographer was with the guys. Ava, Tia, and Maddy slipped into their long, pale pink, strapless gowns, and me . . . my wedding dress.

My heartbeat skipped and cartwheeled as I slid into my white minidress, covered in thousands of sequins, beads, and rhinestones. The short, strapless gown was heavy, but the fitted bodice and skirt molded to my body, hugging my hips and caressing my chest perfectly. *Yep. My boobs look fantastic.* Maddy zipped me in, then Kara draped the detachable train around me and buckled the rhinestone belt at my waist. The long, open skirt of palm-sized chiffon roses cascaded to the floor in billowing waves like a pillow of soft, silky petals. I bobbed down for Maddy to attach my veil above my bun with a rhinestone encrusted hair clip.

"Perfect." Kara admired the gorgeous gown she'd designed for me.

With sparkling, silver high heels adorning my feet, and my diamond necklace, earrings, and bracelet in place, my outfit was complete.

"My God, Sutt. You look beautiful." Maddy's eyes glistened with tears as she straightened my veil.

"Absolutely stunning." Gemma fluffed out my train with Kara's help. "You're going to blow Flint's mind."

"You rock that dress, Sutt. But shit . . ." Tia clutched her boobs. She dashed into the bathroom, then reappeared with a dry face cloth and stuffed it down her top. "I just fed Winter, and my boobs are already leaking. This sucks. Winter cries and my tits run. They hurt all the time. I'm gonna have to wear three absorption pads to make it through the ceremony."

"Tia?" I stepped over to her and rubbed her arms. "You had a baby three months ago. I'm beyond happy that you're here. If you need to have Winter with you, or rush off to feed her, or be with her at any time, that's okay. You do what is best for you and your baby. I love you, no matter what."

"Thank you, but I'll be fine." She stuffed the cloth into her bra and wriggled her strapless dress into place. "I just don't want to ruin my dress before photos."

"Well, we'd better get them done before we head off." Giggling, I waggled a finger in front of her chest. "Stuff a diaper down your top if that helps."

She sighed and slumped her shoulders. "My boobs are big enough without more padding."

"Enjoy them while they last." Ava came over and hugged Tia sideways. "Once you stop feeding, they disappear."

"Winter is the only one who's allowed near them." Tia smirked and arched one fine eyebrow. "Good thing Lewis is more of an ass man. But enough about my tits. It's photo time."

"Yes, it is. But before we go . . ." I grabbed the girls' hands, and we formed a circle. "I have waited for this day for a long time. In case I forget, I want to thank you for being here to celebrate with me. I need you girls to promise me a few things. Promise me you'll have fun. The weather won't stop us from having a fabulous evening. And we're going to dance up a storm all night."

"Guaranteed. Today will be amazing and beautiful, just like you." Maddy hugged me, then took my hand and dragged me toward the door. "Let's go. It's time to get your smile on."

That was already in place. I didn't think I could stop smiling, even if I tried. At the top of the staircase, I hooked up my skirt. The gorgeous, silky chiffon roses swished around my legs and trailed behind me. As I headed down the steps, I felt immaculate. Like a billion dollars. Like a beautiful bride. *I am a bride!*

I was surrounded by my friends on the way to marry the man of my dreams, in a spectacular house overlooking the beach.

Yes . . . it was time.

Time to get married.

*Fuck the stupid weather!*

# Chapter 21



Nerves and excitement flurried in my stomach as we made our way to Malibu in our black stretch limousine. No amount of calm breathing settled them. This was it. My wedding. Steven, my brother, sat beside me, handsome as ever in his black suit. The girls sat opposite us with their pale pink bouquets in hand. My gorgeous skirt filled the space between us like a big white fluffy cloud.

As we approached the mansion, the traffic bordered on chaos, but our police and security escort kept everyone moving. Vehicles occupied every parking space along the road. Paparazzi lined the sidewalk. Cameras flashed as we passed through the secure gates into Andy's place.

It was no secret Flint and I were getting married today. Our wedding had been the headline buzz on celebrity news for weeks. Just the whereabouts had been kept private. We'd only texted our guests yesterday with the address. But clearly that information had leaked.

Flint and I had spent many days of our lives in the public eye, but this wouldn't be one of them. The world could wait to see what we wore and who'd attended. Our guest list rivaled an entertainment industry awards show. The paparazzi would no doubt capture some celebrities coming and going. So be it. I'd originally wanted hundreds of people to attend and an exclusive magazine deal, but that had changed as our plans had unfolded. All we wanted was our closest friends, special colleagues, and family present to share our special day . . . all one hundred and seventy of them.

As the limousine drove toward the house, Ally, the videographer, braved and battled the elements on the driveway to capture our approach. Our chauffeur drew to a halt underneath the awning outside the front door. A temporary black barricade had been erected on the windy side, no doubt to help protect us. Quill had thought of everything. But in this crazy weather, I wasn't sure anything would work.

I closed my eyes and placed my hand on my pounding chest. I took a deep breath, struggling to draw in full lungs of air thanks to my fitted bodice. I'd be fine once I stood.

Maddy reached forward and clutched my hand. "You okay? Are you gonna be sick? Pass out?"

"No." I shook my head and smiled. "I'm excited. I'm resisting the urge to run in there, grab Flint, say *'I do'* and get this over and done with. I'm trying to take things slow and savor every moment."

"Good. But we might have to hurry inside to get out of this rain and wind." Maddy pointed out the window. Every shrub and tree were being whipped about. Our security team's jackets flapped in the gale, and their hair was a tussled mess.

Ava smirked. "At least the weather might keep the paparazzi in helicopters away . . . just not the ones standing on top of their vans outside the fence." She waved to two people standing on top of their vehicles with long range lens aimed our way. Good luck to them.

Quill and two of his team, dressed from head to toe in fine black suits with *EQuill Events* embroidery in gold on the breast pocket, rushed out of the front door. Marlo, our wedding photographer, and Ally followed with their cameras in hand.

With his headset draped over one ear, Quill opened the car door and ducked his head in to talk to us. "Hi, everyone. Perfect timing." Yes, we were ten minutes early, as planned . . . for hair and makeup touchups and a few photos before entering the tent. "Happy wedding day, Sutton. And oh. My. Gosh." He exaggerated every word, scanning everyone in the car. "You. All. Look. Am-a-zing. Is everyone ready?"

"Yes." My palm sweated around the stem of my bouquet, but I was set.

"Excellent." Quill leaned against the door to stop it from blowing shut. He talked loudly over the howling wind. "We're going to take you in, one at a time, into the office on the left. Liliana and Prue are there, ready for any touchups." He waved over his shoulder. "Marlo and Ally will capture every moment, and my boys behind me are going to help shield you from the wind. It's wild out here. But once you're inside, you won't care about the weather. The place looks magical, if I dare say so myself."

"Thank you." My breath skipped and danced against my ribs. "Let's get this party started." I wanted to get married. No delays.

"Absolutely." Quill rolled his hand toward my girls. "Bridesmaids first. Let's go."

One by one, the girls hopped out of the car and were attacked by blasts of wind. In their best efforts to shield them, Quill's team guided them inside. The girls' dresses flapped and flicked against their legs. They held their bouquets close to their chest to protect them from the gusts. Their updos didn't budge thanks to bucket-loads of gel and hairspray.

*My turn.*

Steven hopped out of the car, seeming undeterred by the

wild weather hammering us from every direction. He took my bouquet in one hand and held out his other one for me to take. Quill came in beside me. We took handfuls of my huge skirt and held it up to avoid the dirty, wet ground.

I stepped out of the car. The wind whipped against my face, blasting me from every angle and blowing my veil out to one side. My loose curls slapped my cheeks. This was crazy. Certainly memorable. I laughed and hollered over the wind. "I'm good. Let's get inside."

We dashed through the front door. In the center of the vast foyer, I let my skirt fall to the floor, as did Quill. It floated into place and cascaded behind me. The rhinestones in the center of each chiffon rose glistened in the soft light. I truly felt like a bride.

Quill fluffed out the bottom of my train. "Sutton. This dress is stunning."

"Thank you." I smoothed my hands over my bodice, loving the feel of the gorgeous beading beneath my fingertips.

"Sutt, you're exquisite, but you need to fix your hair." Steven waved toward the office. "Go. I'll wait here with these." He smelled my bouquet and scrunched his nose. The roses did have an overpowering, strong perfume, but they were gorgeous and perfect.

"Thank you." I gave him a kiss on the cheek and a quick hug.

I loved my brother giving me away. We'd grown closer now our father was out of our lives.

But just as I was about to join the girls, Liliana rushed out of the office with her makeup apron around her waist and a portable flat-iron in hand.

As she redid my loose curls and coated my hair in another cloud of hairspray, Chloe and Duke arrived with Winter. They were babysitting while Lewis and Tia performed bridal party duties. Tia gave Winter a quick kiss on her forehead before they wheeled her stroller through the house to join the guests.

"Auntie Sutton!"

I giggled at the sound of Charlotte's voice and looked up. She stood at the top of the grand marble staircase with Josh and Celina, Ava's sister, and waved.

Celina took the kids by the hand and headed down the steps. Cole's daughter wore a princess-inspired flower-girl dress made in the same pale pink fabric as my bridesmaids' gowns. Josh, our ring bearer, looked super smart in a handsome black suit. *Totally adorable.*

Charlotte ran over to me and gave me a big hug. "Wow. You look so pretty, Auntie Sutton."

"And so do you." I tapped the tip of her nose with my fingertip. "Have you been practicing?"

"Uh-huh." She gave me a big nod. "Me and Josh are ready."

"So am I." I straightened the bow in her hair. "Let's get some photos first."

After I had a lipstick touchup, we shuffled into the living room for some quick snaps in front of a wall of pale pink roses. Me with Steven. The girls. The kids. Then with everyone. *So cool.*

Before I could take a breath, Quill clapped his hands. "It's time."

*Whoa!* A hot wave rushed over me. My heartbeat jumped again. *This is it. I'm getting married. It's happening.* Was it possible to be too excited? *Nope. Never.*

Quill pressed a button on his headset. "Wil, are we good to go?" Quill nodded *yes.* "Are all guests seated?" *Yes . . .* "Is the officiant ready?" *Yes . . .* "Are the guys in position?" *. . . Yes . . .* "Excellent. Bridal party is on the way. Clear the path. We'll be there in one minute."

Steven stepped in beside me and held out his bent elbow. "Sutt, we doing this?"

Happy tears stung my eyes, but I wouldn't let one fall. Butterflies danced in my belly but didn't flood me with nausea. My heart thundered against my ribs, but I was calm. I was more than ready to marry Flint. "Yes. Yes, we are."

I hooked my arm around Steven's and held my beautiful bouquet in front of me. I filled my lungs with air and drew my shoulders back, and we followed Quill outside. Instead of a vast expanse of manicured lawn, a newly erected clear tent formed a long corridor across the garden, keeping the rain at bay. Sturdy white flooring kept our feet off the wet ground.

The rain poured, pattering hard against the tent.

The wind gushed, flapping the side panels.

But we were dry.

My gorgeous bridesmaids followed me, past the dazzling array of flower arrangements and white candles that lined the way. Small silver chandeliers hung in a line along the roof. Quill had outdone himself in getting this prepared on short notice. It was the perfect pathway to my future.

Flint and I could handle any storm, any drama, any issue . . . together.

The girls and I gathered outside the closed-curtain entrance to the main tent. Prue and Liliana did one last check. Hair? *Check.* Lipstick? *Check.* Flowers? *Check.*

Celina handed my bridesmaids a little satin bag for them to hook over their wrists.

Surprise? *Check.*

With a lit smile, Maddy bumped her hip against mine. "Are you ready to blow Flint's mind?"

I certainly was. "Yes."

The butterflies that were in my belly swooped and soared like excited sparrows. I leaned against Steven to steady myself and peered through the crack in the curtains. Row after row of guests sat chatting, waiting for us to arrive.

*Oh. My. God. This is it!*

Josh, Charlotte, and the girls lined up before Steven and me, ready to enter the tent.

"All good?" Quill fussed with my veil, making sure it was perfectly in place.

"Yes." I nodded.

"Alright. Let's get you married." He glided over to the curtain and pressed a button on his headset. "Team, we are ready. Cue music. On three. Two. One. Bridal party are go."

Traditional wedding march music boomed through the mounted speakers hanging around the tent. The shuffle and commotion of guests standing filled the air. Quill opened the curtain. Josh and Charlotte led the girls down the aisle, throwing rose petals from their baskets. Steven drew me forward. *Step. Step. Step.*

Everything was surreal. Like a dream.

The twinkle lights. The pale pink flowers. The sea of guests.

But then I saw Flint . . . standing at the front with Cole, Slip, and Lewis.

*Oh, my!* Flint stole every ounce of breath from my lungs.

His black hair was styled, swept back off his face for the first time since I'd known him. His glistening, ice-blue eyes held me captive, making the world around me disappear. He radiated pure sexiness in his black suit, shirt, and tie. His charismatic smile claimed my heart.

His hand shot over his chest, and he mouthed, '*Wow.*'

My heart defied gravity. All my nerves vanished.

But after the girls took a few more steps, and I'd reached the back row of chairs, the music skipped and scratched. Then stopped. Silence hung in the hair. The girls halted. So did the kids. Daunted looks passed across the faces of the concerned guests.

Panic flitted across Flint's face.

I just laughed.

Charlotte struck a pose, hand on hip. She ripped out a pair of sunglasses from her petal basket and put them on her face. Josh grabbed a pair out of his jacket and did the same.

Ava, Tia, and Maddy shrugged, then pulled out sunglasses from their satin bags and put them on.

Steven smiled, blew on his fingertips, then pulled out two sets of shades from his jacket—one for him. One for me. We put them on as *"One Way or Another"* by Blondie blasted through the tent. The hard-rock beat reverberated through my soul and soared through my veins.

The kids, my girls, Steven, and I strutted down the aisle, did some fancy steps and spins, struck some sexy poses, and played it up to the crowd. We'd been practicing our moves in secret for days. I flicked my skirt. Shimmied my shoulders. Showed off my long legs. The guests cheered and clapped along with the music.

Flint gaped and laughed and bobbed his head.

But then Cole slapped him on the shoulder and led Lewis and Slip down the aisle. The guys grabbed their partners around their waists. The girls did a sexy wriggle in front of the guys, then circled around them, flicking their hair in time to the wild rock beat. With a twirl and a skip, they made their way into position at the head of the aisle.

Steven and I grabbed each other around the waist. We held one arm each out in front of us and clasped our hands together. We danced down the aisle and stopped by the front row. I pointed and waggled my finger at Flint. Yep, one way or another, I was going to marry my man.

Flint's smile was everything. His palm splayed over his heart, and laughter made our surprise entrance worthwhile. He stepped forward and took my hand, nodded to Steven, and led me to stand in front of Milford, the officiant.

"Sutt, that was so fucking cool." Flint chuckled quietly. But then he took a deep breath and scanned me from head to toe. "And wow. You're so beautiful. I didn't think it was possible to fall more in love with you, but I just did."

"I'm struggling to breathe just looking at you," I whispered. "I love you so much. But can we get married now?"

"Yeah." His eyes glistened with warmth.

I handed my flowers to Maddy, then turned to Flint. I entwined my fingers with his. *Just breath. Time to say, 'I do.'*

Milford greeted everyone; no one objected to us getting married . . . *I'd freaking kill them if they did* . . . and he said a few words about what a marriage meant. Commitment. Love. Family. Support. Flint and I had that and more.

"The couple have written their own vows." He nodded to Flint. "Flint? When you're ready."

Flint adjusted his grip on my hand and cleared his throat. His vows rolled off his tongue like warm honey. "Sutton, I couldn't breathe before you came into my life. You brought me back to the light. Dragged me out of the darkness. Helped me find music again. Nothing in my past scared you away. We have survived the highs and lows in a ruthless industry . . . *just*. With you by my side, I know we'll handle anything the future throws our way. In this crazy life, you are my constant calm. I fell in love with your kind heart, good soul, patience, and wicked sense of humor. You're beautiful inside and out. I want to continue to grow and be a better man for you each day. You are my rock, my muse, and my reason for living. I can't wait to spend the rest of my days with you. I promise to love you forever."

I dabbed a tear from my eye with my fingertip. Flint's vows had been etched into my heart.

I rejoined my hand with his and recited my vows. "Flint, we had a connection from the moment we met. We helped each other through difficult times and found new paths forward.

You restored my faith in love and showed me the true meaning of family. Your dedication to music and your friends is beyond commendable. Your talent is inspiring. Most of all, you're always there for me. You've kept me grounded when I needed it most. Kept me from drowning in this city that can give you the stars and strip them away just as quickly. You showed me what is important and changed my life. Our love grows stronger and stronger every day. I can't wait to see where our future takes us. I will be by your side each step of the way. I promise to love you and be yours forever and ever."

After we exchanged rings, Flint dipped me backward and gave me a breathtaking kiss. My feet didn't retouch the ground until we'd signed our marriage certificates and were pronounced husband and wife . . . Mr. and Mrs. Glover.

*YES!!!!*

To a sea of cheers, hollers, whistles, and claps, Flint and I ran down the aisle and waited in the corridor tent for everyone to join us.

With aching cheeks, unable to stop smiling, I fell into Flint's embrace and kissed him. "We did it."

"We certainly did. I love you." He kissed me, long and hard, stealing the air from my lungs. God, he could kiss me like that for the rest of the night . . . no, my life. But Cole broke us apart, and the congratulations started as guests streamed out of the main tent and crowded around us.

Following photos with and well wishes from family and friends, Flint and I headed upstairs with our bridal party to have photographs while everyone else enjoyed pre-dinner drinks and appetizers, and mingled. We had formal photos, fun photos, a few sexy ones, and some candid snaps. We made the best of being indoors.

Everyone was seated by eight o'clock for our reception.

With another grand entrance, this time floating on Flint's

arm, I entered the main tent, swirling my skirt around me. Our friends waltzed in behind us and we took seats at the bridal table. Strands of twinkle lights covered every inch of the roof. A gazillion pale pink flower arrangement stood throughout the tent. Round tables set with black tablecloths, crystal glasses, white plates, and centerpieces of pink flowers and a tall candle filled the floor. Friends and family filled the chairs.

The venue had turned out better than I'd ever imagined.

A smile never left my face, nor Flint's.

We drank fine champagne, ate exquisite food, and laughed with our friends.

Hunter, from Everhide, hosted the evening. I didn't know who was more of a show pony . . . Flint or him.

He took to the mic at the top corner of the dance floor.

"Evening, everyone. I'm Hunter Collins. I'll be your master of ceremonies tonight. It is an honor to know The Flintlocks, to call them good friends, and to be here to celebrate Flint and Sutton's wedding." He tilted his head toward Flint and his groomsmen. "I met these guys several years ago at an awards show in Vegas . . . where they lost Best Band, and we won. I'm not sorry about that." He threw them a shit-eating grin. "But it has been exciting to watch their career grow and to be a part of their continued success. On behalf of my fellow Everhiders, Kyle, Gem, and Hayden, and our partners, Flint and Sutton, we wish you a lifetime of happiness. The way to do that is to always make each other laugh, make time for one another, talk about anything and everything . . . and *fuck* every day." An even bigger smile lit his face as everyone laughed. "Right. Let's get this evening on a roll. Flint, the mic is yours."

With champagne in hand, Flint made a speech, thanking everyone for coming. Cole had everyone in fits of laughter as he spilled dirt on Flint. Maddy did the same when she talked about me. I said a few words, reiterating Flint's thanks to everyone for not being deterred by the weather and making our day special.

Then Bruce, Flint's dad, spoke.

"As a father of two boys who dreamed about being rock stars, I was always worried. The gigs, the booze, the drugs, women, and parties turned my hair gray well before my time. Trying to keep them in line was often a lost cause. Audrey, my wife, and I had to trust them to find the right path. Let them follow their dreams. Support and love them. Be there when they needed us. We didn't always manage to do that. When we lost our youngest son, Phil, we failed Flint on an epic scale. For that, I am truly sorry. I'll spend the rest of my days making up for that mistake. But today we stand here, proud. Proud of the man he has become. He's a leader. A talented star. A good man. He turned out alright. Flint, you have found a beautiful woman who loves and supports you. Sutton, you are a delight. Flint adores you. And I wish you both a lifetime of happiness. Welcome to the family. Cheers to the happy couple."

*Wow.* I sniffled and dabbed the tears from my eyes with a napkin. Flint's dad was sweet. My dad? Far from it. He was somewhere in Mexico, no doubt gambling his life away. No loss he wasn't here.

After Flint and I cut our huge, tiered wedding cake with roses billowing down one side, and fed each other a mouthful of fluffy chocolate goodness, Flint took my hand and drew me close. "Surprise time."

"What? What surprise?" We had nothing planned. I balked as he dragged me toward the dance floor.

Hunter dragged a chair out into the middle of the area and handed Flint the mic. Cole, Slip, and Lewis scurried over to Duke's band's instruments and took charge of them before Duke and his guys played their first song.

I clutched onto Flint's hand.

*Oh shit. He wasn't, was he? But . . . yay!*

I'd secretly hoped Flint had written a song and would sing. He never disappointed me.

"Sutt?" Mischief flared to life in his eyes as he tilted his head toward the chair. *What is he up to?* "Please take a seat?"

*Oh boy. What am I in for?* But I was game. I flicked my skirt behind me and slid into the chair. All eyes were on me . . . *us*. Every guest looked intrigued. Good thing I liked being on show. As did my husband.

He spoke to the crowd. "Okay, folks. You know I love to write love songs and pour my heart and soul into my lyrics, so I had to write something for Sutt. But this . . . is a little different." He unbuttoned his jacket and loosened his tie. "A little bird, being Maddy, told me Sutt was very, *very* well-behaved at her bachelorette party . . . Well, don't be fooled. She is far from innocent." He winked at me, then pointed toward the guys.

*What? Oh, my. Heat flushed my cheeks.*

Cole, Slip, and Lewis played, but rather than rolling out a romantic slow tune, they struck a sexy, loud rock beat. Flint turned his back to our guests, swayed his hips, leaned toward me, and cradled my cheek.

> *You may have everyone fooled, girl. But oh no, not me*
> *I saw it in your eyes on the very first night that we met*
> *You wanted me so badly, oh yeah, I knew that you did*

He spun around and thrust his butt toward me. I burst out laughing as he continued to sing:

> *I saw you checking out my ass, girl, as you bit your lip*
> *When I brushed against you, I heard your hot breath hitch*

He straightened, crossed his ankles, and flicked open one side of his jacket.

*I couldn't deny it. My heart skipped a full beat*
*Heat rushed through my body; did strange things inside*
*of me*

He slid his hand down and across his stomach as he swayed his hips from side to side. *Oh, wow . . . so sexy.*

*Butterflies took flight in my stomach, yeah*
*Something was happening to me*
*I thought it was the vodka*
*But then you looked at me*

With a spin and a flick of his foot, he straddled me and slowly lowered onto my thighs. He took my hand, slid it down his chest, and injected a sultry rasp into his voice.

*You wanted to take me home, girl*
*Do dirty things to me*
*Now I'm a gentleman, dear lady*
*But you brought out the bad boy inside of me*
*I had to take you home, girl*
*And see what you did to me*

He glanced over his shoulder at our captivated, laughing audience and threw them a sexy smirk.

*Oh yeah, we went too far*
*All the way, in fact*

He grabbed onto the back of the chair, half stood, and thrust his hips against me. He rose up and down slowly and seductively, giving me a lap dance. Was it wrong that this turned me on? *So hot!* I giggled and clutched his butt. He caught my hand and held it there.

*As I got to know you and all the things you liked*

*I fell in love with you, girl*
*And you know what I just might*
*Keep being bad for you, yeah*
*So we can make sweet love every fucking night*

He drew my hand around to the front and crushed it against his crotch. I arched an eyebrow. I was more than happy to hold him. Grinning, he leaned forward, nuzzled into the side of my neck, and nipped my skin. He wriggled lower and buried his face between my breasts. His soft lips touched my flesh, heating my insides. But then he drew my hand to his mouth and kissed it. Too much flirty fire flared in his eyes as he put the mic to his lips.

*'Cause I like that look you get*
*When I make you . . . oh . . . at night*
*You may have everyone fooled, yeah. But oh no, not me*
*They all think you're innocent and sweet*
*But girl, I've seen you down on your knees*

He stepped off my legs. Still holding my hand, he kneeled on the floor.

*Good thing I married you, 'cause baby when you do that*
*Oh yeah . . . I know we're meant to be*
*You wanted me so badly, oh yeah, I knew that you did*
*I couldn't deny it, I felt the same way*
*I fell in love with you girl, yeah, I'm in ecstasy*
*I get to call you mine forever*
*Yeah, this is destiny*

He jumped to his feet, then sat sideways on my lap. Gosh, he was heavy. He brushed his fingertips down my cheek.

*I'll always be a gentleman, yeah, I'll always treat you right*

*But keep loving me like you do, girl*
*I'll keep being bad for you, all day and every night*
*Oh yeah . . . I'll keep loving you . . .*
*For the rest of my damn life*

"I love you, my beautiful wife." Chuckling, Flint cradled the back of my head and kissed me on the lips. *Perfect.* Slip, Cole, and Lewis ended the song. The crowd erupted with laughter, loud claps, and hollered *woohoo*s.

Flint stood, drew me to my feet, and bowed to the guests.

"That was awesome." I giggled as I slid my arm around his waist. "You're such a show-off."

He nudged his hip against mine. "Yes. But you love me."

"I do." I loved saying that today. "With all my heart."

Hunter came over and stole the mic off Flint. "Well, folks. Flint has another talent we didn't know about . . . or maybe some of us did. Lap dancing is a future career yet to be explored. But right now, before we hit full party mode, please let Mr. and Mrs. Glover take their first spin around the dance floor. Let's pray it's just a waltz." *It will be.* "Join in when you're ready."

As Duke and his boys reclaimed their instruments and played "Love Me Like You Do" by Ellie Goulding, Flint and I had our first dance as husband and wife. My head still spun with an intoxicating high. Our bridal party joined us, twirling across the floor. Flint's parents ventured onto the dance area shortly after them, as did other guests.

At the end of the song, Duke and his band dialed up the volume and the dance beat. More people left their seats to join in, dancing and jumping around.

Halfway through the night, I discarded my detachable skirt so I could move around easily and party with our friends. Flint and I rarely left the dance floor. We were having so much fun.

I didn't want today to end . . . but it had to . . . for Flint and me anyway.

We had a plane to catch.

Flint swept his fingertips down my cheek and met my gaze. He sucked in a deep breath and smiled, like he was absorbing every last moment of our wedding into his memory, just like I was. "I love you, Sutt."

"I love you, too." I linked my fingers behind his neck and raised my eyebrows. "But now I'd like you to show me how much. It's almost one. We have to get out of here, so we don't miss our flight."

"Are you ready for me to whisk you away on our honeymoon?" Hot sexiness shimmered in his eyes.

"Yes, please." Tahiti, here we come.

After a slow, panty-dropping, languid kiss, he eased back just a fraction. "Hmmm. Before this gets X-rated, Mrs. Glover, we'd better go."

We nodded to Hunter. He dragged himself away from the bar and grabbed the mic. "It's that time in the evening, folks. Can everyone form a line near the entrance? The bride and groom are about to leave."

Quill jostled around, shuffling people into some form of organization.

Flint took my hand. We ran beneath everyone's arms as they threw flower petals over us, clapped, and cheered. We didn't stop. We ran out of the tent, through the house, and into our waiting limousine. As my heart raced, we headed for the private airport.

It had finally stopped raining.

We boarded our chartered plane and took off.

Over kisses and hugs, I couldn't stop smiling.

I was so freaking happy.

I'd had the best day.

I was married.

I was Mrs. Glover.

*Finally!*
Let the honeymoon begin.

# Chapter 22



The second we hit cruising altitude, I unclipped my belt. Sutton followed. I'd waited long enough. It had taken my full self-control not to ravish her during our ceremony, or at the reception, or in the car on the way to the airport. She was so freaking beautiful. My wife. *Mine.*

With her hand in mine, I drew her toward the back of the plane and into the private bedroom. I kicked the door shut and guided her toward the queen bed. It nearly took up the entire space, but like the rest of the plane, it was opulent. Cream leather headboard, walnut trim, black bedding. The soft, golden lighting gave the room a warm hue and shimmered in Sutton's eyes. We had eight hours of travel ahead of us . . . I planned to keep my new wife *very* entertained.

"I'm glad we could take off." Sutton slid her hands up my chest and over my shoulders, then linked her fingers behind my neck. "Spending our wedding night at home wouldn't have been the same."

"No. I want to get to our villa as soon as possible so I can have you all to myself for an entire two weeks." Bora Bora, then Tahiti, then home. We'd relax. Swim and snorkel. Ride ATVs. Explore the islands. Have a fuck-ton of sex. It'd be the perfect honeymoon.

"I still can't believe we did it." Her eyes sparkled with glitter. "We're married."

"Yeah. We are." I cradled her cheek, gliding my thumb over her smooth skin. "I meant what I said, Sutt. I promise to love you forever."

"Forever. Now, be a gentleman." Mischief skipped in her low, soft voice. "Take off your clothes. Bring out that bad boy so we can make the most of this gorgeous plane."

I chuckled against the small of her neck and kissed beneath her ear. "You liked my song?"

"I loved it. Since you didn't go all *Magic Mike* on me at our reception, you could do that now. There isn't a lot of room in here, but I'm sure we can improvise."

Grinning, I rolled my hips slowly and seductively against hers. "I can do that."

She laughed. "Good. But first, let's get more comfortable." She untied my tie, tugged it out of my shirt collar, and dropped it on the floor. I slid my fingers into her hair and pulled the hair clips from her bun. The long strands fell in a mass of soft curls down the back of her neck. Once I'd removed every pin, she yanked out the hair tie, ruffled her fingers through her hair, and moaned. "Oh my God. It's so good to have that undone."

I swept her hair back behind her ear and kissed her sweet lips. "Beautiful."

With nimble fingers, she undid my shirt and eased it from my shoulders.

My skin prickled beneath her warm touch, itching to have her beneath me. "God, Sutt. I want to undress you slowly but tear your clothes off so fast my head spins. I want to kiss every inch of your body but can't wait to be inside you. I want to take my time, make slow love to you, but fuck you so hard we shake the shit out of this plane." My cock was already rock solid.

The plane tilted and swayed. A gorgeous giggle escaped Sutton. "Hmmm, you're definitely making the world move."

"Let's create some more turbulence." I snaked my hands around her waist, slid them up her back, and found the top of the zipper. I eased it downward and smirked. "Easy to get you out of. Perfect."

Sutton's gorgeous minidress dropped to the floor. So did my suit pants and briefs. Shoes and socks joined them. I made quick work of my wife's silky lingerie, scooped her up in my arms, and laid her on the bed.

Naked, I hovered over her. "God, you're beautiful."

She swept my hair off my face. "You make me feel that way, too."

I kissed my way down her body and back up again. Tasted her sweet pussy. Relished her hot arousal on my tongue and her body giving in to my touch. I teased and taunted her. Made her come.

My dick ached to be inside her. Every cell craved her caress. I wanted to be close, so there was no air between us. Be connected, to bind our hearts and souls even more. Today had been the best day of my life. I'd had a few mind-blowing moments in my time. Performing in front of sellout crowds. Winning awards. Proposing . . . but it would be hard to top our wedding.

There was only one way to make it even better.

*This.*

I buried my cock inside Sutton. As I rocked my hips, I moaned, low and raspy.

Her hands slid onto my ass. She clutched my butt and drew me toward her. "Now that . . . feels good."

"It certainly does." I drove into her deeper. Her warmth surrounded me, making me harder and harder. "You're mine, Sutt."

The hum of the plane engine matched the one coursing through my veins. The speed we were traveling was as fast as my racing heart. I rocked, slow and hard, into Sutton, reaching for that spot that made her lose control.

She scraped her fingernails up my chest and around my shoulders, then raked them through my hair. Her legs wound around mine. *Fuck!* Her wet pussy felt like home. Her tight body, my sanctuary. Her burning touch, my calm. Every time I drove into her, soft mewls and murmurs passed her lips. She clutched the back of my head and drew my mouth to hers.

"Flint?" She tasted of chocolate wedding cake and champagne. Sweet and delicious. Intoxicating and divine.

"Yeah?" Breathing her in made my head spin. That could have been the alcohol I'd drunk and the high altitude, but I swore it was just the effect Sutton had on me.

"Let's switch."

With a quick roll, I dragged Sutton over with me. As I lay on my back, she straddled my lap and reclaimed my dick. *Damn. I love that.* She loved being on top . . . and I got the perfect view of her tits. I got to play with them, watch them jiggle, touch her thighs, grab her hips, and drive my cock into her depths. I could strum and stroke her clit.

Smiling, she leaned over me and braced her hands beside my head. Her hair curtained our faces. Sexy fire flickered in her eyes as she rode me. "I'm gonna come again fucking you like this."

"Good." I swept her long hair back and clutched it behind her head. "I want you to so I can give you a few more orgasms before we land."

She rolled her hips, rubbing and rocking her pussy against me. Holding onto her waist, I drove into her, meeting each and every move.

"*Mmmm.*" Her eyes fluttered shut. Tiny grooves furrowed

her brow, and I smirked. I knew that look. That one that was a cross between blissful pleasure and agonizing torture. That sign she was closed and burned for release. She rode me faster, not being gentle in any way. Fuck, that got me every time. "There."

It took all my strength not to come. Not without her.

I wanted to feel her shudder and clench around me. Sitting upright, I flattened my hands over her hips, dug my fingertips into her flesh, and pulled her forward, filling her with my cock. She clung onto my shoulders. Her breath panted against my face. I smiled against her lips. "That a good spot?"

"You know it is."

*Yeah, I do.*

I dipped my head and sucked her nipple into my mouth. *Fuck.* Her buds were so hard, covered in tiny goose bumps. I flicked and circled my tongue around each one, making them peak even more. I carefully, gently, caressed and massaged both breasts. Soft. Heavy. *Perfect.* I'd have plenty of time to play with her boobs later. Right now, I wanted to satisfy my wife. Consummate our marriage. Take her completely over the edge.

As she drove downward, I thrust up. Sliding one hand between us, I thumbed her hot, swollen clit.

Her core clenched around me. "Flint?"

"I got you, Sutt. Come with me." Every muscle in my body blazed with fire. My dick ached. My balls cinched, tighter and tighter and tighter, desperate to explode. *Fuck!*

"Yeah."

Her pulse quickened. My thrusts synced in time with her moves. She wrapped her arms around my shoulders, crushed me close, and moaned, "*Ohhhh.* Shit, yes."

Her shudders reverberated through my body. She giggled and smiled and kissed my face. But her pussy, throbbing around my cock, was my undoing.

With a hard thrust, I found my release, filling her with my

love. My body jerked and jolted as electric shots zapped every cell in my system. They coiled up my spine. Tingled the base of my neck. Slammed into my heart. *So. Damn. Good.*

I snaked my hands around Sutton's body, circled her back, and kissed her. "Fuck, I love you."

"And I love you, husband."

"Wife."

Her smile was like a sky full of stars, all glittery and bright. She touched her lips to mine. "You certainly rocked my world."

"I did."

"It might've been the plane. The sways, dips, and jet engines."

"Never. Give me a few minutes and I'll prove to you it was me."

"I'll hold you to that."

"I'll deliver. Trust me."

Collapsing back onto the bed, I drew her into my arms. I kissed her lips, her face, her forehead. Entwining our fingers, I kissed her rings—her stunning engagement ring and new wedding band of diamonds—then held our hands against my chest. Today had been a big day. An emotional high. But this, lying here in bed with my gorgeous wife, in the calm on the way to our honeymoon was pure bliss. Total happiness. I closed my eyes. I'd promised to love, cherish, and adore Sutton for the rest of my days. And I would. I'd always be there for her when she needed me. Give her the best life possible. Make all her dreams come true. Today was just the start of the rest of our lives together.

We were Flintlocks.

Family.

Married.

We'd rock on together . . . forever.

# EPILOGUE 1



I couldn't breathe. My heart beat so fast I was certain my ribs would crack. Underneath the table, I clasped onto Flint's hand so tightly my knuckles ached. To my left, I held onto Maddy's hand for more support.

*This is it. My category at the Golden Globes.*

My stomach was a bundle of knots, twisting and turning. Skipping and swaying.

Meredith Long, a Hollywood TV legend who'd graced our screens for more than forty years, glided up to the mic. She radiated regal elegance in a long navy gown and with enormous diamonds around her neck. "It is with a great honor I get to present the award for Best Actress in a Comedy TV Series. The nominees are: Glenda Port for *Wild Canyons.*"

*Oh my gosh, I so love her. Brilliant actress. She's so popular; surely she's got this.*

"Georgia Burrows for *Blood River.*"

*Ergh!* Nausea bubbled through my gut, but I kept my smile in place. The cameras could be on us at any moment. My former friend who'd betrayed me had held no remorse for her actions after sleeping her way into the role. Georgia's on-and off-screen boyfriend had publicly broken up with her at an after-party a couple months ago and the show hadn't done as well as expected. Rumors were swirling around the industry that it'd be axed after this third season. Karma had hit Georgia hard. I hoped she'd be okay, but my life was certainly much better without her in it.

Meredith kept reading. "Madison Reed for *Vancouver Heights.*"

*Yay . . . So brilliant.* I'd love her to win for her last season on the show.

"And Sutton Summers for *Angels in LA.*"

Smiling from ear to ear, I nudged Flint's arm. Then Maddy's. I was so stoked. I hadn't been nominated for an award in years. I didn't care if I didn't win. Just to be recognized was phenomenal.

Meredith opened the envelope, and a dazzling smile lit her face. "And the winner is . . . Sutton Summers. *Angels in LA.*"

*ARRRRGH!* I covered my mouth with one hand to stop myself from shrieking. I placed my other hand over my heart to stop it escaping. My head spun. Tears sprang from my eyes.

*Holy shit! I won!*

The room erupted with applause. My fellow castmates—Mia, Peyton, and Ethan, at our table and the executives on the one next to us—jumped to their feet and cheered.

"Oh my God!" Maddy cried and hugged me. "Congratulations. I'm soooo happy for you."

Slip clapped and hollered from the seat beside her. "Woohoo. Go, Sutt."

Flint leaned over and kissed my cheek. "Congrats, babe."

*Wow!*

Everything seemed surreal.

Was this really happening?

Flint stood and helped me to my feet. I couldn't believe it. I'd fucking won!

Following a few quick hugs from my castmates, I floated

toward the stage. I hitched up the long skirt on my glittery pale-blue dress and skipped up the steps. As I hit the stage, I let the satin fabric fall to the floor and glided over to Meredith standing by the lectern. *Fuck, please don't trip.*

"Congratulations, Sutton." Meredith handed me my Golden Globe. *Damn, it is heavy.*

"Thank you." In a haze, I stepped up to the mic. My heart thudded so loudly I was certain everyone could hear it. My skin tingled from my head down to my toes. The crowd before me blurred behind my teary eyes. I couldn't stop smiling as the applause died.

"Thank you. This award is truly special." I glanced at the statuette in my shaking hands. *It's perfect. So fucking perfect.* "Congratulations to the other nominees. Ladies, you're all awesome. Please keep up your amazing work. But wow . . . it has been a very long time since I've won an award of any kind. Fifteen years, in fact. Like many people in this industry, especially women, you're typecast, struggle to find new roles, and careers fade. You're too old. Not the right fit. Not the right look. I've been on TV since I was six years old and struggled to find work when I was twenty-two. Everyone saw me as a high school sweetheart. Newsflash—we all grow up. So a huge thank you to Harlow, my fabulous agent, for encouraging me to do something daring to shock the hell out of everyone in Hollywood—not just casting directors. Yes, I went on a date with Flint Glover."

The audience laughed and clapped.

"That night changed my life. I met my soulmate, my now husband." I placed my hand over my heart as I met Flint's gorgeous gaze. We'd gone from one fake date to forever. Life worked in mysterious ways. I was truly blessed. "Thank you, Flint, for your never-ending love and support. I wouldn't be here without you. I love you with all my heart." I stole a glance at Georgia. I wanted to sneer but didn't. I may have done something bold to revamp my career, but I hadn't resorted to dirty tactics to land a role like she'd done. I couldn't deny she was a great actress, but she just wasn't a nice person. So get a load of this! *I won!*

Keeping the sweetest smile in place, I turned to my fellow castmates looking up at me with praise. "Thank you to all the amazing cast and crew on this show. You make every day at work so much fun. Mia, Peyton, and Maddy, this award belongs to you too. You ladies rock. *Angels in LA* wouldn't be the same without you. To Ethan, my on-screen partner in crime, Frank, our director, Shona, our producer, and all the amazing writers, thank you for bringing this show to life and giving four incredible women the opportunity to bring the funny and sometimes serious side of dating in today's world onto the screen. You're all so talented, and I love working with you. Finally, a huge thank you to the fans and for making this show a hit. I love you and can't wait to bring you more laughs in the coming seasons. This really is the best job in the world. Once again, thank you, everyone." I charged my statue into the air and hollered, "This is awesome. Woohoo."

Underneath the glittering stage lights, I linked arms with Meredith, and we headed offstage. The minute I was behind the curtains, I jumped up and down, clutching my Golden Globe against my chest. Meredith congratulated me again before the show's production crew ushered me toward the winners' interview area. Cameras flashed. Lights blinded me. Reporters thrust microphones in my direction and asked questions.

Light on my feet, I savored every incredible moment.

Out of the corner of my eye, I saw Flint make his way through the crowd. I excused myself from the horde of media representatives and rushed over to him.

I flung my arms around him, taking care to avoid knocking

him in the head with my award. I kissed his gorgeous lips. "This is so brilliant. I won. I really won."

"You earned it." He rested his forehead against mine. "You're a star. Never forget that."

I eased back and held my award between us to show him. "I would've never have gotten this if it wasn't for you."

"Yes, you would've. You're determined, ambitious, talented. You would've dated some other loser or shone regardless who stood by your side. I'm just fucking glad it was me. That you made me go on that first date. Otherwise I would've missed out on getting to know you and falling in love with one of the most incredible people I've ever met. I'm thrilled I get to stand beside you as you chase and fulfill every dream."

"I always wanted to be on another hit show. But this . . . this is just incredible." I smoothed my hand over my award. I couldn't wait to get my name engraved on it. "I'm back on top, and it feels amazing."

I didn't need awards or accolades, but it was certainly nice to be recognized by industry peers for my talent and hard work. Once I'd landed the role on *Angels in LA*, I'd been so content and happy I could've burst. I worked with great people. The show was always fun. Maddy had come home. The Flintlocks had become my family, and I had Flint. Life was fantastic. This award was just an added bonus.

"I'm so proud of you." Flint kissed my forehead. "You've earned that Globe. Own it."

"I am." I grabbed his tie and tugged him forward. "And I love you, too. Forever."

"Always." His smiling lips touched mine.

This was a dream come true. All I'd ever wanted.

I was an A-list star.

I'd won a huge award.

I was in love.

Married.
*Happy.*
What could ever top this?

# EPILOGUE 2



Backstage in our dressing room at MetLife Stadium, New Jersey, I stood in a huddled circle with Cole, Slip, and Lewis. Our arms were draped around each other's shoulders. Our focus was connected . . . *one.* Ignoring the hustle and bustle around us . . . our entourage—hair, makeup, and wardrobe stylists—waiting to fuss over us, our management team—Blake and Avril and Falon—talking to the media reps and security personnel, our partners laughing and chatting on the sofas, and the photographers waiting to take more shots of us . . . we took a moment together before life changed yet again. We were minutes away from opening night . . . our fourth world tour, three years on, almost to the day, since our last tour had ended. The butterflies in my stomach resembled dive-bombing, stunt-performing jet planes. They wouldn't settle . . . I didn't fucking care.

The nervous-yet-excited energy fueled me, not hindering me in any way.

Was I ready?

*Hell fucking yes.*

It had been another epic journey to get here.

Once I'd returned from my honeymoon with Sutton, sixteen

months ago, the guys and I had flown to New York to record at Everhide's EH4 Records. Cole, Lewis, Slip, and I had written and finessed most of our songs before the wedding, so we'd been ready to hit the recording studio. We'd spent hours, days, and long nights laying down the tracks. We'd had the best fucking time. It was like we'd never been apart. I'd been worried for no reason. After our songs had been mixed and mastered, album number four was done. Our work had blown Everhide's and Ashlem's minds. The songs weren't just good . . . they were *fucking* great.

The working title for the album had stuck. *Lost and Found* had remained.

We'd released the first single last November. Announced our tour in late January, along with our second single. Our third single had hit the airwaves in March. Each song had hit number one on the charts. *"Feeling the Vibe,"* track three off the album, had remained in the American top ten for twelve weeks. *Totally. Mind-blowing!*

Ashlem, our promotional and touring company, had always said they wanted to make us the next Coldplay. It was an honor and thrilling that they believed we could achieve that status. Years ago, when we were signed with WestTyme Records, we'd been on a successful path, but EH4 Records and Ashlem had put us on a bigger map. They'd taken us to the next level. We were now on a superhighway. Ashlem had delivered. Our stadium tour was a sellout across the globe. For the next twelve months, the guys and I would be traveling. Performing. Living the dream. Sutton and Maddy had six months off as of February, thanks to Mia and Peyton's movie commitments . . . and I was certain that time would be extended thanks to Sutton's new plans. But regardless of what happened with the girls' schedules, the guys and I had ensured we had longer-than-usual breaks between the legs of the tour so our crew could rest and we could spend time with our wives.

*Fuck.*

I couldn't believe we were all married.

Lewis and Tia had tied the knot last September in a small service held in Pasadena. Cole and Ava had gotten married in spring in Hawaii.

We were one big, happy family.

This tour would be epic.

I felt it in my soul.

"Guys? This is it!" With a huge grin stitched onto my face, we shoved, nudged, and jostled about in our circle. Contagious energy bounced and hummed between us. No one could stand still. But the clock was ticking down to showtime. I took a deep breath and drew my shoulders back. Time to be serious. "I need to say a few quick words."

"Just a few?" Across from me, Cole smirked as he hugged Lewis and Slip. He knew I was a man of *many* words—never *just a few.*

"Okay. You know me too well." With a big grin, I flicked my long hair off my face. "But I can't go out there without you knowing what this means to me. To all of us. This is the first night of the long months ahead. Our hard work has paid off again, and now we get to take this epic production on the road."

"Woohoo. I can't fucking wait." Slip howled into the air and slapped Cole on the back. "We're ready. We're pumped. Can't wait."

"Me either." Light filled my chest. I'd never felt so confident about the shows ahead. The past had paved our way here. Each tour got bigger and better. *We* got better. This . . . the four of us . . . this band . . . and Sutton were my everything. I didn't want any of us to suffer or make the same mistakes again. We'd learned a lot about ourselves and each other since we'd lost Phil. We'd become men. "You're my best friends. My family. My life. Each one of us has grown and changed since our last tour. So please, if at any time you need a break, are struggling, feel like shit, want something altered, or want to share how fucking amazing something is, big or small, let me know. I'm here for you. I will do anything and everything in my power to help you, be there for you. I love you guys, no matter what."

"Ditto." Cole dipped his chin. "We're living the dream. Playing and performing with you guys is still as fresh and exciting as it was during our first gig. I live for this shit every day. This tour will be huge. I'm stoked I get to do this with the three of you, Ava, and the kids. I'm one lucky asshole and I promise to give every show my all every fucking night."

"Too right." Slip laughed and ruffled Cole's perfectly styled hair into a tussled mess, then gave him a playful shove. "And do it without the dizzy spells and fainting episodes like last tour."

Cole clipped Slip on the back of the head, then smoothed his fingers through his hair, combing it back neatly. "That's the plan. But I assure you, I'm good. Meds keep my blood pressure under control. I'm fit. Healthy. Fired up and ready to go." He snickered and waggled a finger at Slip as his tone took on a serious edge. "And you? You watch that damn hip of yours. No jumping around too much. And no resorting to hard drugs or pushing yourself over the limit if you're in pain."

My stomach cinched, yanking my guts hard against my spine. My throat tightened, running dry. Images of Slip at his worst toward the end of our last tour, hooked on painkillers and cocaine, flickered through my mind. That was something I never wanted to witness again. Rehab and a new lease on life had him looking better than ever. He was still sober, still the life of the party, and still a wild man on the guitar, but he had a new inner calmness and zest for living each day to the fullest. Being with Maddy, and taking getaways to Bowen Island had restored his mental and physical health. I was thrilled he was here . . . still Slip. Still a Flintlock.

"No. I won't be doing that again." Slip hugged Cole and took in each one of us. "I promise my hip is better. I won't overdo it. I never want to go through hell like last tour again. I have Mads, you guys, and music to live for. I can't wait to rock up a storm on stage night after night."

"Hell yes!" Lewis pumped his fist. The biggest grin lit his face. We'd become such great friends. It was like we'd known each other for ten lifetimes. He was our new brother, sent to us by Phil, my brother in heaven. I was convinced of that. Lewis slapped his hand against his chest. "I can't express how much I love being here." His chest swelled to the size of a balloon. "It will certainly be different traveling with a toddler. Winter is a handful, but she's amazing. Tia's a super mom. But thank God we have Harper." Grinning, he clutched the back of Cole's leather jacket and gave him a shake.

"Fuck yeah." Cole nodded. "She's got her work cut out for her looking after three kids."

Harper was at our hotel on nanny duties with Charlotte, Josh, and Winter. The kids kept her busy . . . and soon there'd be more.

"She certainly has." I dipped my chin. "But we couldn't do this without her." While she took care of the kids, Tia ran our sound and lighting team. And Ava kept us in line, kept us on schedule. My gaze jumped from Lewis, to Cole, to Slip and back again. I absorbed their energy and fire. "We're here because we love music, and have incredible partners and each other. I hope that never changes. This is our time. We're gonna own it and love every second." Excitement skipped through my voice and hummed through the marrow in my bones. "We have so much to be thankful for and look forward to. But right now . . . it's time to rock the shit out of this stadium and give this crowd one hell of a great show."

"Yeeees!" Slip clutched the back of my neck and gave me an overzealous shake, but I didn't stumble. *Fuck*, I loved my friends. "We'll be doing this shit forever."

Cole's eyes shimmered as he cheered. "You bet."

"I'm down for that," Lewis hollered and clapped. "Show one, here we come."

"Alright." I unhooked my arm from around Slip's shoulders, then held my palm out in front of me. The guys followed suit, placing their hands on top of mine. "We're going to have fun. We're going to sing and play our hearts out. We're going to rock this crowd into a fucking frenzy. Are you with me?"

"Yes!" the guys shouted in unison.

"We are The Flintlocks." I yelled. The vibe between us jumped and ricocheted off the ceiling. It slammed into my chest and coursed through my veins. Best feeling ever. "Let's go!"

We shot our hands into the air and laughed. We hugged and slapped each other on the back. With a clap of my hands, we broke our circle. We kissed and hugged our partners, gave a thumbs-up to our team . . . then headed for the door.

*Yep.*

It was showtime.

***

I stuffed my ear-monitors into place, blocking out the chanting crowd waiting for us on the other side of the huge black curtain. Our stage was massive, bigger than I'd imagined. Towering video projection screens loomed either side of the stage and behind me. Arrays of speakers and rows and rows of stage lights mounted on trusses hung above us. A long catwalk, leading out into the middle of the audience, waited for me and the guys to play on.

In front of my mic, in the dim blue light, Falcon, our tour manager, checked an amp via torchlight, then held up two fingers.

*Two minutes to curtain.*

I closed my eyes, took a deep breath, and nodded. Falcon scurried offstage.

Our crew—light and sound engineers, stagehands, and technicians—would see me and the guys on the monitors. It was totally insane. We needed ninety-three people to take this show on the road. Truck drivers, roadies, camera operators, audiovisual specialists, pyrotechnicians, rigging engineers, caterers, wardrobe, medical and health personnel, security, our management team and more . . . I guessed we'd fucking made it to the big time.

I glanced toward Lewis on my left. A nervous grin lit his face as he hooked his bass into position. To my right, Slip, with his guitar in hand, jumped up and down on the spot. Then he rolled his hips and stretched his neck from side to side. He was on fire, ready for a big night. He was back to his old self . . . *no* . . . better than ever. I glanced over my shoulder. Cole sat perched at his drums and pumped his fist in the air.

We were good to go.

This was it.

MetLife. A sold-out stadium. Eighty-nine thousand people.

This was what we'd worked for. We lived for. Were meant to do.

Play music. Tour the world.

I clutched my mic on the stand. My electric guitar hung from my shoulders. The hum in the air was alive. Electric. It coursed through my veins, coiled through my belly, and prickled my skin. But the vision standing offstage stole my breath . . . and owned my heart.

Sutton stood beside a small light. Others mingled around her, but I only had eyes for my wife.

Her long golden hair fell in waves across her shoulders.

She smiled and twinkled her fingers at me. She blew me a kiss, swiveled her hips from side to side, then . . . patted her belly.

My breath skipped through my chest, filling me with warmth from my head down to my toes, like it had done every day for the past several weeks.

I'd never considered having a family of my own. It had never been on my radar. I wasn't a never-say-never kind of guy. But when Sutton had said she wanted a baby, I was there. *We* were ready.

She was three months pregnant. We'd told everyone last week we were expecting. Our baby was due in spring, during the break between our European leg of the tour and our second run of dates in the US.

I was going to be a dad.

*Fuck*! That freaked me out. But I had a few months to prepare and couldn't wait.

I unhooked my guitar and placed it on the stand. I rushed over to Sutton, caught her face between my hands, and kissed her. "I love you."

"Love you too." She swept her fingertips down my cheek. "But go. I'll be here, watching every second."

"Okay." I bent down and kissed her tiny baby bump. "Love you too."

With a skip in my step, I dashed back to my mic and picked up my guitar. The guys chuckled and shook their heads. Yep, they understood how stoked and smitten I was. They were just as bad over their wives.

I had my band. My friends. A gorgeous wife and a child on the way.

There was only one thing that could add to how happy, content, and grateful I was . . . and that was to sing.

Perform.

Play for this crowd.

I hooked my guitar strap over my head and swung my Fender into place. My pulse thrummed with a quickened tempo. My heartbeat thundered against my ribs. *Night one. Let's go.* I gave the thumbs-up to Joel, our head stagehand who was standing stage left, down in our technical pit, surrounded by monitors, spare equipment, and racks of guitars.

He spoke into his headset, giving Tia in the main front-of-house control booth and our sound and lighting crew the cue to proceed.

The pre-show music ended.

There was a silence for less than a millisecond. My heartbeat filled my head. *Thud. Thud. Thud.* The lights in the auditorium went out. The audience screamed and shouted, clapped, and cheered. The video screens flashed to life. The metronome cues clicked in my earpiece. *One. Two. Three.* Cole struck his drums, and the curtain fell away.

As I hit the first note on my guitar, raw vibrations charged through my chest.

A sea of colored LED wristbands lit the huge stadium before me. Phones flashed. People jumped up and down. Arms swayed in the air.

*What a sight!*

I couldn't stop grinning. Laughing. Dancing around. Savoring this epic moment.

This . . . was a dream come true.

I licked my lips. Swallowed hard. Drawing air into my lungs, I stepped up to the mic . . . and sang. We opened the show with our hit, "Feeling the Vibe."

> *You kick-started my heart like no one else*
> *The light in your eyes makes my insides melt*
> *Your smile is like sunshine every day I'm with you*
> *Your love is the cure, nothing else will ever do*

*I need you real bad*
*I need you in my bed*
*I need you at night*
*I need to hold you so tight*
*I'm feeling this vibe*
*Burning deep inside*
*This fever's getting hotter*
*My heartbeat stronger*
*I'm dancing on a high*
*Yeah,*
*I'm feeling this vibe*

After that, I said hello to the crowd, then sang another couple of tracks. We churned out a medley of popular songs from our past albums. Cole pummeled out a solo on the drums. Slip and I dueled on our guitars and Lewis joined us, strumming a wicked rhythm on his bass.

Then it was time to slow things down with our song dedicated to Phil. Our song with a twist—one of his that we'd tweaked, like Phil was talking to us. Slip had insisted we perform it. We couldn't have done this on our last tour; we were still processing his death. Now, the timing was perfect. As we sat on stools at the front of the stage with acoustic guitars in hand, and Cole with a single tom, photos of Phil were projected onto the video screens. I had to dig deep to bury the onslaught of memories and emotions, but I was no longer crippled by grief. We'd had a fun-filled, crazy life together. We'd made music. We were family. I'd love and remember him forever. He'd watch over us . . . always. I drew in a deep breath and sang in a low, sultry voice, slow and husky, just above a whisper:

*Could you not see I was hurting inside?*
*Could you not tell, or were you blind?*
*Did you not know how much I cared?*
*Do you know I loved what we'd shared?*

*I'm sorry I had to leave, yeah, I had to go*
*Leaving you was hard, just so you know*
*Loving you was the best thing I've ever done*
*We had it good, yeah, we had so much fun*
*I see you've moved on with someone new*
*It kills me, but I'm happy for you*
*I wish you were here by my side*
*I miss you always, I cannot lie*
*I hope some days you remember me*
*The good times we had are hard to beat*
*There were times when we were up and we were down*
*We fought and laughed and were foolish clowns*
*But I know . . . we were brothers 'til the end*
*I loved you with everything*
*I loved you with everything*

I closed my eyes, squeezing them tight to ward off the bombardment of emotions. I hauled in another big breath and a new calmness washed over me. *Yeah . . .* Phil was with us. He was here. My voice soared, filling the stadium with unchartered energy.

*Remember the high and feeling alive*
*Together forever. All the good times*
*We were so young, united as one*
*Together forever, searching for love*
*We sang from the heart, right from the start*
*Together forever, never apart*

Then I toned it down, dropping my voice back to a breathy rasp.

*I may not be there, but I'm always here*
*I may not be there, but I'm always here*

*Soaring through the clouds, I'm doing fine*

*Never wanted to hurt you, don't trouble your mind*
*Look to the stars, feel me in your heart*
*I'm always here, we are never apart*
*I'm watching you from up above*
*Showering down on you with all my love*
*I'll see you again one day soon*
*I promise that I'll always love you*
*Please know . . . we were brothers 'til the end*
*I loved you with everything*
*I loved you with everything*

As Slip played the last chord, the crowd roared and erupted into applause.

*Fuck!* I didn't know how I got through that, but I did. The first time singing a heartfelt song live was always rough. I'd be fine after tonight, guaranteed. The guys and I nodded at each other. A silent, solid understanding passed between us. *Yeah, we loved Phil. He'd loved us. He's our guardian angel.*

That song had hit everyone hard. I didn't think there was a dry eye in the stadium. So, it was time to change the mood.

We transitioned into a few sexy I-want-you-girl singles, a couple of seductive I-love-you ballads, several I'm-better-off-without-you songs, then hit our love-living-life party tracks. I'd been singing my heart out, and the boys and I had rocked up a storm for just over two hours, when we slammed out the last beat of our encore. Pyrotechnics lit the stage and sky above the stadium. Coated in sweat, we ran offstage. We hugged, cheered, and hollered with our team. What a fucking epic show! My blood charged through my veins. Fire blazed through my soul. The adrenaline rush was a total high.

I made my way over to my wife. I picked up Sutton, spun her around, and kissed her sweet lips.

She laughed, and her head fell back. "Put me down. You're all sweaty. And hot."

"You love it." I placed her on her feet and kissed her.

"I love you." She wrinkled her nose, covered my face with her hand, and pushed me away.

But I caught her wrist and drew her into my embrace. She wasn't going anywhere. She didn't object.

I threw her a mischievous smile. "Want to show me how much?"

"Maybe. If you behave."

"Not my style."

"Then you'd better take me back to our hotel."

I murmured low into her ear, "Deal. We'll get out of here as soon as possible."

We headed for our dressing room. The guys and their wives followed.

"Wicked show," Slip hollered as he drew Maddy into the room and smothered her with a sweaty kiss. Going by her giggle, she didn't seem to mind the onslaught.

"We totally fucking rocked," Lewis bellowed, scooting over to Tia, who'd joined us. "Thank you for not flashing lights in my eyes."

"You're welcome." She gave him a kiss on his lips. "You were awesome tonight."

"Everyone was." He tugged her against his side. "That show was incredible."

"Totally. One show down. Ninety-three to go. Oh, yeah." Cole pumped his fist into the air, then attacked Ava's face with a ton of kisses. He drove her backward, and her ass connected with the counter at the back of the room. She didn't tackle him to the ground or put up a fight. Guessed she didn't mind his dripping sweat.

"Hmmm." Her eyes glinted as she ran her fingers through his damp hair. "Want to celebrate?"

"Always." Cole lifted her onto the counter and nuzzled into her neck.

*Yep* . . . they'd be banging it out somewhere soon, like they often did when the kids weren't around.

How life had changed.

My band and I were riding another huge wave of success, but we had slowed down. We didn't push ourselves as hard and as fast as we'd done before. We made time for our families.

This tour would be long and tiring, but a hell of a lot of fun.

A total high, performing every night.

I touched the silver bracelet dangling around my wrist— the one I'd gotten from Phil.

I missed him every day. But I remembered the good times. The love and fun we'd had. The songs and music we'd created together. As brothers. As a band. As friends.

The lost lyrics Tia had given us had found their home. His words had been embedded into our hearts and souls and music.

His memory would always live on in us. He was part of our legacy.

I may have lost him, but I'd gained so much. I'd found Sutton. We were about to have a family. I've never been so freaking happy.

"You okay?" Sutton cuddled into my side.

I swept her hair back off her face and pressed my lips to hers. "Yes. I couldn't be better. I have this." I jutted my chin toward my band, friends, and entourage. "And you."

"Are you ready to do this on repeat for the next twelve months?"

"You know I am. I love being on stage."

"And you're so good at it."

"Don't make his head swell any further, Sutt." Slip clipped me on the back of the skull. "His ego is big enough."

"Don't listen to him." Laughing, I drew everyone into a circle. The energy in the air was still electric after our show. "What an epic start to the tour. The crowd was incredible. We didn't have any major fuckups." My transmitter had failed but was fine after a quick swap. Slip had tripped on a cord. Cole had snapped a stick. Lewis had broken a string. Some stage lighting hadn't worked. But otherwise, it had gone off without a hitch. "You guys rocked. Let's grab a drink and celebrate . . . just not too hard, so we can do this all again tomorrow." And again and again over the long months ahead.

"Let's party!" the guys cheered and clapped.

Our wives laughed and hugged us.

With my arm draped around Sutton's shoulders, I absorbed the love in the room.

I couldn't wait to watch my baby grow inside my wife's belly. I couldn't wait to hit the road and perform every night. I couldn't wait to become a father.

I planned to play music for the rest of my life. I was here because I had incredible friends . . . and Phil had been a part of our lives.

We'd never forget him.

I promised to live every day to the fullest, surrounded by those I loved . . . with these people.

This was my family.

This was true friendship.

This was love and happiness.

We were The Flintlocks.

We'd be together for life.

We were on tour.

We'd rock on forever . . .

# THANK YOU

Thank you for reading LOST LYRICS, Book 5 in The Flintlocks Rockstar Romance Series. I hope you loved Flint, Sutton, Lewis, Tia, Cole, Ava, Slip and Maddy as much as I do. I'm sure these characters will make cameos in future books I write.

But for now, that is a series wrap. More stories will be coming your way soon.

PS. If you loved LOST LYRICS, would you kindly take a moment and leave a quick review. They are music for an author's soul. Here is the link: https://www.amazon.com/dp/B0DFFBJKFR Thank you.

# LOOKING FOR YOUR NEXT READ?

Find out how my world of rockstars started with the prequel to the Everhide Rockstar Romance Series for FREE.

**ROCKED – The Price of Dreams** is the origin story of how the band met in high school. It is not imperative to read this before the series. It is a pre-romance of the adult relationships that develop throughout the six books - all Happily Ever Afters, no cliffhangers.

From friends-to-lovers, enemies-to-lovers, accidental pregnancies, roommates-to-lovers and more, the Everhide Rockstar Series will have you falling in love, shedding tears, and laughing out loud. Be prepared for another emotional journey.

Read the prequel, **ROCKED – The Price of DREAMS,** for **FREE** if you subscribe to my newsletter or it is available for purchase at Amazon.

Subscribe at: https://taniajoyce.com/subscribe

# BOOKS BY TANIA JOYCE

## The Flintlocks Series

## The Everhide Series

## Billionaires and College Romance

  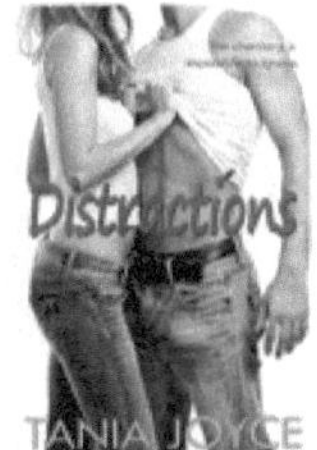

# NEWSLETTER

To stay in touch and to be notified about my new releases, sales, giveaways and more, please subscribe to my monthly newsletter. Join at: https://taniajoyce.com/subscribe
REMEMBER: You get a BONUS BOOK if you join.

***

# FOLLOW TANIA JOYCE

You can follow and find me on the following social media platforms.

Amazon: https://amazon.com/author/taniajoyce
BookBub: https://www.bookbub.com/authors/tania-joyce
Facebook: https://www.facebook.com/taniajoycebooks
Goodreads: https://www.goodreads.com/taniajoyce
Instagram: https://www.instagram.com/taniajoycebooks/
Pinterest: https://www.pinterest.com/taniajoycebooks
TikTok: https://www.tiktok.com/@taniajoyce
Web: http://taniajoyce.com

# FOR MORE INFORMATION
Visit: taniajoyce.com